Charles Kegan Paul

William Godwin

His friends and contemporaries. Vol. 1

Charles Kegan Paul

William Godwin
His friends and contemporaries. Vol. 1

ISBN/EAN: 9783337424107

Printed in Europe, USA, Canada, Australia, Japan

Cover: Foto ©Andreas Hilbeck / pixelio.de

More available books at **www.hansebooks.com**

WILLIAM GODWIN:

HIS FRIENDS AND CONTEMPORARIES.

I.

WILLIAM GODWIN

AFTER A PORTRAIT BY NORTHCOTE

WILLIAM GODWIN:

HIS FRIENDS AND CONTEMPORARIES.

BY

C. KEGAN PAUL.

WITH PORTRAITS AND ILLUSTRATIONS.

VOL. I.

QUI LEGIT REGIT

BOSTON: ROBERTS BROTHERS.
1876.

PREFACE.

My best thanks are due to Sir Percy Shelley, the grandson of William Godwin, for the generous manner in which he has placed at my disposal the whole of the papers in his possession which relate to his grandfather. These included a vast quantity of letters and other MSS., some of which had never been opened since they were laid aside by Godwin's own hand, many years before his death. Mrs Shelley began to arrange them for publication soon after that event, in 1836, but many packets had apparently not been examined by her. This fact renders it the more necessary that I should state that while Sir Percy Shelley has sanctioned my work as a whole, he is in no way whatever answerable for details. I only am responsible for the selections made and inferences drawn from the papers, as well as for every opinion expressed in the book.

A very few of the letters have been already printed— some of Godwin's by Lady Shelley in her "Shelley Memorials," and some of Coleridge's by Mr Garnett in a Magazine article.

In all cases where there appeared to be the smallest doubt in regard to the publication of documents, I have consulted, where possible, the representatives of the persons concerned, and have obtained their permission to print the letters.

C. K. P.

February 1876.

CONTENTS.

PAGE

CHAPTER I.

EARLY LIFE. 1756—1785, . . . 1

CHAPTER II.

LITERARY WORK. 1785—1788, . . 24

CHAPTER III.

POLITICAL WRITINGS. 1788—1792, . 59

CHAPTER IV.

LITERARY LIFE AND FRIENDS. 1793, . , 77

CHAPTER V.

GODWIN'S WORKS AND POLITICS. 1783—1794, . 99

CHAPTER VI.

FRIENDS AND ACQUAINTANCES. 1794—1796, . . 138

CHAPTER VII.

THE WOLLSTONECRAFTS. 1759—1791, . . 161

PAGE

CHAPTER VIII.

MARY WOLLSTONECRAFT. 1791—1796,   .   200

CHAPTER IX.

MARRIED LIFE. 1797,   .   .   231

CHAPTER X.

MARY GODWIN'S DEATH. 1797, .   .   .   272

CHAPTER XI.

A SINGULAR COURTSHIP—FRIENDS. 1798,   292

CHAPTER XII.

ST LEON. MRS REVELEY. 1799,   .   .   328

CHAPTER XIII.

VISIT TO IRELAND—LITERARY SQUABBLES. 1800,   354

LIST OF ILLUSTRATIONS.

WILLIAM GODWIN. After a Portrait by Northcote.   *Frontispiece.*

FACSIMILE OF MARY WOLLSTONECRAFT'S HAND-

WRITING,   .   .   . *p.* 200

WISBEACH.—GODWIN'S BIRTHPLACE, .   387

WILLIAM GODWIN:

HIS FRIENDS AND CONTEMPORARIES.

CHAPTER I.

EARLY LIFE. 1756—1785.

To those conversant with the literary history of the close of the last, and the first quarter of the present century, few names are more familiar than that of William Godwin. The husband of Mary Wollstonecraft, the father-in-law of Shelley, the confidential friend of Coleridge and Lamb, his life was so closely intertwined with the lives of those whose story has been often written, as to render some record of him valuable, even had the man himself been less remarkable than he was. But though the present generation has read his works but little, this age owes more to him than it recognizes ; many opinions now clothed in household words were first formulated by him, and the publication of his " Political Justice," in 1793, marked a distinct epoch in the growth of liberal thought. During a large part of his life younger men looked on him as a kind of prophet-sage, and he exercised a remarkable influence over all with whom he came in contact.

The mere record of his life, would, if written soon after his death, have had a deeper interest than it now can have, the interest being in these days rather antiquarian and

I.   A

literary than personal and social. But to write such a
life was then possible to one alone, to Godwin's daughter,
Mrs Shelley. She only would have known what to preserve and what to reject from the mass of papers left by
one who never willingly destroyed a written line, and whose
life and opinions had clashed to so great an extent with the
susceptibilities of men then living. But from causes into
which there is here no need to enter, Mrs Shelley was only
able in a measure to select those papers which seemed to
her fittest for publication, and to draw up a few valuable
notes, explanatory of otherwise forgotten circumstances.
Much as this is to be regretted, it may yet be that a freer
handling than is possible to a daughter was needed for
such a life and correspondence as is here presented. Not
however that a veil is lifted from particulars which
Godwin's daughter would have desired to hide ; she wished
to conceal nothing of interest except in cases where some
living person might be wounded, or some dear memory of
the dead, and such danger has now almost or wholly ceased.

For the record of Godwin's early years we are mainly
dependent on an autobiographical fragment, drawn up by
him in the year 1800, when he was forty-four years of age.
But interest in the extreme detail in which the facts of his
earlier life are presented in this fragment would at all times
have been restricted to the members of his own family, nor
was there anything especially remarkable in the surround-
ings of his earlier years. For these reasons but a small
portion of his narrative is reproduced in the following pages.
   William Godwin was born March 3rd, 1756, at Wisbeach
in Cambridgeshire, at which place his father was a Dissenting Minister. He sprang on both sides from respectable
middle-class families, that of his father having been estab-

lished for some generations at Newbury in Berkshire, that
of his mother, whose name was Hull, had originally held
landed property in Durham. Mr Hull had married and
settled in Wisbeach, had been originally in the Merchant
Service, and was at the time of his daughter's marriage to
Mr Godwin, the owner of vessels engaged in the coasting
trade ; he also sent an occasional venture to the Baltic.

The earliest traceable ancestor on the Godwin side was
a great-great-grandfather, William Godwin, of Newbury,
described in the Parish Register as " Mr," who died, leaving
six sons and three daughters. The following are among
the family traditions, recorded by William Godwin :—

" Edward, my great-grandfather, was the fifth son of William,
and was born in the year 1661. He married, probably in the
year 1694, Mary ———, fifteen years younger than himself, and
in the year 1706 was chosen Mayor of the town of which he was
a native. He was educated to the profession of an attorney, and
possessed at the time of his death in 1719 the office of town clerk
of the corporation of Newbury.

" Edward," his eldest son, " was born 10th November 1695.
He was destined to the profession of a dissenting minister, and
was placed at a suitable age under the reverend Mr Samuel Jones,
who conducted an academy for preparing young persons for the
profession of the ministry at Tewkesbury in Gloucestershire."

This Samuel Jones was a remarkable man. He was the
son of the Rev. Malachi Jones, a " minister of the gospel
in Pennsylvania," who had emigrated to America early in
life. Samuel was sent to Europe, and received his education in great measure at Leyden, " under the learned Peri-
zonius," Professor of History and Greek, who died 1715.
In 1711 we find him, still quite a young man, taking fifteen
pupils, who were not, however, all constant to the nonconformist training of their tutor. Not only Dr Isaac Watts,

but Thomas Secker, afterwards Archbishop of Canterbury, and Joseph Butler, Bishop of Durham, author of the Analogy, were among his pupils. From Tewkesbury, while still a schoolboy, Butler "conducted a correspondence with Dr Samuel Clarke on the subject of certain propositions in Clarke's treatise, entitled 'A Demonstration of the Being and Attributes of God,' which were afterwards printed as an appendix to that work."

" A ridiculous mistake," says Godwin, " has been fallen into by some persons who have written concerning this Samuel Jones, in supposing that he married the daughter of Mr John Weaver, one of the ministers ejected in the reign of Charles II., who was born about the year 1632, and whose daughter may be supposed to have been about sixty at the time of Mr Jones's marriage." He did in fact marry a young woman named Judith Weaver from Radnorshire.

" To go back to my grandfather. He was a fellow-student of Butler and Secker, and " on the death of Mr Jones in October 1719 "was invited to undertake the conduct of the seminary in which he had been educated." This offer he declined. " On the 12th of April 1721 he married the widow of his late tutor. He resided at this time in his professional character of a minister at Hungerford, in the county of Wilts, and in 1723 was called to take charge of a congregation in Little St. Helens, Bishopsgate Street, London, in which situation he continued for the rest of his life. My grandfather maintained in his advancing years the character he had acquired in early life, and was frequently consulted by his brethren as a reviser of their works. He, in particular, superintended the ' Family Expositor' of Dr Philip Doddridge in its passage through the press."

Edward Godwin had two sons, Edward, who having run " a certain career of wildness and dissipation, became a convert to the tenets and practices of Mr George Whitfield. He was for a short time, for the thread of his life was soon broken, a distinguished preacher in the Methodist connection, and an eager publisher of experiences, devout allegories and hymns." John, the younger of the two sons, was born Feb. 21, 1723. He was a pupil of Dr Doddridge, "for whom he retained during life a more affectionate veneration than for any other human being," became a dissenting minister, as has been said, and the father of William Godwin.

The son's portrait of the father is amusing and characteristic. Aiming at the most scrupulous fairness, he succeeds only in giving a very distinct impression that he had but little love for his father, and no very high opinion of his mental powers.

" My paternal grandfather, as I have said, was esteemed a man of learning ; my father was certainly not a man of learning. But he was something better than a merely learned man can ever be ; he was a man of a warm heart and unblemished manners, ardent in his friendships, eager for the relief of distress whether of mind or of circumstances, and decent and zealous in the discharge of his professional duties. He had so great a disapprobation for the constitution and discipline of the Church of England, as rather to approve of his children's absenting themselves from all public worship than joining in her offices ; yet he lived on terms of friendship with many of her members and of her clergy. He was scrupulous and superstitious respecting most of the succours of religion, particularly the observance of the Lord's day. My father, at the time I was most capable of noticing his habits, was extremely nice in his apparel, and delicate in his food. He spent much of his time on horseback. This habit grew out of a sentiment of duty, when he resided in a village, the scene of my early reveries and amusements, where his flock lay variously dispersed through a circle of from twelve to sixteen miles in diameter. He was attached to the intercourses of society, yet of the most unvaried temperance. He was extremely affectionate, yet at

least to me. who was perhaps never his favourite, his rebukes had
a painful tone of ill humour and asperity. He was fond of reading
aloud in his family, but the age of novels and romances, of Tom
Jones and Cleopatra, was over with him before my memory. I
scarcely ever heard him read anything but expositions and
sermons. His study occupied but little of his time. His sermon,
for in my memory he only preached once on a Sunday, was regu-
larly begun to be written in a very swift short-hand after tea on
Saturday evening. I believe he was always free from any desire
of intellectual distinction on a large scale ; I know that it was with
reluctance that he preached at any time at Norwich, in London,
or any other place where he suspected that his accents might fall
on the ear of criticism. He was regarded by his neighbours as a
wise as well as a good man, and he desired no more. He died at
fifty years of age, but it was with considerable reluctance that he
quitted this sublunary scene. The last time I stood by his bed-
side, two or three days before he expired, he repeated with an
anxious voice a hymn from Dr Watts' collection, the first stanza
of which is as follows :—

> ' When I can read my title clear
> To mansions in the skies,
> I'll bid farewell to every fear
> And wipe my weeping eyes.' "

The notice of his mother is more favourable, and, as will
appear from letters which are extant, not other than
deserved.

" My mother, so long as her husband lived, was the qualifier
and moderator of his austerities. Some of the villagers were impertinent enough to allege that she was too gay in her style of
decorating her person. She was facetious, and had an ambition
to be thought the teller of a good story, and an adept at hitting
off a smart repartee. She was a most obliging, submissive, and
dutiful wife. She was an expert and active manager in the detail
of household affairs. Two persons perhaps never lived against

whom the voice of calumny itself had less to urge than my father and mother. I speak here of her character during the life of my father. After his death it became considerably changed. She surrendered herself to the visionary hopes and tormenting fears of the methodistical sect, and her ordinary economy became teazingly parsimonious."

It may be added, and indeed will hereafter be sufficiently evident, that Mrs Godwin was far from being a highly educated person.

Of this marriage, "which proved extremely prolific," William was the seventh child of thirteen. Mrs Godwin did not suckle her children, and the child was "sent from home to be nourished by a hireling." When he was again taken home at the age, apparently, of two years, there was added to his family circle a first cousin of his father, Miss Godwin, afterwards Mrs Sothren, "who out of her decent income, as it was considered, of £40 a year, paid £16 to my father as a stipend for lodging and board." Miss Godwin had a considerable amount of literary culture, and still more of literary instinct. This, however, was qualified and checked by a strongly Calvinistic turn of mind, which impressed the child whom she made her chief favourite and companion, but increased the breach between them, when in after years he adopted opinions widely different from those in which he had been so carefully nurtured. To this lady William Godwin owed his first teaching and initiation into literature. His earliest books were the "Pilgrim's Progress," and an "Account of the Pious Deaths of Many Godly Children," by James Janeway. "Their premature eminence," he writes, "suited to my own age and situation, strongly excited my emulation. I felt as if I were willing to die with them, if I could with equal success engage the admiration of my friends and mankind." But while thus nursed in a very hotbed of forced piety, he was physically a puny child, and records that the persons about him were much less solicitous for the health of his body than the health of his soul.

In 1758 Mr Godwin, senior, removed from Wisbeach to Debenham, " a small market town in the vicinity of Suffolk. But here his congregation was divided into two factions, Arian and Trinitarian. The Trinitarians had just before expelled an heretical pastor, and the defeated Arians were resolved to grant no suspension of arms to his more orthodox successor." He therefore went in about 1760 to Guestwick, sixteen miles north of Norwich, "one of the smallest order of villages in the county of Norfolk," and here, where it may be hoped the simple villagers did not know the subtle differences of rival creeds, he passed the remainder of his life. The emolument of none of his preferments exceeded the amount of £60 a year.

William Godwin's school-life was subject to the same influences which surrounded him at home. His earliest teacher beyond his own family was the mistress of a dame's school at Guestwick, and, like all the persons who had hitherto had any charge of him, she "was much occupied in the concerns of religion. She was considerably stricken in years, and had seen twenty years of the preceding century. I recollect her bitter lamentations respecting the innovation in the Style," September 1752, "and the alteration of Christmas Day." Under her tuition he read through the whole of the Old and New Testaments, and gained, before he was eight years old, a great familiarity with the phraseology and manner of the Bible ; and this, he himself thought, had a considerable share in the formation of his character. He was a precocious child, in whose mind the most characteristic features "were religion and love of distinction." Having determined even thus early to be a minister, he afterwards recorded that he "preached sermons in the kitchen, every Sunday afternoon, and at other times, mounted in a child's high chair, indifferent as to the muster of persons present at these exhibitions, and undisturbed at their coming and going." His education at this time was puritanically strict. "One Sunday, as I walked in the garden, I happened to take the cat in my arms. My father saw me, and seriously reproved my levity, remarking that on the Lord's-day he was ashamed to observe me demeaning myself with such profaneness."

In March 1764, upon the death of his aged schoolmistress, the boy was sent with one of his brothers to a school at Hindolveston, or Hilderson, about two miles and a half from his home. The school consisted of thirty boarders, and seventy day scholars, among which last were the Godwins. The name of the master was Akers; he was celebrated as "the best, or second best, penman in the county of Norfolk, or, for aught he knew, in England." This will account for the admirable quality of Godwin's own handwriting, which remained, even to the end of his long life, as legible as print, yet with a distinct personal character about it. "Akers was bred a journeyman tailor, and had never had more than a quarter of a year's schooling in his life. The rest was the fruit of his own industry. He was a moderate mathematician, and had a small smattering of Latin. Few men ever excelled him in the rapidity and truth of his arithmetical operations." Godwin says further: "I was perhaps the only one of his scholars that ever loved him;" and this is likely enough from the account given of the master, and of the conduct of his school. All, however, that was taught was well taught, and Godwin was an eager and ambitious pupil.

At this school was also "a poor lad of the village, whose name was Steele," who seemed to Godwin a proper subject on whom to exercise his old practice of preaching. He talked to Steele "of sin and damnation, and drew tears from his eyes." He privily got possession of the key of the meeting-house, that he might preach to and pray over Steele from his father's pulpit. His whole soul was vexed within him, because he thought that very few of his school-fellows discovered any tokens of God's grace.

In the following year Mrs Sothren took the boy on a tour to Norwich, Lynn, and Wisbeach; and as at Wisbeach it was the time of the races, he was then, for the only time in his life, a spectator of that amusement, to which he "attended with great interest and passion." At Norwich he saw the play of Venice Preserved; and it is a curious instance of the changeableness and inconsistency that there is in the repudiation of amusements by those who are very strict in their religious views, that he was taken to the theatre by Mrs Sothren, with the full consent of his parents.

In September 1767 he was sent to Norwich, to become the solitary pupil of Mr Samuel Newton, minister of the Inde-pendent congregation in that city. Of this man he gives a most unpleasant picture, physically and intellectually. But this is evidently the impression of his riper manhood, not of his childhood. For at the time Newton had a great influ-ence over him, and of a kind scarcely possible but where sympathy exists. It is probable that he only grew to detest Newton when he grew to detest Newton's creed. This was "drawn from the writings of Sandeman, a celebrated north country apostle, who, after Calvin had damned ninety-nine in a hundred of mankind, has contrived a scheme for damn-

ing ninety-nine in a hundred of the followers of Calvin."
Of himself at this time he writes as follows, and there is no
reason to doubt the accuracy of his self-introspection :—

" It was scarcely possible for any preceptor to have a pupil more
penetrated with curiosity and a thirst after knowledge than I was
when I came under the roof of this man. All my amusements
were sedentary; I had scarcely any pleasure but in reading; by
my own consent, I should sometimes not so much have gone into
the streets for weeks together. It may well be supposed that my
vocation to literature was decisive, when not even the treatment I
now received could alter it. Add to this principle of curiosity a
trembling sensibility and an insatiable ambition, a sentiment that
panted with indescribable anxiety for the stimulus of approbation.
The love of approbation and esteem, indeed, that pervaded my
mind was a nice and delicate feeling, that found no gratification
in coarse applause, and that proudly enveloped itself in the consciousness of its worth, when treated with injustice."

But his new tutor did not think so highly of the abilities
which thus panted for recognition as Mrs Sothren and
Akers had done. After the fashion of those days, Newton
speedily proceeded to birch his self-complacent pupil, pre-
facing the application of the rod by a long exhortation, full
of facetious metaphor.

"To this discourse," says Godwin, " I listened at first with
astonishment, and afterwards with incredulity. It had never
occurred to me as possible that my person, which hitherto had
been treated by most of my acquaintances, and particularly by Mrs
Sothren and Mr Akers, who had principally engaged my attention,
as something extraordinary and sacred, could suffer such ignominious violation. The idea had something in it as abrupt as a fall
from heaven to earth. I had regarded this engine as the appropriate lot of the very refuse of the scholastic train."

In the spring of the following year, 1768, he had an

attack of the smallpox, having on religious grounds steadily
refused to allow himself to be inoculated ; and during his
illness he was conscious of entire "detachment" from life,
and willingness to die. After his recovery, he found that
his tutor's son had much difficulty and bashfulness in pray-
ing before others, and he therefore used to take the lad to
his own room, and there pray with him. He remained with
Mr Newton three years, and finally left him in 1771. There
had been in this time one short break, during which he
went back to Hindolveston, but returned to Newton at his
own request. It is plain, therefore, that his dislike of his
tutor could not have been great, while his own attainments
in after-life speak well for the teaching he had received.
Godwin also had gained much intellectually from having
been allowed—or at least not checked in—the free range
of his tutor's library.

"The books I read here," he says, "with the greatest transport
were the early volumes of the English translation of the Ancient
History of Rollin. Few bosoms ever beat with greater ardour than
mine did while perusing the story of the grand struggle of the
Greeks for independence against the assaults of the Persian
despot ; and this scene awakened a passion in my soul which will
never cease but with life."

Another extract, and it is one displaying that inordinate
vanity which was traceable through life, amid much that
was loveable, will close this period of mere boyhood.

"When I was about thirteen or fourteen years of age I went by
myself one day at the period of the assizes to the Sessions House.
Having gone early, I had my choice of a seat, and placed myself
immediately next the bench. The judge was Lord Chief-Justice
De Grey, afterwards Baron Walsingham. As I stayed some hours,
I at one time relieved my posture by leaning my elbow on the
corner of the cushion placed before his lordship. On some occa-

sion, probably when he was going to address the jury, he laid his hand gently on my elbow and removed it. On this action I recollect having silently remarked, if his lordship knew what the lad beside him will perhaps one day become I am not sure that he would have removed my elbow."

Thus ends the fragment of detailed autobiography. In 1805 Godwin wrote of this MS.,—" I shall probably never complete it. My feelings on the subject are not what they were. I sat down with the intention of being nearly as explicit as Rousseau in the composition of his Confessions." But finding that so minute a portrait would not be after all the truest which could be written, he hints that posterity will judge him by his works. There remain, however, many short notes of the years 1772–1795, but scarcely more than a summary of the leading events. Such as they are, these notes are almost the only authority for that portion of the life. The greater part of his correspondence with his relatives after he left his father's house was destroyed by his mother shortly before her death, and there were but few letters of interest addressed to him during the period in which he was young and unknown.

Enough has been said to show the school in which the religious opinions of the growing lad were formed. In politics his father was a moderate whig, but in that household politics were rarely discussed. Of Mr Newton his pupil says again—

" Ductility is a leading feature of my mind. I was his single pupil, and his sentiments speedily became mine. He was rather an intemperate Wilkite, but first and principally he was a disciple of the supra-Calvinistic opinions of Robert Sandeman."

Such was the boy, who made an early start in life, at

the age of fifteen, by accepting the post of usher in the
school of his old master, Mr Robert Akers of Hindolveston.
He continued in this occupation during the whole of the
year 1772, and probably during the spring of the following
year. He read during this period the whole of Shaks-
pere, "and planned an epic poem of Brute." Mr Godwin,
senior, died on November 12, 1772, but the event did not
cause his son any profound emotion. The circumstances
in which the family were left were slender, but some small
sum seems to have been available for the completion of
William's education. In April 1773 he came to London
with his mother, intending to enter Homerton Academy,
but was rejected when examined by Mr Stafford and Mr
Noah Hill, at the instance of the former, on suspicion of
Sandemanianism. After spending the summer in Kent
with his mother's relatives, he entered Hoxton College as
a student in September, the authorities being either more
tolerant than those at Homerton, or having a less keen
scent for possible heresy. He planned during that summer
"two tragedies, one on the subject of Iphigenia in Aulis,
and the other of the death of Cæsar, and constructed a harmony of the evangelists from the gospels themselves, without the assistance of any commentators." He procured
also from the circulating library at Rochester the works of
Robert Sandeman, that he might compare them with his
previous habits of thinking, and know whereof he was
accused.

He remained five years at Hoxton, and in long after
days wrote as follows his recollections of that period :—

"During my academical life, and from this time forward, I was
indefatigable in my search after truth. I read all the authors of
greatest repute, for and against the Trinity, original sin, and the
most disputed doctrines, but I was not yet of an understanding

sufficiently ripe for impartial decision, and all my inquiries terminated in Calvinism. I was famous in our college for calm and impassionate discussion ; for one whole summer I rose at five and went to bed at midnight, that I might have sufficient time for theology and metaphysics. I formed during this period, from reading on all sides, a creed upon materialism and immaterialism, liberty and necessity, in which no subsequent improvement of my understanding has been able to produce any variation. I was remarked by my fellow-collegians for the intrepidity of my opinions and the tranquil fearlessness of my temper."

Godwin's tutor at Hoxton was Dr Kippis, editor of " Biographia Britannica," &c., &c., who died in 1795 ; he was very sincerely his friend, did much for him when starting afterwards in literary life, and found him also a fairly lucrative appointment as a private tutor. The then head of the college was Dr Rees, editor of " Chambers's and Rees's Cyclopædia," who died in 1825, and with him Godwin held a very curious and interesting conversation on the eternity of hell torment, in which the pupil, one day to become so heretical, was more orthodox than his teacher. In answer to Godwin's complacent quotation of the stock texts on the matter—

" The doctor argued that in these passages an infinite duration was put merely for one that was unlimited, and that 'for ages of ages' meant only for a very long time. The doctor further maintained that this ambiguous and obscure style was very wisely kept up in the New Testament, since less than the absolute belief in eternal suffering would never retain the lower orders of the community in the path of duty. For himself he was perfectly convinced that such a punishment was never the meaning of Jesus Christ, but he should think it censurable in himself to promulgate the true sense of the New Testament on this point, to the grosser mass of mankind, who if they were acquainted with it would infallibly launch out into the most enormous crimes." Godwin could not agree with him in this, and "was persuaded there was more virtue and less crime in the best ages of Greece and Rome than in any period of the Christian dispensation, and was therefore satisfied that the doctrine of eternal punishment in hell was not absolutely required to prevent men from running out into excesses that would be destructive of the social system."

Of the general tone of the College, Godwin says—

"The prevailing opinions were those of Arminius and Arius, but I endured the fiery trial, and came out in my twenty-third year as pure a Sandemanian as I had gone in; this, however, without any intercourse with the congregation in London distinguished by the name of that leader. A little time before the period of my entering the Dissenting College at Hoxton, I had adopted principles of toryism in government, by which I was no less distinguished from my fellow-students than by my principles of religion. I had, however, no sooner gone out into the world than my sentiments on both these points began to give way; my toryism did not survive above a year, and between my twenty-third and my twenty-fifth year my religious creed insensibly degenerated on the heads of the Trinity, eternal torments, and some others."

In 1777 while spending his last summer vacation in his native county, Godwin preached at Yarmouth every Sunday morning, and at Lowestoft in the afternoon. In the next year after leaving the College and recovering from a severe attack of "putrid fever," he preached, unsuccessfully, as a candidate at Christchurch in Hampshire, and settled at Ware in Hertfordshire as a minister. If, however, it be necessary to have a firm faith before teaching others, as then, for the most part, men would have held, Godwin's fitness for his post, which however he accepted in all seriousness and devotion, may be doubted. He writes :—

" In the last year of my academical life I entered into a curious paper war with my fellow student Mr Richard Evans, an excellent mathematician, and a man of very clear understanding. The subject, the being of a God. Our papers were, I believe, seen by no person but ourselves. I took the negative side, in this instance, as always, with great sincerity, hoping that my friend might enable me to remove the difficulties I apprehended. I did not fully see my ground as to this radical question, but I had little doubt that grant the being of a God, both the truth of Christianity, and the doctrines of Calvinism, followed by infallible inference.

No record is preserved of Godwin's ministry at Ware, nor are any facts now discoverable, but he was there first brought in contact with Joseph Fawcet, whose name is interesting to us as being the first of four persons who at different periods profoundly impressed Godwin, and influenced his mental development. He says :—

" The four principal oral instructors to whom I feel my mind indebted for improvement were Joseph Fawcet, Thomas Holcroft, George Dyson, and Samuel Taylor Coleridge."

Again :—

" In my twenty-third year I became acquainted with the Rev. Joseph Fawcet, a young man of nearly my own age, one of whose favourite topics was a declamation against the domestic affections, a principle which admirably coincided with the dogmas of Jonathan Edwards, whose works I had read a short time before. Mr Fawcet's modes of thinking made a great impression upon me, as he was almost the first man I had ever been acquainted with, who carried with him the semblance of original genius."

Fawcet's very name is now forgotten as well as his writings, but Godwin was not the only one of his contemporaries who esteemed him highly. Hazlitt thus speaks of him :—

I.   B

"The late Rev. Joseph Fawcet, author of the 'Art of War,' &c. It was he who delivered the Sunday Evening Lectures at the Old Jewry, which were so popular about twenty years ago. He afterwards retired to Hedgegrove in Hertfordshire. It was here that I became acquainted with him, and passed some of the pleasantest days of my life. He was the friend of my early youth. He was the first person of literary eminence whom I had then known, and the conversations I then had with him on subjects of taste and philosophy, for his taste was as refined as his powers of reasoning were profound and subtle, gave me a delight such as I can never feel again. Of all the persons I have ever known, he was the most perfectly free from every taint of jealousy or narrowness. Never did a mean or sinister motive come near his heart. He was one of the most enthusiastic admirers of the French Revolution, and I believe that the disappointment of the hopes he had cherished of the freedom and happiness of mankind, preyed upon his mind, and hastened his death."—*Life of Holcroft*, Vol. 2, note to p. 246.

Leaving Ware in August 1779, Godwin resided for four months "with great economy," at a little lodging in Coleman Street. Here he read reports of the speeches of Burke and Fox, "to whom from that time he commenced an ardent attachment, which no change of circumstances or lapse of time was ever able to shake." In this first residence in London he was still uncertain about his career—not yet detached from a set of opinions which his previous training had made so habitual, as to be with difficulty shaken even by his growing liberalism. The next year he left London again, and resumed his ministerial work. In the commencement of the next year, he writes in his notes :—

" I went to reside at Stowmarket in Suffolk, in my profession of a dissenting minister. The only pleasant acquaintance I had here was Mrs Alice Munnings, and her unfortunate son Leonard, a captain of the Suffolk Militia, and a lively, well bred and intelligent man. In 1781 there came to reside at Stowmarket Mr Frederic Norman, deeply read in the French philosophers, and a man of great reflection and acuteness. In April 1782 I quitted Stowmarket, in consequence of a dispute with my hearers on a question of Church discipline. My faith in Christianity had been shaken by the books which Mr Norman put into my hands, and I was therefore pleased in some respects with the breach which dismissed me. I resided during the rest of the year at a lodging in Holborn, and by the persuasions of Fawcet and another friend was prevailed on to try my pen as an author. I drew up proposals for a periodical series of English Biography, but having set down first to the Life of Lord Chatham, I found it grow under my hands to the size of a volume, which I completed by the end of the year. I spent the first seven months of 1783 at Beaconsfield, in the way of my original profession."

It appears however from the records of the "Old Meeting House" at Beaconsfield, now no longer used as such, that Godwin was only a candidate, and was never formally appointed as minister. An old man who was still living forty years ago, "remembered," or thought he remembered, "that on one Sunday morning there was no service, because the minister had gone out coursing," but the tradition is difficult to reconcile with the earlier training from which Godwin had not wholly emancipated himself, and with his apparent total indifference to, if not dislike of such pursuits at other times.

"I found myself," continue the notes, "troubled in my mind on the score of the infidel principles I had recently imbibed, but reading at Beaconsfield the Institutes of Dr Priestley, Socinianism appeared to relieve so many of the difficulties I had hitherto sustained from the Calvinistic theology, that my mind rested in that theory, to which I remained a sincere adherent till the year

1788. On quitting Beaconsfield in August, I formed the plan of a school, for which I was offered some pecuniary assistance, and I actually hired a furnished house for the purpose, at Epsom in Surrey, and published a pamphlet in recommendation of my plan : but I never secured a sufficient number of pupils at one time to induce me to enter upon actual business. This year I may for the first time be considered as an author by profession. My ' Life of Lord Chatham ' was published in the spring. I wrote a defence of the Rockingham party in their coalition with Lord North."

This coalition turned out Lord Shelburne, who had become Prime Minister on the death of Lord Rockingham, made the Duke of Portland Prime Minister in the room of Lord Shelburne, Fox and Lord North the two Secretaries of State, in February 1783.

"For this Stockdale gave me five guineas ; I published my scheme of the seminary at Epsom ; and I composed a pamphlet entitled the ' Herald of Literature,' which was not published till the following year. Soon after the period in which I quitted Beaconsfield, I took lodgings near the New Church in the Strand,"—St Mary Le Strand, consecrated in 1723,—"where I continued during the whole of the following year. I," now " lost the pecuniary assistance which had in some degree smoothed for me the difficulties of the two preceding years, and enabled me to publish on my own account the ' Life of Chatham,' the friend who assisted me going abroad at this period, and leaving me forty pounds in his debt. My principal employment was now writing for the ' English Review,' published by Murray in Fleet Street, at two guineas a sheet, in which employment it was my utmost hope to gain twenty-four guineas per annum. Mr Murray had been won to this contract by the offer of the MS. of the Herald of Literature.' This was probably the busiest period of my life ; in the latter end of 1783 I wrote in ten days a novel entitled Damon and Delia, for which Hookham gave me five guineas, and a novel in three weeks called 'Italian Letters,' purchased by Robinson for twenty guineas, and in the first four months of 1784 a novel called 'Imogen, a Pastoral Romance,' for which Lane gave me ten pounds. Murray published my 'Herald of Literature,' by which I gained nothing, and Cadell published on the same terms and with the same effect a small volume of my Sermons. This volume was dedicated to Dr Watson, Bishop of Llandaff." Richard Watson was a friend but opponent of Gibbon, a liberal and enlightened prelate. He died in 1816, aged 79. "Murray also graciously put into my hands the job of translating from the French MS. the 'Memoirs of Simon Lord Lovat,' which was not published for several years after. For this job he gave me twenty guineas, but the style of the translation was refined and improved in every sentence, almost in every line, by Mr and Mrs Murray. Notwithstanding these resources, for the most part I did not eat my dinner without previously carrying my watch or my books to the pawnbroker to enable me to eat."

In the next year, 1785, he was appointed by Robinson the publisher, on the introduction of Dr Kippis, writer of the historical part of the "New Annual Register," at the stipend of sixty guineas, "and the contract was sealed by a dinner in trio between Mr Robertson, Dr Kippis, and myself at the Crown and Anchor in the Strand." This tavern was opposite St Clement's Church, on a site now occupied by shops.

It was about this time that the prefix of Reverend gradually fell away from his name, and the links were severed between the old life and the new. For some time past he had seen but little of his family. The eldest brother was settled as a farmer at Wood Dalling in Norfolk, with whom, or close to whom Mrs Godwin senior resided.

The conduct of their relations did not gratify this lady and her eldest son, neither did the family letters afford them pleasure, and they therefore destroyed nearly all the correspondence which passed in these years. There are however records of a brother John who settled in London in "sickness and poverty," of another, Nathaniel, in scarce better case, who became a sailor and died at sea, of another, Joseph, who had got into trouble and disgrace, and of a sister Hannah, who wrote poetry, but could not spell—few women then could—and who had settled in partnership with a dressmaker in London. Between her and William Godwin existed a strong affection which survived their not infrequent quarrels.

It may well be supposed that so complete a change of life and views on Godwin's part had given much pain to the honest, homely folk at Wood Dalling, and to Mrs Sothren to whom he was once so dear. The first indication of this is to be found in a letter from her, in answer to a request for some information in regard to his family, and with this—for the letters from his mother will find place hereafter—may close the record of his early life.

Mrs Sothren to William Godwin.

" NORWICH, *March 7th,* 1788.

" DEAR COUSIN,—I was indeed much surprised to receive a letter from you, but on opening it found it to be one of meer curiosity, and what is not in my power to satisfy, as I know not so far as you, for I never knew my grandfather; he being dead before I was born, nor have I anything in my possession relating to it. Am very glad your Sister (for I think that a much more indearing title than Miss G. but suppose 'tis polite, as I know your partiality for your Sister used to be great, and hope she has not done anything to abate it) is to appearance so agreably fixed, sincearly wish them success.

" Wish Joseph may not hurt you ; if report says true he has been very imprudent. There is an old proverb ' Keep your shop, and your shop will keep you,' am very sorry for the poor woman and dear little children. Mary is with your mother.

" You seem to keep out of these troubles. Shure you must want a companion, cannot think how you live. Since I received yours am told you have commenced Novel writer, own it gives me some concern that you that are so capable of turning your thoughts to some thing that would have been for the good of mankind should take that turn.

" Indeed your disposition of maintaining yourself without troubling your friends is very commendable but it has always been a profound secret what the productions of your pen were (to me).

" Young Wilkins seems very happy. Am very sorry for poor Miss Gay ; she is a great favourite of mine, I think her an amiable young lady.—Yours affectionately, HAN. SOTHREN.

" *P.S.*—Hope you will not take it ill what I have wrote, if you can read it. My pens and ink are so bad I am quite ashamed."

Mrs Sothren became a widow in 1785 and died in 1796.

CHAPTER II.

LITERARY WORK. 1785—1788.

IN 1785 Godwin was fairly started as a literary man in London, and became gradually known as a useful political writer on the liberal side. He was a constant contributor to the *Political Herald*, of which Dr Gilbert Stuart was editor, a publication the aim of which is sufficiently described by its title, and which expired at the close of the following year. Some attempts were made to revive it under Godwin's own editorship, and Sheridan, as representing Mr Fox's party, had repeated interviews with Godwin on the subject. It was proposed to him that he should receive a regular stipend from the funds set apart for political purposes by the adherents to the party of Mr Fox, but this he declined, resolving to limit his pecuniary advantages to the fair profits of the pamphlet. He was at this time, and indeed long afterwards, struggling with great pecuniary difficulties, having no fixed income whatever, with the payment for one pupil sent him by Dr Kippis, as the only addition to the small and precarious sum obtained by his fugitive writings.

Through Murray he became known to many literary men, who were accustomed to meet at Murray's, and at the house of Mr Robinson the publisher in Paternoster Row, while through Sheridan he made the acquaintance of some who were already, or were soon to be known in the world of politics. At Sheridan's he met at dinner " Mr Canning, then an Eton schoolboy, just become known to the public by the paper of the Microcosm, &c., &c. Mr Canning was very pressing with me for the cultivation of my acquaintance." Sheridan and his circle, finding him not venal, soon dropped him, but not before he had fairly taken his place in the best London literary and scientific society. Fawcet, the dear and chosen friend of a few years back, was not in London, but his place was soon supplied by Holcroft. This name is the second among those of the four men who profoundly influenced the tone of his mind. The acquaintance was made in 1786, but it was not till the year 1788 that he writes of himself and Holcroft as "extremely intimate." The outward facts of Holcroft's life are well known, or may be read in his life by Hazlitt. The son of a shoemaker, he had been himself a stable-boy, shoemaker, and actor, before he became a dramatic author, and, self-educated as he was, a successful translator of works from French and German. His home life was far from happy, as will in part appear in these pages. He died in 1809, aged 65. Mrs Shelley writes of him :—

" The name of Holcroft at once gives rise to a crowd of recollections to those who are conversant with the history of the times, and that particular circle of literary men of which my father was one. The son of a shoemaker, he rose to eminence through the energy of his character, and the genius with which nature had endowed him. To think of Holcroft as his friends remember him, and to call to mind whence at this day he principally derives his fame as an author, present a singular contrast. He was a man of stern and irascible character, and from the moment that he espoused liberal principles, he carried them to excess. He was tried for life as a traitor on account of his enthusiasm for the objects of the French Revolution. He believed that truth must prevail by the force of its own powers, but he advocated what he deemed truth with vehemence. He warmly asserted that death and disease existed only through the feebleness of man's mind, that pain also had no reality. Rectitude and Courage were the gods of his idolatry, but the defect of his temper rendered him a susceptible friend. His Comedy, 'The Road to Ruin,' will always maintain its position on the English stage, so long as there are actors who can fitly represent its leading characters. He was a man of great industry, unwearied in his efforts to support his family. When they first became acquainted neither he nor Mr Godwin had yet imbibed those strong political feelings which afterwards distinguished them. It required the French Revolution to kindle that ardent love of Political Justice with which both were afterwards, according to their diverse dispositions, warmed."

Godwin had now entirely severed himself from his former faith, and he thus writes of the change :—

"Till 1782 I believed in the doctrine of Calvin, that is, that the majority of mankind were objects of divine condemnation, and that their punishment would be everlasting. The 'Système de la Nature,' read about the beginning of that year, changed my opinion and made me a Deist. I afterwards veered to Socinianism, in which I was confirmed by 'Priestley's Institutes,' in the beginning of 1783. I remember the having entertained doubts in 1785, when I corresponded with Dr Priestley. But I was not a complete unbeliever till 1787."

By "complete unbeliever," however, Godwin must be understood to mean an infidel to Creeds only, and not an infidel to God. That he was at any time a "religious" man may be doubted, if by that term be meant one who has the emotional nature exercised in regard to a Being apprehended by faith alone. Reason, far more than the affections, guided his actions, and while he sought after

One who would satisfy his intellect, he seems to have never felt the need, and therefore never the power of adoration and self-abasement. That he was not at this time an infidel in the vulgar sense, is plain from the following note found among his papers, and dated somewhat *after* the above extract. It is one of several of the same kind, but seems rather to be the digest of the whole, and may be taken as his deliberate answer to the same question as Gretchen put to Faust, " Believest thou in God ?"

" God is a being, who is himself the cause of his own existence.

" His prerogative is to perceive before there was anything to be perceived. He is the creator of the universe, He operated upon nothing, and turned it into something.

" He has not impenetrability, yet can act upon matter which is impenetrable, and moves all things, himself immoveable.

" He produces all things with a word ; all his works are equally easy, and equally instantaneous.

" He is present everywhere, yet has neither parts, figure, nor divisibility : He is all in all, and all in every part.

" With Him is no variableness, neither before nor after ; he is the eternal Now.

" He exists through all time, fills all space, possesses all knowledge, yet is perfectly simple and uncompounded ; his thought is but one, His omniscience a single, all-perfect idea.

" He is for ever the same, without change, yet is perpetually active, beginning, conducting, and ending all the variety of events.

" He desires the happiness of all His creatures, and is averse to their pain ; yet His own felicity is always complete, He neither approves of their good nor is displeased by their misery.

" I believe in this being, not because I have any proper or direct knowledge of His existence,

" But, I am at a loss to account for the existence and arrangement of the visible universe,

" And, being left in the wide sea of conjecture without clue from analogy or experience,

" I find the conjecture of a God easy, obvious, and irresistible. I perceive my understanding to be so commensurate to His nature, and His attributes to be so much like what I know and have observed

" As instantly to convert mystery into reason, and contradictions into certainty."

The following note, in a somewhat more pantheistic key, but still far removed from the no-creed of the "unbeliever," was apparently written about the same time :—

" Religion is among the most beautiful and most natural of all things ; that religion which 'sees God in clouds and hears Him in the wind,' which endows every object of sense with a living soul, which finds in the system of nature whatever is holy, mysterious, and venerable, and inspires the bosom with sentiments of awe and veneration.

" But accursed and detestable is that religion by which the fancy is hag-rid, and conscience is excited to torment us with phantoms of guilt, which endows the priest with his pernicious empire over the mind, which undermines boldness of opinion and intrepidity in feeling, which aggravates a thousandfold the inevitable calamity, death, and haunts us with the fiends and retributory punishments of a future world."

It is plain that this is not orthodox, and though the letter of Mrs Sothren's already quoted is the only expression of dissatisfaction on the part of his family to be found among the papers, there is the draft of a letter from himself to his mother which is interesting as conveying an apology for his declension from his mother's view. It is not dated, but certainly belongs to this time.

" I am exceedingly sorry that you should suffer yourself to form so unfavourable an opinion of my sentiments and character as you express in your last letter. Not that I am anxious so far as relates to myself what opinion may be formed of me by any human being: I am answerable only to God and conscience. But I am sorry, even without deserving it, to occasion you with the smallest uneasiness.

"You seem to regret my having quitted the character of a dissenting minister. To that I can only say, with the utmost frankness, whatever inference may be drawn from it, that the character quitted me when I was far from desiring to part with it.

"With respect to my religious sentiments I have the firmest assurance and tranquillity. I have faithfully endeavoured to improve the faculties and opportunities God has given me, and I am perfectly easy about the consequences. No man can be sure that he is not mistaken, but I am sure that if I am so, the best of beings will forgive my error. If I could ever hope for his approbation, I have now more reason to hope for it than ever. My views, I think, were always right, but they are now nobler and more exalted. I am in every respect, so far as I am able to follow the dictates of my own mind, perfectly indifferent to all personal gratification. I know of nothing worth the living for but usefulness and the service of my fellow-creatures. The only object I pursue is to increase, as far as lies in my power, the quantity of their knowledge and goodness and happiness. And as I desire everything from God, I hope the situation in which I am now placed is that in which I am most likely to be useful. Always anxious to resemble the great Creator, can I be afraid of his displeasure? If he has resolved to punish in another world those who are most sincerely desirous to act properly and uprightly in this, what must we think of his goodness or his mercy?"

The same calm temperament which enabled him to dispense with much which is often thought of the essence of religion, seems to have kept him free also from any feeling which can be called love. Except the one great passion of his life, and even this was conducted with extreme outward and apparent phlegm, friendship stood to him in the

place of passion, as morality was to him in the room of devotion. All the jealousies, misunderstandings, wounded
feelings and the like, which some men experience in their
love affairs, Godwin suffered in his relations with his
friends. Fancied slights were exaggerated ; quarrels, ex-
postulations, reconciliations followed quickly on each other,
as though they were true *amantiam irae.* And his relations
with women were for the most part the same as those with
men. His friendships were as real with the one sex as
with the other, but they were no more than friendships.
Marriage seemed to him a thing to be arranged, "adjusted,"
as Mr Tennyson says of the loves of vegetables. Hence it
was that when settled in London he suggested to his sister
Hannah that she should choose him a wife. Her choice
fell on the lady whom Mrs Sothren calls "a great favourite
of mine," and thus she recommends her friend :—

Hannah Godwin to William Godwin.

29th June '84.

"I send" the letter enclosed "to you by way of introduction to
the only lady upon whom I could fix, since you said you should
like your sister to chuse you a wife. This was one of the thousand things I intended to tell you, that if you had neither fixed
upon any lady yourself, nor sworn to be an old bachelor, I had a
friend whom I thought might in every way meet your approbation,
and that I hoped that if you thought proper to offer your services
they might meet with acceptance, could I but be in London to introduce you. The young lady is in every sense formed to make
one of your disposition really happy. She has a pleasing voice,
with which she accompanies her musical instrument with judgment. She has an easy politeness in her manners, neither free
nor reserved. She is a good housekeeper and a good economist,
and yet of a generous disposition. As to her internal accomplish-

ments, I have reason to speak still more highly of them, good sense without vanity, a penetrating judgment without a disposition to satire, good nature and humility, with about as much religion as my William likes, struck me with a wish that she was my William's wife. I have no certain knowledge of her fortune, but that I leave for you to learn. I only know her father has been many years engaged in an employment which brings in £500 or £600 per ann., and Miss Gay is his only child. Mr Gay is very much of a gentleman, though one whom you would say savours too much of Methodism. . . . I have only mentioned you as my dearest brother, and added that I wished she were acquainted with you, to which she answered, 'need I say how much pleasure I should have in an acquaintance with one who is so high in the esteem of my dear Godwin.'

"I would not have you mention her to Jack, nor let him know that I have such friends in town, lest he should impose upon their kindness, for I know their friendship for me would induce them to behave respectfully to him, at the same time that I am sure he would be far from agreeable to them.

"What do you say now, my dear William, to my living with you? I certainly intend coming to live in London, hiring a couple of rooms, which, if agreeable to you, I should like to be in the same house with you, and taking in millinery work. . . . But where shall I get a little money to begin with? I shall want £20, and I have neither money nor credit. O my dear brother, how I please myself with the thought of living with you; you will read to me sometimes when I am at work (will you not?) and instruct me, and make me a clever girl.

"I am, with all my failings,

Your affectionate Sister,

H. Godwin.

Godwin answered this effusion, when some months had passed, by asking the lady's age and opinions, and after two more months he called upon her. What he wrote to his sister may be gathered from her reply to him.

The Same to the Same.

"*8th Feb.* 1785.

" . . . You have seen Miss Gay. You are not struck with her, but do not think it impossible for you to like her well enough to make certain proposals after a time : let me know the results of your next Interview. I wish to know your sentiments. If you do not approve of her for a wife, but wish to make her your intimate friend, trust me she is worth the trouble it may cost you.

Your obliged Friend and Sister,

H. GODWIN.

Godwin appears to have taken no notice of his sister's rapturous exclamations at the prospect of living with or near him, and he thought no more of the lady of her choice, who accordingly, for the matter was discussed in full family conclave, becomes "poor Miss Gay" in subsequent letters, as though Godwin had really behaved ill to her.

Although during this period of his life Godwin had no settled home, and was constantly changing his lodgings, he yet received a pupil, as has been said, who was apparently a boarder. The lad's name was Willis Webb, of whom nothing is now discoverable save what can be found in the letters which passed between them. He seems to have left a public school—probably Eton—to become Godwin's pupil, and to have gone from him to a large private school at Hitcham, near Eton. Old Hitcham Manor House was one of those many houses said "to have been visited by Queen Elizabeth." It was afterwards for a time the residence of Judge Jeffreys, and about the year 1700 that of Dr Freind, physician to Frederick, Prince of Wales, and afterwards to Queen Caroline. It then became a school, and the house was pulled down, though a part still remains as a cottage.

The grounds which surrounded it are merged in a larger estate. Thence Willis Webb was to go to one of the Universities, but "the Captain," presumably a step-father, did not exert himself about this final step, and kept the young man under tuition longer than the latter thought desirable. The letters show that Godwin was able to inspire genuine enthusiasm in the young, in spite of his somewhat formal manner of writing to his pupil, and they are the first instance of the way in which he was considered one to whom the young might resort as to an oracle. They are interesting also as a picture of school life ninety years ago. He writes to Godwin from Hitcham House, and, after giving an account of his school work, continues :—

Willis Webb to William Godwin.

" October 25, 1787.

.   . "To me, who have enjoyed the liberty of a public school, and experienced the liberality of private tuition, my present situation is extremely irksome and disagreeable. Confined within a narrow pale, I survey a beautiful country, which I am forbid to enter, on the penalty of expulsion from the society. I shudder at the reflexion that for a juvenile indiscretion, which is overlooked at a public institution, not considered as a fault in private education—(the merely taking a walk)—one's character is liable to be blasted by ignominious dismission.

"When, moreover, I consider that most of my contemporaries have finished their classical career, that mathematical knowledge can be acquired elsewhere with as much facility as at my present abode, that my character is hitherto unimpeachable, and by a timely secession from a place in which it is hourly exposed to imminent danger, will be secured, I confess I ardently desire to be admitted at the University, and to leave a society from which little profit and no pleasure is to be derived.

"Nor am I singular in my opinion that the University would be

C

the most advisable plan for my future education. Several men
of learning and experience, friends of my father (who, by-the-by,
had he lived, intended to have sent me this autumn to Oxford),
concur in recommending the same measure. I am now in my
eighteenth year, an age no longer puerile. My friends wish me
to assume the character of a man ; but how is this practicable
whilst they retain me in the shackles of a child ?

"Some people are apt to think that these private seminaries are
free from the vices of the age, but give me leave to assure you
they are grossly mistaken. The same vices that flourish at Eton
or Westminster are practised at Hitcham, with this *glorious* addition
that here deceit is necessary to conceal them; there they gratify
their passions without breach of truth and sincerity.

"Adieu, dear Sir, and believe me,

"Yours sincerely,

"W. WEBB.

"*P.S.*—The Captain intends to send me to Cambridge next
summer, because I shall then be more discreet. *Q.* Are the
passions of a young man of eighteen less strong than those of one
who is seventeen years and six months old ? "

Mr Webb at last got to St John's, Cambridge, where
his gratitude to his former tutor and his priggishness suffered no diminution. He writes from St John's College,
[Cambridge] :—

The Same to the Same.

"*Feb.* 24, [1788].

"I am very much pleased with the academical life ; in the
University one is at liberty to cultivate whatever branch of learning is most congenial to one's disposition. In the University one
has the opportunity of conversation with men of learning and
erudition ; we are indulged in every proper liberty, nor have we
the mortification of being subjected to illiberal and fruitless
restrictions.

"For my part, I chiefly cultivate the classics ; to the other

branch I was never much inclined, and though I shall endeavour
to make myself master of it, yet I am sure I shall never derive
much satisfaction from it. I am surprised that in the present
system of education so much attention should be paid to a science
which can never produce any real advantage in life to one that is
destined for a learned profession.

"I shall conclude, Dear Sir, with my best thanks for the part
you had in this affair, and remain, believe me,

"Yours sincerely,

"W. WEBB." ·

It is not, however, probable that Godwin, considerable as
was his success with Willis Webb, had a gift for the
drudgery of tuition. To write, converse, lecture, and in
these ways exert a great influence over others, and
especially the young, was a wholly different thing from
bearing with the wayward humours, ignorances, and needs
of lads who might not all be as receptive as his first pupil.
In the summer of 1788, while lodging for a while at Guildford, in Surrey, he took as a pupil, gratuitously, his kinsman, Thomas Cooper, then twelve years of age, who had
just lost his father in the East Indies. In the midst of his
own real poverty he was always ready to assist those in
need. Thomas Cooper was a second cousin of Godwin's,
their mothers being first cousins. Mr Cooper, the father,
had entered the service of the East India Company in 1770
as a ship's surgeon; he went two voyages, and was afterwards attached to the army in Bombay. About 1783 he
was appointed surgeon to the factory at Bauleah in Bengal,
where he died in October 1787, just as there appeared a
fair prospect of providing for his family. Some invest-
ments made immediately before his death turned out ill
when there was no one to look after them, "his effects at
Bauleah, and all his papers, books, and accounts were lost

in a great storm which swept over Bengal in November of
that year, while the executor was bringing them from
Bauleah for the greater convenience of arranging and
settling his affairs." Thus it appears that all means of
tracing considerable debts owing to Mr Cooper were lost,
while still further mismanagement in the conduct of the
business reduced the family to indigence. It had been
with them that Godwin passed some part of his Hoxton
vacations, and he now repaid this kindness by taking
charge of the elder orphan boy. The younger boy and a
girl were adopted by other relatives, and Mrs Cooper took
a situation as housekeeper. Mrs Shelley has left an interesting note on the characters of tutor and pupil, the two parties
in this experiment.

"Godwin, who, from the very nature of his opinions, was led
to analyse mind and draw conclusions as to character, had a
sanguine faith in the practicability of improvement, and entertained rigid opinions on the subject of education. Tom Cooper
was a spirited boy, extremely independent and resolute, proud,
wilful, and indolent. Godwin, conscientious to the last degree in
his treatment of everyone, extended his utmost care to the task of
education; but many things rendered him unfit for it. His severity
was confined to words, but these were pointed and humiliating.
His strictness was undeviating; and this was more particularly
the case in early life, when he considered the power of education
to be unlimited in the formation of character, the understanding, •
and temper. He took great pains with his kinsman, and devoted
attention and care to his instruction. To further his endeavours,
he kept notes of the occurrences that disturbed their mutual kindness, evidently as appeals to the lad's own feelings and understanding, endeavouring to awake in him a desire of reparation
when he had done wrong, and also of detailing and remarking on
any defects in his own behaviour. These papers throw light on
his own views of education, and show the conscientious and per-

severing nature of his endeavours. At the same time they display his faults as a teacher. He was too minute in his censures, too grave and severe in his instruction ; at once too far divided from his pupil through want of sympathy, and too much on a level from the temper he put into his lectures."

The following notes in reference to Cooper are taken almost at random from Godwin's diary during the years that the boy remained under his roof.

" Give energy, and mental exertion will always have attraction enough.

" Not to impute affected ignorance, lequel n'existe pas. Not to impute dulness, stupidity.

" Suaviter, oh ! suaviter, sed fortiter excita mentem.

" It is of no consequence whether a man of genius have learned either art or science before twenty-five : all that is necessary, or even desirable, is that his powers should be unfolded, his emulation roused, and his habits conducted into a right channel.

" He ought to love study, science, improvement.

" Is not his temper embittered by sternness ? *i.e.*, over-exactness in lessons and propensity to play the censor on trivial occasions ?

" Do not impute intentional error, lequel n'existe pas.

" It is now again probable that our connection will be permanent."—This was written after a severe illness of Cooper's, during which it was thought probable that there were seeds of consumption in him which might necessitate his removal to a warmer climate.—" Let me, then, again aim at gentleness, kindness, cordiality.

" Chide him for rudeness and impertinence to Mr Marshal : am heard with great sensibility. The rudeness was public in the mercer's shop.

" Take from him the translation of Gil Blas, which I yesterday forbade him to procure. Geometria lacrimans. Takes a walk, being engaged, to the Society's room, Adelphi ; comes home too late ; does not choose to apologise ; insist."

Another quarrel with Mr Marshal, who was at this time residing with Godwin, led to the following letter of apology, which shews the boy's disposition better than a hundred comments :—

Thomas Cooper to James Marshal.

"Sir,—I am convinced that I was wrong in not immediately desisting from that from which you desired me to desist ; I therefore ask your pardon, and I shall endeavour to make amends for my misconduct by my future behaviour.

"We have lived, sir, for some time in the same house, and, I believe, with a certain degree of friendship and good understanding. I am sorry that that friendship and good understanding have received such a shock as they have done to-day. I was certainly wrong, as I have already said, in not complying with your desire ; that non-compliance brought on high words, in course of which you directly called me a liar. You called me so, not by implication ; you said, 'You are a liar.'

"I am glad that I have escaped doing that which your words naturally excited me to do.   T. COOPER."

The same daily—and indeed hourly—squabbling lasted so long as Tom Cooper continued with Godwin, till Cooper was nearly seventeen ; and he from time to time relieved his feelings and refreshed his memory by writing down his tutor's "pointed and humiliating words." Here is one such memorandum :—

"He called me	*a foolish wretch*	in my presence.
"He said	*I had a wicked heart*	ditto.
"He would	*thrash me*	ditto. Does he think I would submit quietly?
"I am called	*a Brute*	in my absence.
"I am compared to	*a Viper*	ditto.
"He went out	*merely to avoid me*	ditto.

" I am	*a Tiger*	in my absence.
" I have	*a black heart*	ditto.
	No justice in it	ditto.
	No proper feelings	ditto.

" He has no enmity to my *person*, yet he hates me. I suppose he means by that that he does not think me very ugly," &c., &c.

This paper he, in a pet, addressed to Mr Godwin, and by design or accident put it in his way.

The following rough draft of a letter in reply throws much light on Godwin's character, and the wishes in respect to his ward by which he was guided :—

William Godwin to Thomas Cooper.

"*April* 19, 1790.

" MY DEAR BOY.—I am more pleased than displeased with the paper I have just seen. It discovers a degree of sensibility that may be of the greatest use to you, though I will endeavour to convince you that it is wrongly applied. I was in hopes that it was written on purpose for me to see ; for I love confidence, and there are some things that perhaps you could scarcely say to me by word of mouth. I have always endeavoured to persuade you to confidence, because you have not a friend upon earth that is more ardently desirous of your welfare than I, and you have not a friend so capable of advising and guiding you to what is most to your interest.

" This confidence would have been of use to you in what has lately passed ; and its continuance would be of use to you in all your future life. If I had seen this paper before last Tuesday, what passed on that day would not have happened. But I am closely engaged in observing what passes through your mind, and I observed a sulkiness and obstinacy growing up in it. You said to yourself, ' When I behave ill, I am only reprimanded ; and I do not mind that.' Thus when I have been endeavouring, in strong language, to point out your errors, and lead you to amend them, you have been employed with all your might in counteracting the impression I sought to make.

"There is in this paper a degree of sensibility that has great merit. The love of independency and dislike of unjust treatment is the source of a thousand virtues. If while you are necessarily dependent on me I treat you with heaviness and unkindness, it is natural you should have a painful feeling of it.

" But harshness and unkindness are relative. The appearance of them may be the fruits of the greatest kindness. In fact, can my conduct towards you spring from any but an ardent desire to be of service to you ? I am poor, and with considerable labour maintain my little family ; yet I am willing to spend my money upon your wants and pleasures. My time is of the utmost value to me, yet I bestow a large portion of it upon your improvement.

"Supposing I should be mistaken in any part of my conduct towards you, can it spring from anything but motives of kindness ? I ask for your confidence, because without it I am persuaded that I cannot do you half the good I could wish. It is not an idle curiosity. I care nothing about myself in this business. If I can contribute to make you virtuous and respectable hereafter, I do not care whether I then possess your friendship, I am contented you should hate me. I desire no gratitude, and no return of favours, I only wish to do you good. W. GODWIN."

The few letters which remain from Mrs Cooper to her son and to Godwin during this period are most touching. They present a sad picture of broken health, of humbled pride, of habits of intemperance resulting in part from her misery, against which the struggles were scarcely effectual, but there is no good gained by dissecting, as it were, a broken heart. What is here said may serve to account still further for the boy's proud, sensitive nature, and indeed to enhance the extreme kindness and forbearance of Godwin, though his judgment may sometimes have been in fault.

At the advice apparently of Holcroft, with the encouragement of Cook the actor, and Godwin's full approval, Tom Cooper determined to devote himself to the stage, but his earlier efforts met with scant success. The following letters record his impressions of John Kemble and Mrs Siddons, and his endeavours to gain a permanent stage engagement. They are all the remaining documents respecting him connected with our present period :—

Thomas Cooper to William Godwin.

"EDINBURGH, *Thursday, July* 27, 1792.

" I arrived here last night at nine, in high health and spirits, but my spirits were damped when upon my arrival I could get no bed nor lodging either at Edinburgh or Leith, on account of the races, which will end on Saturday. I went to Mr Kemble's this morning, at eleven, and he told me that at one he would hear me go through the character of Douglas. At one I went, but he left word (with his compliments) that he was obliged to go to Leith. To-morrow morning at twelve I am to rehearse with Mrs Siddons, and on Monday night am to make my first appearance in the character of Douglas. I am just returned to the inn from my second visit to Mr Kemble, to whom I went to know if I might not go to the play to-night. I *am* going, and Mrs Siddons plays Jane Shore. To-morrow the Road to Ruin is acted (not for the first time), to give some rest to Mrs S., who has acted several nights running. You will receive this Monday morning, and may expect another on Thursday or Friday, and so, hoping you will excuse bad writing on account of haste, I remain, yours everlastingly, T. COOPER.

" Friday, two o'clock.—'Sdeath, I'm sped! I have just rehearsed Douglas with the other actors before Mr Kemble. When I had done he walked aside with me, and told me he was sorry to say that he could not trust me with the character. He then made his individual objections. He said that in two descriptive speeches

I had a great deal too much passion, especially in the last ; and that in the scene with Glenalvon the audience would laugh at me.

" I asked him if he did not think Douglas was very angry ; he answered, Certainly, but that he was angry with good manners, and that he must not vex Mrs Siddons (she was not present) ; and, in short, he thought I was really too young to act a character of such importance, but that he would see about some other characters. Then, having parted, he said that if I would come to him next morning to breakfast, he would see if we could not manage Douglas by reading it together. Perhaps Mrs Siddons will be there, and I shall probably please her better, if she gives me a hearing, for I am certain I rehearsed as well as ever I did to Mr H. I have an infallible rule to judge by—the recollection of my own feelings. I should be glad to hear from you, if possible, by return of post. Direct to me at Mrs M'Lelland's, opposite the general entry, Potterrow St., Edinburgh. Nothing less will answer the purpose, for reasons which I have not room to explain."

The Same to the Same.

"*August*, 1792.

" My courage is as great as you could wish, considering that I stand upon a shaking foundation. Every time Mr Kemble sees me, I perceive, or think I perceive, a kind of discontent, arising from want of determination in his countenance. I do not keep company with any of the actors, except in the green room.

" I wish when you have room in any letter that you would give me some news. I have not heard any of Mr Pavie and France's proceedings since I left London. Let me know of mother's health, &c., soon. Is A. Dyson gone to France ? T. COOPER."

" Monday.—The above was written on Saturday, since which something of importance has occurred. I went this morning into the pay-room to receive my money, and having got it, asked Mr Kemble's advice relative to my manner of travelling to London, whither we remove in the middle of this week. ' Why, really, Mr Cooper, I think the best thing you can do is to go back to Lon-

don.' I told him that I believed if he would give me a hearing in
Lothario I could please him. He said I was not at all fit to play
it. Then he began to talk in a hesitating way about my being of
no use on account of my being inexperienced in stage matters. I
said that if that were true in every instance plays would live as
long as, and no longer than actors at present existing should live.
In short, I argued the case a little with him, told him that I had
learned the characters in London. He then said that he had a
great respect for Mr Holcroft, and must endeavour to bring me
forward little by little.

" To-night I am one of Mrs Siddons's train (dumb as usual) in
the Mourning Bride. On Wednesday I am to be the second
witch in Macbeth. Mr Kemble told me that if he had thought
of it in time, I should have played Malcolm, and desired me to
learn it. On Thursday I believe I shall begin my march to Lan-
caster, arriving there Sunday night. I shall stay there a week, and
then for Sheffield."

The Same to the Same.

" NEWCASTLE, *Aug.* 11, 1792.

" I did leave such directions at Edinburgh as answered the purpose of bringing your letter immediately to hand, which I think it
was most probable I should do, as I had begged you to write by
return of post. I think your observation relative to my being
too loud in rehearsal was the true cause of Mr Kemble's rejection
of my Douglas : but as you say, that belief is of little consequence
(except, indeed, that it will be a warning to my future conduct),
since I have had no second hearing, and I am afraid shall not
have, for Mrs Siddons, on account of her health, is unwilling to
play any characters that require her greatest exertion. She has
already played Jane Shore, Desdemona, to-night Mrs Beverley,
for the last time but two, one of the two is to be Zara, of the
other I am ignorant : so that you perceive there is very little
chance for me. I have learned since that it is to be Lady
Macbeth.

" I am, as you say, at a loss for a subject, the strangeness of

which will vanish when you consider that I am deprived of the
characters in which I expected to shine : that I am obliged to
sit down with a black gown over my shoulders as a dumb
senator (which I have done twice in the plays of Shylock and
Othello ! !) and hear Mr Kemble hold forth with the most im-
petuous rant, with sudden, ill-timed, unmeaning risings and fall-
ings of voice, to astonish the vulgar, and confound the wise by
not articulating a single syllable ; and to hear Mr Woods repeat
his words in one dull, heavy, monotonous sound.   This circumstance is so remarkable in Woods, that having repeated a part of
Lord Hastings' speech with tolerable propriety, and having made
a pause introducing a totally different feeling and passion, and by
his pause, and the length of it, rousing every individual to the
highest pitch of eagerness and expectation, he begins to speak,
and on the instant destroys all pleasure by the repetition of the
very same sound.   I uttered, at the very first syllable, an involuntary groan (this was at the first time of my seeing him), and a
dirty scene-shifter, cursing him, expressed his dissatisfaction in a
very characteristically awkward manner.   Woods speaks with a
remarkably graceful action and easy deportment.   Then to perceive a number of dull fools who scarcely even pretend to know
their right hands from their left, fill up the other characters, without my being considered worthy to utter a syllable ; your astonishment, I say, must vanish when you consider these things, for it is
natural that a mind reflecting on them should withdraw itself to
talk of the height of steeples, the length of streets, the nature of
the soil, &c., &c.

" Mr Woods was to have played Glenalvon, but was obliged to
undertake Douglas, which he had never played before ; in consequence of which a Mr Sparkes took his Glenalvon.   My reception
was such as I could wish : the actors are all very civil, and the
higher are not distant and proud.   Mr Bell, and others of some
consequence, give me advice, in general insignificant enough, but
tolerably good of its kind.   You need be under no apprehension
concerning money, for I get a guinea every Monday."

The Same to the Same.

"NEWCASTLE, *Aug.* 16, 1792.

"The die is cast, and when, having tottered some time, I thought myself firm, at that instant the fate was reversed, and I fell headlong without hopes of recovery. I will now explain my meaning, and I am afraid that the explanation will be more serious than you may expect from this introduction. I told you in my last of the doubtful manner of talking of Mr Kemble, and at last of his saying that he would keep me, and endeavour to bring me forward, on account of his respect for Mr Holcroft. Irresolute blockhead! he has again altered his mind. Now he has got the shadow of a reason for his final determination, to which, although one of the most irresolute, I believe he will adhere; but observe, although I call it the shadow of a reason, I do not mean to say that I was without blame. He desired me to study Malcolm against the next time it was acted. But the next morning I told him that I would undertake it for that time, as I had two before me : he consented. I went through the part very well, and tolerably perfectly, till I came within two lines of the end of the play (I speak the last speech), and there I wanted the word. The noise behind scenes, the play being nearly over, prevented my hearing the prompter, and in an instant some people at the back of the gallery, as I guessed, began to hiss, and immediately everybody else began to clap, which lasted for a minute, and as we were so near the end it was not advisable to wait the conclusion of the bustle to say the few words that remained. The trumpets sounded, and the curtain fell. My blame consisted in want of courage, or recollection, in not skipping to the next line the very instant they began to hiss, and it was impossible to catch the word. Mr Kemble made this his handle, declared I was totally unfit for the profession, and that I had not one single requisite for an actor, and in fine, he said, 'As a friend, I advise you to return to London. I cannot keep you.' I told him that I would undertake anything, however low, if I was not qualified for higher, and in proportion to my little utility would be willing to receive little.

I told him I should be willing to take the salary of Mr Charteris, junr. (a foolish fellow about my age), and he certainly could not deny that I should be of equal, if not more utility than him. He could not deny it, but he did not want a person of that description —that Mr Ch. was going to leave. I thought I had submitted already too much for honesty, and therefore would submit no further. I asked if that was his reason for dismissing him. This question was a home-thrust at his own equivocation. He said, ' he had no business to account to me for his motives.' I answered ironically, begging his pardon that it was an improper question. I believe he understood me literally. I have too much dependence on your sense of justice to think that you will blame me for not stooping to his pride any further than honesty would justify, and altering my manner when I perceived his injustice, which I did with moderation, as appears from his not even understanding my irony (which perhaps you do not, for from hurry I'm afraid I am not very intelligible). I ought to observe, in addition, that Mr Charteris goes away by his own choice with a number of other actors from Mr Kemble's company, who are going to stroll as a sharing company. I have been endeavouring to get admission into it, but have not succeeded, and I suppose shall not. The most disagreeable part of my most disagreeable situation, is that I am afraid I must determine on something without waiting for advice. I write, however. If you can suggest any means by which in London I can earn 10s. 6d. per week, at the expense even of four or five hours a day. 10s. 6d. is sufficient to live on. Write . . . I shall presently be left alone here. It is now Thursday. They play here for the last time on Friday.

T. Cooper."

Mr James Marshal, to whom was addressed Tom Cooper's curious letter quoted above, was a friend who for some time shared Godwin's house, and each would seem to have aided the other when in need, struggling against such difficulties as only those can know whose daily bread depends upon their daily writings. Mrs Shelley speaks of him with affectionate enthusiasm as follows :—

" There was another man, a fellow student, and an aspirant to the honours of literature. The booksellers of London in his day knew him well, and many a contemporary author, fallen on evil days, many a widow and orphan had cause to remember the benevolent disposition, the strenuous exertions, the kind and intelligent countenance of James Marshal. His talents not permitting a higher range, he became a translator and index maker, a literary jobber. In a thousand ways he was useful to Godwin, who, sensitive, proud, and shy, whose powers of persuasion lay in the force of his reasoning, often found the more sociable and insinuating manners of his friend of use in transacting matters of business with editors and publishers. They often shared their last shilling together, and the success of any of his friend's plans was hailed by Marshal as a glorious triumph. Godwin, whose temper was quick, and, from an earnest sense of being in the right, somewhat despotic on occasions, assumed a good deal of superiority and some authority. Marshal sometimes submitted, sometimes rebelled, but they were always reconciled at last, and the good-humoured friend was always at hand to assist to the utmost Godwin's more intellectual exertions in copying, or in walking from one end of town to the other."

He had acted as amanuensis to Godwin at an earlier date, but having got into considerable difficulties, went to the West Indies to seek his fortune. Not having found it, he soon came back again to work for, and quarrel with Godwin once more.

Another man of very different stamp was much with Godwin in those years. George Dyson was a friend of Thomas Cooper. He was a young man whose abilities promised much, and whose ardour for literature and desire to do right seemed to give assurance that such promise would be realised. Unfortunately violent passions and a vehement temper ruined these hopes. Godwin spared neither remonstrance nor censure to keep him straight, and though these were sometimes received with remorseful confessions of their justice, sometimes with bitter resentment, they did not in the end avail. In various disputes which arose between Cooper and Dyson, Godwin seems to have taken, on the whole, Dyson's part; but in the end the breach between these old friends became too wide for healing, and Dyson's name only appears in these pages to give occasion for the touching lines which Godwin addressed to him, later indeed than this date, but as the conclusion of many a fierce paper war.

William Godwin to George Dyson.

"I hope and still strongly incline to believe that I shall one day see you, complete in talent, and free from every stain of those vices which I have always suspected, and now vehemently disapprove in you. You have been one of my prime favourites, and whatever may be the vicissitudes of your character, the deviousness of your conduct, or the fermentation of your uncontrollable passions, they will all be watched by me with affectionate anxiety. You may grieve me, but you cannot inspire me with anger.

" W. GODWIN.

" *Friday Evening.*"

With all his faults, however, Dyson must have been a very remarkable man. He is the third of those of whom Godwin speaks as being "the four oral instructors" to whom he felt his "mind indebted for improvement," thus ranking him with Fawcet, Holcroft, and Coleridge, although he was so much younger than himself, and standing in so evident need of fatherly counsel and control.

We have seen already that in these years Godwin had become "extremely intimate" with Holcroft. It would seem to have been a characteristic of the literary men of those days that the most furious verbal onslaughts on each other brought no real diminution of friendship. Godwin and his friends were typical examples of this. The first of the following notes, which commences the correspondence between Holcroft and himself, is undated, but it would seem to have been written immediately before the other, and they appear to refer to one and the same engagement.

Thomas Holcroft to William Godwin.

"I will certainly not fail you, God willing, on Tuesday. Sentimental hypocrisy you know I treat nearly the same as other hypocrisy, therefore I think you will not blame me for telling you we were yesterday, as I told you we should be, driven, &c. But I know you—what *is* who can resist? Had I but the power to remove difficulties from all of us—oh, there would be rare doings! For heaven's sake do not torment yourself; times and seasons have strange variations, and who knows that the sun will never shine. T. HOLCROFT."

The Same to the Same.

"SIR,—I write to inform you that instead of seeing you at dinner to-morrow I desire never to see you more, being determined never to have *any* further intercourse with you of *any* kind. T. HOLCROFT.

"*Feb.* 28, 1785."

"I shall behave as becomes an honest and honourable man who remembers not only what is due to others, but himself.

I. D

There are indelible irrevocable injuries that will not endure to be mentioned. Such is the one you have committed on the man who would have *died* to serve you."

The estrangement happily did not last long, but no further letters are preserved till the summer of 1788, when Godwin was staying at Guildford, and was glad to receive news from Holcroft in London.

The vacancy for the City of Westminster, the main subject of the following letters, was occasioned by the appointment of Lord Hood, the sitting member, to be a Lord of the Admiralty. He, of course, offered himself for re-election, and was opposed by Lord John Townshend, in the liberal interest. The poll was kept open from Friday, July 18th, till Monday, August 4th, on which day Lord John Townshend was elected by a majority of 823. The excitement during the election was very great, and the compliments bandied on both sides unusual, even for the license of the day. That a lawyer was thrown out of the window of Lord Hood's committee room into a night-cart, was a specimen of the amenities of parties. "This," mildly says the *Public Advertiser*, which supported Lord Hood, "is a species of outrage not easily to be justified in a civilized community. No subjects have a right to take the law into their own hands."

Thomas Holcroft to William Godwin.

"LONDON, *July 24th*, 1788.

"DEAR SIR,—I am greatly obliged by your kind attention, but Trenck—'The Life of Baron F. von der Trenck,' translated from the German by T. Holcroft—"I find, must not go to press yet; there are 250 copies overlooked, so that when you return to town it will be time enough to marginate—yes, marginate. It needs little philosophy to prove that if no man had ever made innovations, we should all have been dumb.

"The tide is turned, instead of Townshend. The whole Town, great and small, old and young, the little vulgar and the great, seem all to be bawling, 'Hood for ever!' 'The beast with two horns (blue and orange) appears to have pushed westward and northward and southward, till behold an he-goat came from the West.' Despatches from Cheltenham, Pitt and Treasury runners, canvassing, Military interference, the potent Magistrate Sir Sampson Wright collared by Sheridan, Bayonets pointed at patriot throats, James Parry, Esq., become a leader from the breakfasting-houses in company with Lord William Russell, &c. Oh, here is the devil to pay! A mad world, my masters! Women murdered, Men with their skulls fractured, sailors with broken arms, Bullies committed, Freedom maintained by battle-array, soldiers polling by hundreds and sent to the house of correction by (oh! no, I had forgotten—bailed by their officers, who commanded them to present, and if occasion were to fire), the Foxites disagreeing and disunited, Liberty Hall in an Uproar, Pitt and prerogative triumphant, &c., &c., &c. For I am quite out of breath. Observe, however, I will not vouch for the truth of a single syllable of all this; but I will cite you most grave and respectable authorities, viz., Herald and Post. This, however, you may, if so it you shall please, affirm from me, sir, namely, that scandal (and, I believe, falsehood), pitiful, mean, mutual scandal, never was more plentifully dispersed; and that electioneering is a trade so despicably degrading, so eternally incompatible with moral and mental dignity, that I can scarcely believe a truly great mind capable of the dirty drudgery of such vice. I am at least certain no mind is great while thus employed. It is the periodical reign of the evil nature or Demon. A most paltry apology, but the best I can make.

"Since writing the above, having the advantage of an exquisitely dizzy headache, I strolled, in company with this delightful associate, to the hustings, and thence into Westminster. ''Fore heaven, they are all in a tune.' I must indeed except three

unities, whom in my traverse sailing progress I encountered
between the Garden and the Horse Guards, *i.e.*, a Barber's boy,
a Lamplighter's Do., and a young Chimneysweeper, who all had
the singularity to wear '*Townshend for ever*' pinned in front. No:
two of them were in Hedge Lane. One thing amazes me: the walls
abound in squibs and pasquinades, many of them keen and excellently adapted to the capacity of their serene worships the worthy
Electors of Westminster, all for Lord Hood, and no sign of any
such in behalf of Townshend. This is the very reverse of what
might have been expected. 'Tis plain the Hoodites have been
most remarkably active, and I suspect the adverse party has been
very foolishly lulled to sleep by Mrs Security. To afford you
some small comfort, however, let me tell you an active Foxite has
laid 10 Guineas to five that Townshend is 100 ahead at the poll,
and affirms that he shall himself go up to the Hustings to-morrow
(Friday) at the head of 400 voters. In the meantime the state of
the poll yesterday was —

" July 23d. — Hood,   2892
Townshend, 2741

———

Majority,   151

and according to the account I have just received, for I sent expressly to afford you as much of that information which your aunt
Abigail desires as possible—

" July 24th, 5 P.M. — Hood,   3380
Townshend, 3258

———

Majority,   122

" The Lord knows when I wrote so long a letter before, or
when I shall again.—I am, dear sir, very sincerely,

" T. HOLCROFT."

The Same to the Same.

"LONDON, *August 4th*, 1788.

"As I know, Dear Sir, you interest yourself in the present
desperate (I had almost said despicable) contest, I take it for

granted you will be glad to hear that your favourite, Lord John Townshend, is elected. I have sent to know the exact state of the poll, but it was impossible to obtain it with certainty. I hear the balance is 823 in favour of Lord John. The universal cry of the Hood party at present is bad votes and Parliamentary scrutiny. I imagine this scene is soon again to be renewed, *i.e.*, at the General Election. The Hoodites publish such long lists of bad votes, and exclaim so loudly, that the vulgar opinion is that the present election will be declared void, which, however, I think improbable. I imagine you received the strange olio I wrote before in the form of a letter. Affairs took another turn, I believe the very day after I wrote. The cry of the mob has uniformly gone with the majority, but this is no newly discovered principle in man. Though my letter required no answer, I begin to fear lest, wanting a more accurate direction, you have not received it; pray be so much of an Irishman as to write an answer to this, whether you receive it or no. I intend to ride down and pay you a visit, if I can, in the course of next week; but I do not suppose it will be more than the visit of a day.—I am, dear Sir, very sincerely yours,   T. HOLCROFT."

" Mr Godwin,
   at Mr ——, Upholsterer,
      Guildford, Surrey."

William Godwin to Thomas Holcroft.

"GUILDFORD, *August 5th*, 1788.

"DEAR SIR.—Though I am flattered by your attention, and must acknowledge that you have touched upon my hobbyhorse, yet I am sorry that your politeness led you to give yourself a moment's trouble for the sake of gratifying the silly impatience of your humble servant. I owe you a thousand apologies for not having answered your letter of a fortnight since; but the fact is I wrote to you and another gentleman, immediately after my arrival, by the same post, and was answered by said gentleman that I was a man of leisure and could write letters; he was engaged in active life, and could not. No man is less willing to be guilty of the sin of intrusion than I am : I therefore took this rebuff in dudgeon, and forswore the writing of any letters but of mere business for a fortnight. Will you accept this apology ? If you do, in gratitude I will damn you, and say you have more good-nature than wit.

"If you did but properly reflect upon my desolate situation, banished from human society, and condemned to eat grass with the beasts, you surely would not tantalize me with the visit of a day. But be it as it will, for I can adapt to myself the words of Addison with true Addisonian fire, and say—

> " ' A day, an hour, of intellectual talk
> Is worth a whole eternity of solitude.'

Only upon this occasion keep the reins in your own hands, and do not fetter yourself too much with domestic stipulations before you set out.

"Sir, had you remembered the letter of the Chinese Mandarin, which had no other address than ' Dr Boerhaave, Europe,' you surely would not have insulted me with the supposition that I must borrow lustre from a petty upholsterer in such a town as Guildford, and not be seen by own radiance. I would have you to know that I am as much of a poet as either Dr Boerhaave, or even Van Swieten, his commentator. Nay, if you provoke me, I do not know but I shall enter the lists with Mynheer Van Haaren, the Homer of the whole Dutch nation.

"Lord John Townshend for ever ! Huzza !

"Yours sincerely,

"W. GODWIN.

"Present my compliments to Robinson and Hamilton. Tell the latter (if you see him, and if you like it) that he has forgotten me."

The only other letter of special interest relating to this time is the following from Mrs Godwin senior, to which may also be added one of somewhat later date, since it fits in more appropriately here, with the notices of the Coopers and of Hannah Godwin. Hull Godwin was Mrs Godwin's eldest son, with whom she was residing.

Mrs Godwin senior to William Godwin.

"*May* 29, 1788.

" DEAR WILLIAM,--Your letter to be sure could not fail of being pleasing and acceptable to me, who delights to hear from my children, espetially when they are going on comfortably and are likely to be a blessing to their connections and an ornament to Religion w^h is not the least part of w^t we are sent into the World for. poor dear Hannah once made it her Chief concern and happiness but now I fear it is otherwise, God grant It may revive again And y^t she may not be as the fig-tree whome the master of the vinyard came seeking fruit and found none. Is my daily prayer for her and all of you poor Jack once made a profession two but him I have no hopes off. I may say the same of Joseph how cuting a Stroke it is to be the means of bringing Children into the world to be the subjects of the kingdom of Darkness to dwell with Divils and Damned Spirits from whence as I have heard you mention in your Prayers there is no redemption. Sometime agoe I lent Hannah a book of Sermons that was not my own, but not without the owner's live Mr Copland, I red them myself and was Charmed with them, espetially as there was one about declention having lost their first love which I hoped might have a better effect than all I could say. please from me to desire her to return the first privat opportunity y^t will be safe directed to Mrs Sothrens, she have miss'd Mr Burchan who would have brought it safe. You say Miss Anna Trench is going to be married and I suppose by what you mention to live the Partnership to her Sister Miss Frances Trench and your Sister as with Miss Trench why can't you call your Sister Hannah as you call Miss Trenches Nancy and Fanny and me Hon'd Mother, as well as Mad'm it would be full as agreeable.

" You say by great luck Joseph has got a comfortable Place I wish it may Prove so and he deserving of it but If He prospers I shall think it strange indeed that one could use a Woman as he has, an agreeable Woman his own Choice and brought him some fortune and also her friends always doing for her.—and of Jack he is still the unfortunate man. It is not Scripture Language I do not as I know off read of luck or fortune then I think it rather the Language of Heathens and that it should be owned as the smiles or frowns of Providence or in other words God.

"but I don't want to enter into arguments with you ab¹ it for perhaps I might not find words or time to go thro it, therefore if its not agreeable to your notion it will be better to pass it by and you keep yours and I mine. I had Jackey's letter but could not find an opportunity to send the 20ˢ he was out of pocket for Natty when he was hiding from yᵉ Press Gang till now, and this acquaints you that I have sent yᵉ guinea by the hand of Mr Jⁿᵒ Johnson which is the second on Natty's account and the full of what I promiss'd and I dont thank Jackey for taking him into good company as he calls it every Evening and two or three Sunday's executions. I like your Conduct to him much better Jackey says you gave him 5ˢ at parting—my kind love to my dear Hannah.

I remain yʳ affecate Mother.

"Cousin Sothren Mrs Hull and Hully are well I hope I am at Norwich and parted with the 2 last mentioned yesterday."

The Same to the Same.

"DALLING, *Sep*. 5, '92.

"DEAR WILLIAM,—I earnestly pray you may be making progress Heavenward, that is my fear and question on account of the little apearance of religion in those that are left as well as those yᵗ are departed this life. my life is bitter, am obliged to cry out with David Ps. 13 How long wilt thou forget me O Lord forever, How long wilt thou hide thy face from me. I may say I pray without ceasing for you, 3 times a Day, besides the sleepless Hours of the night, and my strength is so feble that I know not how to sustain myself in the day some times. I know that its God's work to make the hart suseptable of divine Impressions. Not ye most Eloquent preachers, for they are but Earthen Vesels, Paul and Apolos may water, but without God gives the increase no fruit will spring up. God's word is full of promisses to those that seek in sincerity, relying on Christ as the atoning sacrifice and intercesor, for sure I am that sinners cannot be justified and accepted by any righteousness of their own. His word declares that by the works of the Law shall no flesh be justified and for that reason Christ came to make a propitiation to Offended justis that all who believe in him might be saved. You know its not ment without showing their faith by their Obedience as far as we in our fallen and depraved state are capable, but its not said that his affronted and despised patience will last always, a bare crying for mercy at last is a dangerous experiment. I'm obleged to you for the respect you profsess for me. If I could see my children walk in ye truth I should be happy, my Happiness is bound up in theirs. It would sweeten my expiring moments, with Views of meeting those I have been ye Instrument of bringing into life, in the happy regions of blesedness where all perplecty will for ever cease. Thank y^o for ye information you gave me respecting Natty, as to ye name of ye Ship Capt &c. am sorry he has not a better constitution, for he can have but few indulgencies in the way of life He is in. the tempers of seafairing men are generaly like the boisterous Element. I hope there will come a time when he will fare better, tho I dont think Mr Hurry have been so kind to him as might be expected considering he had been so many years in his service. his perseverance is a good sign, for what could be done with him otherwise I dont know. Am realy sorry John should accept an iniquitous imployment. I think he might make a living of the two clarks places without the Lottery. I gave him my advice before I rec^d yours or knew anything about it, not to disoblige Mr Finch least he should loose his place. but would have you use all the influence you have to prevale with him to keep the two places, and never more to Ingage in the Lottery. I think he might do exceeding well with his pay and the perquisites. I sincerely wish Mrs Cooper cou'd meet with an agreabl sittuation, believe they are hard to be met with, believe there is something in her temper that forbids happiness. It must give Miss Cooper much uneasiness. Miss Cooper is I think a very senceable, prudent agreable Girl. Poor Hannah wrote me of the unlucky accident that befel her of her being push'd down in the street, and her Cloths being Spoil'd. It was a great mercy she escaped so well as She did, and was able to get home. I hope it will be a warning not to be out of an Evining, at least not to come home alone. Intend writing to her soon. am glad she has got such an agreable Girl as Miss Green to bare her company. I was exceeding hurt that you should have borrow'd 5 guineas of Mr Venning so long and then say to me when I was in Town he was so mean as to mention it. What would you have him do, or what would you have done in such a predicament. However I have paid it, and shall expect your note for it. You can inquire at Fish Street Hill when its likely Mr Jacob will be in town for you to meet him, and give a proper note. These things so often repeated with all the œconemy I am mistress of shall not be able to do anything for the young ones.

"I have a few friends that I highly value, Mrs Sothren and Mrs Foster, and Mrs A. Hill is a comfort and help to me, but Mrs Sothren is a person you ought to Rever as your second Mother, who nurtured you in your infancy. I did not expect she would got this winter over, she is so assmatic, thro divine mercy she is yet spared, and I hope shall see her in the course of the summer. Mrs Hill was confined near 6 weeks, has a bad complant of her neck, otherwise is much as usual. She and Hully desire to be remember'd to you.

"from your Affec^ate Mother,

"A. GODWIN."

CHAPTER III.

THE notes already mentioned, which are mainly the authority for the facts of this portion of Godwin's life, are supplemented by a diary begun by him on the 6th of April 1788, and continued to the end of his life. It was contained in thirty-two small notebooks, all of which have been preserved. They are ruled and dated most carefully in black and red ink, for those were not days in which such diaries could be purchased ready to hand, and are marvels of neatness and method. This record is extremely concise, and contrary to the usual practice of journal keepers, is even more laconic at the beginning than towards the end. The use made of this diary was to mention the portion of writing accomplished each day, the books read, the persons seen, the places visited. In the earlier volumes many days, and even weeks are sometimes left without an entry, and the most full account extends to but a few words. But for the last forty years of his life there is no omission of even a single day. It appears that he was at this time widely extending his circle of acquaintance, and nearly all the names mentioned are those of men worth knowing.

The following specimens of two weeks may prove of interest :—

"*Apr.* 6. Su.
" 7. M. Called at Webb's.
" 8. Tu. Brand Hollis called. The Ton written by La
      Wallace acted.
" 9. W.
" 10. Th. Hasting's trial resumed.
" 11. F. Dined at Leg of Pork. Dr Priestley in London.
" 12. Sa.
"*May* 4. Su. Dine at Holcroft's. Call on Mr Close, Tower Hill.
" 5. M.
" 6. Tu.
" 7. W. Hear Sir G. Elliot. Dine at Holcroft's.
" 8. Th. Tea Holcroft's. Dinner at Cadel's, and on Gib-
      bon's birthday and day of publication.
      Sheffield, Fullarton, Reynolds, Gillies, Kippis,
      Cour Plénière.
" 9. Fr. Exhibition. Nunducomar 55 to 73. Speak with
      O'Brien. Priestley from London.
" 10. Sa. Wilson calls. Correct for him Graham's Letter
      to Pitt on Scotch Reform."

Much of this diary has now become simply enigmatical,
such as the entries—"Aug. 4. Th. Jour de mauvaise nouvelle. Marshal for Southampton." "Nov. 22. Sa. Meilleur
nouvelle. Robinson calls," and much which touches on the
mere opinion of the day proves unhistorical, as " Nov. 7.
F. Dine at Hamilton's with Robinson, Arch^{d.}, Holcroft,
Nicholson, and Mercier, Le roi mourant." The king's illness was his first temporary seizure, from which he entirely
recovered. But to those who have turned over the pages
of the diary, with their short unimpassioned records of forgotten sorrows and forgotten joys, of keen political struggles
and of eloquent voices hushed, there rises a very vivid picture of the dead past, far more life-like than they have
gained from more elaborate histories.

Godwin, calm as he seemed, was stirred to his depths by politics. Holcroft knew his friend when he wrote him the details of the Westminster election, and to eager hearts at the close of the last century it seemed an easier thing to undo admitted evils than we now find it, who are the children and grandchildren of those who were roused by the sound of the first French Revolution. The following is the note on the year 1789 :—

"'This was the year of the French Revolution. My heart beat high with great swelling sentiments of Liberty. I had been for nine years in principles a republican. I had read with great satisfaction the writings of Rousseau, Helvetius, and others, the most popular authors of France. I observed in them a system more general and simply philosophical than in the majority of English writers on political subjects ; and I could not refrain from conceiving sanguine hopes of a revolution of which such writings had been the precursors. Yet I was far from approving all that I saw even in the commencement of the revolution. . . . I never for a moment ceased to disapprove of mob government and violence, and the impulses which men collected together in multitudes produce on each other. I desired such political changes only as should flow purely from the clear light of the understanding, and the erect and generous feelings of the heart."

The diary of this year, though written with the same extreme brevity, shows that he followed with keen interest the course of events in France, as "June 23. Tu. Difference of Necker and the king : he proposes to resign. Dine at Hollis's with the Garbets. 24. W. Necker is restored." "July 11. Sa. Necker is dismissed." "15. W. King of France submits to the National Assembly." Under "Nov. 5. W.," is the following entry :—"Dine with the Revolutionists : see Price, Kippis, Rees, Towers, Lindsay, Disney, Belsham, Forsaith, Morgans, Listers, S. Rogers, and B.

Wits." " Present Earl Stanhope, Beaufoy, H. Tooke, and Count Zenobio. See B. Hollis, Jennings, Lofft, and Robinson. Sup with Fawcet." " The Revolutionists " were the members of one among many clubs existing at that day composed of men who sympathised more or less with the friends of liberty in France. Their President at this time was Charles, Earl Stanhope. Dr Price had preached— Nov. 4th, 1789—a sermon before them at the Old Jewry Meeting House, and their proceedings generally had attracted considerable attention, which was heightened by the eloquence of Burke, directed against them. The following draft of a communication from English to French Republicans belongs to this time. It bears no date, and is evidently only a rough copy in Marshal's handwriting, but the words are the words of Godwin.

" GENTLEMEN,—We acknowledge with the utmost pleasure the communication you have made us of sentiments honourable to the country of which you are natives, and calculated to advance political society to a state of enviable felicity. The Revolution Society of London does not pretend to the authority of being the organ of the national sentiment. We are a body of private individuals, who can claim little other distinction than what we derive from a love of freedom, reason, and humanity. With no desire to be regarded as of great political importance, we do not scruple to do everything in our power for the dissemination of benevolence, liberality, and truth.

" We join with you, gentlemen, in the most ardent wishes that that freedom which for several centuries appeared to have fixed her last retreat in the island of our birth, may, by your example, be diffused over Europe and the world. So admirable and illustrious an example cannot be lost. The proceedings of the people of France will secure tranquillity, and all the virtues of patriotism to themselves, and a dawn of justice and moderation to surrounding nations. The inhabitants of Great Britain in particular may expect to derive the most essential benefit from the Revolution of France; and united as we are to you by congeniality of sentiment, by the cultivation of science and truth, and by the love of that freedom for which our ancestors bled, we trust it is scarcely possible for any occasion to offer that can lead two such nations to engage in mutual hostilities."

Godwin lived much in society during this year, being a very constant visitor at the house of Miss Helen Maria Williams, where many literary people congregated almost every night at tea-time. There are repeated notices of intimacy with Willis Webb, his old pupil, and of almost daily meetings with Holcroft. On this friend fell the great sorrow of the death of his son in November 1789.

His son was a lad of sixteen, who had long shown a wild and wandering disposition, and, young as he was, had several times run away from home. He had, however, seemed of late more steady, and had been in consequence praised and rewarded by his father. But the old disposition again showed itself. On Nov. 8 he broke open his father's desk, stole from it £40 and a pair of pistols, and set off to join a friend who was sailing for the West Indies. He was pursued to Gravesend, but there for a time all trace was lost. A few days after he was found to be at Deal, on board the " Fame," and on a search being made he concealed himself in the steerage. He had said that he would shoot whoever came to take him, unless it was his father, in which case he would shoot himself. This his father considered to be a mere threat. He was called, but did not answer. A light was procured, but as soon as the lad heard his father advancing, with the ship's steward and some of the crew, he suddenly shot himself, unable to bear the shame of open detection. The shock to Holcroft was very great. For a whole year afterwards he seldom left his house, and the impression was never wholly effaced from his mind.

The entries in Godwin's journal show that he was the friend who accompanied the father first to Gravesend and afterwards to Deal to seek the fugitive. They are as follows:—

> " Nov. 8. Tu. Dine at Holcroft's—Elopement de son fils.
> " 9. M. To Gravesend.
> " Nov. 15. Su. Dine at Holcroft's: set out for Deal. Call upon Crosdil W. Holcroft.
> " 16. M. Mort de son fils.
> " 17. Tu. Funerailles : to have drank tea with Holcroft at Miss Williams's.
> " Nov. 22. Su. Dine at Holcroft's : Crosdil calls.
> " 27. F. Dine at Holcroft's: write a paragraph sur son fils."

Mrs Shelley has left a short note on this occurrence :

" The youth was of an unfortunate disposition, and his conduct was very reprehensible, at the same time it is certain that Holcroft carried further than Godwin a certain unmitigated severity, an exposition of duty and truth, and of the defalcation from these in the offender, conceived in language to humiliate and wound, a want of sympathy with the buoyant spirit of youth when conjoined to heedlessness and, it may be added, dissipation, all of which tended to set still wider the distance too usually observed between father and child. Something of this Godwin detected in himself in his conduct towards Cooper. I mention this circumstance the more particularly, as it, several years afterwards, caused the breach between Holcroft and Godwin which was never healed until the death of the former."

Under the year 1790 Godwin writes :

" My mind became more and more impregnated with the principles afterwards developed in my Political Justice ; they were the almost constant topic of conversation between Holcroft and myself; and he, who in his sceptic and other writings had displayed the sentiments of a courtier, speedily became no less a republican and a reformer than myself. In this year I wrote a tragedy on the story of St. Dunstan, being desirous, in writing a tragedy, of developing the great springs of human passion, and in the choice of a subject of inculcating those principles on which I apprehend the welfare of the human race to depend."

The Diary becomes somewhat more full, recording here and there scraps of conversation. He took the same vivid interest in foreign politics, and he also attended the debates in the House of Commons. Some fragments which belong to this period show that the ambition to be himself a Member was not strange to him, and he mentions with pleasure that Sheridan had once said to him, "You ought to be in Parliament." He speaks of another dinner with the "French Revolutionists," at which were present "Stanhope, Sheridan, Tooke, O'Brien, B. Hollis, Geddes, Lindsey, Price, Paradise," and one of the party said to him, "We are particularly fortunate in having you among us; it is having the best cause countenanced by the man by whom we most wished to see it supported." There was a dinner with the "Anti-Tests," among whom are, as might be expected, some of the people we have seen among the Revolutionists: "Fox, Beaufoy, Hoghton, Sawbridge, Adair, Watson, Heywood, B. Hollis, Shore, Geddes, Vaughan, Fell, Stone, Woodfall, Listers."

There is also the record of a correspondence with the Bishop of Llandaff and the Archbishop of Canterbury in reference to a vacancy in the Natural History Department of the British Museum, of which correspondence Dr Watson's letters remain. It is curious that when applying, without success, for the vacant post, Godwin still calls him-

I.   E

self, "The Rev. William Godwin" in a letter to Lord
Robert Spencer. It would appear, however, that he did so
rather with a view of identifying himself with the person
whom Lord Robert had known in former years, than with
any wish of resuming a character which, as he said, had
completely quitted him. He had, as will be remembered,
dedicated his sermons to the Bishop of Llandaff, who had
by no means forgotten him. The Bishop's letter is curious,
as evidence that a liberal Bishop even in those days was
somewhat suspect.

The Bishop of Llandaff to William Godwin.

"SIR,—I would not have hesitated a moment writing to the
Archbishop in your favour, if I had not been of opinion that *my*
appearing in support of a *Dissenter* would rather have tended to
obstruct than to promote your wishes. The enclosed is written in
such a manner that if you think it can serve you, it may be sent
as from yourself, as a kind of confirmation that you had used my
name with propriety. I sincerely wish you success, and am your
most obedient Servant, TH. LLANDAFF.

"CALLGARTH, KENDALL,
"*May* 18, 1790."

The last entry in the Diary for the year is under date of
Dec. 31 : " It was in this year that I read and criticised
'The Simple Story' in MS." This was probably at the
instance of the publisher, for Godwin does not appear to
have made Mrs Inchbald's personal acquaintance till the
autumn of 1792.

Godwin's autobiographical note for the year 1791 is
somewhat longer than usual, and must be given in full, as
showing the growth of his political views, and giving his
first conception of his great work, the " Enquiry concerning Political Justice."

" On the 29th of April in this year Mr Holcroft and I wrote two anonymous letters, he to Mr Fox, and I to Mr Sheridan. Mr Fox, in the debate on the bill for giving a new constitution to Canada, had said that he would not be the man to propose the abolition of a House of Lords in a country where such a power was already established ; but as little would he be the man to recommend the introduction of such a power where it was not. This was by no means the only public indication he had shown how deeply he had drank of the spirit of the French Revolution. The object of the above-mentioned letters was to excite these two illustrious men to persevere gravely and inflexibly in the career on which they had entered. I was strongly impressed with the sentiment that in the then existing circumstances of England and of Europe great and happy improvements might be achieved under such auspices without anarchy and confusion. I believed that important changes must arise, and I was inexpressibly anxious that such changes should be effected under the conduct of the best and most competent leaders.

" This year was the main crisis of my life. In the summer of 1791 I gave up my concern in the New Annual Register, the historical part of which I had written for seven years, and abdicated, I hope for ever, the task of performing a literary labour, the nature of which should be dictated by anything but the promptings of my own mind. I suggested to Robinson the bookseller the idea of composing a treatise on Political Principles, and he agreed to aid me in executing it. My original conception proceeded on a feeling of the imperfections and errors of Montesquieu, and a desire of supplying a less faulty work. In the first fervour of my enthusiasm, I entertained the vain imagination of " hewing a stone from the rock," which, by its inherent energy and weight, should overbear and annihilate all opposition, and place the principles of politics on an immoveable basis. It was my first determination to tell all that I apprehended to be truth, and all that seemed to be truth, confident that from such a proceeding the best results were to be expected."

The diary shows many and various literary labours besides the composition of " Political Justice," which, when fairly started, was written very slowly : six or seven pages of MS. are recorded as being the utmost written in a day, but far more often a page, half a page, or even a paragraph or a sentence written twice, are proofs of the extreme care which was bestowed on the work. Godwin took also Italian lessons, and his reading in all branches, from Greek plays and Greek philosophy to modern belles lettres, was vast. But he was an extremely discursive reader, and had several books in hand at once, carefully noting how many pages of each were read as the day's task. He visited the theatre frequently, and took great interest in all that related to the stage. Here are a few of the entries for this year :—

> " March 16, W.   Robinson calls ; proposes a ' Naval History.'
> "19, S.   Wrote to Robinson ; propose £1050, *i.e.*, £525 per volume.

It is perhaps not surprising to find that the publisher declined to accede to these terms, or that in consequence there is an entry :—

> " Mar. 25, F.   Démélé avec Robinson.
> " June 30, Th.   Dine with Robinson ; propose ' Political Principles.'
> " July 10, M.   Close with Robinson.
> " Aug. 31, W.   Holcroft dines, Fawcet expected ; démélé faintness.
> " Nov. 30, W.   Holcroft at tea ; un peu de démélé sur Davis."

It would not be fair to suppress these very characteristic notes of hot temper, and quarrels with his best friends, which also appear only too often in the letters. It must, however, be said that the vehemence of temper soon exhausted itself, and did not affect the real regard which Godwin felt for those with whom he disputed the most.

And during this and the next year, during which the word "démêlé" so often occurs, we also have notices in this plain-spoken diary of various forms of ill-health, resulting apparently from Godwin's very sedentary habits, no symptom being serious in itself, but all of a kind which are frequently found most trying to the nerves and temper of the patient.

In the spring of 1791, Thomas Paine, whose acquaintance Godwin had made at the house of Mr Brand Hollis, published his celebrated pamphlet, "The Rights of Man," in answer to Burke's "Reflections on the French Revolution." Godwin and Holcroft had both seen much of this in MS., and the former wrote of it in terms of great though measured praise. Holcroft—never so cautious—addressed to Godwin a little twisted note, worth insertion here as some evidence of the fervour of spirit which animated men in days when such eager utterances escaped from a press, over which hung the terrors of the pillory, and of prosecutions for high treason.

Thomas Holcroft to William Godwin. [*No date.*]

"I have got it—If this do not cure my cough it is a damned perverse mule of a cough—The pamphlet—From the row—But mum—We don't sell it—Oh, no—Ears and Eggs—Verbatim, except the addition of a short preface, which, as you have not seen, I send you my copy—Not a single castration (Laud be unto God and J. S. Jordan!) can I discover—Hey for the New Jerusalem! The millennium! And peace and eternal beatitude be unto the soul of Thomas Paine."

The pamphlet had been originally printed for Johnson of St Paul's Churchyard, who, on seeing it in print, de-

clined to publish it. The unexpected refusal caused a
month's delay. A few copies, however, got into private
hands, one of which, bearing Johnson's name as publisher,
is in the British Museum. Some of those most anxious
for the appearance of the tract urged the excision of certain passages, and it was commonly believed that it was
not issued after all in its original form. A "Life of Thomas
Paine, by Francis Oldys, A.M. of the University of Pennsylvania"—a Pseudonym for George Chalmers, one of the
Clerks of Plantations, the real author of the book—has the
following passage on "The Rights of Man :"—

"The men mid-wives determined to deprive the child of its
virility, rather than so hopeful an infant should be withheld from
the world. At length, on the 13th of March 1791, this mutilated
brat was delivered to the public by Mr J. S. Jordan, at No. 166
Fleet Street."

Holcroft, however, was quite right ; he and Godwin were
members of the Committee, of which Mr Brand Hollis was
the leading spirit, to whom had been entrusted the revisal
of the work.

One more entry in the diary of this year calls for attention, for it records Godwin's first meeting with Mary
Wollstonecraft.

"Nov. 13, Su. Correct. Dyson and Dibdin call ; talk of
virtue and disinterest. Dine at Johnson's with Paine, Shovet,
and Wolstencraft ; talk of monarchy, Tooke, Johnson, Voltaire,
pursuits, and religion. Sup at Holcroft's."

The autobiographical note for 1792 is concerned with the
preparation of his work on Political Justice. That he was

engaged on it was already well known to a not inconsiderable number of persons likely to be interested in the subject, and it appears that the work received during its preparation the imprimatur of men whose views still carry weight. Godwin writes :—

" During this year I was in the singular situation of an author, possessing some degree of fame for a work still unfinished and unseen. I was introduced on this ground to Mr Mackintosh, David Williams,"—founder, and afterwards a pensioner of the Literary Fund, died 1816,—"Joel Barlow,"—afterwards American ambassador to Napoleon, died at Wilna, Dec. 26, 1812; the translator of Volney,—" and others, and with these gentlemen, together with Mr Nicholson,"—a mathematical teacher, foreign agent for Wedgwood, civil engineer, died 1815,—"and Mr Holcroft, had occasional meetings, in which the principles of my work were discussed. Towards the close of the year I became acquainted with Mr Horne Tooke, to whose etymological conversation and various talents I am proud to acknowledge myself greatly indebted, though these came too late to be of any use to me in the concoction of my work, which was nearly printed off before I had first the pleasure of meeting this extraordinary and admirable man."

From the Diary, however, it appears that the foregoing paragraph must be understood with limitations. Godwin and Horne Tooke had met from time to time at the meetings of the " Revolutionists," and had been thus slightly acquainted, though no degree of intimacy had sprung up, nor had they met in private. The entries also record in increasing detail the topics of the conversations held day by day with friends, as " Dyson at tea, talk of ancient virtue, and respect for other men's judgment;" "Tea at Barlow's with Jardine, Stuart, Wolstencraft, and Holcroft : talk of self-love, sympathy, and perfectibility, individual and general;" "Sup at Nicholson's, talk of ideal unity."

Godwin saw much of his sister Hannah in this year, much of Mrs and Miss Cooper; his brothers were not unfrequently his guests; but the only entries which are especially interesting are a few which shew how warmly he and his friends welcomed to England any one who represented the leaders of the Revolution in France. Thus—

"Sep. 6. Th.   Dine at Holcroft's avec Noel et le cousin de Danton, Merget.

"Oct. 14. Su.   Dine at Holcroft's with Crosdil: adv."—advenæ — "Merget, Danton jun^r et Pinard.

"Oct. 21. Su.   Dine at Holcroft's with Major Waller, Merget and Recordat; History of Danton."

On Nov. 25 are the words, "Debating Society silenced," which, taken with the political trials so soon to follow, make us wonder how Englishmen remained quiet while France rebelled.

Since Godwin came to London he had been living in various lodgings, the greater part of the time having one or two persons to share his chambers—the boys Willis Webb, and Cooper, and often his friend Marshal. In the next year he took a house to himself, and in a district where he could be more free from interruptions. As this year was therefore in a degree the end of his nomad existence, a note may be inserted from among his papers giving the various changes of abode.

"Holborn,	Apl. 1782.	"Newman St.,	June 1786.
"Beaconsfield,	Dec. ,,	"Berkeley St.,	Sep. ,,
"Porter St.,	Aug. 1783.	"Norfolk St.,	Mar. 1787.
"Strand,	Sep. ,,	"Guildford,	June 1788.
"Norfolk St.,	Dec. 1784.	"Marylebone St.,	Sep. ,,
"Tavistock Row,	Mar. 1785.	"Titchfield St.,	Dec. 1790.
"Broad St.,	June ,,	"39 Devonshire St.,	1792."

Mrs Inchbald, whose more intimate friendship and correspondence with Godwin began in 1792, was the well-known
authoress of "The Simple Story." This was, as we have
seen, criticised by Godwin; and the plot was in a measure
altered in deference to his advice.

Mrs Shelley has left the following note relative to Mrs
Inchbald :—

"She was one of a numerous family, orphaned of their father,
whose mother had to struggle with poverty. She was exceedingly
beautiful. The spirit of adventure natural in youth seems to have
developed itself in her with unusual vigour, but it was joined by
a certain saving grace of self-command and self-possession that
bore her through nearly unharmed. She married early an actor,
and went also on the stage. She was left a widow at the age of
six-and-twenty, and from that time had to struggle alone with the
world. She continued her career as an actress for some time
under many disadvantages, an impediment in her speech preventing all hope of excellence, till at length her success as an author
enabled her to retire from the stage.

"Nothing can be more singular and interesting than the picture
of her life as given in her biography. Living in mean lodgings,
dressed with an economy allied to penury, without connections,
and alone, her beauty, her talents, and the charm of her manners
gave her entrance into a delightful circle of society. Apt to fall in
love, and desirous to marry, she continued single, because the men
who loved and admired her were too worldly to take an actress
and a poor author, however lovely and charming, for a wife. Her
life was thus spent in an interchange of hardship and amusement,
privation and luxury. Her character partook of the same contrast: fond of pleasure, she was prudent in her conduct; penurious
in her personal expenditure, she was generous to others. Vain of
her beauty, we are told that the gown she wore was not worth a
shilling, it was so coarse and shabby. Very susceptible to the
softer feelings, she could yet guard herself against passion ; and
though she might have been called a flirt, her character was unim-

peached. I have heard that a rival beauty of her day pettishly complained that when Mrs Inchbald came into a room, and sat in a chair in the middle of it as was her wont, every man gathered round it, and it was vain for any other woman to attempt to gain attention. Godwin could not fail to admire her; she became and continued to be a favourite. Her talents, her beauty, her manners were all delightful to him. He used to describe her as a piquante mixture between a lady and a milkmaid, and added that Sheridan declared she was the only authoress whose society pleased him."

One letter of Mrs Inchbald's may here be given, the first apparently written by her to Godwin: it relates to her tragedy called "The Massacre," which was never acted, but may be found in the Appendix to Boaden's Memoirs of her Life.

Mrs Inchbald to William Godwin.

"*3rd Nov.* 1792.

"Sir,—There is so much tenderness mixed with the justice of your criticism, that, while I submit to the greatest part of it as unanswerable, I feel anxious to exculpate myself in those points where I believe it is in my power.

"You accuse me of trusting to newspapers for my authority. I have no other authority (no more, I believe, has half England) for any occurrence which I do not *see:* it is by newspapers that I am told that the French are at present victorious; and I have no doubt but you will allow that (in this particular, at least) they speak truth.

"*2ndly.* There appears an inconsistency in my having said to you, 'I have no view to any public good in this piece,' and afterwards alluding to its preventing future massacres: to this I reply that it was your hinting to me that it might do harm which gave me the first idea that it might do good.

"*3rdly.* I do not shrink from Labour, but I shrink from ill-health, low spirits, disappointment, and a long train of evils which attend on Laborious Literary work. I was ten months, unceasingly, finishing my novel, notwithstanding the plan (such as you saw it) was formed, and many pages written. My health suffered much during this confinement, my spirits suffered more on publication; for though many gentlemen of the first abilities have said to me things high in its favour, it never was liked by those people who are the readers and consumers of novels; and I have frequently obtained more pecuniary advantage by ten days' labour in the dramatic way than by the labour of this ten months.—Your very much *obliged* humble servant,   E. INCHBALD.

"LEICESTER SQUARE, 24*th.*"

It does not appear that the letters by Godwin and Holcroft to Sheridan and Fox were printed, but the MS. copy is among the Godwin papers, as from "a well-known literary character." The following paragraphs are noteworthy:—

"You would willingly promote the true interests and happiness of the human race. You would willingly enrol your name with the benefactors of mankind, or, which is still better, would rejoice in the extension of justice, though your efforts in promoting that extension should never be acknowledged. Can you really think that the new constitution of France is the most glorious fabric ever raised by human integrity since the creation of man, and yet believe that what is good there would be bad here? Does truth alter its nature by crossing the Straits, and become falsehood? Are men entitled to perfect equality in France, and is it just to deprive them of it in England? Did the French do well in extinguishing nobility, and is it right that we should preserve hereditary honours? Or are these questions so very trifling in their nature, so uninteresting to the general weal, that it is no matter which side of them we embrace? If you speak out you must be contented to undergo a temporary proscription. That proscription you at present suffer, and the period of the obloquy which the true friend to mankind must endure will be very short. Had you rather be indebted for your eminence to the caprice of a monarch than to the voice of a whole nation, accumulating its gratitude on

the head of the general benefactor? Had you rather have the
nominal possession of power, with your hands free for the purposes of corruption, but chained up from the exertion of every
virtuous effort, than have the real possession of power, able to
make every act of your administration a blessing to Britain, to
Europe, and to mankind."

Again:—

" Liberty strips hereditary honours of their imaginary splendour,
shows the noble and the king for what they are—common mortals,
kept in ignorance of what other mortals know, flattered and encouraged in folly and vice, and deprived of those stimulations
which perpetually goad the hero and the philosopher to the acquisition of excellence. Liberty leaves nothing to be admired
but talents and virtue, the very things which it is the interest of
men like you should be preferred to all the rest. Pursue this
subject to its proper extent, and you will find that—give to a state
but liberty enough, and it is impossible that vice should exist
in it."

This sweeping, and somewhat astounding statement,
proves the excess of Godwin's enthusiasm on the subject
of political liberty. Mrs Shelley writes with respect to the
passage just quoted :—

" It may seem strange that any one should, in the sincerity of
his heart, believe that no vice could co-exist with perfect freedom
—but my father did—it was the very basis of his system, the very
keystone of the arch of justice, by which he desired to knit together the whole human family. It must be remembered, however, that no man was a more strenuous advocate for the slow
operation of change, no one more entirely impressed with the
feeling that opinions should be in advance of action. Perhaps
even to a faulty degree he desired that nothing should be done
but by the majority, while he ardently sought for every means of
causing the majority to espouse the better side."

CHAPTER IV.

LITERARY LIFE AND FRIENDS—1793.

IN 1793 Godwin published " Political Justice," and it becomes necessary to examine this important work, as well as the various writings which preceded it. Any attempt to form an estimate of his literary labours has hitherto been deliberately set aside, and the next chapter will be devoted to the task. In the meantime Godwin shall give his own account of his mode of life at this period :—

" In the beginning of the year 1793 I removed to a small house in Challon Street, Somers Town, which I possessed entirely to myself, with no other attendance than the daily resort of a bedmaker for about an hour each day. No man could be more desirous than I was of adopting a practice conformable to my principles, as far as I could do so without affording reasonable ground of offence to any other person. I was anxious not to spend a penny on myself, which I did not imagine calculated to render me a more capable servant of the public, and as I was averse to the expenditure of money, so I was not inclined to earn it but in small portions. I considered the disbursement of money for the benefit of others as a very difficult problem, which he who has the possession of it is bound to solve in the best manner he can, but which affords small encouragement to any one to acquire it who has it not. The plan, therefore, I resolved on was leisure—a leisure to be employed in deliberate composition, and in the pursuit of such attainments as afforded me the most promise to render me useful. For years I scarcely did anything at home or abroad

without the enquiry being uppermost in my mind whether I could
be better employed for general benefit; and I hope much of this
temper has survived, and will attend me to my grave. The frame
in which I found myself exalted my spirits, and rendered me more
of a talker than I was before or have been since, and than is
agreeable to my natural character. Certainly I attended now,
and at all times, to everything that was offered in the way of
reasoning and argument, with the sincerest desire of embracing
the truth, and that only. The 'Enquiry concerning Political
Justice' was published in February. In this year also I wrote the
principal part of the novel of 'Caleb Williams,' which may, perhaps, be considered as affording no inadequate image of the fervour
of my spirit; it was the offspring of that temper of mind in which
the composition of my 'Political Justice' left me. In this year
I acquired the friendship of many excellent persons—Thomas
Wedgwood, Richard Porson, Joseph Gerrald, Robert Merry, and
Joseph Ritson."

Of these, Porson's name needs no remark; of Gerrald
and Wedgwood more hereafter. Merry was a Harrow and
Cambridge man, afterwards in the Guards. He wrote
plays and poetry, now forgotten, under the signature "Della
Crusca." He married Miss Brunton, a well-known actress,
emigrated to America, and died there in 1798.

Ritson was a lawyer, but better known as the collector
of old English songs and ballads. He was a vegetarian,
and died in 1803, aged fifty-one.

Mrs Shelley's affectionate note on Wedgwood demands
insertion :—

"Godwin cemented this year his acquaintance with a man
known to himself and all his literary contemporaries, as the most
generous, the most amiable of men; Thomas Wedgwood of
Etruria, in Staffordshire, a name dear to all who reverence virtue
and goodness. His enthusiasm in the cause of knowledge, his
earnest desire to serve his fellows, rank him high among good

men. He was afflicted with bad health, which acted on his nerves, and frequently rendered him low-spirited to a painful degree. At one time he and Godwin contemplated making a common household together; their establishment was to be conducted on the most economical plan, as suited the narrow circumstances of the one, and the generous views of the other, which led him to limit his personal expenses, that he might have more to spare for others."

This scheme, however, fell through, and Godwin continued to live, now alone, as he tells us, in Challon Street, Somers Town. He furnished only a part of his house, and keeping strictly to his intention of earning little and spending little, he lived during three successive years on the several annual sums of £110, £120, and £130.

His habits were exceedingly regular, and remained the same to the end of his life.

"He rose," says his daughter, "between seven and eight, and read some classic author before breakfast. From nine till twelve or one he occupied himself with his pen. He found that he could not exceed this measure of labour with any advantage to his own health, or the work in hand. While writing 'Political Justice,' there was one paragraph which he wrote eight times over before he could satisfy himself with the strength and perspicuity of his expressions. On this occasion a sense of confusion of the brain came over him, and he applied to his friend Mr Carlisle, afterwards Sir Anthony Carlisle, the celebrated surgeon, who warned him that he had exerted his intellectual faculties to their limit. In compliance with his direction, Mr Godwin reduced his hours of composition within what many will consider narrow bounds. The rest of the morning was spent in reading and seeing his friends. When at home he dined at four, but during his bachelor life he frequently dined out. His dinner at home at this time was simple enough. He had no regular servant; an old woman came in the morning to clean and arrange his rooms, and if necessary she prepared a mutton chop, which was put in a Dutch oven."

The diary shows the same amount of reading as heretofore, chiefly in English, Latin, and French. It tells of work contemplated as well as accomplished, as, for instance, under Oct. 20. " Plan a treatise on God," and he notes also that he made a proposal to Robinson to write a history of Rome, "from the building of the city by Romulus to the Battle of Actium," the demand for which he considered would be "immense." There is the same eagerness about foreign and home politics, but the most exciting events, such as the sentence on and death of Louis XVI., Horne Tooke's trial [Jan. 24th], the debate whether Political Justice should or should not be prosecuted [May 25th], are told in the fewest words.

In reference to this last event Mrs Shelley says that from

" A government fearful and suspicious in the extreme, ready to use any measures for pulling down the spirit of innovation which had spread abroad, every man who publicly announced liberal opinions anticipated prosecution. I have frequently heard my father say that Political Justice escaped prosecution from the reason that it appeared in a form too expensive for general acquisition. Pitt observed, when the question was debated in the Privy Council, that 'a three guinea book could never do much harm among those who had not three shillings to spare.'"

In publishing the book at this high price

" Godwin acted in strict conformity to his principles. He was an advocate for improvements brought in by the enlightened and sober-minded, but he deprecated abrupt innovations, and appeals to the passions of the multitude."

The publisher, however, expected a large sale of the book, and his expectations were realised. The agreement between author and publisher, "William Godwin, of Challon Street, in the parish of St Pancras, Middlesex, gentleman, and George Robinson, of Paternoster Row, bookseller," is extant. Seven hundred guineas was paid down by Robinson for the copyright, and a further sum of three hundred guineas was covenanted to be paid, and was paid, after the sale of 3000 copies in quarto, or 4000 in quarto and octavo added together. The work was first brought out "in two volumes quarto, containing one hundred and twenty sheets, or thereabouts."

The only entry at this time which calls for special remark in regard to the list of friends and acquaintances, is that of the name of Mrs Reveley, which meets us now for the first time, and from the first very frequently.

"Maria Reveley," writes Mrs Shelley, "was the daughter of an English merchant at Constantinople, named James. Her education had been wild and singular, and had early developed the peculiar and deep-seated sensibility which through life formed her characteristic. Her father had left her in infancy with her mother in England—he might be said to have deserted them, for they lived in great penury. She remembered once asking her mother for a farthing to buy a cake, which was given her with such reluctance, on the score of poverty, that with a passion of tears she returned it. Mrs James at length took a desperate resolution, and sailed to Constantinople with her daughter, then eight years old. Mr James had no inclination to renew his conjugal duties. He had in his house the wife of one of his skippers as housekeeper, and it was generally believed she stood to him in a more intimate relation. He was, however, delighted with his little daughter, and had her stolen from her mother, and secreted in the house of a Turk, till he had persuaded Mrs James, by the promise of an annuity, to return to England alone. The little Maria was then taken home, and brought up with sedulous care. Many accomplishments were taught her, and on one of the first side-saddles which appeared in the East, she accompanied her father in his rides in the environs of Constantinople. While yet a

F

mere child she looked womanly and formed, and entered into the
society of European merchants and diplomatists. Having no
proper chaperon, she was left to run wild as she might, and at a
very early age had gone through the romance of life. When she
was fifteen her father left Constantinople and went to Rome.
She had shown great talent for painting, and it was her wish that
she should cultivate this art under the tuiton of Angelica Kauffman.
Her studies were, however, interrupted by her early marriage.
Her beauty attracted the admiration of Mr Reveley, a young
English architect travelling for improvement; they married and
came to England.

"Mr Reveley's means were small, his father being still alive,
and his marriage imprudent, for Mr James, who acted ill in all
the relations of life, refused to consent to the match, only, as it
would seem, as an excuse for giving his daughter no fortune.
From the genial climate, the luxuries, the gay and refined society
which had surrounded her, Mrs Reveley found herself transported
to a situation but little removed from penury, demanding an
economy and self-denial in expenditure of the most painful kind.
She found herself among the middling class of English people—
ignorant, narrow-minded, and bigoted. She felt fallen on evil
days, the fairy lights had disappeared from life; sedulous occupation bestowed on the necessaries of life was varied only by society
which did not possess a ray of intellect, and had but little refinement.

"She was very young and very beautiful, and possessed a peculiar charm of character in her deep sensibility, and an ingenuous
modesty that knew no guile : this was added to ardour in the pursuit of knowledge, a liberal and unquenchable curiosity. Parties
ran high in those days. Her husband joined the liberal side, and
entered with enthusiasm into the hopes and expectations of political freedom, which then filled every heart to bursting. The
consequence of these principles was to lead to his acquaintance
with many of their popular advocates, and among them with Godwin and Holcroft. There was a gentleness, and yet a fervour in
the minds of both Mrs Reveley and Godwin that led to sympathy.

He was ready to gratify her desire for knowledge, and she drank eagerly of the philosophy which he offered. It was pure but warm friendship, which might have grown into another feeling, had they been differently situated. As it was, Godwin saw only in her a favourite pupil, a charming friend, a woman whose conversation and society were fascinating and delightful ; but his calm and philosophic heart was undisturbed by any of those feelings which in natures less happily tempered would too readily have crept in to disturb and injure."

A considerable part of the correspondence for this year turns, as might be expected, on Political Justice. The letters to and from Newton, Godwin's old schoolmaster, explain themselves, and they substantiate also what has been already surmised, that the extreme dislike of the pupil for the master in later years dated, not from the time of their early intercourse, but from the misunderstanding which arose when each became conscious of the wide chasm which separated their opinions. The chasm appeared to widen, the breach in feeling was the greater, because, though he would not afterwards admit it, Godwin had really been conscious of great intellectual indebtedness to his old teacher, not unmixed with affection on both sides.

William Godwin to the Rev. Samuel Newton.

" SIR,—I have been informed that you have delivered it as your judgment of the work I have published on Political Justice, that, upon attempting the perusal, you found in it matters so peculiarly censurable that you could not bear to read any farther.

" I confess I am strongly inclined to believe that there has been some mistake on the part of my informant, and that the story I have heard is untrue. If so, you will thank me for giving you an opportunity to contradict it.

"Having written thus much, I will trouble you with the reasons that persuade me you never delivered the opinion ascribed to you.

"When I knew you, you were an ardent champion for political liberty. I cannot easily suppose that you have changed your sentiments on that head.

"It is impossible that you shouldnot have perceived that the book in question is intended to promote that glorious cause. Granting that I have the misfortune to differ from you in your theological creed, I am well assured that at the period to which I allude, you had the candour and discernment to do justice to the political writings of people of all persuasions in religion and philosophy. The indulgence in this respect that you would grant to all other men, I cannot suppose you would deny to me. The subject of the book is not religion, but politics : if it be calculated to produce any effect, it is infinitely more probable that that effect will relate to its express object, than its incidental allusions ; to the politics which I imagine you will allow to be generally right, than to the theology which you perhaps suspect to be wrong.

"There is a view which I am strongly inclined to entertain upon this subject, that I will take the liberty to mention. We have all of us our duties. Every action of our lives, and every word that we utter, will either conduce to or detract from the discharge of our duty. We cannot any of us do all the things of which mankind stand in need ; we must have fellow-labourers. Hence it seems to follow that it is one of our most important duties to do justice to the good qualities of every man and every book that falls under observation, that thus we may enlarge the opportunity of others for discharging those parts of public service which we cannot perform ourselves. It is unworthy of any real friend to mankind to depreciate any well conceived endeavour from a too painful feeling of the incidental defects that may accompany it.

"I make no apology for want of ceremony. We are both of us, I conceive, enemies to that servility under which the species have so long laboured."

Samuel Newton to William Godwin.

" DEAR SIR,—I naturally contract a friendship, feel an attach-ment, and interest myself in the welfare of those who have for any time lived with me, though their sentiments and habits may be different from mine. Sincerely can I say that I have been very solicitous for your reputation and welfare ; and when I saw your publication advertised, I told several gentlemen of my acquaint-ance of different persuasions, that from what I knew of your abilities and application, I presumed it was a production that merited attention. When I was lately at my son's at Witham, I was determined, as he had procured it for a book-club there, I believe on my recommendation, to read it attentively through, though it was in a library at Norwich some time before, to which I belonged, but I had not time then to investigate its contents. In the perusal I was charmed with your language, with many of your sentiments, and with your general idea of political justice and liberty. I said that there were some descriptions, reasonings, and ideas, that for simplicity, elegance, force, and utility, seemed to me to surpass all that I had ever read in Tacitus, Polybius, Mon-tesquieu, Barbeyrac, Grotius, Robertson, Price, or Priestley.

" But I will ingenuously confess to you (and I have, you know, a right to think for myself) that there were several things that you advanced concerning moral obligation, gratitude, any public test of marriage, Christianity, and one or two more subjects, that very much disgusted me. My indignation was raised, not so much that you differed from me, but because I considered it would damn the book, which contained in it so many useful and interest-ing sentiments. Towards the close, or about the middle of the second volume, I found something of this kind, and I did throw by the book, with some such sentence as you have heard, but it was from an impulse, I can assure you, arising from the preceding views. Truth I revere, though it condemns my own conduct.

" I believe Christianity, you may not; but as I am convinced that it is the most friendly system to the equality and liberty of mankind that ever was published, I think justice requires me to resent a person's suggesting that I am not as strongly attached to the rights of man as any one who does not believe it.

"In short, Sir, permit me to intimate that when you publish another edition, I think you can better the arrangement, and make the general method more perspicuous; and if you should think proper to change your expressions, and leave out certain sentences on some subjects, which are, as I conceive, no ways essential to your general system, your performance will be more extensively perused, and it will wonderfully add, I doubt not, to that torrent of political light which is pouring in upon an oppressed world.

"Thus much I thought it my duty to suggest to you, but whether you think it worthy your attention or not, I shall think I am bound by immutable justice to wish you well, and really to esteem you without giving way to the least degree of base servility.

"S. NEWTON."

This letter, courteous and moderate as is its tone, does not appear to have satisfied Godwin. His reply is lost, but the tenor of it is sufficiently clear from Newton's second letter:

The Same to the Same.

"*Dec.* 14*th*, 1793.

"Since, Sir, you have been so condescending as to favour me with another epistle, I think it, from our former connection, my duty (and I annex a real meaning to the term) to reply with all due respect, but with all simplicity and integrity. I have often said that there might be a volume collected from your work which would make, in my opinion, one of the most valuable political systems that I ever perused, and, as far as justice, equality, and liberty are recommended in it, I heartily wish the motives and arguments were impressed upon the heart of every human being, particularly on the rich, the powerful, and the learned. Viewing it altogether, I own it is a wonderful production; but I must confess that it has such a cast of character in it from its author, that

I am inclined to think I should have known it to have been yours, had not your name stood in the title page.

"I never affected the reputation of a philosopher, nor have I ever courted the countenance and recommendations of the reputed Literate ; but I have for a number of years thought for myself, read productions on all sides of religious and political questions, and been very particular in my observations on the associations, habits, and character of my species. The result of my observations has been this :—Two sets of men have appeared to my view which I wish *not* to imitate. The one is composed of those who seek popularity, reputation, and interest by embracing the most fashionable systems in the religion and policy of the age, and by following the esteemed great with a sort of implicit confidence and submission. I suspect these have no genuine sincerity. The other set is composed of those who affect in everything singularity, who delight in contradiction, whose fort is objection, whose aristocracy is dictation, and whose pride is that of superior genius, accuracy, and judgment to all others. These may boast of sincerity, and treat the bulk of mankind as the swinish multitude who are not capable or worthy of examining and judging on the subject of religion and policy with themselves. In this spirit there is something in my view truly despicable ; yea, I smile at a Johnson, or a Hume, when they assume the air of the latter set of men, and as I conceive resentment and indignation virtues, if properly, that is *proportionably* directed against vice and usurpation, without wishing to injure persons, I think myself justified by immutable justice, in allowing these sensations to pass in my mind. Yes, I feel not any remorse for indulging them, though I have as firm a belief as you can have in the most certain and indissoluble connection between moral causes and effects. But I use not the word *necessarian* because I think the philosophers who have adopted it are guilty of a vulgar error, in appropriating a word to a sense contrary to its general acceptation.

"That Goliath of critical and moral censure, Johnson, would, perhaps, have thought me a most seditious and dangerous Sectary for rejecting all establishments of religion, and for seriously

ridiculing every order of priests constituted by the reigning powers.
Hume would have deemed me a servile, implicit, narrow soul, for
believing a religion which was embraced by my parents, though I
think I have as fairly examined it as any man in the island. But
I laugh at his conceit, and pity his prejudices, guessing, from what
I know of his life, how his associations of ideas were formed ; for
as a philosopher pretending to the most accurate and deep investigations, he should have accounted for this phenomenon, how
the books containing the Hebrew and Christian systems of
religion came to be published. If they were forgeries, who were
their authors, and what their motives and ends in publishing such
singular schemes, so different from all the fine conceptions and
sublime notions of all politicians and philosophers that ever
existed ? I can resolve questions of this sort with regard to the
Coran, and every other pretended revelation from God, but I
never saw this done with respect to the Bible.

" Our associations of thought, and habits of mind are so totally
different, that it is no wonder we should determine very oppositely
one to the other on many subjects, and therefore you will not be
surprised if I should affirm, as I do with the greatest sincerity :
the evidence for the being of a God from analogy, or arguing
from the effect to the cause, and of a future state from our desires,
and from the supposed justice of the divine government, does not
strike my mind so forcibly, nor afford it so much satisfaction as
that which it is impressed with, for the undoubted truth of the
Hebrew and Christian religions. You may think I have not
examined as fairly and impartially as you have done. I must
think the same of you. Here your right to judge is the same as
mine. Here is the equality I would maintain. And if you think
you have far superior genius, that is a point I cannot dispute with you. Those of this character I have found committing
as many blunders, and run into as many extravagant absurdities as
any of more moderate abilities. In short, Mr Godwin, my views
of mankind, the little knowledge I have of myself, the account my
religion gives me of man, which I find confirmed by fact, prevent
my boasting with an aristocratical air of any superior talents, lead

me to think I am not so great a man as I once thought myself to be, and compel me so conscientiously to impress it in your thoughts, that you and I, and all mankind are more upon an equality with respect to a capacity for the most certain and useful knowledge in politics, morals, and religion than you are perhaps in the habit of admitting. As your friend really thought, so he has discharged his duty, in wishing to convince you of it, thinking this to be the greatest friendship without servility or prejudice."

With this letter, as was not unnatural, ended all inter-course between the Rev. Samuel Newton, and his distinguished but unorthodox pupil. There appears in this correspondence Godwin's extreme sensitiveness to criticism, which rendered so much of his intercourse with his friends subject to those unfortunate *démêlés* of which his journals speak so often. The following note, written by Godwin, and the letter from Marshal in reference to the same affair belong to the same year, and illustrate in an amusing way this extreme touchiness, though it must be admitted that the friendly critic seems to have pushed his candour to its furthest bounds.

" When I had written nearly three-fourths of the first volume of Caleb Williams, I was prevailed on, with much reluctance by the importunity of a very old friend, to entrust him with the perusal of my manuscript. In three days he returned it to me with a note nearly in these words :—' If you have the smallest regard for your own reputation or interest, you will immediately put the enclosed papers in the fire. I was strongly tempted to have done this friendly office for you, but that I recollected, I had placed myself under a promise to return them.' It is hardly necessary to say that the receipt of this note was the means of disturbing me. It was three days before I fully recovered my elasticity and fervent tone of mind required for the prosecution of my work."

James Marshal to William Godwin.

"*Friday, May* 31, '93.

"I enclose you three guineas; the rest you shall have very shortly. I take this opportunity of saying a word or two on the affair of Tuesday. It was not I, but somebody else, who exhibited marks of intoxication, or more properly of insanity—for upon no principle of sound intellect is it to be accounted for. I came like a rational being, from motives of the purest kind, to discharge what I believed to be a duty. But Sir Fretful was in a humour to hear nothing but commendation, and tyrant Procrustes would admit no duty in another of which he should himself be the object, and which did not square precisely with his own ideas. Yet this is a philosopher teaching the firm discharge of duty to mankind! Whip me such philosophers, whose precepts and practice are eternally at variance.

"So far from being told twenty times, previous to reading the MS., that I was not to give my opinion, I do not remember being once told it; but had it been so, I do not see that it ought at all to have altered my conduct.

"One word respecting the MS. itself, and I have done. The incidents are ill chosen; the characters unnatural, distorted; the phraseology intended to mark the humorous ones inappropriate; the style uncouth; everything upon stilts; the whole uninteresting; written as a man would make a chair or a table that had never handled a tool. I got through it, but it was as I get over a piece of ploughed-up ground, with labour and toil. By the way, judging from the work in question, one might suppose some minds not to be unlike a piece of ground. Having produced a rich crop, it must lie fallow for a season, that it may gain sufficient vigour for a new crop. You were speaking for a motto for this work—the best motto in my opinion would be a *Hic jacet;* for depend upon it, the world will suppose you to be exhausted; or rather what a few only think at present, will become a general opinion, that the Hercules you have fathered is not of your begetting.

"Your note to me is written to justify yourself from a charge of weakness; and it contains an additional confirmation of that weakness. The meaning of it is that if I cannot have the forbearance to avoid mentioning a syllable or breathing a censure upon this 'work of works,' I must not approach you till it be finished. Fie, fie! what name does this deserve?

"JAS. MARSHAL."

It is pleasant to hear of Tom Cooper again, whose relations with Godwin were now those of a steady and grateful friendship. The letters from him, which conclude the correspondence for this year, show how Godwin's stern training had at least enabled him to keep courage and a stout heart under difficulties. Undeterred by his trip to the North in Kemble's company, he had fairly taken up the profession of an actor, and had joined a company of strollers on their provincial tour.

Thomas Cooper to William Godwin.

"PORTSMOUTH, *March* 1, '93.

"Well, here I am! 'My fortune smiles and gives me all that I dare ask!' I called on Mr Collins this morning. He received me very politely, desired me to call on him at three o'clock, and he would go over with me to the theatre. Mrs C. proposed an amendment, that I should dine with them, and go after dinner. So I did. Mr Collins was very pleased with my rehearsal. I walked with their son to a lodging which he knew. When I went out of the room Mrs C. said that she should expect me back to tea. To tea back I came, having agreed for a remarkably nice room at 9s. a week; and now I am writing in their apartment, which is the reason for my writing so laconically.

"Inform my mother, if you can, of what I write. Inform Mr Marshal that I play for the first time on Monday the 4th inst. If he have a mind to come down, I can procure him an order. I can write no more. I am obliged thus to write. If I did not, I should be unable to write till Monday.

"My next letter shall keep up better appearances.

"THOMAS COOPER."

The Same to the Same.

"PORTSMOUTH, *March* 11, '93.

"I gave my mother all the information you require in the letter I sent yesterday, and I thought that might save the additional trouble and expense of postage, for I have a great deal to do. Though I play seldom, whenever I play I have to study the character; but as necessary information cannot in London be conveyed half a mile, I will with pleasure endeavour to do it from seventy miles' distance. You desired to be acquainted with some of the gentlemen of the company. Their names are as follows :— Tyler, Curtis, Stanewix, Gill, Kelly, Woolley, Baker, Davies, Barrett ; Mesdames Tyler, Maxfield, Kelly, Davies, Collins, Balls, and Lings. Mr Tyler is the chief singer, and has £1, 11s. 6d. salary a week. He plays, besides, in middling parts, is good-natured and rather formal, and about thirty-eight years of age. Mr Curtis is a kind of pompous fool, never seems to attempt anything in acting, stands always in one position, and as erect as if he had a spit thrust through him. Mr Gill is — nobody. Mr Stanewix is a young beginner—he has been but nine months on the stage. I do not well know what to make of him. His understanding is above mediocrity, but I believe he will never be a good actor. He plays French parts and fops. Mr Maxfield is the tragedy hero. It so happened that he did not till last night play one of his best castes, when he played 'George Barnwell' with some merit ; but though this man is their Richard III., their Essex, &c., such is the nature of this company that last night, after playing 'George Barnwell,' he went on as a sailor in 'Captain Cook,' without a word to say, or anything to do. Kelly is a Jack in all parts — a young man who would have merit in some caste, if he did not undertake all. Woolley, Baker, and Davies are low comedy men, and all have an equal and middling share of merit. Perhaps Woolley is the best. Barrett is the auxiliary to the company in the same manner as Holman was, but in my mind a very bad actor. He is about forty-seven years of age, plays genteel comedy, Plune, Kerger, Lord Townley, &c. He has been a manager somewhere, played ' Don Juan ' at the Royalty, and is six foot high. He is a wit, but of all the dull who profess that character, I never knew a duller. I will give a specimen. Somebody asked whether Mrs Inchbald's play was *cast*. Another replied that if he had the direction of it, it would be cast into the fire. ' Then,' rejoined Barrett, ' it would be an *outcast*.' He was complaining one day of a dilemma to which he was reduced. ' I am in a damned scrape ; I almost think I am a fiddle, I am in such a scrape,' running his stick backwards and forwards across his arm by way of illustration. When Mrs Davies, Mrs Laing, and Mrs Rivers are mentioned, I have mentioned all the women who are not non-entities. I have, since I wrote last, played Worthy and Philip in ' The Brothers.' The salary is only 15s. a week, not to me only, but to everybody except Tyler and Barrett. Next week is Passion Week, during which there are no plays, and no pay.

" Thomas Cooper.

" I expect every day to be pressed, and neither appearance nor friends can save me. Masters of houses have been taken away. I know a common sailor who sometime ago was a player."

The Same to the Same.

" Winchester, *July* 13, '93.

" You say in your last letter that you are obliged to adopt my mode of correspondence. I agree with you that your mode would be far preferable; but from my situation, it is impossible to adopt it.

" Since about June 10th we have travelled from Portsmouth to Chichester ; from thence, after ten days, back to Portsmouth, and having stayed there four days, have taken our departure for Winchester, where we have now been about a fortnight, and our managers think of dissolving the company till we play at Southampton, which will be at the end of this month. In all our journeys we bear our own expenses, and they have allowed nothing extra for our continual removings. We are paid only nightly. In this town our salary is only 4s. a-night. This last week we have only played once, so that we are going to receive this morning a shilling a-head; and if we are not dismissed till Southampton, there is no probability of our playing more than once in that town, which I suppose will be upwards of a fortnight. From the above circumstances you may conclude that we are all chop-fallen. It is your maxim that a little wholesome adversity is a very good thing for a young man to encounter, so that I trust you will give me credit for a little wisdom : that a few of the dregs of folly are purged away by the purifying physic of bread and water. You may expect, if we are dismissed, to see me in London in a few days, towards the latter end of next week. So much for that subject. Mr Quicke was with us at Chichester, and the four days at Portsmouth. He is a very pleasant man in company, and very familiar. We expect Incledon at Southampton, and I believe Holman, but of him I am not certain.

"I received a day or two ago a very strange letter from my sister about her situation. A kind of despondency runs throughout it. Has she written to you in the same style lately? I returned a pretty sharp answer immediately, which I hope will cure her of her disorder, whatever it is. You have never informed me anything of your affairs—how your book sells, whether you like your way of living, &c.

"Write to me as soon as convenient ; but observe that I shall perhaps not be here long. I am in perfect health, as I hope this will find you. T. COOPER."

The Same to the Same.

"WINCHESTER, *July* 19, 1793.

" ' It must be so.   O guts, ye reason well,
Else whence those painful gripes, those inward workings,
This craving after something good to eat ?

.   .   .   .   .

.   .   .   Why shrinks the belly
To the back bone, and 'tween leaves no vacuum ?
'Tis this damned *nothing* that commoves within.
'Tis starving's self that stares us in the face
And indicates non-entity to man.'

" I am just come from the theatre, where we dismissed two
from the theatre and one from the pit.

" I shall not come to London after all.   We have played once
this week, having got a bespeak from the Marquis of Buckingham :
we are to open at Southampton on Monday week, so that it would
not be worth while to come for so short a space ; besides that, our
managers mean to open their doors next week, as the week
before.

" There are a few mistakes in your letter.   When I say that my
situation renders impracticable a diligent correspondence, I did
not mean that it has that effect at present, for if I did, my actions
would belie my words ; but that it had in our frequent movings,
and during the benefit time at Portsmouth.   You are to write to
me at full, as you need not expect to see me.   In the next paragraph you say, ' Not a word about your health,' but that's a mistake, for the last words of my letter are, ' I am in perfect health,
as I hope this will find you ;' but I suppose you had not patience
to get through my bad handwriting.

" I'll now relate a theatrical incident.   George Barnwell was
played : you recollect that the uncle comes on, and makes a
soliloquy on death.   The uncle had not, or did not choose to
have leisure to learn the soliloquy, but thought, if he carried on a
book of the play, that he might read it.   He did not reflect that
the stage would be darkened, and when he looked in the book, he
found he could not read.   He recollected the first words, ' O

death !' and repeated them three or four times in great agitation, calling at the same time for George Barnwell to come and kill him, but George was laughing so heartily behind the scenes that for some time he could not relieve his uncle, and his uncle said no more than ' O death—do—do '—till his nephew came and stabbed him, and laughed at him in the agonies of death.

" I have just received information that the Coldstream is all killed except fifteen, and that the Duke is in the number of the slain. Among the rest of the information you are to give me, let the sale of your pamphlet and the title be included—what Mr Holcroft has lately written—what Mr Marshall is about. In short, tell me something about everybody. Do you know anything concerning the Dysons now?

" Remember me to all my acquaintance in London : say something for me to each, what you shall judge proper, just the same as if I had written.   T. COOPER."

The Same to the Same.

"SOUTHAMPTON, *Oct.* 18, 1793.

"Glory be to Thee, O God, for all the manifold goods which day after day Thou bestowest upon me ! Would you believe it ? I have had a *benefit*—such a benefit—a kind of Irish one, by which I have lost upwards of six pounds—at least I remain that much indebted to our managers. How strange, how despicable are the dispositions of tyrants ! The morning after my night, this Davies came to me to do something for him in a pantomime which is performed to-night for his benefit. I readily consented. Things have turned out that I am not of much consequence to him to-night, and this morning, instead of the smiling, smirking face of yesterday, he addressed me with a stiff Hibernian frown—' Mr Cooper, I want some money—I must have money. I'll not pay the salaries, sir, till you have paid me. Blood, sir, why am I to pay money out of my own pocket ?' The absent politician, too, has attempted to speak to me. ' Mr Tyler, have you heard any news to-day ? Oh, Mr Cooper, about your night (a pause). I have not seen the *Star* to-day. Sir, walk this way, if you please.' I was going to follow but Mrs Somebody met him, and he immediately began to settle the business of the nation. He dared imagine that it was for me to wait his pleasure. About half-an-hour afterwards he repeated his request, and I told him I was engaged.

"The usual method of payment in cases of deficiency of the changes is by stopping 3s. or 4s. per week out of the salary; but on account of my great deficiency, he says he will stop the whole week's salary until it is paid. In case he attempts it, it is my present intention to leave him immediately, not secretly. No; what I dare do, I dare do openly. If he pursues other steps, I have arrived at such a happy disregard of my personal affairs, that it will scarcely give me a moment's concern.

"You will wonder, perhaps, how I came to fail so much. There are three or four sufficient reasons. The first is, that the interest of a man of long standing and unusual acquaintance carries everything before it; next, that though the other weak interests are supremely blessed with the happy gifts of fawning servility, yet I have not so much of the spaniel about me; I cannot take my hat off to the great man's servant. If I were to lose £50 and fifty benefits, I cannot bow to flatter the man I despise. The third was that I was between two fires—one manager's daughter before, the other manager's wife after me.

"I now want you or Mrs Holcroft to inform me whether Mr H. himself spoke to Mrs Wood relative to an engagement for me with her husband; or if not, who was it. "T. COOPER."

The Same to the Same.

"SOUTHAMPTON, *Nov.* 2, '93.

"If there were an appearance of reserve in my letters, relative to my present situation, it could be only an appearance; for I have not, nor have I ever had, the least wish to conceal anything. If I did not expatiate at large on the subject, it was because I had no desire to excite any man's compassion; for I feel no compassion for myself; or in other words, I am quite indifferent about it, as I have told you before. I have lived partly upon a little money which I had saved, and partly upon credit, which has involved me in debt near £2. But I shall considerably decrease it by means of about a guinea, which I got last night, by joining with two others who had failed, and buying a bad stock-night of the managers at an under-price. This, with the loan of a guinea, which you are so kind as to offer me, will pretty well bring me about, so that I shall probably still remain with Messrs C. and D., if they promise to allow me a salary after this town, and will pay the bill for printing the tickets for my benefit. But if he refuses, my former resolution will remain unbroken. You may depend on seeing me in London very soon—how soon will in some measure depend on Mr Davies's acceptance or rejection of my proposals. If he refuse, I shall not stay to play for his benefit. At all events, you will see me in less than a fortnight.

"If you can oblige me with this guinea, direct to me in any small parcel, at Mr Ling's, 15 Butcher Row, and send it by Mr Cox's coach, which sets out every morning from the Saracen's Head, Snow Hill.

"When I spoke relative to the School for Arrogance to Mr Davies, he said, 'If Mr Holcroft had really been inclined to serve me, he certainly could not have refused so small a favour.' I smiled within myself at the confined ideas of a selfish man.

"I should be glad if you would not make it public that I am coming to town. 'Tis, I grant, a childish wish, but it would be a pleasure to surprise my friends. Though childish, it is innocent, and as it would be a pleasure, I hope it will be a sufficient reason with you to comply with my request.

T. COOPER.

CHAPTER V.

GODWIN'S WORKS AND POLITICS. 1783—1794.

WITH the publication of "Political Justice" Godwin first became known as an author, and appeared before the world under his own name, except so far as the "Sketches of History" were an exception.

The six sermons which bear that wholly inappropriate title are on the characters of Aaron, Hazael and Jesus— four sermons being devoted to the last. They are fair specimens of Nonconformist pulpit oratory, and, with the exception of one or two sentences, are remarkable chiefly for the extreme lucidity of style. Then, as always, it was impossible to mistake Godwin's meaning. Simple and straightforward, his language rose sometimes to a rare eloquence, not because he desired it, or valued rhetoric for its own sake, but because the words he used were the fittest to clothe his most intimate convictions, and therefore appealed to the hearts of other men. An early and a diligent student of French literature, there is something in his own style of the characteristics of the better French writers, where the thoughts are seen through rather than in the language, like pebbles in a deep well, and invested with a beauty beyond their own.

Other points for which the Sermons are noticeable are these. Writing nominally as a strong Calvinist, and believing himself to uphold the absolute sovereignty of God, he yet strikes a note which, though he knew it not, was dissonant to all the rest. "God himself," he says in   . .'

Sermon I., "God himself has no right to be a tyrant." Of this passage the *English Review*, in a very favourable article, says: "In some instances his vivacity transports him beyond the bounds of decorum." It was the enuncia-tion of a principle from which he was afterwards to draw unexpected conclusions.

Again, writing as an orthodox believer, he no doubt thought that he held that Jesus Christ was God, and by that fact different from all men, not to be compared or placed on the same level with them. But at the bottom of his mind was the feeling that if Jesus were to be loved and venerated, it was not as God, but for his likeness to, and his oneness with, humanity. And this found ex-pression in the sentence which ends the Sermon on the Resignation of Aaron.

"May we all of us exemplify the quietness of an Aaron, and the unresentful mildness of a redeemer, that so we may be united with these great and illustrious characters for ever hereafter."

Little can here be said of the three novels which issued in such rapid succession from Godwin's brain and pen during the years 1783-4 — "Damon and Delia," "The Italian Letters," and "Imogen ; a Pastoral Romance," pro-fessing to be a translation from an old Welsh MS. These appear to have vanished into nothingness as well as forget-fulness, and the most diligent researches have as yet obtained only slight indications that once they were deemed interesting. But this need scarcely be regretted. The emotional part of Godwin's nature had never as yet been stirred, while he had gained no such experience of life as was his when he wrote "Caleb Williams."

It is, however, a real misfortune that much else which Godwin wrote at this date is buried in the pages of reviews, some of them extinct and hard to discover, and some, like the older volumes of the Annual Register, reposing dusty, worm-eaten, and seldom handled, on the more inaccessible shelves of libraries. The sketch of English History which Godwin contributed to the *Annual Register* from 1785 onward is well worthy to stand alone and to live. It is entitled "The History of Knowledge, Learning, and Taste in Great Britain," and the portion contributed by him begins with the reign of Henry VII. In addition to his invariable clearness and method in the grouping and presentation of his facts, there is much curious learning and research displayed, much wide reading, sympathy with art, keen power of criticism, and a kindly toleration for views the most opposed to his own. It may be suspected that the apparent research of some of his contemporaries is really Godwin's research alone. It is scarcely likely that he, Charles Lamb, and Coleridge were all reading the Schoolmen at the same time, all picking out the same absurd questions from Albertus Magnus and Thomas Aquinas! yet there is a most suspicious resemblance in the selections made by all three, ending with the enquiry whether a million of angels might not sit upon a needle's point ; and these selections certainly appeared first in the *Annual Register.*

The paragraphs in which the Schoolmen and their influence are dismissed after a fairly full account may serve to show the calm and judicial tone of the writer, and the work done for the *Annual Register* is an adequate specimen of the manner in which he performed the whole of that class of work, anonymous, underpaid, and almost unnoticed.

"With all the misapplication of their talents, the school divines and philosophers were many of them great men. Thomas

Aquinas in particular had extraordinary abilities which, if they had been properly directed, might have rendered him very useful to mankind.   Nor is it to be imagined that everything in him is trifling and ridiculous.   There are, it is believed, parts of his works which might even now be read with pleasure and advantage.

"So far as it is an honour to have produced the Schoolmen our own country had its full share in that honour.   Not to mention Lanfranc and Anselm, Duns Scotus was a Briton, probably born in Scotland, and William Occam was an Englishman. Alexander Hales, John Baconthorpe, Thomas Bradwardine, and a large list of names might be produced, if it were necessary to rescue them from the oblivion in which they have long slept."— *New Annual Register*, 1786, p. viii.

Though, however, the "Sketches of History" were the firstfruits of Godwin's pen, his first published work was the "Life of Lord Chatham."   It was issued anonymously, probably because it was a first effort, and its author was as yet uncertain of his own powers, as well as his own opinions; and even up to the date at which these lines are written, it stands in the British Museum catalogue with a query as to whether it is really Godwin's.

The book is rare, but, for those who can lay hands on it thoroughly worth reading in itself, and also as showing how the commanding figure of the great tory statesman drew the enthusiastic admiration of one who was so soon to startle his contemporaries, by asserting in "Political Justice" that all government whatever was an infringement of the Rights of Man.   A few sentences of the concluding chapter may be given.

"Like the first king of the Jews, he walks, elevated by the head above his compatriots, who seem as they were born his subjects.   Men of genius and attraction, a Carteret, a Townshend, and I had almost said, a Mansfield, however pleasing in a limited

view, appear evidently in this comparison to shrink into narrower
dimensions, and walk a humbler circle. All that deserves to
arrest the attention in taking a general survey of the age in which
he lived is comprised in the history of Chatham.

"No character ever bore the more undisputed stamp of originality. Unresembled and himself, he was not born to accommodate
to the genius of his age. While all around him were depressed
by the uniformity of fashion, or the contagion of venality, he stood
aloof. He consulted no judgment but his own, and he acted from
the unstained dictates of a comprehensive soul. He loved fame
too much, but it was the weakness of a noble mind. He loved
power too much, but it was power of a generous strain. And he
had passions that had nothing selfish in their texture. No spirit
ever burned with a purer flame of patriotism."

Life of Chatham, pp. 287, 288.

These writings were, however, one and all, provisional
and preparatory. They were soon forgotten; the fate,
with the rarest exceptions, of all anonymous writing. But
the publication of "Political Justice" marked an epoch in
English thought. It was coincident with the rise of a
school of philosophic radicals, and in large measure
placed in clear words the views of that school, on
many, though perhaps not all, of the subjects treated.
There were, however, very few who carried out logical conclusions so consistently and unshrinkingly as Godwin. He
alone formulated, among his political judgments, the extreme severity of social principles, the denial of all play to
feeling and affection, which Fawcet and Holcroft had more
loosely held as matters for informal discussion.

By the words "Political Justice," the author meant "the
adoption of any principle of morality and truth into the
practice of a community," Vol. I. p. 19, and the book was
therefore an enquiry into the principles of society, of govern-

ment, and of morals. The first volume deals with principles
only; the second with the mode in which those principles
would exhibit themselves in politics and in society.

Twelve years before he wrote his preface, that is, when
living under the influence of Mr Frederic Norman at Stowmarket, Godwin "became satisfied that monarchy was a
species of government unavoidably corrupt," Vol. I. p. viii.
The ideas suggested by the French Revolution induced
him to desire a government of the simplest construction,
and he gradually became aware that "government, by its
very nature, counteracts the improvement of original mind,"
Vol. I. p. x. Believing in the perfectibility of the race, that
there are no innate principles, and therefore no original
propensity to evil, he considered that "our virtues and our
vices may be traced to the incidents which make the history
of our lives, and if these incidents could be divested of
every improper tendency, vice would be extirpated from
the world," Vol. I. p. 18. Education, literature, and political justice "are three principal causes by which the human
mind is advanced towards a state of perfection," Vol. I.
p. 19; hence what is really required is that the truth
should be placed before men, and free discussion allowed;
they would then, in the widest sense of the words, "know
the truth, and the truth would make them free." Hence
all control of man by man is more or less intolerable,
and the day will come when each man, doing what
seems right in his own eyes, will also be doing what is
in fact best for the community, because all will be
guided by principles of pure reason. But all was to be
done by calm discussion, and matured change resulting
from discussion. Hence, while Godwin thoroughly approved of the philosophic schemes of the precursors of the
Revolution, he was as far removed as Burke himself from

agreeing with the way in which they were carried into practical life, and he strongly disapproved of the mode in which some English politicians of his own school from time to time endeavoured to hasten the course of events. He says, in a note to his first chapter, that the foregoing "arguments are for the most part an abstract, the direct ones from Locke on the 'Human Understanding,' those which relate to experience from Hartley's 'Observations on Man,' and those respecting education from the 'Emile' of J. J. Rousseau." In these views he never wavered, and his life was thoroughly consistent. He never allowed himself to be converted to the expediency of giving and taking in politics, or to see that principles can be applied to facts only by losing a portion of their gloss and of their truth. He never could have been a worker on the active stage of life. But he was none the less a motive power behind the workers, and " Politi-cal Justice " may take its place with the " Speech for Unlicensed Printing," the " Essay on Education," and " Emile," among the unseen levers which have moved the changes of the times.

The first edition of the book—to which all references are made—so well deserves reading for its own sake, even at this date, that no exhaustive extracts need here be given : it is enough to describe the scope of the book. But some points in which the writer touched on matters still under discussion, and full of interest for us, may yet detain us awhile. In the chapter on the Perfectibility of Man, entitled " Human Inventions capable of perpetual improvement," Godwin found himself face to face with the problem of the origin of language. It would be difficult even now to put forward the interjectional, and probably sound theory on this subject more clearly and excellently than is here done :—

"Its beginning was probably from those involuntary cries which infants, for example, are found to utter in the earliest stages of their existence, and which, previously to the idea of exciting pity or procuring assistance, spontaneously arise from the operation of pain upon our animal frame. These cries, when actually uttered, become a subject of perception to him by whom they are uttered, and being observed to be constantly associated with certain preliminary impressions, and to excite the idea of those impressions in the hearer, may afterwards be repeated from reflection, and the desire of relief. Eager desire to communicate any information to another will also prompt us to utter some simple sound for the purpose of exciting attention. This sound will probably frequently recur to organs unpractised to variety, and will at length stand as it were by convention for the information intended to be conveyed. But the distance is extreme from those simple modes of communication which we possess in common with some of the inferior animals, to all the analysis and abstraction which languages require."—Vol. I., p. 45.

Again, when discussing the effect that climate and other physical influences have on the character of man, Godwin recognised in the frankest way the animal nature which can thus be affected, even while he combats the view that man is unable to triumph over those physical environments.

"'Breed, for example, appears to be of unquestionable importance to the character and qualifications of horses and dogs. Why should we not suppose this or certain other brute and occult causes to be equally efficacious in the case of men? How comes it that the races of animals perhaps never degenerate if careful'y cultivated, at the same time that we have no security against the wisest philosopher's begetting a dunce?'

"I answer that the existence of physical causes cannot be controverted. In the case of man, their efficacy is swallowed up in the superior importance of reflection and science. In animals, on the contrary, they are left almost alone. If a race of negroes were taken, and maintained each man from his infancy, except so far as was necessary for the propagation of the species, in solitude; or even if they were excluded from an acquaintance with the improvements and imaginations of their ancestors, though permitted the society of each other, the operation of breed might perhaps be rendered as conspicuous among them as in the different classes of horses and dogs. But the ideas they would otherwise receive from their parents and civilized or half civilized neighbours would be innumerable, and if the precautions above mentioned were unobserved, all parallel between the two cases would cease."— Vol. I., pp. 58, 59.

It was, of course, impossible that the writer of the above should, in the then state of science, be aware how large a part exterior causes play in influencing the breeds of man, nor the vast time in which such causes may have been at work; but the fact that the above sentences could not be written now, by no means detracts from their value then.

So logical and uncompromising a thinker as Godwin, so plain spoken and unequivocal a writer, could not go far in the discussion of abstract questions without coming into collision with received opinions. The chapter on justice is interesting, as showing how largely he was still under the influence of Fawcet, and Fawcet's teacher, Jonathan Edwards. He says :—

"Justice is a rule of conduct originating in the connection of one percipient being with another. A comprehensive maxim which has been laid down upon the subject is 'that we should love our neighbour as ourselves.' But this maxim, though possessing considerable merit as a popular principle, is not modelled with the strictness of philosophical accuracy.

"In a loose and general view I and my neighbour are both of us men, and of consequence entitled to equal attention; but in reality it is probable that one of us is a being of more worth and importance than the other. A man is of more worth than a beast, because, being possessed of higher faculties, he is capable of a more refined and generous happiness. In the same manner the illustrious Archbishop of Cambray was of more worth than his chambermaid, and there are few of us who would hesitate to pronounce, if his palace were in flames, and the life of only one of them could be preserved, which of the two ought to be preferred.

. . . .

" Supposing I had been myself the chambermaid, I ought to have chosen to die rather than that Fenelon should have died. The life of Fenelon was really preferable to that of the chambermaid. But understanding is the faculty that perceives the truth of this and similar propositions, and justice is the principle that regulates my conduct accordingly. It would have been just in the chambermaid to have preferred the Archbishop to herself. To have done otherwise would have been a breach of justice.

" Supposing the chambermaid to have been my wife, my mother, or my benefactor, this would not alter the truth of the proposition. The life of Fenelon would still be more valuable than that of the chambermaid, and justice, pure unadulterated justice, would still have preferred that which was most valuable. Justice would have taught me to save the life of Fenelon at the expense of the other. What magic is there in the pronoun 'my' to overturn the decisions of everlasting truth? My wife or my mother may be a fool or a prostitute, malicious, lying, or dishonest. If they be, of what consequence is it that they are mine?

" ' But my mother endured for me the pains of childbearing, and nourished me in the helplessness of infancy.' When she first subjected herself to the necessity of these cares, she was probably influenced by no particular motives of benevolence to her future offspring. Every voluntary benefit, however, entitles the bestower to some kindness and retribution. But why so? Because a voluntary benefit is an evidence of benevolent intention, that is of virtue. It is the disposition of the mind, not the external action that entitles to respect. But the merit of this disposition is equal whether the benefit was conferred upon me or upon another. I and another man cannot both be right in preferring our own individual benefactor, for no man can be at the same time both better and worse than his neighbour. My benefactor ought to be esteemed, not because he bestowed a benefit on me, but because he bestowed it upon a human being. His desert will be in exact proportion to the degree in which that human being was worthy of the distinction conferred. ... Gratitude therefore ... is no part either of justice or virtue. By gratitude I understand a sentiment which would lead me to prefer one man to another from some other consideration than that of his superior usefulness or worth ; that is which would make something true to me (for example this preferableness), which cannot be true to another man, and is not true in itself."—Vol. I., p. 84.

Much more, however, was to come which ran still more counter to the feelings of society. The propriety of allowing or not allowing play to the affections might seem to most persons a purely abstract question. But no abstract speculation was advanced when in a day in which the penal code was still extremely severe Godwin argued gravely against all punishments, not only that of death. He considered that the only true end of punishment is correction—a proposition which may well be disputed— and that the only proper way of conveying to any understanding a truth of which it is ignorant, or enforcing a truth imperfectly held, is by an appeal to reason. And as no two men were ever guilty of the same crime, positive law was an evil in that it levels all characters and tramples on all distinctions.

Yet, however faulty might the law be, however vicious the state of society, however tyrannical the government enforcing the one and upholding the other, no conceivable state of things would justify any violent change, plot or conspiracy, still less tyrannicide or the execution of the malefactor to the State, for

" If the attempt prove abortive it renders the tyrant ten times
more bloody, ferocious, and cruel than before. If it succeed and
the tyranny be restored, it produces the same effect on his succes-
sors. In the climate of despotism some solitary virtues may spring
up but in the midst of plots and conspiracies there is neither truth
nor confidence, nor love nor humanity."—Vol. I., p. 228.

In all this Godwin was in fact ignoring what every
statesman must face, and what history as yet has ever
proved true, that to carry any principle into practical life
some part of the principle must of necessity be lost, that
there is no progress whatever without attendant circumstances which fall hard on some of the community. Godwin approved the French Revolution so long as he had to
consider only the problems presented to him by Rousseau,
and the reforms urged by Turgot ; he shrank not only from
the violence of the Terror, but even from the political
associations which sought to mature possible changes
before they were openly suggested, and from such healthy
popular risings as the destruction of the Bastille.

Before passing from the strictly theoretical portion of the
work, whence the foregoing extracts have been taken,
Godwin paused in order to consider those general principles
of the human mind, which were most intimately connected
with his subject. None of these principles seemed of
greater moment than that which affirms that all actions are
necessary. The chapters on the doctrine of necessity are
among the most interesting and lucid in the whole book,
nor is the interest diminished by his admission that the
substance of a large part of his arguments may be found in
Hume's " Enquiry concerning Human Understanding," and
in Jonathan Edwards's " Enquiry into the Freedom of the
Will." The arguments on either side of the controversy
must in any age be much the same in all the writers of

that age, and their immediate intellectual descendants, but
the clearness and precision of the words in which they are
clothed is Godwin's own.

When these principles, as laid down in the first five books,
were to be applied to existing society, Godwin came most
decidedly into collision with all opinion which was con·
sidered respectable, orderly, and religious. Not only did he
assail all government, even that then considered by the
liberal party as full of promise—the government by National
Assemblies; not only did he assail religious establishments
and tests, but property itself, and marriage, were not to
him sacred things, apart and unassailable. His observations on property include some suggestive hints on his
whole scheme of political justice, if, indeed, the word
"scheme" can apply in any sense to his theory of life in a
community.

"The subject of property is the key-stone that completes the
fabric of political justice. According as our ideas respecting it
are crude or correct, they will enlighten us as to the consequences
of a *simple form of society without government*, and remove the pre·
judices that attach us to complexity. There is nothing that more
powerfully tends to distort our *judgment* and *opinions* than erroneous
notions concerning the goods of fortune. Finally, the period that
shall put an end to the system of *coercion* and *punishment* is intimately connected with the circumstance of property being placed
upon an equitable basis.

.   .   .   .

"To whom does any article of property, suppose a loaf of bread,
justly belong? To him who most wants it, or to whom the possession of it will be most beneficial. Here are six men, famished with
hunger, and the loaf is, absolutely considered, capable of satisfying
the cravings of them all. Who is it that has a reasonable claim to
benefit by the qualities with which this loaf is endowed? They
are all brothers, perhaps, and the law of primogeniture bestows it

exclusively on the eldest. But does justice confirm this award? The laws of different countries dispose of property in a thousand different ways; but there can be but one way which is most conformable to reason.

. . . .

"The doctrine of the injustice of accumulated property has been the foundation of all religious morality. The object of this morality has been to excite men by individual virtue to repair this injustice . . .

"But while religion inculcated on mankind the impartial nature of justice, its teachers have been too apt to treat the practice of justice, not as a debt, which it ought to be considered, but as an affair of spontaneous generosity and bounty. They have called on the rich to be clement and merciful to the poor. The consequence of this has been that the rich, when they bestowed the most slender pittance of their enormous wealth in acts of charity, as they were called, took merit to themselves for what they gave, instead of considering themselves as delinquents for what they withheld.

"Religion is in reality, in all its parts, an accommodation to the prejudices and weaknesses of mankind. Its authors communicated to the world as much truth as they calculated that the world would be willing to receive. But it is time that we should lay aside the instruction intended only for children in understanding, and contemplate the nature and principles of things. If religion had spoken out, and told us it was just that all men should receive the supply of their wants, we should presently have been led to suspect that a gratuitous distribution to be made by the rich was a very indirect and ineffectual way of arriving at this object. The experience of all ages has taught us, that this system is productive only of a very precarious supply. The principal object which it seems to propose, is to place this supply in the disposal of a few, enabling them to make a show of generosity with what is not truly their own, and to purchase the gratitude of the poor by the payment of a debt. It is a system of clemency and charity, instead of a system of justice. It fills the rich with unreasonable pride by the spurious denominations with which it decorates their acts, and the poor with servility by leading them to regard the slender comforts they obtain, not as their incontrovertible due, but as the good pleasure and the grace of their opulent neighbours."—Vol. II., pp. 788-798.

There is one institution which is in the minds of most men—or at least most men would have it supposed to be so—yet more sacred than that of property, namely, marriage. It is generally assumed that whoever would strike a blow at this relation can only do so in a spirit of lawless lust. Such, however, was evidently not the case with Godwin. He was a man to whom passion was unknown, who could discuss the relation of the sexes quite apart from any special application. And this very fact made his opinions more important than they would otherwise have been. To marriage he at this time objected altogether, and his objections are extremely curious, when, and in so far as, they go beyond those superficial ones easily made, and as easily refuted. These are such as that the inclinations of two human beings do not coincide through any length of time, that thoughtless and romantic youth of each sex do not know their own minds, and are reduced to make the best of an inevitable mistake. But the real objections felt by Godwin are those which are bound up with the whole idea of his book. Thus—

"Marriage is law, and the worst of all laws. Whatever our understandings may tell us of the person from whose connection we should derive the greatest improvement, of the worth of one woman, and the demerits of another, we are obliged to consider what is law, and not what is justice.

"Add to this that marriage is an affair of property, and the worst of all properties. So long as two human beings are forbidden by positive institution to follow the dictates of their own mind, prejudice is alive and vigorous. . .

I.   II

"The abolition of marriage will be attended with no evils. We
are apt to represent it to ourselves as the harbinger of brutal lust
and depravity. But it really happens in this, as in other cases,
that the positive laws which are made to restrain our vices irritate
and multiply them. . . . . The intercourse of the sexes will fall
under the same system as any other species of friendship. . . . I
shall assiduously cultivate the intercourse of that woman whose
accomplishments shall strike me in the most powerful manner.
' But it may happen that other men will feel for her the same preference that I do.' This will create no difficulty. We may all
enjoy her conversation, and we shall all be wise enough to consider the sensual intercourse a very trivial object."—Vol. II.,
pp. 849-851.

But perhaps the most striking instance of Godwin's
thorough consistency is to be found in the fact that he
does not shrink from applying his doctrine to the case
even of the young. It will of course follow that if in an
ideal community the child, however wise, cannot know his
own father, education will be the business, not of the family,
but of the state. But

"The task of instruction under such a form of society as that
we are contemplating will be greatly simplified and altered from
what it is at present. It will then be thought no more legitimate
to make boys slaves than to make men so. The business will not
then be to bring forward so many adepts in the egg-shell that the
vanity of parents may be flattered in hearing their praises. No
man will then think of vexing with premature learning the feeble
and inexperienced, for fear that when they come to years of discretion they should refuse to be learned. Mind will be suffered to
expand itself in proportion as occasion and impression shall excite
it, and not be tortured and enervated by being cast in a particular
mould. No creature in human form will be expected to learn
anything but because he desires it, and has some conception of
its utility and value ; and every man, in proportion to his capacity,

will be ready to furnish such general hints and comprehensive views as will suffice for the guidance and encouragement of him who studies from a principle of desire."—Vol. II., pp. 853, 854.

Portions of this treatise, and only portions, found ready acceptance in those minds which were prepared to receive them. Perhaps no one received the whole teaching of the book. Every strong reformer, religious or political, states general principles which must be accommodated to the existing state of things, only those are accepted in which he gives a voice to opinions which are "in the air," while the originality and independence of thought gain for him the hearing which would not be his did he *merely* put forward thoughts which were struggling for expression. The book gave cohesion and voice to philosophic Radicalism; it was the manifesto of a school without which the milder and more creedless liberalism of the present day had not been. Godwin himself in after days modified his communistic views, but his strong feeling for individualism, his hate of all restrictions on liberty, his trust in man, his faith in the power of reason remained; it was a manifesto which enunciated principles modifying action even when not wholly ruling it. Perhaps none but the founder of any system ever believes that it can be maintained in its entirety, and among such founders few have been so consistent and uncompromising as Godwin.

But while his friends and admirers allowed to slip that which they could not accept, it was far other with his political opponents. He who was to the one party all but an inspired teacher, though the source of the inspiration would have been hard to define, was to the other party a revolutionary Atheist, who went in daily danger of a prosecution for treason. He had the affection of a small and growing band of friends, but he was a mark for the scorn of all who were, or desired to be considered, orthodox and respectable.

In a separate note-book headed "Supplement to Journal," Godwin has recorded conversations of various friends, partly in regard to his book. Under date of 1793, March 23, he writes :—

" Dr Priestley says my book contains a vast extent of ability— Monarchy and Aristocracy, to be sure, were never so painted before—he agrees with me respecting gratitude and contracts absolutely considered, but thinks the principles too refined for practice—he felt uncommon approbation of my investigation of the first principles of government, which were never so well explained before—he admits fully my first principle of the omnipotence of instruction and that all vice is error—he admits all my principles, but cannot follow them into all my conclusions with me respecting self-love—he thinks mind will never so far get the better of matter as I suppose ; he is of opinion that the book contains a great quantity of original thinking, and will be uncommonly useful.

" Horne Tooke tells me that my book is a bad book, and will do a great deal of harm—Holcroft and Jardine had previously informed me, the first, that he said the book was written with very good intentions, but to be sure nothing could be so foolish ; the second, that Holcroft and I had our heads full of plays and novels, and then thought ourselves philosophers."

"Caleb Williams," the first of Godwin's novels which was destined to survive, was published in May 1794. Very many years afterwards, he wrote a short notice of his intention in this book :—

" I believed myself fortunate in the selection I had made of the ground-plot of that work. An atrocious crime committed by a man previously of the most exemplary habits, the annoyance he suffers from the immeasurable and ever-wakeful curiosity of a raw youth who is placed about his person, the state of doubt in which the reader might for a time be as to the truth of these charges and the consequences growing out of these causes, seemed to me to afford scope for a narrative of no common interest."

Advertisement to "St Leon," ed. of 1831.

He was not disappointed; the novel had very great success, and was dramatized by Colman under the name of "The Iron Chest." In spite of the amazing impossibilities of the story and its unrelieved gloom; in spite of the want of almost any character to admire—since Mr Clare, by whom Godwin probably intended to represent his friend Fawcet, dies early in the tale; though there is no real heroine and scarcely mention of love, the story has survived and has probably been read by very many persons who, but for it, have never heard of Godwin. It is a very powerful book, and the character of Falkland the murderer is unique in literature.

In the year 1794 Godwin found it his duty to fling himself to a greater extent than he had hitherto done into the stream of active politics. He came out of his study to stand by prisoners arraigned of a crime of which the terrors then were real—High Treason. His own note best sums up the circumstances—

"The year 1794 was memorable for the trial of twelve persons, under one indictment upon a charge of high treason. Some of these persons were my particular friends; more than half of them were known to me. This trial is certainly one of the most memorable epochs in the history of English liberty. The accusation, combined with the evidence adduced to support it, is not to be exceeded in vagueness and incoherence by anything in the annals of tyranny. It was an attempt to take away the lives of men by a constructive treason, and out of many facts, no one of which was capital, to compose a capital crime. The name of the

man in whose mind the scheme of this trial was engendered was
Pitt. Mr Horne Tooke was apprehended on the 12th of May.
The novel of "Caleb Williams" was then ready for publication,
and appeared about a fortnight after. In the following month I
paid a visit to Mr Merry at Bracon Ash, near Norwich, and to my
friends and relatives in Norfolk, whom I had not visited for twelve
years. In October I went into Warwickshire on a visit to Dr
Parr, who had earnestly sought the acquaintance and intimacy of
the author of "Political Justice." My position on these occasions
was a singular one: there was not a person almost in town or
village who had any acquaintance with modern publications that
had not heard of the "Enquiry concerning Political Justice," or
that was not acquainted in a great or small degree with the contents of that work. I was nowhere a stranger. The doctrines of
that work (though if any book ever contained the dictates of an
independent mind, mine might pretend to do so) coincided in a
great degree with the sentiments then prevailing in English
society, and I was everywhere received with curiosity and kindness. If temporary fame ever was an object worthy to be coveted
by the human mind, I certainly obtained it in a degree that has
seldom been exceeded. I was happy to feel that this circumstance
did not in the slightest degree interrupt the sobriety of my mind.

"On the 6th of October, the day after that on which I left
London for Warwickshire, the grand jury found a bill of indictment against the twelve persons who had been accused before
them. Among the names in the indictment were included not
only the persons known to me who were already in confinement,
but also that of my friend Holcroft, and others who were at large.
Holcroft immediately surrendered himself, and was committed to
Newgate: he wrote me word of his situation, and requested my
presence. I left Dr Parr on Monday the 13th, and reached town
on that evening. Having fully revolved the subject, and examined
the doctrines of the Lord Chief Justice's charge to the grand jury,
I locked myself up on Friday and Saturday, and wrote my stric-
tures on that composition, which appeared at full length in the
Morning Chronicle of Monday, and were transcribed from thence

into other papers. During the progress of these trials I was present at least some part of every day. Hardy's trial lasted eight,
and Horne Tooke's six days. Among the many atrocities witnessed on that occasion, perhaps the most flagitious was the
speech of the Attorney-General, now Lord Eldon, at the close of
the trial of that extraordinary man. In his peroration he burst
into tears, and entreated the jury to vindicate by their verdict his
character and fame; he urged them by the consideration of his
family to co-operate with him in leaving such a name behind to
his children as they should not look upon as their disgrace. It
was in the close of this year that I first met with Samuel Taylor
Coleridge, my acquaintance with whom was ripened in the year
1800 into a high degree of affectionate intimacy."

The Diary does no more than confirm the above, adding
some touches of detail. Thus it is recorded, that during his
stay with Dr Parr he went to church, and had an altercation with Mrs Parr about the Lord's Supper, or, in his own
curious mixture of Latin and French, "altercation de
Madame de cœnâ dom." He was very regular in attendance at the "Philomaths," a society which met every Tuesday and discussed abstract questions, such as, taken at
random, "Fame," "Tribunes," "Marriage," "Incest," "a
God." His interest in the political trials was most keen
and unselfish, though he must have felt the force of the
"tua res agitur paries quum proximus ardet."

The real charge against the prisoners, when divested
of amplifications and technicalities, was that they had
endeavoured to change the form of Government established,
by publishing, or causing to be published, divers books or
pamphlets, and by belonging to political societies having
the same object.

Mrs Shelley has left, as was natural in the daughter of
such a father and the wife of such a husband, very full

notes in reference to the political trials, which may be quoted at length, for they clearly represent not only her own mind, but the impression left on her by the conversation of her father in his later years. Though the circumstances of which she speaks occurred before her birth, she yet had a knowledge of them at second-hand in a way impossible to those of us who can only read them in the dry pages of annual registers and biographical dictionaries.

The trials of Palmer, Muir, and others in Scotland for treason, or, as it was then called in Scotland, "leasing making," took place in the autumn of the year 1793.

"In these years," she writes, "the collision between Government and the advocates for reform, or something more, was at its height. While one set of men saw an opening for their endeavours for political freedom, another became panic-struck, believing that the horrors of the French Revolution were about to overflow into this island. There were many whose zeal transported them with a wish to excite the multitude to use their numerical strength to force Government to adopt liberal measures; nor can we wonder that Ministers considered it right to put down such appeals, rendered trebly dangerous by the state of excitement into which the country was thrown.

"As the ministers of those days were in no degree favourable to the extension of the liberty of the subject, they became exasperated by the attempts of the reformers, and yet were not sorry to see them come to such a head as would admit of their taking vindictive measures. They resolved not to be sparing in their punishments, and to use the whole force of the law against such as should become their victims. Their first operations were entered on in Scotland, where the laws against sedition were severer than here, and juries more entirely under the direction of the court. Messrs Palmer, Skirving, and Muir were apprehended for various seditious practices. They were found guilty, and sentenced to be transported for seven and fourteen years. This sentence was put into execution soon after, and by its atrocity, and the horror excited by the idea that men of good education were to be subjected to the treatment of felons excited universal compassion. Their case was brought forward in Parliament, but without effect, and called forth also the following indignant letter from Mr Godwin to the *Morning Chronicle*:—

" ' *To the Editor of the ' Morning Chronicle.*'

" ' MUIR AND PALMER.

" ' SIR,—The situation in which Messieurs Muir and Palmer are at this moment placed is sufficiently known within a certain circle, but is by no means sufficiently adverted to by the public at large. Give me leave, through the channel of your paper, to call their attention to it.

" ' All the consolations of civilized society are pertinaciously refused to them. Property, whether originally their own or the gift of their friends, is to be rendered useless. Supplies of clothing, it seems, have been graciously received on board the vessels ; but stores of every kind and *books* have constantly been denied admission. The principle which has been laid down again and again by the officers of Government is—*they are felons like the rest.*

" ' This, sir, is a species of punishment scarcely precedented in the annals of mankind. Tiberius, and his modern antitype, Joseph the Second, are mere novices in the arts of cruelty compared with our blessed administration. Joseph took judges from the bench, men accustomed to reflection, to deference and elegant gratification, and made them scavengers in the streets of Vienna. Mr Pitt probably took the hint from this example. But he has refined upon his model, inasmuch as he has sent the victims of his atrocious despotism out of the country. If I must suffer under the barbarian hand of power, at least let me suffer in the face of day. Let me have this satisfaction, that my countrymen may look on and observe my disgrace. Let them learn a great lesson from my suffering. It is for them to decide whether it shall be a lesson of aversion to my guilt, or abhorrence against my punisher.

On that condition, I will stand on their pillories, and sweep their
streets with satisfaction and content. But to shut me up in
dungeons and darkness, or to transport me to the other side of
the globe, that they may wreak their vengeance on me unobserved,
is base, coward-like, and infamous.

" 'Perhaps, Mr Editor, I may be told that, in holding up these
proceedings to the indignation of my countrymen, I am guilty of
sedition. You know, sir, that there is not in the Island of Great
Britain a more strenuous advocate for peaceableness and forbearance than I am. But I will not be the partaker of their secrets of
State. What they dare to perpetrate, I dare to tell. Do they not
every day assure us that the great use of punishment is example,
to deter others from incurring the like offence? And yet they
delight to inflict severities upon these men in a corner, which they
tremble to have exposed in the eyes of the world. I join issue
with administration on this point : I, too, would have the punishment of Messieurs Muir and Palmer serve for an example. Sir,
there are examples to imitate and examples to avoid.

" 'Mr Dundas told Mr Sheridan, when that gentleman applied
to him officially upon this subject a few months ago, that *he saw
no great hardship in a man's being sent to Botany Bay*. Observe
that in this sentence, as now appears, is meant to be included an
exclusion from all the means of intellectual pleasure and improvement, a reduction of men of taste and letters to the condition of
galley-slaves. I can readily believe that to a man so obdurate in
feeling and unhumanised in manners as Mr Dundas, a privation
of the sources of intellectual pleasure may appear no hardship.
Let me appeal, then, to Mr Burke. Who knows so well as he
what is due to elegance of education, delicacy of manners, and
refinement in literature? Who has declaimed so powerfully
against those systems, by which all classes of society are confounded together, and all that is venerable for antiquity, lovely
in cultivation, and elevated by imagination and genius, is overwhelmed by the iron hand of a barbarous usurpation? Never
was the principle of taking lessons from an enemy so extensively
adopted as at present. We declaim against the French, and we

imitate them in their most horrible atrocities. Administration is desirous of conducting themselves with respect to Messieurs Muir and Palmer as the Germans have acted towards M. de la Fayette, who, we are told, in consequence of the rigours he has endured, is reduced to the state of an idiot.

" ' And who are the men that are destined to this treatment, that are to be considered as *felons like the rest?* I hear the moderate and respectable friends of Government perpetually confessing that they are *men of excellent character and irreproachable manners.* What is it by which they have incurred this punishment? I learn from the same quarter that it is *by an ill-directed zeal for what they thought a good cause.* I agree to that statement ; I think they did wrong. Let us suppose that for that wrong, that well-meant but improper zeal, they ought to be punished. In what manner punished? Not, sir, *as if they were felons.* A mild and temperate punishment might, for aught I know, have operated upon others to induce them to act with more becoming deliberation. But a punishment that exceeds all measure and mocks at all justice, that listens to no sentiment but revenge, and plays the volunteer in insolence and cruelty—a punishment the purpose of which is to inflict on such men slavery, degradation of soul, a lingering decay and final imbecility—can do nothing but exasperate men's minds, and wind up their nerves to decisive action.

" ' You will perceive, sir, that in this letter I have entered into no comment upon the justice of the sentence of the Court of Session, and that the baseness of which I complain belongs exclusively to the Secretary of State for the Home Department and the rest of the Cabinet junto.'

" But on March 10th, 1794, occurred another trial in which Mr Godwin was far more deeply interested, that of Joseph Gerrald for sedition. Gerrald was a West Indian, and a man of property. He had been a pupil of Dr Parr, who regarded him with warm and affectionate interest. Every one who knew him loved him, but his character was unguarded, ardent, and even dissipated. His property became involved, and his health was injured by his irregularities and extravagance ; and yet, in spite of his conduct, his friends were enthusiastically attached to him on account of his brilliant talents, and his nice sense of honour, and an unconquerable ardour in the pursuit of objects which seemed to him the noblest in the world. He had emigrated to America early in life, and had practised as an advocate in the courts of Pennsylvania. Returning to England a confirmed republican, he entered into societies founded for the spread of his favourite doctrines. He was arrested with several others who had met in what they called a Convention of Delegates at Edinburgh, on a charge of sedition, and brought for trial before the High Court of Justiciary.

" The high spirit and generous sense of honour of this unfortunate man are shown by the fact that his friends offered him every means of easy escape, of which he refused to avail himself. He was at large, and on bail in London, when intelligence came of the trial and conviction of several of his associates. Dr Parr, and others of his friends, implored him to fly, promising to indemnify his bail. He indignantly refused, resolving that his lot should be the same as that of his partners in a cause, which he looked upon as sacred, and considered it as a base desertion to refuse to share their fate.

"Such noble feelings, which mirrored the devotion and honour of his favourite heroes of Greece and Rome, excited the deepest interest in Godwin ; he always spoke of Gerrald with affectionate admiration, and his feelings were strongly excited by the peril his friend incurred. During the January of 1794, while the trial was expected, there is frequent mention in the journal of seeing Gerrald ; he conversed with him on his trial, the conduct he ought to hold in regard to it, and the defence he ought to make. To render his advice more impressive, he wrote to him. The tone of his letter is calculated to encourage and animate. Godwin, who knew the human heart so well, was aware that nothing so inspires courage and magnanimity as a belief in the sufferer that he is regarded with respect by his fellow-men. In his letter, therefore, he casts into the shade the sad and fearful evils attendant on conviction, and endeavours to bring forward only such ideas as would animate Gerrald to self-complacency and fortitude.

"Gerrald's defence was eloquent and good, but the judge did not hesitate to interrupt it to tell him it was seditious, adding the singular assertion that, taking his, Gerrald's, account of the matter to be just, supposing that he acted from principle, and that his motives were pure, he became a more dangerous member of society than if his conduct had been really criminal, springing from criminal motives. Thus urged, the jury found him guilty, and the court showed no mercy; he was sentenced to be transported for fifteen years, which, in his precarious state of health, was considered, as it proved to be, equivalent to a sentence of death. When Gerrald, in his defence, professed himself ready to sacrifice his life for the cause he espoused, he was well aware that he made no empty boast, and that his life would indeed expire under the severities to which he was exposed.

"In April Gerrald was removed to London, and committed to Newgate, where Godwin and his other friends were allowed to visit him. It is said that he refused the offer of a pardon made him by the Secretary of State, because coupled with conditions which he felt it impossible to accept. In May 1795 he was suddenly taken from his prison, and placed on board the hulks, and soon afterwards sailed. He survived his arrival in New South Wales only five months. A few hours before he died he said to the friends around him, 'I die in the best of causes, and, as you witness, without repining.'"

This extract is a fitting introduction to the very noble letter addressed by Godwin to Gerrald, of which Mrs Shelley speaks. Its lofty tone takes us back alike to the dangers and the enthusiasm of the time.

William Godwin to Joseph Gerrald.

"*Jan.* 23, 1794.

"I cannot recollect the situation in which you are in a few days to be placed without emotions of respect, and I had almost said of envy. For myself I will never adopt any conduct for the express purpose of being put upon my trial, but if I be ever so put, I will consider that day as a day of triumph.

" Your trial, if you so please, may be a day such as England, and I believe the world, never saw. It may be the means of converting thousands, and, progressively, millions, to the cause of reason and public justice. You have a great stake, you place your fortune, your youth, your liberty, and your talents on a single throw. If you must suffer, do not, I conjure you, suffer without making use of this opportunity of telling a tale upon which the happiness of nations depends. Spare none of the resources of your powerful mind. Is this a day of reserve, a day to be slurred over in neglect—the day that constitutes the very crisis of your fate ?

" Never forget that juries are men, and that men are made of penetrable stuff: probe all the recesses of their souls. Do not spend your strength in vain defiance and empty vaunting. Let every syllable you utter be fraught with persuasion. What an event would it be for England and mankind if you could gain an acquittal! Is not such an event worth striving for? It is in man, I am sure it is, to effect that event. Gerrald, you are that man. Fertile in genius, strong in moral feeling, prepared with every accomplishment that literature and reflection can give. Stand up to the situation—be wholly yourself. 'I know,' I would say to this jury, 'that you are packed, you are picked and culled from all the land by the persons who have at present the direction of public affairs, as men upon whom they can depend ; but I do not fear the event ; I do not believe you will be slaves. I do not believe that you will be inaccessible to considerations irresistible in argument, and which speak to all the genuine feelings of the human heart. I have been told that there are men upon whom truth, truth fully and adequately stated, will make no impression. It is a vile and groundless calumny upon the character of the human mind. This is my theory, and I now come before *you* for the practice.'

" If you should fail of a verdict—but why should I suppose

it?—this manner of stating your defence is best calculated to persuade the whole audience, and the whole world, for the same
reason that it is best calculated to persuade a jury.

"It is the nature of the human mind to be great in proportion
as it is acted upon by great incitements. Remember this. Now
is your day. Never, perhaps never, in the revolution of human
affairs, will your mind be the same illustrious and irresistible mind
as it will be on this day.

"You stand on as clear ground as man can stand on. You are
brought there for meeting in convention to deliberate on griev-
ances. Do not fritter away your defence by anxiety about little
things; do not perplex the jury by dividing their attention. Depend upon it, that if you can establish to their full conviction the
one great point—the lawfulness of your meeting—you will obtain
a verdict.

"That point is fully contained in the Bill of Rights, is the
fundamental article of that constitution which Englishmen have
been taught to admire. Appeal (for so upon your principles you
can) to an authority paramount to the English constitution, to all
written Law and parchment constitutions; the Law of universal
Reason, authorising men to consult. Ireland was always the least
emancipated part of the British Empire. In Ireland they thought
proper to pass a tyrannical law taking away this inalienable privilege. But in Britain they do worse; ministers are said to have it
in contemplation to pass a similar law here, and in the meantime 'you, the jury, are called upon to act as if the law were already
in existence. Was ever so atrocious a breach of equity and reason?
They pride themselves in having drawn us, and a great part of the
Scottish nation, into the snare, and overwhelmed us with a destruction which no prudence could foresee, and no innocence
avert.'

"The next point I would earnestly recommend to your attention is to show that you and the reformers are the true friends of
the country, that you are actuated by pure philanthropy and
benevolence, and have no selfish motives, that your projects lead
to general happiness, and are the only means of averting the scene

of confusion which is impending over us. 'Our whole effort is
directed to the preventing mischief, and the sparing every drop of
blood. The longer the confederates of foreign despots among us
go on in their present impious career, the more you will want us.
We place ourselves in the breach to snatch your wives and children from destruction. Will the present overbearing and exasper-
ating conduct of government lead to tranquillity and harmony?
Will new wars and new taxes, the incessant persecution, ruin, and
punishment of every man that dares to oppose them heal the
dissensions of mankind? No! Nothing can save us but moderation, prudence and timely reform. Men must be permitted to
confer together upon their common interests, unprovoked by
insult, counteracting treachery, and arbitrary decrees. It is for
this antidote to the madness of men in power that we have made
every sacrifice, and are ready to sacrifice our lives. If you punish
us, you punish us because we have watched for your good.'

"Above all, let me entreat you to abstain from harsh epithets
and bitter invective. Show that you are not terrible but kind, and
anxious for the good of all. Truth will lose nothing by this.
Truth can never gain by passion, violence, and resentment. It is
never so strong as in the firm, fixed mind, that yields to the
emotions neither of rage nor fear. It is by calm and recollected
boldness that we can shake the pillars of the vault of heaven.
How great will you appear if you show that all the injustice with
which you are treated cannot move you: that you are too great to
be wounded by their arrows; that you still hold the steadfast
course that becomes the friend of man, and that while you expose
their rottenness you harbour no revenge. The public want men
of this unaltered spirit, whom no persecution can embitter. The
jury, the world will feel your value, if you show yourself such a
man: let no human ferment mix in the sacred work.

"Farewell; my whole soul goes with you. You represent us
all.   W. GODWIN."

Mrs Shelley's note on the English State Trials is also
fortunately extant, and is here mainly reproduced. After

mentioning that on learning that the grand jury had found a true bill against the twelve men, among whom were Holcroft, Horne Tooke, and several other of his personal friends, Godwin immediately started for London, and sent in a formal application to be allowed to visit the prisoners. Mrs Shelley continues :—

" Godwin well understood, that had these trials been followed by a verdict of 'guilty,' he would have subsequently shared their fate as their friend and intimate associate. Neither the difference of his own opinion from those of his friends, in some points considerable, nor his own personal risk, could prevent a man so enthusiastic and intrepid as my father, from exerting all his powers in their cause.

" That ministers should have accused of high treason men whose crime could not by any perversion be interpreted beyond sedition, might excite his indignation, but not surprise, but that Grand Jury should have given their sanction to the proceeding seemed extraordinary and overwhelming. These sentiments were increased by the charge of Chief-Justice Eyre. Godwin, on returning to London, lost no time in writing an answer to the charge. On this occasion, speed being a main ingredient of success, he wrote by dictation, his old and tried friend Marshal being his amanuensis. As he warmed in his subject, he paced the room with quick, eager steps, pouring out his arguments with an animation and fervour which sat well on features and manner usually too quiet and undemonstrative. He looked on this crisis as one of awful moment to all Englishmen. The law of high treason, accurately defined by the statute, and ably commented on by the best lawyers, was to be stretched and bent for the destruction of these men. Because they had entered upon a line of conduct which, if carried to its utmost extent by the worst of men, might be supposed in the result as tending to overthrow the monarchy, they whose motives were pure, and who abhorred blood, were to be condemned as traitors. Nay more. Their ostensible object was confessedly legal, and it was behind this avowed and

I.   I

innocent intention that hidden and treasonable acts were to be
discovered and punished.

"They had met in convention for the sake of furthering a plan
to obtain annual parliaments. This was their apparent crime ; it
remained to discover the guilt of high treason behind so innocuous
an outside. Chief-Justice Eyre explained the law of treason
according to the statute 25 Edward III., which is the law of England. He set forth what an overt act was, and that it was necessary to prove by two witnesses the committing of an act, which
had in its intent and effect the compassing and imagining the
death of the king. He allowed that meeting in convention for the
sake of obtaining annual parliaments was not treasonable, but he
averred that a secret and evil design was in the present instance
most probably concealed by this pretext. He said that if the convention had for its intention the enforcing annual parliaments of
its own authority, that was an act of treason. He further observed
that whether the project of convention, having for its object the
collecting together a power which should overawe the legislative
body and extort a parliamentary reform, would, if acted upon,
amount to high treason, and to the specific treason of compassing
and imagining the death of the king was a more doubtful question,
and he added, ' If charges of high treason are offered to be maintained on this ground only, perhaps it may be fitting that, in
respect of the extraordinary nature, and dangerous extent, and
very criminal complexion of such a conspiracy, that case, which I
state to you as a new and doubtful case, should be put into a
judicial course of inquiry, that it may receive a solemn adjudi-
cature whether it will or will not amount to high treason, in order
to which the bills must be found to be true bills.'

"In short, after sketching and rendering as vague as possible
the narrow and defined limits of the law of treason, the judge set
up a new case, not acknowledged as treason by the law of the
land, but of which, when the criminals were found guilty, the
judges, against whom it is a principle of our constitution to guard
the accused, were to decide upon, and determine whether they
were or were not to be hanged, thus erecting the mere executive

into legislative, and giving an awful stretch of power, which would have placed every disaffected Englishman in the hands of government to be dealt with as it chose, and the mercy to which it was inclined was manifested in the present trials.

"Godwin's keen and logical mind easily detected the flaws in Sir James Eyre's reasoning, and his eloquence set them forth clearly and forcibly. He repeated and praised the first exposition of the Law of Treason by the Judge. 'In all this preamble of the Chief Justice,' he says, 'there is something extremely humane and considerate. I trace in it the language of a constitutional lawyer, a sound logician, and a temperate, discreet, and honest man. I see rising to my view, a Judge resting upon the law as it is, and determinedly setting his face against new, unprecedented, and temporizing constructions. I see a Judge that scorns to bend his neck to the yoke of any party or any administration, who expounds the unalterable principles of justice, and is prepared to try by them, and them only, the persons that are brought before him. I see him taking to himself, and holding out to the jury, the manly consolation that they are to make no new law, and force no new interpretation, that they are to consult only the statutes of the realm, and the decisions of those writers who have been the luminaries of England. Meanwhile, what shall be said by our contemporaries, and by our posterity, if this picture be reversed, if these promises were made only to render our disappointment more bitter, if these high professions merely served as an introduction to an unparalleled mass of arbitrary constructions, of new-fangled treasons, and doctrines equally inconsistent with history and themselves.' He then proceeds to argue that the thing to be proved was not whether the accused were guilty of a moral crime, but of a crime against law. 'Let it be granted,' he says, 'that the crime is, in the eye of reason and discretion, the most enormous that it can enter into the heart of man to conceive, still I have a right to ask, is it a crime against law? Show me the statute that describes it; refer me to the precedent by which it is defined, quote me the adjudged case in which a matter of such unparalleled magnitude is settled.'

"Mr Godwin then proceeds to analyse the various modes in which the Chief Justice supposes it possible that these men, associated for the purpose of obtaining Parliamentary Reform, were guilty of High Treason. 'One mode,' he says, 'is by such an association, not in its own nature, as he says, simply unlawful too easily degenerating, and becoming unlawful in the highest degree.' It is difficult to comment upon this article with the gravity that may seem due to a magistrate delivering his opinion from a bench of justice. An association for Parliamentary Reform may degenerate, and become unlawful in the highest degree, even to the enormous extent of the crime of High Treason. Who knows not that? Was it necessary that Chief Justice Eyre should come in 1794, solemnly to announce to us so irresistible a proposition? An association for Parliamentary Reform may desert its object, and become guilty of High Treason. True ; so may a card club, a bench of justice, or even a Cabinet Council. Does Chief Justice Eyre mean to intimate that there is something in the purpose of a Parliamentary Reform, so unhallowed, ambiguous, and unjust, as to render its well-wishers objects of suspicion rather than their brethren and fellow subjects? What can be more wanton, cruel, and inhuman than thus to single out the purpose of Parliamentary Reform, as if it were of all others most especially connected with degeneracy and treason.

"'But what is principally worthy of attention is the easy and artful manner in which the idea of treason is introduced.' After commenting with extreme severity on the insinuation of intention, of which there was not a particle of truth, he continues : 'But the authors of the present prosecution probably hope that the mere names of Jacobin and Republican will answer their purposes, and that a jury of Englishmen will be found who will send every man to the gallows without examination to whom these appellations shall once have been attributed.'

"Mr Godwin then comments on the Chief Justice's observations on a convention, a word brought into disrepute by its adoption in France, but by no means foreign to English History. Because of the present use of the name, the Judge declared that it 'deservedly became an object of jealousy to the law.' 'Can anything,' exclaims Godwin, 'be more atrocious than the undertaking to measure the guilt of an individual and the interpretation of a plain and permanent law by the transitory example that may happen to exist before our eyes in a neighbouring country.'

"After much more on this and on other heads, Mr Godwin comes to the last point of the charge—that in which he bids the Grand Jury find a true bill, if they should discover on the part of the accused a design to overawe King and Parliament, so that afterwards it might be subjected to a judicial course of enquiry. 'The Chief Justice,' he says, 'quits in this instance the character of criminal judge and civil magistrate, and assumes that of a natural philosopher, or experimental anatomist. He is willing to dissect the persons that shall be brought before him, the better to ascertain the truth or falsehood of his preconceived conjectures. The plain English of his recommendation is this. Let these men be put on their trial for their lives, let them and their friends be exposed to all the anxieties incident to so uncertain and fearful a condition; let them be exposed to ignominy, to obloquy, to the partialities, as it may happen, of a prejudiced Judge, and the perverseness of an ignorant jury; we shall then know how we ought to conceive of *similar cases*. By trampling on their peace, throwing away their lives, or sporting with their innocence, we shall obtain a basis on which to proceed, and a precedent to guide our judgment in future instances.'

"The effect of this appeal, of which the passages quoted may give a sufficient notion, when it became widely spread through the papers, was memorable. Hitherto men had heard that the King's Ministers had discovered a treasonable conspiracy, and had arrested the traitors. They believed this. No project was believed too wild or wicked for those who had imbibed the infection of the French Revolution, nor could any believe that the highest and most solemn council of the State would have proceeded against twelve subjects of the realm but on clear and undoubted grounds. The charge of the Chief Justice did not dissipate the illusion. It is true that all he said was wrapped in

' May-be,' and the Grand Jury was told that they were to discover
secret, treasonable designs; but still Mr Pitt was a man of high
character and vast talents—men leant on him with confidence,
and readily saw gigantic dangers in the shadowy images of treason
that were evoked. They could not believe that for the sake of an
experiment, for the purpose of overawing the country, and extending his power beyond the limits of the constitution, he would put in
slight account the lives and liberties of twelve men, his fellow subjects, whom he knew that there was no law to condemn, whom he
only hoped to destroy through the influence of the panic which the
proceedings in France had engendered in this country. But these
remarks dissipated the mist that clouded men's understandings;
they who before believed that the accused were undoubtedly
guilty of treason began to perceive that a design to reform Parliament was not treasonable, and that however wrong-headed, and
even reprehensible it might be to associate for such a purpose,
this was no cause why men, otherwise innocent, should, themselves and their families, be subjected to the frightful pains and
penalties of treason.

" Impartial men now looked forward to the event of these trials
with very different expectations, both as to the nature of the charges
to be brought, and the result. The friends of the accused, now
that they dared hope for a fair trial, confided in an acquittal.
The event shewed how reasonable and just were Godwin's reasonings; how strained, tyrannical, and barbarous the proceedings of
ministers.

" Hardy, a shoemaker by trade, was the man first selected by
the Attorney-General to be placed at the Bar. The trial lasted
eight days; the evidence brought was complicated and vast, but
vague and inconclusive. He was acquitted. The trials of Horne
Tooke and Thelwal followed; but the whole force of Government
had been directed against Hardy, and when these also were acquitted, the public accusers felt their task ended. They allowed
verdicts of acquittal to be recorded in favour of their other
prisoners.

" Godwin, as he says, attended the trials every day, though he

knew himself to be a marked man, had his friends been found
guilty. He was present when the Attorney-General announced
that he gave up his intention of proceeding against Holcroft, who,
on being liberated, left the dock, and, crossing the court, took his
seat beside Godwin. Sir Thomas Lawrence, struck by the happy
combination and contrast exhibited in the attitude and expression
of the two friends, made a spirited sketch of them in profile.

"The feeling of triumph among the friends of liberty was universal. Even now there lingered on the English shores Gerrald,
Muir, Palmer, and Skirving, who, victims of Scottish law, were
sentenced to be transported to Botany Bay. Their fate filled
their friends with grief and indignation; but worse had been since
attempted, and it was a matter of virtuous triumph to find that the
attempt failed, that our country was restored to the protection of
its laws, and a boundary placed to the encroachments of arbitrary
power. Godwin never forgot the delightful sensations he then
experienced; it was his honest boast, and most grateful recollection, that he had contributed to the glorious result, by his letter to
Chief-Justice Eyre."

The panic which was felt by some, who, belonging
to the liberal party, feared they might be compromised
by their accused friends, is reflected in a letter from Mrs
Reveley, whom Holcroft had proposed to call as a witness,
to what special point in his defence does not appear.

Mrs Reveley to William Godwin.

"SOUTHAMPTON ROW, EDGWARE ROAD,
"*Monday Morng.*, **27** *October.*

"I was very much surprised last night, to hear your statements
of Mr Holcroft's determination concerning me, as it differed
materially from what had been represented to me before; hitherto
I have had no opportunity of conversing with you on the subject,
and it is necessary that I should inform you of the exact state of
my mind. Should it appear that Mr Holcroft's life is at all in

danger, and that my evidence would tend in the least to avert that misfortune, far from repining, I profess myself, without hesitation, ready calmly to encounter every odium, every public or private resentment—in a word, ruin—to save him.

"But if, on the other hand, he means to sacrifice me, with scarcely a possibility of advantage to himself, and the evidence I am able to give should have nothing singular and particular, or out of the power of any other person to produce ; from what could such conduct arise, but wanton cruelty or insanity ?

"If this should be his determination, I declare to you, as I did last night, that I will not expose myself to the evils which this puerile conceit is thus preparing for me.

"What could be more tyrannical than Mr Holcroft's assertion, that whatever might be my dislike, he would force me to do my duty ? As if he were to be the judge of it. The Despots say no more ! His treatment of Mr Reveley excites in me the most unpleasant feelings ; I believe I shall ever think of it with detestation.

"I feel a doubt that, from many circumstances which have lately occurred, you should imagine that any change has taken place in my opinion of you. Be assured that the high esteem and veneration which your virtues and genius entitle you to, have not suffered the smallest diminution in the sentiments of

"MARIA REVELEY."

When Hardy's trial was over, Godwin received a letter from the friend from whose house he had hurried to help his friends.

Dr Parr to William Godwin.

"*Nov.* 10, 1794.

"Your anxiety, dear Mr Godwin, during Hardy's trial could not be more intense than mine, your joy at the close of it was not more rapturous, your approbation of the jury is not more warm, and your indignation against the judge seems to be less fierce. Is it possible, my friend, that any baseness can be more foul, any injustice more

pernicious, any treason more atrocious, than the deliberate, techni-
cal, systematic perversion of law? My bosom glowed with honest
rage when I saw the snares that were laid for men's lives in that
odious address to the Grand Jury; but I doubt whether the dagger
of an assassin, reeking with blood, would have given a more violent
shock to my feelings than the close of Eyre's speech at the Old
Bailey. I can make great allowances for the projects of statesmen,
the errors and prejudices of princes, and even the outrages of con-
querors; but when I see the ministers of public justice thirsting
with canine fury for the blood of a fellow-creature, my soul is all
on fire . . . I very strongly disapproved of the Convention; I
would oppose the doctrine of universal suffrage; I look with a
watchful, and perhaps with an unfriendly, eye upon all political
associations; I wish to see the people enlightened, but not in-
flamed; I would resist with my pen, and perhaps with my sword,
any attempts to subvert the constitution of this country, but I am
filled with agony when laws, intended for our protection, are
stretched and distorted for our destruction . . . I am glad the
charge was published, because it has been answered; and as I
think the answer luminous in style, powerful in matter, and solid
in principle, I am extremely desirous of knowing who is the author.
He is entitled to my praise as a critic, and my thanks as an Englishman. I shall not be satisfied till Mr Fox takes up, in Parliament,
the subject of constructive treason; and I trust that, by perseverance, he will be no less successful than we have already seen him
in vindicating the rights of juries. He is a sound and sober statesman, a real lover of his country, and a friend to the collective
interests of social man . . . Remember me kindly to Mr Holcroft.
Come again to see me at my parsonage, when the weather is finer,
the days longer, the roads cleaner, and the aspect of public affairs
less gloomy.—Believe me, dear sir, with great respect, your well-
wisher and obedient servant, T. PARR."

CHAPTER VI.

FRIENDS AND ACQUAINTANCES. 1794 – 1796.

IN all the storm and stress of politics, when his male friends were almost all more or less in trouble, when Mrs Reveley was putting herself into the semi-hysterical state in which we have seen her, the friendship of Mrs Inchbald, who was no politician but only a very clever and very charming woman, was a great comfort to Godwin. Their correspondence was frequent, as also were their meetings; all Mrs Inchbald's letters are worth reading, but only a few can be given. Godwin sent the proofs of "Caleb Williams" to her, and her opinion of it must have pleased him as much as Marshal's criticism displeased him. The early tales from his pen had been forgotten, and he appeared before the world as a new novelist.

The letters which follow were written while the story was still in reading, and she wrote in far too hot haste to dream of dating her letters, and usually to sign them.

Mrs Inchbald to William Godwin.

(*No date.*)

"God bless you !

"That was the sentence I exclaimed when I had read about half a page.

"Nobody is so pleased when they find anything new as I am. I found your style different from what I have ever yet met. You come to the point (the story) at once, another excellence. I have now read as far as page 32 (I was then interrupted by a visitor) and do not retract my first sentence. I have to add to your praise that of a most *minute*, and yet most *concise* method of delineating human sensations.

"I could not resist writing this, because my heart was burthened with the desire of saying what I think, and what I hope for.

"My curiosity is greatly increased by what I have read, but if you disappoint me you shall never hear the last of it, and instead of 'God Bless,' I will vociferate, God ——m you."

The Same to the Same.

"Monday evening.

"Sir,—Your first volume is far inferior to the two last. Your second is sublimely horrible—captivatingly frightful.

"Your third is all a great genius can do to delight a great genius, and I never felt myself so conscious of, or so proud of giving proofs of a good understanding, as in pronouncing this to be a capital work.

"It is my opinion that fine ladies, milliners, mantua-makers, and boarding-school girls will love to tremble over it, and that men of taste and judgment will admire the superior talents, the *incessant* energy of mind you have evinced.

"In these two last volumes, there does not appear to me (apt as I am to be tired with reading novels) one tedious line, still there are lines I wish erased. I shudder lest for the sake of a few sentences, (and these particularly marked for the reader's attention by the purport of your preface) a certain set of people should hastily condemn the whole work as of immoral tendency, and rob it of a popularity which no other failing it has could I think endanger.

"This would be a great pity, especially as these sentences are trivial compared to those which have not so glaring a tendency, and yet to the eye of discernment are even more forcible on your side of the question. . . . . But if I find fault it is because

I have no patience that anything so near perfection should not be perfection."

She could take as well as give criticism in a thoroughly good-humoured manner. She had sent Godwin a MS., which was probably afterwards destroyed. It is, however, no doubt that to which a letter from Mr Hardinge, quoted in Boaden's "Life of Mrs Inchbald," alludes, under the title, "A Satire on the Times," and about which Boaden remarks that Hardinge's remark is unintelligible. "Oh! that I may be for ever called stupid by the person who wrote 'A Satire on the Times,' by setting a ship on fire and burning every soul in the book except a Lord of the Bedchamber, by whom she meant the k——."—*Memoirs of Inchbald*, Vol. I., p. 328.

The Same to the Same.

"I am infinitely obliged to you for all you have said, which amounts very nearly to all I thought.

"But indeed I am too idle, and too weary of the old rule of poetical justice to treat my people, to whom I have given birth, as they deserve, or rather I feel a longing to treat them according to their deserts, and to get rid of them all by a premature death, by which I hope to surprise my ignorant reader, and to tell my informed one that I am so wise as to have as great a contempt for my own efforts as he can have.

"And now I will discover to you a total want of *aim*, of *execution*, and every particle of genius belonging to a writer, in a character in this work, which from the extreme want of resemblance to the original, you have not even reproached me with the fault of not drawing accurately.

"I really and soberly meant (and was in hopes every reader would be struck with the portrait) Lord Rinforth to represent his Most Gracious Majesty, George the 3rd.

"I said at the commencement all Lords of Bedchambers were

mirrors of the Grand Personage on whom they attended, but having Newgate before my eyes, I dressed him in some virtues, and (notwithstanding his avarice) you did not know him.

"The book is now gone to Mr Hardinge. Mr Holcroft is to have it as soon as his play is over, and though I now despair of any one finding out my meaning, yet say nothing about the matter to Mr Holcroft, but let my want of talent be undoubted, by his opinion conforming to yours.

"And there, (said I to myself as I folded up the volumes) how pleased Mr Godwin will be at my making the King so avaricious, and there, (said I to myself) how pleased the King will be at my making him so very good at the conclusion, and when he finds that by throwing away his money he can save his drowning people he will instantly *throw it all away* for flannel shirts for his soldiers, and generously pardon me all I have said on *equality* in the book, merely for giving him a good character.

"But alas, Mr Godwin did not know him in that character, and very likely he would not know himself."

Some extracts from a letter to a young man, whose name is not preserved, may be interesting, for they represent Godwin in yet another light, and show at once his versatility, and his unceasing desire to help others in all their various needs. There is no date, but it belongs to this time, and seems to have been written to an Oxford man who was in some trouble of mind.

William Godwin to ————.

(*No date.*)

". . . I am glad that my writings have in any degree contributed to your pleasure in moments of dejection and gloom. I should be much more glad if I could point out to you a remedy for your disease. Dr Darwin, you say, assures you it is a disease of the mind. There is perhaps some deception in that way of distributing the disorders of the human species. The mind and the animal frame are so closely connected, that scarcely anything can unfavourably affect the one without deranging the other. I think it not improbable that your unhappiness may be connected with some vice of organization, as far as I can annex a distinct meaning to that term. But in these subtle diseases, take insanity for an example, it seems as if the remedies might sometimes be found in material, sometimes in mental applications. I see no good reason to doubt, that a certain discipline of the mind may have a powerful tendency to restore sanity to the intellect, and consequent vigour to the animal frame. I know a young man, subject in a considerable degree to the same evil under which you labour, and of a strong understanding, who has in some measure found out the remedy for himself, and has considerably added to his happiness by watching resolutely the operations of his own mind.

"The first thing you have to guard against, as the most pernicious error into which you can fall, is the feeling yourself flattered by your own misery as something honourable and delicate. Do not from this, or other motives, cherish and indulge painful sensations. Resolutely expel them, if possible, from your mind. Determine vehemently and hardily to be as happy as you can. . . . Break abruptly the thread of painful ideas. Set your face as much as possible against a spirit of timidity and procrastination. Endeavour to be always active, always employed. Walk, read, write, and converse. Seek variety in this respect. Whatever you engage in, engage in firmly, and give no quarter to the inroads of irresolution and listlessness. . . . Do not indulge in visions, and phantoms of the imagination, or place your happiness in something you may perhaps never obtain, but endeavour to make it out of the materials within your reach. Adopt some course of improvement, and impress yourself with some ardour of usefulness, which will never wholly elude the grasp of him who seeks it with ingenuousness and simplicity. . . .   W. GODWIN."

The remaining letters of value during this year are those from Tom Cooper, which follow. They relate, as will be seen, to different periods of the year, but equally to his professional engagements, and are best presented consecutively. The most truculent game preserver may, at this distance of time, feel tenderly towards the poor stroller, who would not have dined at all but for his venial poaching.

Thomas Cooper to William Godwin.

" CHICHESTER, *January* 12, 1794.

" On inquiring into the causes that guide our actions, I am greatly puzzled to discover the reason why I have not written before to London. Can it be indolence? I have been in other respects very industrious. It cannot be indifference or inattention, for a day has never passed over without my thinking on the subject. Whatever was the cause, such is the fact, which cannot be removed by an inquiry, however long. I will therefore dismiss it at once, and proceed to my purpose.

" I left Hyde Park Corner at five o'clock on the Sunday. I left you at two. I proceeded some twenty or thirty miles when I was overtaken by the Southampton mail. I got a four shilling cast on the outside, and arrived at Southampton, gloriously wet, at ten o'clock on Monday night. I set off to Cowes the next morning at seven by the mail packet, which was opposed both by wind and tide, and could make no way. The mail was obliged to shift to an open boat, and as I could row, I got into the boat, leaving the rest of the passengers on board. I now pulled against wind and tide for upwards of twelve miles, without one minute's rest, and I do not recollect ever to have undergone so great fatigue before. I arrived at Newport, however, by 3 P.M. on Tuesday, according to my promise, when, contrary to my expectation, I had nothing to do in the evening's entertainment. I have since been on a salary of 10s. a week, and we have had one idle week between Newport and this place, where we have been three weeks, and are likely to continue four more. Hence we go immediately to Portsmouth. . . . I have pursued the plan Mr Holcroft mentioned as much as possible, consistently with almost continual moving,

but that will for about a month receive a considerable check. On
account of some of the company taking benefits here, and the
manager's great impatience to open the Portsmouth Theatre, the
company is obliged to divide. I am ordered to Portsmouth, and
have a great deal of study on my hands. Mr Collins, in addition
to other things, told me yesterday to study George Barnwell and
Irwin. Of a morning, since I have been here, from about seven
to nine, I have amused myself by shooting, and have in utter
defiance of the laws of the constitution under which I exist, dined
twice or thrice on partridges.

"I beg you will make a point of showing this to my mother
immediately, as I have not written to her since I left town. My
love to her and Betty and Miss Godwin. Is Nat at Spithead?

"THOMAS COOPER"

"STOCKPORT, *October* 21, 1794.

"Whether the God of Wisdom presided in my brain at the
time I made the resolution of joining these strolling players at
Stockport I know not. Whether you may think the step wise
(which is not the same quære, however paradoxical my supposing
a difference may appear to you), I am equally ignorant. But well
I know that it is now a fortnight since we closed at Liverpool, and
that in the interim I have travelled fifty miles, bag and baggage,
across the country, and that by this means my stock of cash is
so reduced, that without a supply before to-morrow at twelve
o'clock, I shall be obliged to dine with a certain duke with whom
I have kept company before to-day (but heartily despising everything, and titles among the rest, that put me in mind of usurpation and inequality), whose company I would very willingly re-
nounce for the time to come. Nevertheless I stand prepared to
encounter any tricks or mischief Fortune may be inclined to put
upon me, continually repeating the first lines of that ode of Horace,
beginning, 'Justum et tenacem propositi virum.'

"By means of reduction in my pocket, having now taken the
step of coming here, it is impracticable to recall it, and here I
must remain. But in eight or ten weeks, unless I should meet

with any great success, I shall again think of coming to London. Though, indeed, if Mr Holcroft's trial comes on, and a consequence which I tremble to think of should take place, I shall be in London on the instant.

"Thus, then, I am. We open to-morrow. I do not play till Saturday, when I make my appearance in Barnwell. I have no doubt of my success, for what trifling degree of merit I may have, will derive additional lustre from the extreme dullness of the set of devils I have got among. We are to play in a theatre, to be sure, that is, in a place built for that purpose only, but we shall come under the Vagrant Act. But the sweets of superiority! 'Oh, 'tis better to reign in hell, than serve in heaven!'

"I will thank you for a letter, containing as much circumstance as you can contrive. How do yours' and Mr Holcroft's novels sell? How is Mr H.'s family governed in his absence. Tell me any occurrences relative to Mr H.'s imprisonment, if any there is, not mentioned in the papers. Is George Dyson yet out of his swaddling clothes? that is, does he yet live entirely as his own master, or is he still at home with papa and mamma? How does Jack go on? Remember to give my love to my mother, Miss Godwin, &c. Likewise let the Holcroft family know I have not forgotten them. And though last, not least, mention me, 'after what flourish your nature will,' to Mrs Reveley—I believe—but it is, however, the lady who supped with you at Mr Holcroft's the last night I was in town. She is a painter. Tell her I would come to London, all the way barefoot, to see her perform the office of hangman to Mr P., which I recollect she said she should have no objection to.

"THOMAS COOPER."

" STOCKPORT, *Oct.* 28, 1794.

"All the devils in hell seem to conspire against me. When success seemed placed within my reach, and I had nothing left to do but to nod my head and become a hero, some damned untoward accident prevents it. Barnwell could not be played, as I informed you it would. But last night, to forward the manager's business,

I.   K

I undertook to play Holdam, in Columbus, at a short notice, and to give up an appearance part. The consequence of which was, that the manager, relying upon a continued obligingness in doing his dirty work, this morning gave me a list of parts, and grinning, told me I promised very well, but that I must do all the parts there specified. There were, to be sure, a great many *good* parts, and most of them respectable ; but he told me that in my turn I must also deliver messages. I told him that the parts expressed in his list would satisfy me very well indeed ; but that as to the delivering of messages, I would not do it in heaven.

" If it were a respectable company, I would gladly accept the good parts he gave me, though a few messages were thrown in with them, because it was really a good line ; but in that situation I hardly think it would be right to stay, even if I did nothing else but the good parts. They are such a wretched set of mummers. Perhaps you will say that I can do my business properly, though they did not. I say no. They seldom speak a word of the author. The business is a jest, and likewise the man who attempts to treat it seriously.

" I shall leave this place before you can possibly return an answer. I am now 170 miles from town. I shall start from hence with 5s. in my pocket. I shall see you shortly. I will black shoes at the corner of Goodge Street for 1s. a-day sooner than be anything but the leader among a set of wretches I despise.

" Io Triumphe,

"THOS. COOPER."

The note for the year 1795 records that Godwin's literary work during the course of it consisted mainly in the revision of his two lately published works. He continues :—

" In the beginning of this year I accepted the offer of a certain degree of acquaintance with a man, in doing which I thought myself right, but in which I did not escape censure. The man was John King, a notorious Jew money-lender, who was married to the Countess Dowager of Lanesborough. My motive was simple—the study to which I had devoted myself was man, to analyse his nature as a moralist, and to delineate his passions as an historian, or a recorder of fictitious adventures ; and I believed that I should learn from this man and his visitors some lessons which I was not likely to acquire in any other quarter. My system prompted me to express my thoughts of him as freely, though without the same scurrility and ill-temper, as Apemantus at the table of Lord Timon. An incident worthy to be mentioned occurred to me on the 21st of May in this year. I dined on that day with Mr Horne Tooke and a pretty numerous company at the house of a friend. The great philologist had frequently rallied me in a good-humoured way upon the visionary nature of my politics—his own were of a different cast. It was a favourite notion with him that no happier or more excellent Government had ever existed than that of the English nation in the reigns of George the First and George the Second. From disparaging my philosophy, he passed by a very natural transition to the setting light, either really or in pretence, by the abilities for which I had some credit. He often questioned me with affected earnestness as to the truth of the report that I was the author of the 'Cursory Sketches on Chief Justice Eyre's Charge to the Grand Jury,' of which pamphlet he always declared the highest admiration, and to which he repeatedly professed that he held himself indebted for his life. The question was revived at the dinner I have mentioned. I answered carelessly to his enquiry that I believed I was the author of that pamphlet. He insisted on a reply in precise terms to his question, and I complied. He then requested that I would give him my hand. To do this I was obliged to rise from my chair and go to the end of the table where he sat. I had no sooner done this than he suddenly conveyed my hand to his lips, vowing that he could do no less by the hand that had given existence to that production. The suddenness of the action filled me with confusion ; yet I must confess that when I looked back upon it, this homage thus expressed was more gratifying to me than all the applause I had received from any other quarter.

Another detached note contains fragments of a conversation at Horne Tooke's during another dinner party about the same time ; it has some small value as bearing on the controversy about the authorship of "Junius' Letters."

"WIMBLEDON.—For several years after the commencement of the present reign (except the 'Daily Advertizer') there were but two newspapers, the 'Gazetteer' and the 'Public Advertizer:' afterwards started up the 'Ledger,' expressly ministerial.

"Horne Tooke knows who was the author of 'Junius' Letters.' He wrote a few years before letters under the signature of 'Lucius,' collected in two volumes, and intended a series under the signature of 'Brutus;' he designed the coincidence of the three for a clue to his secret. He sunk 'Junius' at last—by law arguments, a science in which he was uninformed, and city politics, which he did not understand; he is still living. Tooke speaks of his style with the highest commendation.

"H. T., born 1737 ; goes abroad with Elwes, heir to Sir Harvey Elwes (whose estate afterwards descended to Megget, alias Miser Elwes, 1763) ; staid abroad four years.

"Burke came to England before Tooke went abroad ; he had previously a pension of £200 for writing a speech [for single-speech Hamilton.

"Tooke was to have for his services with Elwes £300 a-year for life, or a provision in the Church to the amount of £900 ; his (Tooke's) father was a tradesman in the city.

"Tooke brought home his ward from the South of France in a fit of insanity, the young man at the bottom of the chaise, and Tooke on the seat armed with pistols. The young man was not allowed knife or fork."

The diaries add little worth recording. They show an ever increasing number of acquaintances, among whom the most noticeable are Lord Lauderdale, who was afterwards Plenipotentiary to France in 1806, and died in 1839 ; Mrs

Siddons, and Basil Montagu. This gentleman was for many years a warm friend and devoted admirer of Godwin. He was Q.C., Commissioner of Bankruptcy, and author of "A Digest of the Bankruptcy Laws." He died in 1851, aged 81. Opie the painter, R.A., buried in St Paul's 1807, also became an acquaintance of Godwin first in this year. With Amelia Alderson, who became Mrs Opie, he had formed a fast friendship during his visit to Norwich in 1793, and many letters had already passed between them. He paid another and a more extended visit to Dr Parr at Hatton, near Warwick, in the summer of this year. Though Mrs Shelley records that he had become disgusted with the excesses of the French Revolution, it must not be supposed that he had in any degree wavered in his allegiance to its principles, or shrunk from such of its acts as sprung from deliberation. Thus we find an entry: "June 9th, The Young Capet dies," showing that he acquiesced at least in the deposition of Louis XVI., and the degradation of his family from all royal titles.

Holcroft had gone to Exeter during Godwin's absence from London, and from Broadclyst, near Exeter, he addressed the following letter to his friend :—

Thomas Holcroft to William Godwin.

"CLIST, *July* 22*d*, 1795.

"Had I not forgotten the place of Dr Parr's residence, you would have received the 'Lamentations of Jeremiah' from me. You would have heard how I fell from a slip ladder, and broke it fairly in two; how, with difficulty, I kept what your friend at Hatton calls soul and body together; how I endeavoured to overcome the extreme pain, but at last was obliged, partly by entreaty and partly by precaution to send for a village surgeon; how he took a full basin of blood from me; how, half an hour after his departure, the spasms with which I had before been seized assaulted me with two-fold, or, for aught I know, with ten-fold malignity; how I was obliged to send to Exeter for another Dr in search of ease; how he affirmed my ribs were broken; how I believe they were not, but am not quite certain; how he made me swallow potions which proved to be opiates, and which indeed relieved me in part from spasm, but consigned me over to drowsy stupidity, which to me appeared a more intolerable evil; how I was roused from this lethargic struggle after existence by a severe fit of the gout; how I lay with my joints burning and my muscles cramped and twisted, during which I had full leisure for the display of my system 'of resistance to pain;' how I persuaded myself, in spite of my tormentors, that my system was true; how it induced me to laugh and joke, and exercise my little wits on all that came within my sphere of action; how some believed I was in pain, and some believed I was not; and how difficult I found it to define to myself what pain is. In short, like my predecessor Grumio, I would have told you a very tragical tale, had not my ignorance of your local existence prevented me.

"The gout has not yet left me, though I carry it about in a very clandestine kind of a manner; and till it has disappeared, I am advised not to bathe again; being further advised that bathing would be very good for me. Hence you will perceive I have not escaped that Tyrant Necessity—(if you can tell me when I shall, pray send me the intelligence by express, I will venture the expense)—and that the Necessity of which I am now the slave is uncertainty.

"I have had occasion to talk of you, or rather of your essence, your 'Political Justice,' and your 'Caleb.' If you suppose I understand you, I need not tell you in what terms I spoke. I sometimes doubt whether it be right, i.e., necessary, to declare sentiments of personal affection; yet I still seem more strongly to doubt whether it be right totally to omit such declarations; for impossible as it is that men should perceive utility, or if you will virtue, and not love it, yet the temporary uncertainties to which the clearest minds appear to be subject, may render declarations concerning our feelings necessary. To what accidents you or I shall hereafter be liable is more than either of us can *positively* determine ; but it seems to me our minds have proceeded too far for there to be any *probability* that our sentiments respecting each other should suffer any great change. Still, if it be pleasure to remind each other that we deserve and possess something more than mutual esteem, I see no good motive for abstaining from the enjoyment of this pleasure.

"I hope you have renewed your visits in Newman Street. As this letter will perhaps be a more circumstantial narrative of my late disaster than any they have yet received, be kind enough to communicate the contents at home.

"Mr Cooper, partly in consequence of my desire, and partly, as I suppose, from the decisions of his own judgment, remains near me some time to pursue his studies. I wish, perhaps more than a wise man ought, to be at home. Whether this impulse, or the hope of re-establishing my health shall prevail, must be left to future circumstances : my return, however, cannot be very distant.
"T. HOLCROFT."

"How came I to omit saying that you have a few warm admirers here, and that the report of your second edition has committed homicide upon the first? In my opinion, should the publishing be delayed, both will be injured."

Holcroft's faith that death and disease existed only through the feebleness of man's mind, must have been rudely shaken, unless we accept the dictum of Jean Paul, that no man really believes his creed till he can afford to laugh at it.

The only other letters of special interest preserved during his year are two from Cooper. He had not yet made the

figure on the stage which he and his friends alike hoped
that he would do : life was sustained with difficulty on ten
shillings a week and a chance partridge. Hence he
accepted a clerk's situation in an office, and appears to
have been under a regular agreement. He was ill-treated,
or thought himself so, and discharged himself by running
away. No trouble, however, was taken by Mr Dorset, his
employer, to recover the young man, who probably had not
been the most docile of clerks, and he then went to study
his chosen profession with Holcroft. How he supported
himself, or if Godwin again helped him, does not appear.
With these few words the letters speak for themselves.

Thomas Cooper to William Godwin.

"*January* 20, 1795.

" The die is, I believe, now finally cast, and if it be, the result
is insignificance, nonentity, death to the hopes my ambition has
oftentimes formed, and on which my mind has continually
brooded with enthusiasm. The little portion of mind I (perhaps)
have hitherto retained has now yielded. It receives its fetters, not
indeed without murmuring, but the curses it pours forth and the
tortures it endures are equally unavailing. The love of fame,
which you consider a bad motive for praiseworthy conduct, has
been with me the only spur to intellectual exertion. Perhaps it is
for want of the better motive for action that my mind has now
given up the contest, and that I consent to become totally an
everyday man. Your last words to me on Sunday night were,
' And thou become a mere vegetable.' The damned idea has
harassed me ever since. . . . . But why do I complain ?
Have I not given my consent to become a slave ? Have I not even
sought for the means of becoming so ? What right then have I
to assume the phraseology or to pretend to the feelings of a man ?
They are the last faint struggles of an expiring mind, and to you
therefore I address them, as being the first cause of producing

that mind. . . . . I feel half inclined to go and quarrel
with Mr Holcroft. I do not know, and have not inquired, why I
feel that inclination (I state facts : of causes I am ignorant), though
at the same time I have the utmost veneration and love for him.
. . . . The purport of my present letter is to tell you that I
am under treaty with Mr Dorset (fiends !) to become a clerk in his
house, and by this means I intend to advance towards riches. . .
. . . . "THOMAS COOPER."

The Same to the Same.

"EXETER, *July* 25, 1795.

"I am at a loss to discover wherein consists the singularity of
requesting a letter from one I have been in the habit of considering my most immediate and intimate friend. That you should
think it singular, I do not wonder, as you presently take care to
inform me that in so considering I labour under a mistake . . .
You say that I shall probably be sorry for having asked you to
write, when I have read a certain portion of your letter. This
would be the case, perhaps, if anything any man could say to me
would make me sorry. But I am not easily moved to contrition
or repentance, either by falsehood or truth ; and it does not in the
least operate in that way. When truth is presented to me, I hope
I shall grow better under the perception of it. When falsehood
blows her foul breath upon me, it passes by like the idle wind I
regard not. Since, therefore, I am invulnerable, I rejoice rather
than repent that I requested a letter, as the reception of it has, in
some measure, let me into the state of your feelings.

"You say that my *pretence* of a ten days' ramble appears to be a
cloak for a visit to Bath. What criminality there is in a visit to
Bath that should require a cloak, I cannot perceive ; but take my
word for it, whatever desperate villany I may engage in shall not
be under a *cloak ;* and when, as you express it, I sink into vice, it
shall not be into its sourness ; it shall be into the dashing whirlpool
that openly destroys everything around it. Therefore, whenever
vice becomes my object, notorious shall be the fact.

. . . . . .
"THOMAS COOPER."

Godwin writes, of 1796 :—

"In the preceding year the Earl of Lauderdale had requested the favour of my acquaintance, and now I was almost a regular attendant at his most select parties. The persons I met at them were Mr Fox, General Fitzpatrick, Lord Derby, Sir Philip Francis, Mr Adam, Mr Tierney, Mr Courtenay, Mr Dudley North, Mr William Smith, Mr Robert Adair, &c., &c. In my little deserted mansion I received, on the 22d of April, a party of twelve persons, the most of whom good-humouredly invited themselves to dine with me, and for whom I ordered provisions from a neighbouring coffee-house. Among this party were Dr Parr and his two daughters, Mr and Mrs Mackintosh, Mr Holcroft, Mrs Wollstonecraft, and Mrs Inchbald. I was also introduced about this time by Merry, the poet, to a most accomplished and delightful woman, the celebrated Mrs Robinson. In the course of this summer I paid a second visit to Norfolk, in the company of Merry, and had the happiness, by my interference and importunity with my friends, to relieve this admirable man from a debt of £200, for which he was arrested while I was under his roof, and would otherwise have been thrown into jail."

To this the Diary adds but little. It records, in scarce intelligible private notes, the increasing intimacy with Mary Wollstonecraft, of which more hereafter ; and there is some evidence that Godwin during this year might, even at his mature age, have said in reference to her as Proteus said of Julia—

> "Thou hast metamorphos'd me,
> Made me neglect my studies, lose my time ;"

for the record of work is slender, and there is less evidence of interest in public questions.

Two letters, however, claim insertion. King, the Jew bill-broker already named, was concerned in a trial arising out of his not altogether creditable business. He wrote to Godwin, requesting him to appear as his friend and supporter, and to use his influence with "some nobleman" to do the same. This letter is worded somewhat vaguely; and it does not appear whether he wanted evidence to character given in his favour, or merely the moral support in the eyes of the public which would have been afforded by such appearance of distinguished men in court by his side. The following very characteristic letter is an answer to this application :—

William Godwin to John King.

"*Jan.* 24, 1796.

"I am extremely surprised at the note I have just received from you, and hasten to oppose the false statement it contains. From the first moment I was acquainted with you, it was a contest between me and several of my friends, and partly in my own mind, whether or no I ought to be acquainted with a man, of whom, to say the least, the world entertained a very ill opinion, respecting the justice of which I could be no competent judge. Upon what grounds, do you think, I decided that contest? I said, 'It would be absurd for me to attempt to associate only with immaculate persons ; nor do I believe that the right way to attempt to correct the errors of the vicious, is that all honest men should desert them.' As to the frequency of my visits, I appeal to your own memory whether I ever sought that frequency. Did you imagine that your dinners were to be a bribe, seducing me to depart from the integrity of my judgment? That would be a character meaner than that of the poorest pensioner of the vilest court that ever existed.

"You seem to insinuate that I ought to appear in court as your friend and supporter. I have always avoided connecting myself with any set of men, even though Charles Fox should be at their head. I will stand or fall by my own character, and my own principles. Are you ignorant that, if I were to show myself as your supporter, it would be considered as a declaration, not merely that I thought you injured by Alex. Champion, Esq., of Winchester Street, but that I approved of the general spirit of your transaction with Philips, and other similar transactions? If I were asked in open court whether, upon the whole, I believed that your money transactions were immaculate, or that they had in some instances been very exceptionable, what do you think would be my answer?

"You call upon me for an act of friendship, and the act you demand would be scarcely of any imaginable use to you. At the same time you show very little friendship in the demand. Why should my character be involved with yours, which however as you may conceive undeservedly labours under a very extensive odium? Why should I bring obloquy upon all my future, and all my past labours? No sir, I will retain my little portion of usefulness undiminished. Whatever may be my share of good opinion with the world, it shall be injured by no man's vices but my own. Should I not be both fool and knave if I did otherwise?

"You oblige me to treat you unceremoniously. But I must venture that rather than be misunderstood. Otherwise I certainly would have refused to give you pain, especially at the present moment. If there were anything I could do for your service that I could be brought to think reasonable, I would most cheerfully do it. I wish you all imaginable happiness, but I cannot sacrifice my independence and my judgment. Upon this footing, and this explanation being given, I am willing that our acquaintance should either cease or continue, as best suits your inclinations. It is perhaps impossible that one human being should have a repeated good humoured intercourse with another, without increasing in kindness towards him. But, remember, I can dine at a man's table, without being prepared to be the partisan of his measures and proceedings.

"What a strange dilemma do you create for your acquaintance! If I had ceased to visit you, you would have censured me, as unnecessarily squeamish and fastidious. I have continued to visit you, and you conclude that I ought to be ready to proceed all lengths with you.

" W. GODWIN."

The intimacy was continued. King's reply has in it something of bluster, mixed with a great desire not to quarrel with Godwin, and ends thus ;

J. King to William Godwin.

"24 PICCADILLY, *Janry. 26th*, 1796.

". . . I am ashamed of the illiberality about dining with me. Do I expect every man to be my partizan who dines with me, or desist my invitations when he differs from me in opinion? I say I understand you now, but I still like you, and perhaps you will hereafter like me better when you know me more, and the impracticability of your own theory. Merry and Este dine with me to-morrow when I expect you will join them. JOHN KING."

It appears from the diary that the invitation was accepted.

Godwin's fearlessness to offend his own friends and supporters, if duty called him to oppose them in any degree, appears in a nobler manner in a letter to Erskine in reference to his defence of political prisoners, in which he thought Erskine compromised principle for the sake of results, and there are many other letters of criticism to Faweet and others showing the same fearlessness, but these have not in them otherwise anything to call for special remark. The same may be said of a correspondence which began to be frequent between himself and Miss Alderson. Godwin's replies to the lady's letters are not extant, and hers do not at this period show any great literary power. They are lively and pleasant, and show Miss Alderson as she was in days which afterwards seemed to her frivolous, and in which she was unconverted. An extract from one may here be transcribed, as it gives the last glimpse of an old friend.

Miss Alderson to William Godwin.

"NORWICH, 5*th of F.bry.*, 1796.

" . . . I called on your old friend Mrs Southern about a month
ago, and asked her opinion of 'Caleb Williams :' now, pray let
not thy noble courage be cast down when I inform you that both
Mrs S. and her daughter think you talk too favourably of wicked
men, and that 'Italian Letters' (your first novel), are vastly
prettier than 'Caleb Williams.' Console yourself, my good friend,
by reflecting on the fable of the old man and his ass."

Mrs Sothren had become more tolerant since in 1788
the fact that Godwin had turned novel-writer had given
the good lady "serious concern."

There is some reason to suppose that Godwin had at
one moment seriously thought of asking Amelia Alderson
to be his wife, and that not long before his intimacy with
Mary Wollstonecraft, but whether the lady or her father
declined the alliance, or whether no offer was actually
made, it is plain that the feeling between the two was at no
time warmer than a sincere friendship. Nor was there a
shade of pique or jealousy to come between Miss Alderson
and Mary Wollstonecraft. They were no sooner acquainted,
in the spring of this year, than they became fast friends,
and in one of the letters still preserved from Miss Alderson
to Mrs Imlay (Mary Wollstonecraft) is this curious sentence,
that whatever Miss Alderson had seen before for the first
time had always disappointed her, "except Mrs Imlay and
the Cumberland Lakes." She was one of the persons who
always looked with interest on the intimacy between
Godwin and Mary Wollstonecraft, and rejoiced when their
marriage was declared.

The relation in which this remarkable woman stood to Imlay and to Godwin, and the light in which the very exceptional nature of the case may present itself to us, will be presently considered. No doubt, however, not only she, but Mrs Inchbald and others, may be in some degree compromised by the association with one who has been mentioned in Godwin's notes—Mrs Robinson. This lady, whose maiden name was Darby, had married very young, and her marriage had proved unhappy. She went on the stage, and while acting Perdita in the Winter's Tale, had the ill fortune to attract the notice of the Prince of Wales, whose mistress she became. This connection was short, but was not the only one she formed. At this time she was living on a pension from the Prince, and was received in a certain society, chiefly literary and theatrical.

There is a radical difference between the life of one who honestly believed, on moral grounds, that marriage as usually understood is a mistake, and that true marriage can dispense with outward forms, and is an union of the heart and mind, and one who necessarily and avowedly was only the object and ministress of a fleeting passion of the basest sort. Yet even republicans were then dazzled by the name of a prince, and the shame of a royal amour was felt less then than perhaps it now would be. The day had gone by, if indeed it ever had been, save in the imagination of a song writer, when such a connection would be repudiated with the scorn expressed in the fine old ballad of " Mary Ambree," nor had that day dawned, if now it has, in which to be the mistress of a prince is held to be the lowest and most fatal degradation, because in that case alone must the mistress abandon all hope of ever being made "an honest woman " by him who has wronged her.

With this halo of false stage light around her, Mrs

Robinson appears to have been a very agreeable woman, and her society was eagerly cultivated.

The record of the year may close with the following letter:

Mrs Godwin sen. to William Godwin.

[No date, but Mrs Sothren died Dec. 12, 1796. The top of the page is wanting.]

" Mrs Sothren pass'd out of this life in a serene Slumber. She had been down stairs the day before; eat some minc'd turkey, and, with taking hold of ye maids arm, walked about the room. Departed abt. 4 o'clock Thursday morng., 22 inst. Mr Sothren sent a messinger yt same morning to acquaint me of the Awful event; your brother Hully attended ye funeral on Lord's Day morng.; a Hears and mourng Coach; Mr and Mrs Sothren, Mr and Mrs Hatton, H. G. and Miss Jane, in ye coach; barers 5s. a piece. She said she thought she would be too heavy to be carried on men's sholders : your brother slept at the Widow Nutter's, a very nice woman : the deare Creature was a pattern of strict piety, Humility, patience, doing good to all as far as she had ability and opportunity; tho' not rich in this world's goods, was rich in the promises, disclaiming all merit of her own, owning she had nothing but what she had recieved. Others have a loss, a great one, but myself the greatest; to die is her gain, as St Paul saith of himself. It now remains that we keep her steps in mind, that we may meet her, with all our pious friends, in the realms of Joy and Peace. She has desired yo sh'd have her watch, yr Sister can give yo further particulars. She did not mean to make a will, as her Estate was not at her Disposal after her death. I sent you a Hare 13 Instant, did yo receive it, was it good and of any use ; sh'd you like anything else better. If you have a few spare minutes, sh'd like to receive a letter fr you, and to be informed if there is any alteration for the better in Josh. respecting his family. I hear a poor account of his aunt Barber, yt is, that she is a kept Miss to Mr H. Hall. I shall inclose this in a goose for my daughter Joseph, directed to Son John.—I am, with sincear affection, yours,

" A. GODWIN."

CHAPTER VII.

THE WOLLSTONECRAFTS. 1759—1791.

GODWIN'S increasing intimacy with Mary Wollstonecraft has been already noticed. She had not made any great impression on him at their earliest meetings, nor, when he first knew her, had she ceased to consider herself as virtually the wife of Imlay, whose name she bore. The treatment she had received from this person, however, was such that when the connection was finally dissolved, the bitterness of parting was already past, and the affectionate friendship existing between herself and Godwin passed easily into a warmer feeling. There were, however, many reasons on both sides which rendered the idea of marriage distasteful. Mrs Shelley has left a note in regard to her father which must be given at length.

" He was very averse to marriage. Poverty was a strong argument against it. When he concocted a code of morals in 'Political Justice,' he warmly opposed a system which exacted a promise to be kept to the end of life, in spite of every alteration of circumstance and of feeling. Objections to marriage are usually supposed to infer an approval, and even practice, of illicit intercourse. This was far from being the case with Godwin. He was in a supreme degree a conscientious man, utterly opposed to anything like vice or libertinism, nor did his sense of duty permit him to indulge in any deviation from the laws of society, which, though he might regard as unjust, could not, he felt, be infringed without deception and injury to any woman who should act in opposition

I. L

to them. The loss of usefulness to both parties, which the very stigma brings, the natural ties of children, entailing duties which necessitate the duration of any connection, and which, if tampered with, must end in misery, all these motives were imperative in preventing him from acting on theories, which yet he did not like to act against.

"Among his acquaintance were several women, to whose society he was exceedingly partial, and who were all distinguished for personal attraction and talents. Among them may be mentioned the celebrated Mary Robinson, whom to the end of his life he considered as the most beautiful woman he had ever seen, but though he admired her so greatly, their acquaintance scarcely attained intimate friendship. It was otherwise with Mrs Inchbald; he saw her frequently, he delighted in her manners, her conversation, her loveliness; yet he was not in love, and, above all, never thought of marrying her. He was intimate with Miss Alderson, afterwards Mrs Opie, but their friendship is purely such as is formed every day in society. He admired her beauty and sprightliness. She liked his conversation and respected his talents.

"There was yet another favourite. She was married, and this circumstance was a barrier to every sentiment except friendship, but he certainly experienced for her more of tenderness and preference than for any other among his acquaintance."

It will be plain from what has been already said that Mrs Shelley may possibly have been misinformed about Miss Alderson. There seems reason to believe that Godwin did contemplate marriage with her, and did make a proposal on the subject to Dr Alderson, if not to the lady herself. The lady to whom Mrs Shelley alludes in the last paragraph is of course Mrs Reveley, afterwards Mrs Gisborne. It may be added that Godwin's dislike of what in "Political Justice" he terms "co-habitation," *i.e.*, in his use of the word, the living perpetually in the same house with another person, and having no time or place which can be considered absolutely one's own, without unkindness or incivility, worked greatly in aid of his graver theoretical objections to marriage. It is now necessary to give a detailed account of her who broke the even tenor of Godwin's passionless existence, who for his sake altered not a little her own views, and whose character has been a mark for severer censure than those of women who to a far greater extent than herself have run counter to the prejudices and instincts of ordinary society.

Mary Wollstonecraft, who was born April 27, 1759, was the eldest daughter of a large family, the children of a man who had inherited and spent a considerable fortune. The family appear to have been originally of Irish extraction, but Mary's grandfather was a respectable manufacturer in Spitalfields, and realized the property which his son squandered. Her mother's maiden name was Elizabeth Dixon. She was Irish, and of good family. Mr Wollstonecraft was not bred to any profession, but after he had come to the end of his money he left Hoxton, where he had lived for a short time, and after many changes of residence—to Essex and to Beverley, in Yorkshire, among others—he went to live at Laugharne in Pembrokeshire, where he had a farm. He soon, however, returned to London for a time. Mary Godwin's mother died in 1780, leaving six children—Edward, an attorney, settled near the Tower in London; Mary, Everina, and Eliza, James, afterwards in the Navy; and Charles, who finally emigrated to America. Mr Wollstonecraft speedily married again, but though his wife seems to have done what she could to keep him out of difficulties, he was a man of idle and dissipated habits, and dropped ever lower in fortune and respectability.

His home became no fit place for his daughters, who indeed were obliged to endeavour to earn their own livelihood.

Mary had a friend in Fanny Blood, a girl of her own age, and whose circumstances were somewhat similar. Fanny Blood supported her family as an artist, and lived for some time at Walham Green, where Mary joined her, and earned her livelihood by helping Mrs Blood, who took in needlework. She looked to an independent career as a teacher in a school ; Everina went to keep her brother's house ; and Eliza married, when circumstances occurred which threw on her a far greater amount of responsibility and difficulty.

Eliza Wollstonecraft had married a Mr Bishop, but the marriage had proved from the first an unhappy one. It is more than probable there were faults on both sides. All the Wollstonecraft sisters were enthusiastic, excitable, and hasty - tempered, apt to exaggerate trifles, sensitive to magnify inattention into slights, and slights into studied insults. All had bad health of a kind which is especially trying to the nerves, and Eliza had in excess the family temperament and constitution. With a great desire for culture and self-improvement, she had less actual education than Everina, and very far less than her gifted sister Mary, so that there was little to counteract the waywardness of a hasty disposition. Yet with all this there can be no doubt that Bishop was a man of furious violence, and from the letters which remain it would seem that many of the painful scenes in Mary's unfinished novel, "The Wrongs of Women," are simple transcriptions of what she had known or even witnessed in her sister's married life.

Mary, much attached to all her brothers and sisters, was devoted to Eliza, and considered no sacrifice too great to make for her. To save her from her misery, she at once gave up all hopes for the time of an independent career,

and so soon as it was determined that Eliza should leave
her husband, resolved to make a home for her. On Mary
fell the real responsibility of urging so strong a step as
her sister's flight not only from Mr Bishop, but also from
their child. But Mrs Bishop's reason had all but given way
under her trials, and to escape was the immediate and only
course which presented itself. As soon as a final separation
from Bishop had been effected, Mary took lodgings at
Islington with Fanny Blood. The scheme proposed was
that Mary and Eliza should obtain daily pupils, and that
Fanny Blood should maintain herself as an artist. This
plan was tried for a very short time, but with no success,
and the sisters then removed to Newington Green, where
they had some influential friends, and soon obtained about
twenty day-scholars. A relation, Mrs Campbell, and her
little son, came to board with them, as well as another lady
and her three children. This flash of prosperity induced
Mary to take a larger house, the expense of which involved
her in serious difficulties. The sum due for the board of the
three children was irregularly paid, and the Green proved
too small a place in those days to support a day-school,
which should prove remunerative. It subsisted, however, in
a languishing state for two years and a half.

George Blood, Mrs Skeys' younger brother, had also a
great share of her affection. His disposition and the unfortunate condition of his home, since his father was a
drunken spendthrift, attracted her to the lad, and she felt
also much for him because he entertained a hopeless,
unrequited love for her sister Everina, who was considerably older than herself. Somewhat wild and reckless while
a mere lad, and somewhat unsettled, he accepted a situation as clerk near Lisbon, with hopes of promotion, but
abandoned it almost at once. He then returned to Ire-

land, where his father was settled in a situation far beyond
his deserts, gained some good appointment, and appears
to have done very well. During several years Mary's
correspondence with George Blood was frequent and intimate, and some of her letters to him, as well as those to
her sisters, will at once fill up details, and receive illustration from this sketch of her life at Newington. Those who
have known Mary Wollstonecraft only by reports which
may have reached them of her after career, and by second-
hand criticism on her writings, will be astonished to find in
them so strong a vein of piety of the type that would now
be called evangelical.

.   *Mary Wollstonecraft to Everina Wollstonecraft.*

" *Saturday Afternoon* [*November* 1783].

" I expected to have seen you before this, but the extreme coldness of the weather is a sufficient apology. I cannot yet give any
certain account of Bess, or form a rational conjecture with respect
to the termination of her disorder. She has not had a violent fit
of frenzy since I saw you, but her mind is in a most unsettled
state, and attending to the constant fluctuation of it is far more
harassing than the watching those raving fits that had not the least
tincture of reason. Her ideas are all disjointed, and a number of
wild whims float on her imagination, and fall from her unconnect-
edly, something like strange dreams when judgment sleeps, and
fancy sports at a fine rate. Don't smile at my language, for I am
so constantly forced to observe her—lest she run into mischief—
that my thoughts continually turn on the unaccountable wander-
ings of her mind. She seems to think she has been very ill used,
and, in short, till I see some more favourable symptoms, I shall
only suppose that her malady has assumed a new and more distressing appearance.

" One thing, by way of comfort, I must tell you, that persons
who recover from madness are generally in this way before they are

perfectly restored, but whether Bess's faculties will ever regain their former tone, time only will show. At present I am in suspense. Let me hear from you or see you, and believe me to be yours affectionately, M. W.

"Mr D. promised to call last night, and I intended sending this by him. We have been out in a coach, but still Bess is far from being *well*. Patience—Patience. Farewell.

"*Sunday, noon.*"

The Same to the Same.

"[*December* 1783].

"I don't know what to do. Poor Eliza's situation almost turns my brain. I can't stay and see this continual misery, and to leave her to bear it by herself without any one to comfort her, is still more distressing. I would do anything to rescue her from her present situation. My head is quite confused with thus being to so little purpose. In this case something desperate must be determined on. Do you think Edward will receive her? Do speak to him; or if you imagine that I should have more influence on his mind, I will contrive to see you, but you must caution him against expostulating with or even mentioning the affair to Bishop, for it would only put him on his guard, and we should have a storm to encounter that I tremble to think of. I am convinced that this is the only expedient to save Bess, and she declares she had rather be a teacher than stay here. I must again repeat it, you must be secret; nothing can be done till she leaves the house. For his friend Wood very justly said that he was 'either a lion or a spaniel.' I have been some time deliberating on this, for I can't help pitying B., but misery must be his portion at any rate till he alters himself, and that would be a miracle.

"To be at Edward's is not desirable, but of the two evils she must choose the least. Write a line by the bearer, or by the post to-morrow—don't fail. I need not urge you to use your endeavours; if I did not see it was absolutely necessary, I should not have fixed on it. I tell you she will soon be deprived of reason.

B. cannot behave properly, and those who would attempt to reason with him must be mad, or have very little observation. Those who would save Bess must act and not talk."

The Same to the Same.

"I have nothing to tell you, my dear girl, that will give you pleasure. Yesterday was a dismal day, long and dreary. Bishop was very ill, &c., &c. He is much better to-day, but misery haunts this house in one shape or other. How sincerely do I join with you in saying that if a person has common sense they cannot make one completely unhappy. But to attempt to lead or govern a weak mind is impossible ; it will ever press forward to what it wishes, regardless of impediments, and, with a selfish eagerness, believe what it desires practicable, though the contrary is as clear as the noonday. My spirits are hurried with listening to pros and cons ; and my head is so confused, that I sometimes say no, when I ought to say yes. My heart is almost broken with listening to B. while he reasons the case. I cannot insult him with advice, which he would never have wanted, if he was capable of attending to it. May my habitation never be fixed among the tribe that can't look beyond the present gratification—that draw fixed conclusions from general rules—that attend to the literal meaning only, and because a thing ought to be, expect that it will come to pass. B. has made a confidant of Skeys; and as I can never speak to him in private, I suppose his pity may cloud his judgment. If it does, I should not either wonder at it or blame him. For I that know, and am fixed in my opinion, cannot unwaveringly adhere to it ; and when I reason, I am afraid of being unfeeling. Miracles don't occur now, and only a miracle can alter the minds of some people. They grow old, and we can only discover by their countenances that they are so. To the end of the chapter will their misery last. I expect Fanny next Thursday, and she will stay with us but a few days. Bess desires her love ; she grows better, and of course more sad."

The Same to the Same.

[*January* 1784.]

" Here we are, Everina ; but my trembling hand will scarce let me tell you so. Bess is much more composed than I expected her to be ; but to make my trial still more dreadful, I was afraid in the coach she was going to have one of her flights, for she bit her wedding-ring to pieces. When I can recollect myself, I'll send you particulars ; but, at present, my heart beats time with every carriage that rolls by, and a knocking at the door almost throws me into a fit. I hope B. will not discover us, for I could sooner face a lion ; yet the door never opens, but I expect to see him panting for breath. Ask Ned how we are to behave if he should find us out, for Bess is determined not to return. Can he force her ?—but I'll not suppose it, yet I can think of nothing else. She is sleepy, and going to bed ; my agitated mind will not permit me. Don't tell Charles or any creature. Oh ! let me entreat you to be careful, for Bess does not dread him now so much as I do. Again, let me request you to write, as B.'s behaviour may silence my fears. You will soon hear from me again. Fanny carried many things to Lear's, brush-maker in the Strand, next door to the White Hart.—Yours, MARY.

" Miss Johnston—Mrs Dodds, opposite the Mermaid, Church St., Hackney.

" She looks now very wild. Heaven protect us !

" I almost wish for an husband, for I want somebody to support me."

The Same to the Same.

" *Sunday Afternoon January* 1784].

" Your welcome letter arrived just now, and we thank you for sending it so soon. Your account of B. does not surprise me, as I am convinced that, to gratify the ruling passion, he could command all the rest. The plea of the child occurred to me, and it was the most rational thing he could complain of. I know he will tell a plausible tale, and the generality will pity him and blame me; but, however, if we can snatch Bess from extreme wretchedness, what reason shall we have to rejoice. It was, indeed, a very disagreeable affair; and if we had stayed a day or two longer, I believe it would never have been effected. For Bess's mind was so harassed with the fear of being discovered, and the thought of leaving the child, that she could not have stood it long. I suppose B. told you how we escaped; there was full as much good luck as good management in it. As to Bess, she was so terrified, that she lost all presence of mind, and would have done anything. I took a second coach, to prevent his tracing us. Well, all this may serve to talk about and laugh at when we meet, but it was no laughing matter at the time. Bess is tolerably well; she cannot help sighing about little Mary, whom she tenderly loved; and on this score I both love and pity her. The poor brat! it had got a little hold on my affections; some time or other I hope we shall get it. Yesterday we were two languid ladies; and even now we have pains in all our limbs, and are as jaded as if we had taken a long journey . . . All these disorders will give way to time, if it brings a little tranquillity with it; and the thought of having assisted to bring about so desirable an event, will ever give me pleasure to think of. I hope you sent the letters I enclosed to you, as Bess writ a few very proper lines to B. I am very glad you are in town, as I depend on you for keeping Ned firm. B. would make a more determined person flinch. This quiet portends no good; he will burst out at last, and the calm will end in the usual manner. Tell my brother that Bess is fixed in her resolution of never returning; but what will be the consequence? And if a separate maintenance is not to be obtained, she'll try to earn her own bread. Write to us an account of everything; you cannot be too particular. She carried off almost all her clothes, but we have no linen. I wish you could contrive to send us a few changes at the first opportunity, it matters not whom they belong to. We have neither chemise, handkerchief, or apron, so our necessities are pressing."

The Same to the Same.

[January 1784]

[After discussing the possibility of keeping a school.] "With economy we can live on a guinea a week, and that we can with ease earn. The lady who gave Fanny five guineas for two drawings will assist us and we shall be independent. . . . If Ned makes us a little present of furniture it will be very acceptable, but if he is prudent, we must try to do without it. I knew I should be the Mrs Brown—the shameful incendiary, in this shocking affair of a woman's leaving her bed-fellow, they thought the strong affection of a sister *might* apologize for my conduct, but that the scheme was by no means a good one. In short 'tis contrary to all the rules of conduct that are published for the benefit of new married ladies, by whose advice Mrs Brook was actuated when she with grief of heart gave up my friendship. Mrs Clare too, with cautious words approves of our conduct, and were she to see B. might advise a reconciliation. . . . .

"Don't suppose I am preaching, when I say uniformity of conduct cannot in any degree be expected from those whose first motive of action is not the pleasing the Supreme Being, and those who humbly rely on Providence will not only be supported in affliction, but have a Peace imparted to them that is past all describing. This state is indeed a warfare, and we learn little that we don't smart for in the attaining. The cant of weak enthusiasts has made the consolations of Religion and the assistance of the Holy Spirit appear ridiculous to the inconsiderate, but it is the only solid foundation of comfort that the weak efforts of reason will be assisted and our hearts and minds corrected and improved till the time arrives when we shall not only see *perfection*, but see every creature around us happy. . . . "

Fanny Blood to Everina Wollstonecraft.

" WALHAM GREEN, *Febry. 18th*, 1784.

"MY DEAR EVERINA.—The situation of our two poor girls grows ever more and more desperate. My mind is tortured about them because I cannot see any possible resource they have for a maintenance. The letter I last night received from Mary disturbed me so much that I never since closed my eyes, and my head is this morning almost distracted. I find she wrote to her brother informing him that it was our intention to live all together, and earn our bread by painting and needle-work, which gives me great uneasiness, as I am convinced that he will be displeased at his sister's being connected with me, and the forfeiting his favour at this time is of the utmost consequence. I believe it was I that first proposed the plan, and in my eagerness to enjoy the society of two so dear to me, I did not give myself time to consider that it is utterly impracticable. The very utmost I could earn, one week with another, supposing I had uninterrupted health, is half-a-guinea a week, which would just pay for furnished lodgings for three people to pig together. As for needle-work, it is utterly impossible they could earn more than half-a-guinea a week between them, supposing they had constant employment, which is of all things the most uncertain. . . . I own with sincere sorrow that I was greatly to blame for ever mentioning such a plan before I had maturely considered it; but as those who know me will give me credit for a good intention I trust they will pardon my folly and inconsideration. " [She then suggests that a small haberdashery shop should be taken and stocked for the sisters, and proceeds.] "If your brother should be averse to assisting them from a notion that I should live with them. . . . I wish you would take the earliest opportunity of assuring him from me *that on no* account whatever will I ever live with them unless fortune should make me quite independent, which I never expect. My health is so much impaired that I should be only a burthen on them, and for my own part I don't spend a thought on what may become of me. All I wish is to see them provided for comfortably; but I will neither add to their distress, situated as they now are, nor meanly gain a subsistence by living with them hereafter, if fortune should smile on them. This is my fixed resolve. I beseech you to let me hear from you as soon as possible, for I am impatient to know whether there is the least

prospect of comfort for our dear girls. Believe me to be, dear
Everina, yours sincerely,   F. Blood."

In the spring of the following year Fanny Blood
married Mr Hugh Skeys, a merchant, and went with
him to Lisbon. Mr Skeys had played fast and loose for
some time, the uncertainty had greatly injured her health,
and her new found happiness was to be of short duration. She left behind great sorrows. Her sister Caroline had disgraced her family, and her father drank.
George, who was steady and respectable, had yet been
mixed up with some discreditable associates, and had gone
to Ireland only in time to avoid being seriously compromised by his association with them. Mary's letters throw
light on the trials of the Blood family as well as on her
own.

Mary Wollstonecraft to George Blood.

"Newington Green, *July* 3*d* [1785].

" The pleasure I felt at hearing of your safe arrival [in Ireland]
was a good deal damped by the account you gave of the captain's
brutality. By this time I hope all the effects of so disagreeable a
voyage are gone off, except your being a little weather-beaten or
so ; and you and I don't think that of much consequence, we have
met with so many rough blasts that have sunk deeper than the
skin. You need not have made any apology to me about the old
man. When I entreated you, my dear George, to be prudent, I
only meant to caution you against throwing your money away on
trifling gratifications, but I did not wish to narrow your heart or
desire you to avoid relieving the present necessities of your fellow-
creatures, in order to ward off any future ill which might happen to
self. It would give me great pleasure to hear there was any
chance of your getting some employment. In the meantime give
way to hope, do your duty and leave the rest to Heaven, forfeit
not that sure support in the time of trouble, and though your want

of experience and judgment may betray you into many errors, let not your heart be corrupted by bad example, and then, though it may be wounded by neglect, and torn by anguish, you will not feel that most acute of all sorrows, a sense of having deserved the miseries that you undergo.

" Palmer has been respited, and of course will be pardoned. I have made many inquiries concerning the affair that alarmed us so much, and find that Palmer's servant has sworn a child to you, and that it was on that account those men came to our house. The girl was waiting at a little ale-house near us, so that if you had stayed, you would have been involved in a pretty piece of business that your innocence could not have extricated you out of. I suppose the child is P.'s, or many fathers may dispute the honour. Let that be as it will, the recent affair of Mary Ann would have given this some colour of truth. How troublesome fools are ! Mrs Campbell—who has all the constancy that attends on folly, and in whose mind, when any prejudice is fixed, it remains for ever—has long disliked you, and this confined ill-humour has at last broken out, and she has sufficiently railed at your *vices*, and the *encouragement* I have given them. . . . I have been very ill, and gone through the usual physical operations, have been bled and blistered, yet still am not well ; my harassed mind will in time wear out my body. I have been so hunted down by cares, and see so many that I must encounter, that my spirits are quite depressed. I have lost all relish for life, and my almost broken heart is only cheered by the prospect of death. I may be years a-dying tho', and so I ought to be patient, for at this time to wish myself away would be selfish. Your father and mother are well, and desire their love ; the former has received a letter from Fanny, but her letters to your father are seldom satisfactory to me. I am trying to get your father a place, but my hopes are very faint. I forgot to tell you that Palmer's servant says she followed you one day in town and raised a mob, but that you ran away. God bless you, and believe me sincerely and affectionately your friend. I feel that I love you more than I ever supposed that I did. Adieu to the village delights. I almost hate the Green, for it seems the grave of all my comforts. Shall I never again see your honest heart dancing in your eyes?"

Palmer, whose name is mentioned in the foregoing letter, was an attorney, whose clerk, it would seem, George Blood had been. He was induced to forge documents for a client of his, one Mrs Jones, with the intent to represent her as a clergyman's widow, and her son, therefore, a fit recipient for a charity for clergy orphans. For this he was tried and sentenced to death, but was, as the letters show, afterwards respited.

The Same to the Same.

"NEWINGTON GREEN, *July 20th*, [1785].

. . . . "I am not a fair weather friend; on the contrary, I think I love most people best when they are in adversity, for pity is one of my prevailing passions. I am not fond of possessions, yet, once for all, let me assure you that I have a mother's tenderness for you, and that my heart dances when I make any new discovery of goodness in you. It gives me the sincerest satisfaction to find that you look for comfort where only it is to be met with, and that Being in whom you trust will not desert you. Be not cast down while we are struggling with care, life slips away, and, through the assistance of Divine Grace, we are obtaining habits of virtue that will enable us to relish those joys that we cannot now form any idea of. I feel myself particularly attached to those who are heirs of the promises, and travel on in the thorny path with the same Christian hopes that render my severe trials a cause of thankfulness when I *can* think. . . . I often see your father and mother; they desire to be remembered to you in the kindest manner, and entirely acquit you of the crime that is laid to your charge, as do the girls. . . . I have no creature to be unreserved to. Eliza and Everina are so different that I could as soon fly as open my heart to them. How my social comforts have dropped away—Fanny first, and then you went over the hills and far away. I am resigned to my fate, but 'tis that gloomy kind of resignation that is akin to despair. . . . Your affectionate friend, MARY."

The Same to the Same.

"NEWINGTON GREEN, *July 25th* [1785].

" My dear George,—I have received the long expected packet.
. . . The account Fanny gives of her health is far from pleasing
me, though I imagine that her complaints arise from a new cause
that you can easily guess. . . . She has received several of our
letters, and read in the papers an account of Palmer, which made
her very uneasy lest your name should be mentioned, which would
have been an effectual bar to your settling in Lisbon. . . . Skeys
has received congratulatory letters from most of his friends and
relations in Ireland, and he now regrets that he did not marry
sooner. All his mighty fears had no foundation, so that if he had
had courage to have braved the world's dread laugh, and ventured
to have acted for himself, he might have spared Fanny many
griefs, the scars of which will never be obliterated. Nay more, if
she had gone a year or two ago, her health might have been perfectly restored, which I do not now think will ever be the case.
Before true passion, I am convinced, everything but a sense of
duty moves ; true love is warmest when the object is absent. How
Hugh could let Fanny languish in England, while he was throwing money away at Lisbon, is to me inexplicable, if he had a
passion that did not require the fuel of seeing the object. I much
fear he loves her not for the qualities that render her dear to my
heart. Her tenderness and delicacy are not even conceived by a
man who would be satisfied with the fondness of one of the general
run of women. . . .—Your affectionate friend,   MARY."

The Same to the Same.

"NEWINGTON GRREN, *Sept. 4th* [1785].

" By this time, my dear George, I suppose you have received
Fanny's letter, informing you that your fortune has at last taken a
turn. I only heard of it yesterday, and I most sincerely rejoice,
as I earnestly wish to hear of your arrival at Lisbon, on Fanny's
account as well as your own. I hope to see you before the year

is out, as I am determined to be with her on a certain occasion if
I can possibly contrive it. . . . Palmer has hatched up some story
to my discredit, in order to be revenged on me for opening Mrs
D.'s eyes to his villanies. He is still in prison. I believe I forgot
to tell you that the girl laid the child to him when she could get
no one else to father it. . . .—Your ever affectionate friend.

"MARY WOLLSTONECRAFT."

Fanny Skeys wrote from Lisbon entreating her friend
to be with her during her confinement, and Mary
Wollstonecraft, then, as always, utterly unselfish, complied, leaving her scholars and house in Mrs Bishop's
charge. She arrived only to nurse her friend in what
proved the last hours of her life, and returned almost
heart-broken, for her friendship for Fanny Blood was even
more than a sister's love, to find matters at Newington worse
than before. All chance of future success was at an end,
and the school was given up.

Mary Wollstonecraft to Mrs Bishop.

[LISBON, *Nov. or Dec.* 1785.]

" My dear Girls,—I am beginning to awake out of a terrifying
dream, for in that light do the transactions of these two or three last
days appear. Before I say more, let me tell you that, when I arrived
here, Fanny was in labour, and that four hours after she was
delivered of a boy. The child is alive and well, and considering
the *very very* low state to which Fanny was reduced, she is better
than could be expected. I am now watching her and the child.
My active spirits have not been much at rest ever since I left
England. I could not write to you on shipboard; the sea was so
rough, and we had such hard gales of wind, the captain was afraid
we should be dismasted. I cannot write to-night, or collect my
scattered thoughts, my mind is so unsettled. Fanny is so worn
out, her recovery would be almost a resurrection, and my reason

I.   M

will scarce allow me to think it possible. I labour to be resigned,
and by the time I am a little so, some faint hope sets my thoughts
again afloat, and for a moment I look forward to days that will,
alas ! I fear, never come.

"I will try to-morrow to give you some little regular account of
my journey, though I am almost afraid to look beyond the present
moment. Was not my arrival providential ? I can scarce be
persuaded that I am here, and that so many things have happened in so short a time. My head grows light with thinking
on it.

"Friday morning.—Fanny has been so alarmingly ill since I
wrote the above, I entirely gave her up, and yet I could not write
and tell you so : it seemed like signing her death warrant. Yesterday afternoon some of the most alarming symptoms a little abated,
and she had a comfortable night ; yet I rejoice with trembling
lips, and am afraid to indulge hopes : she is very low. The sto-
mach is so weak it will scarce bear to receive the slightest nourish-
ment ; in short, if I were to tell you all her complaints, you would
not wonder at my fears. The child, though a puny one, is well.
I have got a wet-nurse for it. The packet does not sail till the
latter end of next week, and I send this by a ship. I shall write
by every opportunity. We arrived last Monday. We were only
thirteen days at sea. The wind was so high, and the sea so
boisterous, the water came in at the cabin windows, and the ship
rolled about in such a manner, it was dangerous to stir. The
women were sea-sick the whole time, and the poor invalid so oppressed by his complaints, I never expected he would live to see
Lisbon. I have supported him for hours together, gasping for
breath, and at night, if I had been inclined to sleep, his dreadful
cough would have kept me awake. You may suppose that I have
not rested much since I came here, yet I am tolerably well, and
calmer than I could expect to be. Could I not look for comfort
where only 'tis to be found, I should have been mad before this,
but I feel that I am supported by that Being who alone can heal
a wounded spirit. May He bless you both.—Yours,

                                                      "MARY."

Before the date of the next letter, poor Fanny was in her grave, Mary Wollstonecraft had returned, as also had George Blood, who had thrown up his situation, without a word to any one but his correspondent. It is probable that, after his gentle sister's death, he did not get on so well with his brother-in-law, on whom he was in great measure dependent. Shortly after Mary's return, she made her first essay in literature, publishing a small, and in no way remarkable pamphlet called " Thoughts on the Education of Daughters," for the copyright of which Mr Johnson, the Bookseller in Fleet Street, gave her ten guineas. This sum she applied to enable Mr and Mrs Blood to carry out their desire of going to Ireland and settling in Dublin.

Mary Wollstonecraft to George Blood.

" NEWINGTON GREEN, *Feby. 4th,* [1786].

" I write to you, my dear George, lest my silence should make you uneasy, yet what have I to say that will not have the same effect? Things do not go well with me, and my spirits seem for ever flown. I was a month on my passage, and the weather was so tempestuous, we were several times in imminent danger. I did not expect ever to have reached land. If it had pleased Heaven to have called me hence, what a world of care I should have missed. I have lost all relish for pleasure, and life seems a burden almost too heavy to be endured. My head is stupid, and my heart sick and exhausted. But why should I worry you? and yet, if I do not tell you my vexations, what can I write about?

" Your father and mother are tolerably well, and enquire most affectionately concerning you. They do not suspect that you have left Lisbon, and I do not intend informing them of it till you are provided for. I am very unhappy on their account, for though I am determined they shall share my last shilling, yet I have every reason to apprehend extreme distress, and of course they must be involved in it. The school dwindles to nothing,

and we shall soon lose our last boarder, Mrs Disney. She and
the girls quarrelled while I was away, which contributed to make
the house very disagreeable.   Her sons are to be whole boarders
at Mrs Cockburn's.   Let me turn my eyes on which side I will, I
can only anticipate misery.   Are such prospects as these likely to
heal an almost broken heart?   The loss of Fanny was sufficient of
itself to have thrown a cloud over my brightest days : what effect
then must it have, when I am bereft of every other comfort?   I
have too many debts.   I cannot think of remaining any longer in this
house, the rent is so enormous, and where to go, without money
or friends, who can point out?   My eyes are very bad and my
memory gone.   I am not fit for any situation, and as for Eliza, I
don't know what will become of her.   My constitution is impaired,
I hope I shan't live long, yet I may be a tedious time dying.

"Well, I am too impatient.   The will of Heaven be done !   I
will labour to be resigned.   'The spirit is willing, but the flesh is
weak.'   I scarce know what I write, yet my writing at all when
my mind is so disturbed is a proof to you that I can never be lost
so entirely in misery as to forget those I love.   I long to hear that
you are settled.   It is the only quarter from which I can reasonably expect any pleasure.   I have received a very short, unsatis-
factory letter from Lisbon.   It was written to apologize for not
sending the money to your father which he promised.   It would
have been particularly acceptable to them at this time, but he is
prudent, and will not run any hazard to serve a friend.   Indeed,
delicacy made me conceal from him my dismal situation, but he
must know how much I am embarrassed. . . .

"I am very low-spirited, and of course my letter is very dull.
I will not lengthen it out in the same strain, but conclude with
what alone will be acceptable, an assurance of love and regard.

"Believe me to be ever your sincere and affectionate friend,

"MARY WOLLSTONECRAFT."

It was soon quite clear that the school must be altogether abandoned, or rather it abandoned the teachers, and
all three sisters determined to seek their livelihood as

governesses. Everina's home with her brother was comfort-less, and the shelter grudgingly given ; they could none of them find a home with their father and step-mother. Mr Wollstonecraft had again retired on very small means to Laugharne in Pembrokeshire, with his wife and younger children James and Charles. James soon afterwards went to sea, and Charles, after suffering great privations at home, emigrated, with, as will be seen, indifferent success. At Laugharne Mr Wollstonecraft led an obscure, besotted life, which could bring nothing but misery on his children, and the constant harassing thought of his daughters was how they could best help him, and wring from their brother Edward the support he had promised to give. Mrs Bishop and Everina obtained and abandoned many situations, the changes of which are not important, nor need any of them interest us except one which Mrs Bishop held in Pembrokeshire, from which were dated letters worthy to be quoted hereafter.

Mary Wollstonecraft obtained a situation as governess in the family of Lord Kingsborough in Ireland, through some friends of one of her chief patrons at Newington, and sailed for Ireland with these friends, Mr and Mrs Prior, who were crossing to Dublin, in the autumn of 1787. Mr Prior, at this time Assistant Master at Eton, was a grandson of a former college porter, had obtained a King's Scholarship first at Eton and afterwards became Fellow of King's College, Cambridge. He built the red house opposite the west doorway of the chapel at Eton. One of his daughters became the wife of Dr Goodall, Provost of the College. Mary's life in Ireland will be sufficiently detailed in the letters she wrote thence, and little need be said beyond what she tells us. The "dear Margaret," to whom she was so sincerely attached, became afterwards Lady Mountcashel, was her close friend through life and Godwin's correspondent in after years. It is necessary however to draw particular attention to Mary Wollstonecraft's own religious views at this time, and to point out the tone of earnest orthodox piety which pervades them, and the high morality which also is their characteristic. For one of the chief slanders brought against the governess in long after days, was that she had corrupted the minds of her pupils, teaching them lax morality and false religion. On the contrary, her whole endeavour was to train them for higher pursuits, and to instill into them a desire for wider culture than fell to the lot of most girls in those days. Her sorrow was deep that her pupils' lives were such as to render sustained study and religious habits of mind alike difficult. The tone of Society in Ireland at that date, even in the highest families, would now scarcely be credited. Most of the women with whom Mary Wollstonecraft came in contact were frivolous, and most of the men were coarse. It is not wonderful that her spirits and health flagged, and that in spite of the affection of the one child to whom she was attracted she saw almost everything round her in gloomy colours.

The letters will now speak for themselves, or rather extracts from them, the lines omitted referring to domestic details devoid of interest.

Mary Wollstonecraft to George Blood.

"NEWINGTON GREEN, *May* 22*d* [1787].

"By this time, my dear George, I hope your father and mother have reached Dublin. I long to hear of their safe arrival. A few days after they set sail, I received a letter from Skeys. He laments his inability to assist them, and dwells on his own embarrassments. How glad I am they are gone." [It will be remembered that their voyage to Dublin, where Mr Blood hoped to obtain a situation, was brought about wholly through Mary's exertions, and in great measure by her money, ill able as she was to afford such assistance.] "My affairs are hastening to a crisis. . . . Some of my creditors cannot afford to wait for their money ; as to leaving England in debt, I am determined not to do it. . . Everina and Eliza are both endeavouring to go out into the world, the one as a companion, and the other as a teacher, and I believe I shall continue some time on the Green. I intend taking a little cheap lodging, and living without a servant, and the few scholars I have will maintain me. I have done with all worldly pursuits and wishes ; I only desire to submit without being dependent on the caprice of our fellow creatures. I shall have many solitary hours, but I have not much to hope for in life, and so it would be absurd to give way to fear. Besides, I try to look on the best side, and not to despond. While I am trying to do my duty in that station in which Providence has placed me, I shall enjoy some tranquil moments, and the pleasures I have the greatest relish for are not entirely out of my reach. . . . I have been trying to muster up my fortitude, and labouring for patience to bear my many trials. Surely when I could determine to survive Fanny, I can endure poverty and all the lesser ills of life. I dreaded, oh ! how I dreaded this time, and now it is arrived I am calmer than I expected to be. I have been very unwell ; my constitution is much impaired ; the prison walls are decaying, and the prisoner will ere long get free. . . .—Remember that I am your truly affectionate friend and sister,

"MARY WOLLSTONECRAFT."

The Same to the Same.

"NEWINGTON GREEN, *July 6th* [1787].

". . . Lady Kingsborough has written about me to Mrs Prior, and I wait for further particulars before I give my final answer. Forty pounds a year was the terms mentioned to me, and half of that sum I could spare to discharge my debts, and afterwards to assist Eliza. . . . I by no means like the proposal of being a governess. I should be shut out from society and be debarred the pleasures of imperfect friendship, as I should on every side be surrounded by unequals. To live only on terms of civility and common benevolence without any interchange of little acts of kindness and tenderness would be to me extremely irksome, but I touch on too tender a string. I said just now friendship, *even* friendship, the medicine, the cordial of life, was imperfect, and so is everything in a world which is meant to educate us for a better. Here we have no resting-place, nor any stable comfort, but what arises from our resignation to the will of Heaven, and our firm reliance on those precious promises delivered to us by Him who brought light and immortality into the world. He has told us not only that we may inherit eternal life, but that we shall be changed, if we do not perversely reject the offered grace. Your letters, my dear boy, afford me great pleasure. . . .—Yours,

"MARY."

Mary Wollstonecraft to Everina Wollstonecraft.

"ETON, *Octr. 9th, Sunday,* 1787.

[After saying that Mr and Mrs Prior do not leave for Ireland quite as soon as they had intended, she continues.] "'The time I spend here appears lost. While I remained in England I would fain have been near those I love. . . . I could not live the life they lead at Eton; nothing but dress and ridicule going forward, and I really believe their fondness for ridicule tends to make them affected, the women in their manners and the men in their conversation, for witlings abound and puns fly about like crackers, though you would scarcely guess they had any meaning in them, if you did not hear the noise they create. So much company without any sociability would be to me an insupportable fatigue. I am, 'tis true, quite alone in a crowd, yet cannot help reflecting on the scene around me, and my thoughts harass me. Vanity in one shape or other reigns triumphant. . . . My thoughts and wishes tend to that land where the God of love will wipe away all tears from our eyes, where sincerity and truth will flourish, and the imagination will not dwell on pleasing illusions, which vanish like dreams, when experience forces us to see things as they really are. With what delight do I anticipate the time when neither death nor accidents of any kind will interpose to separate me from those I love. . . .—Adieu ; believe me to be your affectionate friend and sister, "MARY WOLLSTONECRAFT."

The Same to the Same.

"THE CASTLE, MITCHELSTOWN, *Oct.* 30, 1787.

"Well, my dear Girl, I am at length arrived at my journey's end. I sigh when I say so, but it matters not. I must labour for content, and try to reconcile myself to a state which is contrary to every feeling of my soul. I can scarcely persuade myself that I am awake ; my whole life appears like a frightful vision, and equally disjointed. I have been so very low spirited for some days past, I could not write. All the moments I could spend in solitude were lost in sorrow and unavailing tears. There was such a solemn kind of stupidity about this place as froze my very blood. I entered the great gates with the same kind of feeling as I should have if I was going into the Bastille. You can make allowance for the feelings which the General would term ridiculous or artificial. I found I was to encounter a host of females—My Lady, her stepmother, and three sisters, and *Mrses.* and *Misses* without number, who of course would examine me with the most minute attention. I cannot attempt to give you a description of the family, I am so low ; I will only mention some of the things which particularly worry me. I am sure much more is expected from me than I am equal to. With respect to French, I am certain Mr P. has misled them, and I expect, in consequence of it, to be very much mortified. Lady K. is a shrewd, clever woman. a great talker. I have not seen much of her, as she is confined to her room by a sore throat ; but I have seen half a dozen of her companions, I mean not her children, but her dogs. To see a woman without any softness in her manners caressing animals, and using infantine expressions is, you may conceive, very absurd

and ludicrous, but a fine lady is a new species to me of animals.
I am, however, treated like a gentlewoman by every part of the
family, but the forms and parade of high life suit not my mind.
. . . I hear a fiddle below, the servants are dancing, and the rest
of the family are diverting themselves, I only am melancholy and
alone. To tell the truth, I hope part of my misery arises from
disordered nerves, for I would fain believe my mind is not so very
weak. The children are, literally speaking, wild Irish, unformed
and not very pleasing ; but you shall have a full and true account,
my dear girl, in a few days. . . .—I am your affectionate sister
and sincere friend,   " MARY WOLLSTONECRAFT."

The Same to Mrs Bishop.

"MITCHELSTOWN, *Nov.* 5*th* [1787].

". . . Now to introduce the *castle* to you, and all its inhabitants, a numerous tribe, I assure you. The castle is very pleasantly
situated, and commands the kind of prospect I most admire. Near
he house, literally speaking, is a cloud-capped hill, and altogether
he country is pleasant, and would please me when anything of the
kind could rouse my attention. But my spirits have been in continual agitation, and when they will be at rest, heaven only knows.
I fear I am not equal to the task I have been persuaded to undertake, and this fear worries me.

" Lady K. is a clever woman, and a well-meaning one, but not
of the order of being that I could love. With his Lordship I have
had little conversation, but his countenance does not promise more
than good humour, and a little *fun* not refined. Another face in
the house appears to me more interesting, a pale one, no other
than the author of 'Shepherds I have lost my love.' His wife is
with him—a gentle pleasing creature, and her sister, a beauty and
a sensible woman into the bargain. Besides them and several
visitors, we have resident here Lady K.'s stepmother, and her
three daughters, fine girls, just going to market, as their brother
says. I have committed to my care three girls, the eldest fourteen, by no means handsome, yet a sweet girl. She has a wonderful

capacity, but she has such a multiplicity of employments it has not room to expand itself, and in all probability will be lost in a heap of rubbish, miscalled accomplishments. I am grieved at being obliged to continue so wrong a system. She is very much afraid of her mother,—that such a creature should be ruled with a rod of iron, when tenderness would lead her anywhere ! She is to be always with me. I have just promised to send her love to my sister, so pray receive it. Lady K. is very civil, nay, kind, yet I cannot help fearing her. . . . You have a sneaking kindness, you say, for people of quality, and I almost forgot to tell you I was in company with a Lord Fingal in the packet. Shall I try to remember the titles of all the lords and viscounts I am in company with, not forgetting the clever things they say ? I would sooner tell you a tale of some humbler creatures ; I intend visiting the poor cabins ; as Miss K. is allowed to assist the poor, and I shall make a point of finding them out.

> " Adieu, my dear girl,
> " Yours affectionately,
> " MARY WOLLSTONECRAFT."

Mary Wollstonecraft to Everina Wollstonecraft.

"MITCHELSTOWN, *Nov.* 17, [1787].

. . . "Confined to the society of a set of silly females, I have no social converse, and their boisterous spirits and unmeaning laughter exhaust me, not forgetting hourly domestic bickerings. The topics of matrimony and dress take their turn, not in a very sentimental style—alas, poor sentiment ! it has no residence here. I almost wish the girls were novel readers and romantic ; I declare false refinement is better than none at all, but these girls under-stand several languages, and have read *cartloads* of history, for their mother was a prudent woman. Lady K.'s passion for animals fills up the hours which are not spent in dressing. All her children have been ill—very disagreeable fevers. Her ladyship visited them in a formal way, though their situation called forth my tenderness, and I endeavoured to amuse them, while she lavished awkward fondness on her dogs. I think now I hear her infantine lisp. She rouges—and in short is a fine lady, without fancy or sensibility. I am almost tormented to death by dogs. But you will perceive I am not under the influence of my darling passion— pity ; it is not always so, I make allowance and adapt myself, talk of getting husbands for the *Ladies*—and the *dogs*, and am wonderfully entertaining ; and then I retire to my room, form figures in the fire, listen to the wind, or view the Gotties, a fine range of mountains near us, and so does time waste away in apathy or misery. . . . I am drinking asses' milk, but do not find it of any service. I am very ill, and so low-spirited my tears flow in torrents almost insensibly. I struggle with myself, but I hope my Heavenly Father will not be extreme to mark my weakness, and that He will have compassion on a poor bruised reed, and pity a miserable wretch, whose sorrows He only knows. . . . . I almost wish my warfare was over." . . . [*The rest is lost.*]

The letters after this date show some improvement, both in health and spirits, though she was much troubled about family matters, which it is not very easy to understand in full from the allusions in the letters. It would appear, however, that Edward Wollstonecraft, the elder brother, not only refused to contribute anything to the support of his father, which fell almost wholly on Mary, but declined to afford a home any longer to Everina, who had been with him for some time. He also retained in his hands a sum of money, apparently a legacy, which the sisters conceived should have been divided between them all. He seems to have been selfish and extravagant, though doing a fair business as an attorney. The letters which passed be- tween the sisters are either of no special interest or harp on the same string as those already quoted. In the winter of 1787 the Kingsborough family went to Dublin, and the letters thence again afford suitable extracts.

Mary Wollstonecraft to Everina Wollstonecraft.

"DUBLIN, *March 24th*, 1788.

" . . . I believe I told you before that as a nation I do not admire the Irish, and as to the great world and its frivolous ceremonies I cannot away with them. They fatigue one; I thank Heaven that I was not so unfortunate as to be born a lady of quality. I am now reading Rousseau's 'Emile,' and love his paradoxes. He chooses a common capacity to educate, and gives as a reason that a genius will educate itself. However he rambles into that chimerical world in which I have too often wandered, and draws the usual conclusion that all is vanity and vexation of spirit. He was a strange, inconsistent, unhappy, clever creature, yet he possessed an uncommon portion of sensibility and penetration. . . . Adieu, yours sincerely,

"MARY."

The Same to [the Same or Mrs Bishop].

"DUBLIN, *March 14th*, 1788.

" . . . I am very weak to-day, but I can account for it. The day before yesterday there was a masquerade; in the course of conversation some time before, I happened to wish to go to it. Lady K. offered me two tickets for myself and Miss Delane to accompany me. I refused them on account of the expense of dressing properly. She then to obviate that objection lent me a black domino. I was out of spirits, and thought of another excuse; but she proposed to take me and Betty Delane to the houses of several people of fashion who saw masques. We went to a great number, and were a tolerable, nay, a much admired group. Lady K. went in a domino with a smart cockade; Miss Moore dressed in the habit of one of the females of the new discovered islands; Betty D. as a forsaken shepherdess, and your sister Mary in a black domino. As it was taken for granted the stranger who had just arrived could not speak the language, I was to be her interpreter, which afforded me an ample field for satire. I happened to be very melancholy in the morning, as I am almost every morning, but at night my fever gives me false spirits : this night the lights, the novelty of the scene, and all things together contributed to make me *more* than half mad. I gave full scope to a satirical vein and suppose . . . " [*The rest is lost*].

From Dublin Lord and Lady Kingsborough and their family went to Bristol, Hotwells, and Bath, and from these places again the letters complain bitterly of the tone of society in which Mary found herself. She speaks of the " dissipated lives led by the women of quality," and finds that " in many respects the great and little vulgar resemble each other, and in none more than in the motives which induce them to marry." Her health was better away from Ireland, yet the employment continued to be thoroughly uncongenial to her nature, while she had nothing in common with her employers. It is, therefore, not wonderful that in the autumn of this year Lady Kingsborough dismissed her governess. In addition to the long standing want of cordiality Lady Kingsborough had a new grievance because the love which her children were unable to give to her was bestowed on a stranger. In one of her letters Mary Wollstonecraft speaks of one of the younger children having cried herself sick because she was to go into the country with her mother alone, and Margaret above all the others showed the great affection she felt for one who in return was devoted to her. During the year spent with Lady Kingsborough, Mary wrote a tale called by her own name "Mary," and devoted in a measure to the record of her own deep friendship with Fanny Blood.

Mr Johnson, the Publisher, had been struck with the promise Mary Wollstonecraft had shown before she went to Ireland. By his strong advice she had greatly improved her knowledge of French, and he now proposed to her that she should settle in lodgings not far from his house of business, and promised her constant literary work, chiefly to consist in translating from the French. This offer she at once accepted, and Lady Kingsborough having parted with her in London, whither the family had come for the winter, the dismissal and the new life were communicated to her sister in one and the same letter.

Mary Wollstonecraft to Everina Wollstonecraft.

" LONDON, *Nov. 7th,* 1788.

". . . I am, my dear girl, once more thrown on the world; I *have* left Lord K.'s, and they return next week to Mitchelstown. I long since imagined that my departure would be sudden." [From another letter. " The regret Margaret showed, when I left her for a short time, was Lady K.'s pretext for parting with me. They had frequent quarrels, and the consequence was this determination."] "I have not *seen* Mrs Burgh, but I have informed her of this circumstance, and at the same time mentioned to her, that I was determined not to see any of my friends till I am in a way to earn my own subsistence. And to this determination I *will* adhere. You can conceive how disagreeable pity and advice would be at this juncture. I have two other cogent reasons. Before I go on will you pause, and if, after deliberating, you will promise not to mention to any one what you know of my designs, though you may think my requesting you to conceal them unreasonable, I will trust to your honour, and proceed. Mr Johnson, whose uncommon kindness, I believe, has saved me from despair and vexation, I shrink back from, and feared to encounter, assures me that if I exert my talents in writing I may support myself in a comfortable way. I am then going to be the first of a new genus; I tremble at the attempt, yet if I fail *I* only suffer, and should I succeed my dear girls will ever in sickness have a home, and a refuge, where for a few months in the year they may forget the cares that disturb the rest. I shall strain every nerve to obtain a situation for Eliza nearer town : in short, I am once more involved in schemes, heaven only knows whether they will answer! yet while they are pursued life slips away. I would not on any account inform my father or Edward of my designs—you and Eliza are the only part of the family I am interested about, I wish to be a mother to you both. My undertaking would subject me to ridicule, and an inundation of friendly advice to which I cannot listen ; I must be independent. I wish to introduce you to Mr Johnson, you would respect him, and his sensible conversation would soon wear away the impression that a formality, or rather stiffness of manners, first makes to his disadvantage. I am sure you will love him, did you know with what tenderness and humanity he has behaved to me. . . .

" I cannot write more explicitly. I have indeed been very much harassed. But Providence has been very kind to me, and when I reflect on past mercies, I am not without hope with respect to the future. And freedom, even uncertain freedom, is dear. . . . This project has long floated in my mind. You know I am not born to tread in the beaten track, the peculiar bent of my nature pushes me on.—Adieu, believe me ever your sincere friend and affectionate sister, MARY WOLLSTONECRAFT."

" Seas will not now divide us, nor years elapse before we see each other."

The Same to the Same.

[No date, but a few days later.]

. . . [Mr Johnson] "has now settled me in a little house in a street near Blackfriars Bridge, and he assures me I may earn a comfortable maintenance if I exert myself. I have given him ' Mary,' and before your vacation I shall finish another book for young people, which I think has some merit. . . . Whenever I am tired of solitude I go to Mr Johnson's, and there I meet the kind of company I find most pleasure in. . . . I spent a day at Mrs. Trimmer's, and found her a truly respectable woman. I intend to try to get Bess a situation near me, and hope to succeed before the summer vacation ; at any rate, she shall spend the approaching one in my house. Mr J. knows that, next to obtaining the means of life, I wish to mitigate her and your fate. I have done with the delusions of fancy, I only live to be useful ; benevolence must fill every void in my heart. I have a room but not furniture. J. offered you both a bed in his house but that would not be pleasant. I believe I must try to purchase a bed, which I shall reserve for my poor girls while I have a house. If you pay any visits, you will comply with my whim, and not mention my place of abode or mode of life. I shall have a spur to push me forward, the desire of rendering two months in the year a little pleasanter than they would otherwise be to you and poor uncomfortable Bess. . . ."

The "other book for young people" is called "Original Stories from Real Life," and is intended to lead the minds of children to truth and goodness. It is beautifully written, though in a style now obsolete, and for which children in these days would not care, but it ought not to be quite unknown, since it was illustrated by some of Blake's most striking and beautiful woodcuts. The frontispiece, a simple composition of three figures standing in a doorway, up either side of which climbs a creeper; and another, in strong contrast, of a father standing over a bed on which lie his two children, who have died of want, can never be forgotten by those who have seen them.

A MS. note in Mr Johnson's writing gives an account of her work and life at this time :—

"She entered upon her house in George St. at Michaelmas 1787, and continued there till Michaelmas 1791.

"Here she wrote the 'Rights of Woman.' A translation from the Dutch of 'Young Grandison' was put into her hands, which she almost re-wrote. She translated 'Necker on Religious Opinions,' compiled the 'French Reader,' introducing some original pieces, and prefixed a preface to it. She began a novel under the title of the 'Cave of Fancy,' wrote many articles in the

'Analytical Review,'—'Answer to Burke,' 'Elements of Morality
from the German,' which she first studied here, and a translation
of 'Lavater's Physiognomy' from the French.

"Her brothers and sisters were occasionally with her when they
were unsettled. Her's was their home; and she took every
method to improve and prepare them for respectable situations.
She consulted with Mr Barlow on the probability of getting a farm
in America for Charles, which was determined upon, and he was
placed with a farmer here for instruction. He left England the
latter end of 1792. James, who had been at sea, was sent to
Woolwich for a few months to be under Mr Bonnycastle, and
afterwards on board Lord Hood's fleet as a midshipman, where he
was presently made a lieutenant. Much of the instruction which
all of them obtained was obtained under her own roof, and most,
if not all the situations which her sisters had were procured by her
exertions. In the beginning of 1788 she sent Everina to Paris for
improvement in the language.

"During her stay in George Street she spent many of her after-
noons and most of her evenings with me. She was incapable of
disguise. Whatever was the state of her mind, it appeared when
she entered, and the tone of conversation might easily be guessed.
When harassed, which was very often the case, she was relieved by
unbosoming herself, and generally returned home calm, frequently
in spirits.

"In a part of this period, which certainly was the most active of
her life, she had the care of her father's estate, which was attended
with no little trouble to both of us. She could not during this
time, I think, expend less than £200 on her brothers and sisters.

"At Michaelmas 1791 she went to Store Street, and continued
till Decr. 1792. She then went to Paris."

The correspondence with her family grew far more infrequent after the date of the last letter. Nor is there much
which needs extraction. The sisters were for some time at
Putney, when intercourse was more easy. Mary Wollstonecraft was very hard at work, and her sisters had little sym-

pathy with the direction in which her thoughts were now turning. It is not quite so clear why the correspondence with George Blood grew slack—indeed, who can tell why their own correspondence with one and another friend waxes and wanes?—but from the tone of the few that remain, the intimacy was less cordial than in former years. The little coolness, from whatever cause, passed away, and George Blood, now in a good position, seems to have written to Mary Wollstonecraft to ask if there were any hope that Everina would become his wife. The following extract shows the ill-success of his wooing:—

Mary Wollstonecraft to George Blood.

" LONDON, *Feb. 4th*, '91.

. . . " Now, my dear George, let me more particularly allude to your own affairs. I ought to have done so sooner, but there was an awkwardness in the business that made me shrink back. We have all, my good friend, a sisterly affection for you; and this very morning Everina declared to me that she had more affection for you than for either of her brothers; but accustomed to view you in that light, she cannot view you in any other. Let us then be on the old footing, love us as we love you, but give your heart to some worthy girl, and do not cherish an affection which may interfere with your prospects when there is no reason to suppose that it will ever be returned. Everina does not seem to think of marriage, she has no particular attachment, yet she was anxious when I spoke explicitly to her, to speak to you in the same terms, that she might correspond with you as she has ever done, with sisterly freedom and affection. . . .—Your affectionate friend,

" MARY WOLLSTONECRAFT."

It has been mentioned that Mrs Bishop and Everina Wollstonecraft were wanderers during these years. Mrs Bishop was teacher in a school at Market Harborough, at Putney, and at Henley; while her sister was at the same school at Putney, in Ireland, for a short time in France—now and then resident with her brother Edward, and then again for a time with Mary. But few letters are preserved from them during this time, nor have those which remain any special interest. In 1791 Mrs Bishop obtained a more permanent engagement in Pembrokeshire, near Laugharne, the town in which her father, supported by Mary, was now living. Extracts from the letters from this place will prove of interest. They will shew the wretchedness of the home of these three sisters, and the utter impossibility that they should ever permanently return to it in case of ill-health or other misfortune ; they will make it clear that the sisters had to frame for themselves a theory of life ; and, with such a training, how little likely it was this should be the usual one, about the sanctity of home, and of home relations and ties. They give a curious picture of the savagery still existing in far corners of the land among those who yet required a cultivated woman as governess, of ignorance and prejudice, and, towards the end of the series, the view taken by the family of Mary Wollstonecraft's change of life and opinions.

The situation at Upton Castle had been obtained for Mrs Bishop by Mr Woods, a Welsh clergyman, and an old friend of the family.

Mrs Bishop to Everina Wollstonecraft.

"[LAUGHARNE], *Tuesday Night, May* [30], 1791.

"My dearest Everina,—Here I am at Laugharne, without being recollected by anybody. Neither Miss Brown nor her mother have condescended to call on me. Many of the inhabitants have left it, others are dead, or else have quite forgotten Miss Betsy. Mrs Larne is the only one who wished to recollect me, but the old face she, sighing, says is quite gone. In fact, the town is now full of decayed people of fashion. Not one eye have I met that glistened with pleasure at meeting me unexpectedly, and I revisit our old walks with a degree of sadness I never felt before. The cliff-side, the churchyard, &c., &c., are all truly romantic and beautiful—a thousand times more so than I imagined ; yet all creates a sadness I cannot banish.

"The sight of my father's ghastly visage haunts me night and day ; for he is really worn to a mere skeleton, and has a dreadful cough that makes my blood run cold whenever I listen to it, and that is the greater part of the night, or else he groans most dreadfully ; yet he declares he has good nights. There cannot be a more melancholy sight than to see him, not able to walk ten yards without panting for breath, and continually falling ; still he is able to ride ten miles every day, and eat and *drink* very hearty. His neighbours think, as he has had such a wonderful escape, he will quite recover, though his death-like countenance tells me it is impossible. I am harassed to the last degree how to advise him to act ; if he gives up his horse *now*, he is a dead man in a very short time. When I beg of him to be more careful in money matters, he declares he will go to London, and force Ned ; or when I tell him how Mary has been distressed, in order to make him save in trifles, he is in a passion, and exhausts himself. He is mad to be in London. I represented matters as they are, that he might abridge himself of some unnecessary expenses ; but now he is too weak in mind and body to act with prudence. She is truly a well-meaning woman, and willing to do the little she can to lessen the debts.

"Charles is half naked, and is treated by my father in the way that he deserves, for he is at him perpetually ; he never even tried to get him into the Excise, or anywhere else. He is actually altered rather for the better, drinks never anything but water, and is much thinner, and all submission. . . . He now talks of listing for a soldier ; if he does, there is an end of him. . . . I am very cool to Charles, and have said all I can to rouse him ; but where can he go in his present plight ? Thanky, my dear, for your kind letter. I am afraid this will not raise your spirits. Pray tell M. my father received the note. I have many things to chat over with you when I get to my *Haven.* Shall I find peace when I get to the end of my journey? Good night."

The Same to the Same.

"UPTON, *June* 12, 1791.

". . . But were you to see my father's countenance. It is now, I really think, the most dreadful face I ever beheld! It appears constantly convulsed by ill-humour, and every unamiable feeling that can be expressed; his face is quite red, his hair grey and dirty, his beard long, and the clothes he wears not worth sixpence. In this plight he arrived at Upton the third night after my arrival, fearing my portmanteau was lost. I was strolling out with the girls, and was surprised to meet Mr Rees coming to meet us, and not less so when he stretched out his friendly hand to shake mine, saying, 'Who do you think is come to Upton? Your father! in his old clothes too, poor man! He thought you had lost your box.' The good man really thought I should be alarmed at my father's appearance, and was anxious to see me first. After keeping me awake the whole night, he went to Laugharne in the morning, displeased, I believe, at not being asked to spend the day. If you had seen the good old man trying to behave so that I might think he was pleased with my father. He is in truth a most amiable man, though not a very sensible one. He has Mrs Cotton's blush, and none of the tricks of old age. He was tutor to Tom" [name illegible]. "Molly was in his way, as she was waiting-maid in the same house, and he married her, from what motive I will not pretend to say. . . ."

The Same to the Same.

"UPTON, *June* 19, 1791.

". . . The only thing here that resembles man is a noble New-foundland dog, and a fine greyhound. Neptune and his friend Shark have contrived to find a corner in my heart, contrary to my reason. I look on them as *Friends;* indeed, when with them I am not quite alone ! They render my walks still more delightful. The situation of this spot is truly picturesque. The way to the house is through a fine wood, dreadfully neglected, so much so, that one can hardly find a path in it—surrounded by hills. Close to the castle is an old chapel, and near it is a cross, shaded by a yew tree, and many a lofty ash at a distance. The castle joins the house. In one of its turrets is my room, which is furnished in the Eastern manner, though half the ornaments must not be used, for the Captain gave them to Maria, and she must keep them for his sake. The library no one values, though it is a most excellent one. The arm-chair, however, and spacious bed, none of them claim. My room leads into a large drawing-room, which contains all that might be made useful. It has a door at one end that opens, and gives a full view of the woods. . . . There I often sit when all are fast asleep, as it is quite away from their *roosting* places. For though the kitchen was made fit for a nobleman, and the coach-house, stalls, laundry, &c., &c., are all rendered truly commodious, the good family here did not like to have their bed-rooms altered, no ! nor even the common sitting-parlour, which is a dark hole. . . . Their room is quite filled with chest upon chest, which are filled with trumpery sixty years old; and though they have hardly room to turn themselves, they will not let their boxes remain in the garret. Here is a strange medley ! a farthing candle, or one as thick as my wrist. Though they have drawers loaded with everything, they still make the shifts that necessity compelled them to in former times. . . . The girls have dozens of gowns never worn, which they only look at, and everything else that might be made useful. . . . They never have been permitted to walk, on account of wearing out shoes. I am certain I shall break the old woman's heart if I take them out a-walking. . . . Send me a few wax tapers, for a farthing one often falls to my share, and we go to bed very early. . . . Adieu."

IN her lonely lodging near Blackfriars, Mary Wollstonecraft had been writing an original work during the scant time she could give to it from her labours of translation. It was one which has ever been more known by name than by perusal, on a subject which even now excites acrimony rather than calm discussion. The very words, " A Vindication of the Rights of Woman," which was the title of the book, are held, without examination, to claim emancipation alike from law, from custom, and from morality. Yet it is evident that the writer, as she has shown herself in her letters, must have changed far more suddenly than is wont to be the case, if such were indeed the object she set before her in writing her treatise.

It is not among the least oddities of this singular work that it is dedicated to M. Talleyrand Perigord, late Bishop of Autun. Mary Wollstonecraft, always confiding and always charitable, still believed in him. She little knew how unstable was the liberalism for which she gave him credit, and though well aware that some of her opinions were opposed to those which Talleyrand had put forward in his pamphlet on National Education, she yet thought him quite sincere and working in the same direction as herself. Mary Wollstonecraft, like so many others, turned to France as the land from which was rising the day-star of a

I am obliged to recollect that I am writing to Fanny's brother — and this reflected affection will prevent my coldly subscribing myself a well wisher, in the style humanity dictates — for while I remember the friend of my youth I shall ever be particularly <u>interested</u> about your—and therefore shall a)) that I am

Yours <u>affectionately</u>
Mary Wollstonecraft

new time, yet, unlike many, she was far from considering
that all French manners were worthy of imitation. Even
in the Dedication to Talleyrand are some noble words in
defence of English cleanliness in life and talk, even of
seeming prudery, rather than much which is still tolerated
in France.

"The main argument" of the work "is built on this simple
principle, that if woman be not prepared by education to become
the companion of man, she will stop the progress of knowledge, for
truth must be common to all, or it will be inefficacious with respect
to its influence on general practice. And how can woman be
expected to co-operate, unless she know why she ought to be
virtuous?—unless freedom strengthen her reason till she compre-
hend her duty, and see in what manner it is connected with her
real good. If children are to be educated to understand the true
principle of patriotism, their mother must be a patriot; and the
love of mankind, from which an orderly train of virtues springs, can
only be produced by considering the moral and civil interest of
mankind; but the education and situation of woman at present
shuts her out from such investigations."—P. viii.

In the carrying out of this argument the most noticeable
fact is the extraordinary plainness of speech, and this it
was which caused all or nearly all the outcry. For Mary
Wollstonecraft did not, as has been supposed, attack the
institution of marriage, she did not assail orthodox religion,
she did not directly claim much which at the present day
is claimed for women by those whose arguments obtain
respectful hearing. The book was really a plea for equality
of education, a protest against being deemed only the play-
thing of man, an assertion that the intellectual rather than
the sexual intercourse was that which should chiefly be
desired in marriage, and which made its lasting happiness.
In maintaining these theses, in themselves harmless and to

us self-evident, she assailed the theories not only of
Rousseau in "Emile," which would have been easily borne,
but those of Dr Fordyce, whose sermons had long made a
part of a young woman's library, of Dr Gregory and others
whose words were as a gospel to the average English
nation, when she would teach her daughters less from her
own experience than in sounding periods whose gravity
simulated real authority.   She did but carry out what
Day had sketched in "Sandford and Merton," and Miss
Simmons was a young lady who might have been trained
by Mary Wollstonecraft herself.

It may, however, be admitted that her frankness on some
subjects is little less than astounding, and that matters are
discussed which are rarely named even among members of
the same sex, far less printed for both, while side blows are
administered to much which was then unquestioned, at
least in the society to which a woman's book would gain
admission.   The insistance on the reception of the Sacra-
ment in our colleges, the relics of Popery retained in them,
the weekly services she had noticed the Eton boys unwill-
ingly attend, which was "only a disgusting skeleton of the
former state," in which "all the solemnity that interested
the imagination if it did not purify the heart is stripped
off"—in fact, the whole system which had come before her
in her residence with Mr Prior was rudely criticised.   Nor
were other sacred institutions dealt with more gently than
our schools and universities.   The fallacy by which virtue
is confounded with reputation was laid bare, and she by no
means shrinks from uncovering the worst sores of society.

Yet for extreme plain speaking, there was much reason
and excuse.   The times were coarser than ours, the days
were not so far distant when the scenes were possible and
the dangers real which Richardson's novels pourtray.   The

very book she assails, "Dr Fordyce's Sermons," contains words spoken from the pulpit to young women which would now be considered an outrage on the congregation. Mary Wollstonecraft shrunk from no directness in dealing with the most dangerous and explosive subjects.

It was not only the plain speaking which alarmed, and not only that a woman spoke, but every page showed that she too was affected by the thoughts which claimed rights for men, and the demand for these had issued in the French Revolution.

The faults of the book are grave over and above those of the time ; it is ill-considered, hasty, and rash, but its merits are great also ; there is much that is valuable for these days also—it is fresh, vigorous, and eloquent, and most remarkable as the herald of the demand not even yet wholly conceded by all, that woman should be the equal and friend, not the slave and the toy of man.

One passage only shall here be quoted. It is one in which Mary Wollstonecraft gives her views on elementary education, and in favour of mixed schools.

"Day schools should be established by Government in which boys and girls might be educated together. The school for the younger children, from five to nine years of age, ought to be absolutely free, and open to all classes, . . . where boys and girls, the rich and the poor, should meet together. To prevent any of the distinctions of vanity, they should be dressed alike, and all obliged to submit to the same discipline, or leave the school. The school-room ought to be surrounded by a large piece of ground, in which the children might be usefully exercised, for at this age they should not be confined to any sedentary employment for more than an hour at a time. But these relaxations might all be rendered a part of elementary education, for many things improve and amuse the senses when introduced as a kind of show, to the principles of which dryly laid down children would turn a deaf ear. For instance, botany, mechanics, and astronomy. Reading, writing, arithmetic, natural history, and some simple experiments in natural philosophy might fill up the day, but these pursuits should never encroach on gymnastics in the open air. The elements of religion, history, the history of man, and politics might also be taught by conversations in the Socratic form.

"After the age of nine, girls and boys intended for domestic employments or mechanical trades ought to be removed to other trades, and receive instruction in some measure appropriated to the destination of each individual, the two sexes being still together in the morning, but in the afternoon the girls should attend a school where plain work, mantua making, millinery, &c., would be their employment.

"The young people of superior abilities or fortune might now be taught in another school the dead and living languages, the elements of science, and continue the study of history and politics, on a more extensive scale, which would not exclude polite literature.

"Girls and boys still together? I hear some reader ask. Yes. And I should not fear any other consequence than that some early attachment might take place, which, whilst it had the best effect on the moral character of young people, might not perfectly agree with the views of the parents, for it will be a long time, I fear, before the world is so enlightened that parents only anxious to render their children virtuous will let them choose companions for life themselves."—*A Vindication of the Rights of Woman*, pp. 386-389.

That the publication of "The Rights of Woman" should prove startling and even shocking to the author's sisters as it did to many other people, is not surprising, but the exhibition of small spite which is to be found in the following letter is unworthy of one for whom the writer had made, and was again ready to make, such great sacrifices.

Charles the worthless had been taken to London, wholly
by the kindness of his sister Mary, who, since the issue of
her book, which had made her in some degree a public
character, took the brevet rank of *Mrs* Wollstonecraft.

Mrs Bishop to Everina Wollstonecraft.

" UPTON CASTLE, *July* 3*d*, 1792.

". . . He" [Charles] "informs me too that *Mrs Wollstonecraft*
is grown quite handsome ; he adds likewise that being conscious
she is on the wrong side of thirty she now endeavours to set off
those charms she once despised to the best advantage. This
entre nous, for he is delighted with her kindness and affection
to him.

"So the author of ' The Rights of Woman' is going to France !
I dare say her chief motive is to promote poor Bess's comfort, or
thine, my girl, at least I think she will thus reason. Well, in spite
of reason, when Mrs W. reaches the Continent she will be but a
woman ! I cannot help painting her in the height of all her
wishes, at the very summit of happiness, for will not ambition fill
every chink of her Great Soul (for such I really think hers) that is
not occupied by love? After having drawn this sketch, you can
hardly suppose me so sanguine as to expect my pretty face will be
thought of when matters of State are in agitation, yet I know you
think such a miracle not impossible. I wish I could think it at
all probable, but, alas ! it has so much the appearance of castle-
building that I think it will soon disappear like the ' baseless fabric
of a vision, and leave not a wrack behind.'

"And you actually have the vanity to imagine that in the
National Assembly, personages like M. and F[useli] will bestow a
thought on two females whom nature meant to 'suckle fools and
chronicle small beer.' "

The scheme of going to France, of which Mrs Bishop
speaks above, had been announced. to her sister Everina
shortly before. Everina Wollstonecraft had spent a few

weeks in France for the sake of perfecting her French
accent; and there was a plan that Mrs Bishop also should
go for the same purpose.

Mary Wollstonecraft to Everina Wollstonecraft.

"LONDON, *June* 20*th,* '92.

". . . I have been considering what you say respecting Eliza's
residence in France. For some time past Mr and Mrs Fuseli, Mr
Johnson, and myself have talked of a summer excursion to Paris;
it is now determined on, and we think of going in about six weeks.
I shall be introduced to many people, my book" ["A Vindication
of the Rights of Woman"] "has been translated, and praised in
some popular prints, and Mr Fuseli of course is well known; it is
then very probable that I shall hear of some situation for Eliza,
and I shall be on the watch. We intend to be absent only six
weeks; if then I fix on an eligible situation for her she may avoid
the Welsh winter. This journey will not lead me into any extraordinary expense, or I should put it off to a more convenient
season, for I am not, as you may suppose, very flush of money,
and Charles is wearing out the clothes which were provided for his
voyage" [to America at her expense], "still I am glad he has
acquired a little practical knowledge of farming. . . ."

A candid friend who published anonymously in 1803,
"A Defence of the Character and Conduct of the late Mary
Wollstonecraft Godwin," but whose "Defence" is mingled
with a good deal of venom, says that "though we are not
expressly informed," there seems a probability that she
had experienced a disappointment in her earlier years, and
that such disappointment "tended to increase her irrit-
ability." The writer goes on to say,

"The first sexual attachment that is plainly avowed was towards
Mr Fuseli. . . . She had reason to esteem him as a particular
friend, but on finding that her regard for him had gradually
assumed a more interesting form, mark her prudence and resolu-

tion. No sooner had she analysed her feelings, traced them to
their real source, discovered their tendency, and weighed them in the
balance of moral obligation, than, with a just respect for herself as
well as for the other parties interested, she determined to make a
sacrifice of her private desires upon the altar of Virtue; and in
order to snap the tie that seemed likely to occasion uneasiness
either to herself or her friends, she prudently resolved to retire
into another country, far remote from the object who had uninten-
tionally excited the tender passion in her breast."—(Pp. 58-60.)

The same story, told with much greater circumstance,
appears in Knowles's "Life of Fuseli," and is supposed to
be confirmed by extracts from her letters which are given.
But one of them, the last written after her return from
France, most certainly does not refer to any attachment to
Fuseli; and Mr Knowles is so extremely inaccurate in
regard to all else that he says of her, that his testimony
may be wholly set aside, finding, as it does, no confirmation whatever from her correspondence, and very little from
a few ill-natured remarks of Mrs Bishop, which do not
justify the malignant gossip.

Godwin himself, in his Memoir of his wife speaks also of
her intimacy with Fuseli, saying that had he been unmarried, he would probably have been the man of her
choice. He goes on to declare that the friends were only
friends, but his mention of the matter at all is only one
of those strange instances of his somewhat morbid habit
of dwelling on matters of which it would have been well
to take no notice. It is probable that he had only heard
of the more unfavourable version of the story at second-
hand, and, even after careful attention to her husband's
words, the correspondence and the uninterrupted friendship
with Mrs Fuseli would seem wholly to clear Mary Wollstonecraft's memory from the imputation of any feeling for

Fuseli in which there is reason for blame even by the most censorious.

The Fuselis and Mr Johnson having given up the tour, Mary went to France alone in December, and certainly no object whatever finds place in her letters but the one of rendering herself as good a French speaker as she was already a reader, and incidentally of finding a situation for her sister, Mrs Bishop, among the many leading Frenchmen who were then so eager for all that was English. She found a home at first in the house of Madame Filiettaz, *neé* Bregantz, the daughter of Madame Bregantz, in whose school at Putney Mrs Bishop and Everina Wollstonecraft had both been teachers. The following extract gives her first impressions of Paris at a critical time, though none then knew *how* critical.

Mary Wollstonecraft to Everina Wollstonecraft.

"Paris, *Dec. 24th,* '92.

"To-morrow I expect to see Aline" [Mme. Filiettaz] ; "during her absence the servants endeavoured to render the house—a most excellent one—comfortable to me, but as I wish to acquire the language as fast as I can, I was sorry to be obliged to remain so much alone. I apply so closely to the language, and labour so continually to understand what I hear that I never go to bed without a headache, and my spirits are fatigued with endeavouring to form a just opinion of public affairs. The day after to-morrow I expect to see the King at the bar, and the consequences that will follow I am almost afraid to anticipate.

"I have seen very little of Paris—the streets are so dirty, and I wait till I can make myself understood before I call upon Madame Laurent, &c. Miss Williams has behaved very civilly to me, and I shall visit her frequently, because I *rather* like her, and I meet French company at her house. Her manners are affected, yet the simple goodness of her heart continually breaks through the varnish, so that one would be more inclined, at least I should, to love than admire her. Authorship is a heavy weight for female shoulders, especially in the sunshine of prosperity. Of the French I will not speak till I know more of them. They seem the people of all others for a stranger to come amongst, yet sometimes when I have given a commission which was eagerly asked for, it has not been executed, and when I ask for an explanation, I allude to the servant-maid, a quick girl, who, an't please you, has been a teacher in an English boarding-school, dust is thrown up with a self-sufficient air, and I am obliged to appear to see her meaning clearly, though she puzzles herself, that I may not make her feel her ignorance ; but you must have experienced the same thing. I will write to you soon again, meantime let me hear from you, and believe me yours sincerely and affectionately, "M. W."

Two days afterwards she addressed a letter to Mr Johnson. It has already been printed in the "Posthumous Works of Mary Wollstonecraft Godwin: London, 1798." These volumes were edited by Godwin, but are so very unlikely to be known to many readers at the present day, that the letter deserves quotation here.

Mary Wollstonecraft to Mr Johnson.

"PARIS, *December* 26, 1792.

"I should immediately on the receipt of your letter, my dear friend, have thanked you for your punctuality ; for it highly gratified me, had I not wished to wait, till I could tell you that this day was not stained with blood. [Wednesday, Dec. 26th, was the day on which the King appeared to plead, by his advocate Desèze.] Indeed, the prudent precautions taken by the National Convention to prevent a tumult, made me suppose that the dogs of faction would not dare to bark, much less to bite, however true to their scent ; and I was not mistaken ; for the citizens, who were all called out, are returning home with composed countenances,

I.   O

shouldering their arms. About nine o'clock this morning the King passed by my window, moving silently along—excepting now and then a few strokes on the drum, which rendered the stillness more awful—through empty streets, surrounded by the National Guards, who, clustering round the carriage, seemed to deserve their name. The inhabitants flocked to their windows, but the casements were all shut; not a voice was heard, nor did I see anything like an insulting gesture. For the first time since I entered France, I bowed to the majesty of the people, and respected the propriety of behaviour, so perfectly in unison with my own feelings. I can scarcely tell you why, but an association of ideas made the tears flow insensibly from my eyes, when I saw Louis sitting, with more dignity than I expected from his character, in a hackney-coach, going to meet death, where so many of his race have triumphed. My fancy instantly brought Louis XIV. before me, entering the capital with all his pomp, after one of the victories most flattering to his pride, only to see the sunshine of prosperity overshadowed by the sublime gloom of misery. I have been alone ever since; and though my mind is calm, I cannot dismiss the lively images that have filled my imagination all the day. Nay, do not smile, but pity me; for once or twice lifting my eyes from the paper, I have seen eyes glare through a glass door opposite my chair, and bloody hands shook at me. Not the distant sound of a footstep can I hear. My apartments are remote from those of the servants, the only persons who sleep with me in an immense hotel, one folding-door opening after another. I wish I had even kept the cat with me! I want to see something alive, death, in so many frightful shapes, has taken hold of my fancy. I am going to bed, and, for the first time in my life, I cannot put out the candle. M. W."

The news which reached England from France was of the most scanty kind, and little was heard of individuals after the troubles in Paris really began. Mrs Bishop's letters are full of complaints that she so seldom has news of Mary; for, in her ignorance of what was really occurring, she even professes herself ready to join her. Those among whom she lived did not wish to hear more, and marvelled that anyone, especially a woman, should take any interest in politics.

Mrs Bishop to Everina Wollstonecraft.

"UPTON CASTLE, *January* 20, 1793.

". . . I never can get to see a paper; and if anyone of our Bears call, the whole family leave the room when I say a word about Politics, or else order them to talk of something else; and, of course, the conversation turns on *Murphy* or *Irish Potatoes*, or Tommy Paine, whose effigy they burnt at Pembroke the other day. Nay, they talk of immortalizing Miss Wollstonecraft in the like manner; but all end in Damning all Politics: what good will they do men? and what rights have men that three meals a-day will not supply? So argues a Welshman. I heard a clergyman say that he was sure there was no more harm in shooting a Frenchman, than in lifting his piece at a Bird. And a gentleman—I cannot find out who—sent me this receipt:—

"'An effectual cure for the bite of a Mad Frenchman: Mix a grain of common sense in the milk of human nature with two grains of honour, and half-a-dram of loyalty; let the patient take this night and morning, and he will be in his senses all day.'"

The Same to the Same.

"UPTON CASTLE, *February* 10, '93.

". . . I should like to know what you felt on first hearing Louis's death. I own I was shocked, but not deluged in tears. In short, I could bear to hear it read, and hoped they had some motive for such an act of cruelty that our newspapers did not explain. But to hear him cried up as the *best* of men, and that no man's sufferings or *fortitude* equalled the King of France's, is to me quite novel. The depth of his understanding and the

goodness of his heart, is all the men here can talk of. Was he
really that innocent kind of man they here represent him? The
military men at Pembroke, who have left the service, furnish
opinions for the people, who declare, with one voice, that the
French are *all* Atheists, and the most bloody Butchers the world
ever produced. Rees is pale with passion if the subject is introduced, declaring the world is going to be at an end ; that the
Assassins are *Instruments* in the hands of Providence. I can
hardly tell you, then, with what delight I read Fox's manly
speech, or how clear and replete with good sense it appeared to
me ; in short, every word carried conviction with it ; yet this man
is condemned, with Paine, as an unworthy wretch. I was obliged
to sit up till three this morning, to read the debates ; for a gentleman had lent the paper to R., and I could not have it.

"God bless you.—Yours affectionately,   ELIZA."

In the following year some refugee French priests were
lodging at Pembroke, and Mrs Bishop went from Saturday
to Monday in each week to that town, spending nearly all
her time with two of them, an aged bishop and his brother,
for the sake of learning French more thoroughly. The
following extract describes their reception in Pembrokeshire :—

The Same to the Same.

"UPTON CASTLE, *May 24th,* '94.

". . . I believe I told you they fled from wretched France.
They landed near Haverford West, and were used worse, they
declare, than if they had been in Paris. The P[rimat], though he
had fainted among the savages, had a stone flung at his head, and
[was] guarded all night—though he expected every moment to be
his last ; for, in spite of the letter to Government, they were
treated as Republicans. This good creature was compelled to
walk three miles, though nearly fainting at every step he took,
surrounded by men, women, and children, gazing, not at his pale
face, but at a handkerchief that supplied the place of a wig that

the waves had stolen from him. The moment he was housed at
Pembroke, all the children were admitted into the room, where he
sat for many hours, his head sunk on the table, till at last he was
allowed to go to bed. . . .

"He was for a year and a half concealed by friends from the
Republicans, and was so narrowly watched, that neither of the
brothers saw daylight during that period. They at last made their
escape, merely with the hope of saving the family who had sheltered
them. At fifty, it is dreadful to be snatched from the lap of
abundance, for M. Graux had his carriage and every elegance of
life, and to feel all the horrors of dependence in a strange country."

In the meantime, Mary Wollstonecraft's position in France
had become extremely difficult, if not precarious. It was
impossible that she should receive remittances from England, nor could she return when once war was declared.
It was at this juncture, at some time in the spring or summer of 1793, that she met Mr Gilbert Imlay, an American
then living in Paris. He had been a captain in the
American army during the late war, and was afterwards a
commissioner for laying out land in the back settlements.
He appears to have been a speculator in many ways, without real fortune, but with some command of money, and to
have been an attractive person. He certainly was an able
man, for a work published by him, called "A Topographical
Description of the Western Territory of North America,"
is a model of what a monograph on a new country should
be. It is clear, full, and condensed, yet not so much as to
hinder the reader even now from finding it an interesting
work, and in its own day it went through many editions.
The kindness he showed Mary Wollstonecraft disposed
her to look on him favourably, and she soon gave him
a very sincere affection. Opposed as were her views to

those of the majority of women in her own, and even
in this day, yet they were those which now are, except
on one point, held by very many cultivated women,
without a shadow of blame attaching to them. .Her
opinions on the equality of the sexes, on the social and
political position of women, might now be held without
remark, and it would not be too much to say that she
was simply in advance of her age in giving expression
on those subjects to thoughts which are held increas-
ingly by men and women of advanced political views,
but of many shades of devout religion. On the question
alone of the relation of the sexes, there is no indication
of any approximation to her theories. Her view had now
become that mutual affection was marriage, and that the
marriage tie should not bind after the death of love, if love
should die. It must be remembered that her own experience
of family life was not likely to ennoble it in her eyes. Her
father, Mr Blood, Mr Bishop, and Lord Kingsborough, in
whom chiefly she had seen what husbands may be, were not favourable specimens ; her sister was living as an unwived wife,
without any prospect of such a separation as would enable
her to form another tie. Men who were far from acting on
these theories as did Rousseau, yet who were moving the
minds of men to an unprecedented extent, were proclaiming
that man should return to a more " natural" system ; the
accidental defects of certain marriages were pointed out as
the inherent vices of all.

Yet it is probable that what Mary Wollstonecraft held,
as a theory, in common with others who did not put their
theories into act, would have been held by her most blame-
lessly, had it not been for the untoward circumstances which
seemed to claim that she should act upon them. A legal
marriage with Mr Imlay was difficult, if not impossible,

Her position as a British subject was full of danger ; a marriage would have forced her openly to declare herself as such. It may be doubted whether the ceremony, if any could have taken place, would have had validity in England. Under the protection of Imlay, and passing as his wife without such preliminary declaration, her safety was assured. Imlay, long after this period, declared her to be his wife in a document which in some cases would be considered as constituting a marriage. She believed that his love, which was to her sacred, would endure. No one can read her letters without seeing that she was a pure, high-minded and refined woman, and that she considered herself, in the eyes of God and man, his wife. Religious as she was, and with a strong moral sense, she yet made the grand mistake of supposing that it is possible for one woman to undo the consecrated custom of ages, to set herself in opposition to the course of society and not to be crushed by it. And she made the no less fatal mistake of judging Imlay by her own standard, and thinking that he was as true, as impassioned, as self-denying as herself.

Mary Wollstonecraft was living with Imlay as his wife in August 1793, in Paris, but he was soon afterwards called to Havre on business, and was absent for some months. During this period letters passed between them, of which her own were afterwards returned to her, and were published after her death. " They are," as Godwin said of them, " the offspring of a glowing imagination, and a heart penetrated with the passion it essays to describe." But they are the letters of a tender and devoted *wife*, who feels no doubt of her position. Towards the close of 1793, Imlay had established himself in some commercial business at Havre, where Mary joined him, and there, in the spring of 1794, she gave birth to a

girl, who received the name of Fanny, in memory of the
dear friend of her youth.

Some rumours of all these circumstances had reached the
sisters in England, but only such as to render them extremely perplexed as to the true state of the case.

Charles Wollstonecraft to Mrs Bishop.

" PHILADELPHIA, *June 16th* 1794.

[After saying he was doing extremely well, and making an offer
of a home or assistance to his sisters, he continues] " I heard
from Mary, six months ago, by a gentleman who knew her at
Paris, and since that have been informed she is married to Captain
Imlay of this country." . . .

Mrs Bishop to Everina Wollstonecraft.

" UPTON CASTLE, *August* 15th 1794.
[Enclosing copy of the above.]

. . . " Can this be a dream, my heart's best friend ?   I would I
could fancy these things matters of fact.   I mean the poor fellow's
wonderful good luck in so short a time.   I own I want faith" [her
want of faith was justified ; since Charles's account of himself proved
pure brag], " nay, doubt my senses, so I have sent you word for
word, to spell and put together. . . . If Mary is *actually* married
to Mr Imlay, it is not impossible but she might settle there" [in
America] " too.   Yet Mary cannot be *Married !!*   It is natural
to conclude her protector is her *husband*.   Nay, on reading Charles's
letter, I for an instant believed it true.   I would, my Everina, we
were out of suspense, for all at present is uncertainty and the most
cruel suspense ; still Johnson does not repeat things at random,
and that the very same tale should have crossed the Atlantic
makes me almost believe that the once M. is now Mrs Imlay, and
a mother.   Are we ever to see this mother and her babe ?"

In September 1794, business called Mr Imlay to London,
and Mary returned to Paris.   A separation of some months

chilled his affection, and though they met again, his desertion of her had now really begun.

Mr Imlay to Mrs Bishop.

[LONDON, *November* 1794.]

"MY DEAR MADAM.—Mr Johnson gave me your acceptable favor
inclosing one to Mrs Imlay, saying it was for her, which leaving
me ignorant of being included, I could not return an immediate
answer; since which time I have been out of town. I hope
this circumstance will appear to you a sufficient apology for my
silence, and that you will be pleased to consider it a good reason
for preventing a forfeit of that claim to humanity or at least
respect and esteem for a person so affectionately loved by my
dear Mary as yourself, which you say had already been impressed
on your mind.

"As to your sister's visiting England, I do not think she will
previous to a peace, and perhaps not immediately after such an
event. However, be that as it may, we shall both of us continue
to cherish feelings of tenderness for you, and a recollection of
your unpleasant situation, and we shall also endeavour to alleviate
its distress by all the means in our power. The present state of
our fortune is rather" [word omitted]. "However you must know
your sister too well, and I am sure you judge of that knowledge
too favourably to suppose that whenever she has it in her power
she will not apply some specific aid to promote your happiness. I
shall always be most happy to receive your letters, but as I shall
most likely leave England the beginning of next week, I will thank
you to let me hear from you as soon as convenient, and tell me
ingenuously in what way I can serve you in any manner or respect.
I am in but indifferent spirits occasioned by my long absence from
Mrs Imlay, and our little girl, while I am deprived of a chance
of hearing from them.—Adieu, yours truly,

"G. IMLAY."

Mary Wollstonecraft to Everina Wollstonecraft.

"HAVRE, *March* 10*th* '94.

"MY DEAR GIRL.—It is extremely uncomfortable to write to you
thus without expecting, or even daring to ask for an answer, lest I
should involve others in my difficulties, and make them suffer for
protecting me. The French are at present so full of suspicion that
had a letter of James's imprudently sent to me been opened, I
would not have answered for the consequence. I have just
sent off great part of my MS., which Miss Williams would
fain have had me burn, following her example; and to tell
you the truth, my life would not have been worth much had
it been found. It is impossible for you to have any idea of
the impression the sad scenes I have been witness to have left on
my mind. The climate of France is uncommonly fine, the country
pleasant, and there is a degree of ease and even simplicity in the
manners of the common people which attaches me to them. Still
death and misery, in every shape of terror, haunt this devoted
country. I certainly am glad that I came to France, because I
never could have had a just opinion of the most extraordinary
event that has ever been recorded, and I have met with some uncommon instances of friendship, which my heart will ever gratefully
store up, and call to mind when the remembrance is keen of the
anguish it has endured for its fellow-creatures at large—for the
unfortunate beings cut off around me, and the still more unfortunate survivors. If any of the many letters I have written have
come to your hands or Eliza's, you know that I am safe, through
the protection of an American, a most worthy man, who joins to
uncommon tenderness of heart and quickness of feeling, a sound-
ness of understanding and reasonableness of temper rarely to be
met with. Having also been brought up in the interior parts of
America, he is a most natural, unaffected creature. I am with
him now at Havre, and shall remain there, till circumstances
point out what is necessary for me to do. Before I left Paris, I
attempted to find the Laurents, whom I had several times previously sought for, but to no purpose. And I am apt to think that

it was very prudent in them to leave a shop that had been the resort of the nobility.

"Where is poor Eliza? From a letter I received many many months after it was written, I suppose she is in Ireland. Will you write to tell her that I most affectionately remember her, and still have in my mind some places for her future comfort. Are you well? But why do I ask? you cannot reply to me. This thought throws a damp on my spirits whilst I write, and makes my letter rather an act of duty than a present satisfaction. God bless you! I will write by every opportunity, and am yours sincerely and affectionately,   MARY."

The Same to the Same.

[PARIS, *September* 1794.]

"As you must, my dear girl, have received several letters from me, especially one I sent to London by Mr Imlay, I avail myself of this opportunity just to tell you that I am well and my child, and to request you to write by this occasion. I do indeed long to hear from you and Eliza. I have at last got some tidings of Charles, and as they must have reached you, I need not tell you what sincere satisfaction they afforded me. I have also heard from James, he too talks of success, but in a querulous strain. What are you doing? Where is Eliza? You have perhaps answered these questions 'in answer to the letters I gave in charge to Mr I., but fearing that some fatality might have prevented their reaching you, let me repeat that I have written to you and to Eliza at least half a score of times, pointing out different ways for you to write to me, still have received no answers. I have again and again given you an account of my present situation, and introduced Mr Imlay to you as a brother you would love and respect. I hope the time is not very distant when we shall all meet. Do be very particular in your account of yourself, and if you have not time to procure me a letter from Eliza, tell me all about her. Tell me too what is become of George, &c., &c. I only write to ask questions and to assure you that I am most affectionately yours,

"MARY IMLAY."

[*P.S.*]—

"Should peace take place this winter, what say you to a voyage in the spring, if not to see your old acquaintance, to see Paris, which I think you did not do justice to. I want you to see my little girl, who is more like a boy. She is ready to fly away with spirits, and has eloquent health in her cheeks and eyes. She does not promise to be a beauty, but appears wonderfully intelligent, and though I am sure she has her father's quick temper and feelings, her good humour runs away with all the credit of my good nursing.

" I managed myself so well that my lying-in scarcely deserved the name. I only rested, through persuasion, in bed one day, and was out a-walking on the eighth. She is now only four months old. She caught the small-pox at Havre, where they treat the dreadful disorder very improperly. I however determined to follow the suggestions of my own reason, and saved her much pain, probably her life, for she was very full, by putting her twice a-day into a warm bath. Once more adieu. The letter not being sent for as soon as I expected, gave me an opportunity to add this prattling postcript. You will see the last vol. I have written, it is the commencement of a considerable work. Tell Mrs Skeys, who could not fulfil her promise respecting her portrait, that it was written during my pregnancy."

Imlay was now involved in a multitude of speculations which rendered him restless and dissatisfied with the competency which it seems that at one time he had secured. The plan that he and Mary Wollstonecraft had proposed to themselves was to settle on a farm either in France or America, but he now embarked in trade connected with Norway and Sweden, which was, he considered, to bring him a large fortune. His interest in Mary and his child sensibly cooled, and though he allowed them to join him in England, her letters to him show that she did so with a heavy heart, and gloomy forebodings of coming sorrow.

Mr Rowan, to whom the following letter is addressed on her departure from France, was just about to settle in America, where Charles Wollstonecraft already was established in Philadelphia.

Archibald Hamilton Rowan, Esq., Secretary of the Society of United Irishmen, was prosecuted January 29, 1794, for having published a seditious libel. After a trial at Bar, in which he was defended by Curran, he was found guilty, was sentenced to pay a fine of £500, to be imprisoned for two years, and at the end of this time to give security for his good behaviour for seven years, himself in £2000 and two sureties in £1000 each. Within four months he escaped from gaol, and found his way to Havre, then called Havre Marat, in lieu of its old name Havre de Grace.

Mary Wollstonecraft to Archibald Hamilton Rowan, Esq.

"HAVRE, *April* 1795.

"MY DEAR SIR,—I wrote a few hasty lines to you just now, before we entered the vessel, and after hurrying myself out of breath—for as I do not like exaggerated phrases, I would not say *to death*—the awkward pilot ran us aground, so here we are in an empty house ; and with the heart and imagination on the wing, you may suppose that the slow march of time is felt very painfully. I seem to be counting the ticking of a clock, and there is no clock here. For these few days I have been busy preparing, now all is done, and we cannot go. If you were to pop in I should be glad, for in spite of my impatience to see a friend who deserves all tenderness, I still have a corner in my heart, where I will allow you a place, if you have no objection. It would give me sincere pleasure to meet you at any future period, and to be introduced to your wife. Pray take care of yourself, and when you arrive let me hear from you. Direct to me at Mr Johnson's, St Paul's Churchyard, London, and wherever I may be the letter will not fail to

reach me. You will not find a very comfortable house; but I
have left a little store of provisions in a closet, and the girl who
assisted in our kitchen, and who has been well paid, has promised
to do everything for you. Mr Wheatcroft has all your packages,
and will give you all the information and assistance he can. I
believe I told you that I offered Mr Russell's family my house,
but since I arrived I find there is some chance of letting it. Will
you then, when Mr Wheatcroft informs you in what manner he
has settled it, write the particulars to them. I imagine that the
house will be empty for a short time to come at any rate, but I
found it necessary to take my linen with me, and the good people
here sold my kitchen furniture for me. Still I think, as they have
many necessaries, they will find this house much more comfortable
than an inn. I neither like to say or write *adieu*. If you see my
brother Charles, pray assure him that I most affectionately remember him. Take every precaution to avoid danger.—Yours sincerely.

                                        " MARY IMLAY."

Mary Wollstonecraft to Everina Wollstonecraft.

                                        April 27th [1795].

" When you hear, my dear Everina, that I have been in London
near a fortnight without writing to you or Eliza, you will perhaps
accuse me of insensibility, for I shall not lay any stress on my not
being well in consequence of a violent cold I caught during the
time I was nursing; but tell you that I put off writing because I
was at a loss what I could do to render Eliza's situation more
comfortable. I instantly gave Jones ten pounds to send, for a
very obvious reason, in his own name to my father, and I could
send her a trifle of this kind immediately, were a temporary assistance necessary. I believe I told you that Mr Imlay had not a
fortune when I first knew him ; since that he has entered into very
extensive plans, which promise a degree of success, though not
equal to the first prospect. When a sufficient sum is actually
realized, I know he will give me for you and Eliza five or six
hundred pounds, or more if he can. In what way could this be

of the most use to you? I am above concealing my sentiments, though I have boggled at uttering them. It would give me sincere pleasure to be situated near you both. I cannot yet say where I shall determine to spend the rest of my life; but I do not wish to have a third person in the house with me; my domestic happiness would perhaps be interrupted without my being of much use to Eliza. This is not a hastily-formed opinion, nor is it in consequence of my present attachment, yet I am obliged now to express it, because it appears to me that you have formed some such expectation for Eliza. You may wound me by remarking on my determination, still I know on what principle I act, and therefore you can only judge for yourself. I have not heard from Charles for a great while. By writing to me immediately you would relieve me from considerable anxiety. Mrs Imlay, No. 26 Charlotte St., Rathbone Place.--Yours sincerely,   " MARY."

Mrs Bishop to Everina Wollstonecraft.

" PEMBROKE, *April* 29, 1795.

" Read the following letter: ' I arrived in town near a fortnight ago, my dear girl, but having previously weaned my child on account of a cough, I found myself extremely weak. I have intended writing to you every day, but have been prevented by the impossibility of determining in what way I can be of essential service to you. When Mr Imlay and I united our fate together, he was without fortune; since that, there is a prospect of his obtaining a considerable one; but though the hope appears to be well founded, I cannot yet act as if it were a certainty. He is the most generous creature in the world, and if he succeed, as I have the greatest reason to think he will, he will, in proportion to his acquirement of property, enable me to be useful to you and Everina. I wish you and her would adopt any plan in which five or six hundred pounds would be of use. As to myself, I cannot yet say where I shall live for a continuance. It would give me the sincerest pleasure to be situated near you. I know you will think me

unkind, and it was this reflection which has prevented my writing
to you sooner, not to invite you to come and live with me. But,
Eliza, it is my opinion, not a readily formed one, the presence of
a third person interrupts or destroys domestic happiness. Excepting this sacrifice, there is nothing I would not do to promote
your comfort. I am hurt at being obliged to be thus explicit, and
do indeed feel for the disappointments which you have met with
in life. I have not heard from Charles, nor can I guess what he
is about. What was done with the £50 he speaks of having sent
to England? Do, pray, write to me immediately, and do justice
to my heart. I do not wish to endanger my own peace without a
certainty of securing yours. Yet I am still your most sincere and
affectionate friend,   MARY.'

'26 CHARLOTTE ST., RATHBONE PLACE, LONDON.'

" 'This I have just received. My Everina, what I felt, and shall
for ever feel! It is childish to talk of. After lingering above a
fortnight in such cruel suspense. Good God! what a letter!
How have I merited such pointed cruelty? When did I wish to
live with her? At what time wish for a moment to interrupt their
domestic happiness? Was ever a present offered in so humiliating
a style? Ought the poorest domestic to be thus insulted? Are
your eyes opened at last, Everina? What do you now say to our
goodly prospects? I have such a mist before my lovely eyes that
I cannot now see what I write. Instantly get me a situation
in Ireland, I care not where. Dear Everina, delay not to
tell me you can procure bread, with what hogs I eat it,
I care not, nay, if exactly the Uptonian breed. Remember
I am serious. If you disappoint me, my misery will be
complete. I have enclosed this famous letter to the author
of the 'Rights of Women' without any reflection. She
shall never hear from *poor Bess* again. Remember, I am as
fixed as my misery, and nothing can change my present plan.
This letter has so strongly agitated me that I know not what I
say; but this I feel, and know, that if you value my existence you
will comply with my requisition, for I am positive I will never tor-

ment our amiable friend in Charlotte Street. Is not this a good spring, my dear girl? At least poor Bess can say it is a fruitful one. Alas, poor Bess!"

Mrs Bishop to Everina Wollstonecraft.

"PEMBROKE, *May* 10, 1795.

" MY DEAR EVERINA,—Though I know it is impossible for you to have answered either of my last letters, yet I feel vexed at not hearing from you. I am so eager for you to say you have pro-cured a situation for me in Dublin. I now have only ten days to spend at Pembroke, yet am quite uncertain what ' poor Bess's ' future fate is to be. I mean to stay with my father a week, or little more, so write and tell me the price of the new stage from Waterford to the capital. Also inform me from what inn it sets off, not forgetting the hour. There is no vessel now that can sail for Ireland, so I must send my box to London, and from thence to our mother country. What say you to Mrs Imlay's friendly epistle? I told you I returned it with only these words : ' Mrs B. has never received any money from America.' Nine days have now elapsed, and here I am waiting for your letter, my dear Everina. Can you blame me for returning Mrs I.'s letter? I am sick of thinking on the subject, and weary of anticipating ought from to-morrow. If it is impossible to procure me bread imme-diately, perhaps George would permit me to remain with him until you succeed. Recollect I value not what situation you get me— agreeable or disagreeable will be equally acceptable to the sister of the author of the ' Rights of Women.' I now have not the smallest wish to quit Wales, nor are my prospects in the least cheered by the idea of seeing you so soon. For I am sick to death of arguing and accounting for the unaccountable events of this wretched life, and as thoroughly tired of the lingering exist-ence I have dragged on year after year, spring after spring. To receive aught now from your Mary appears to me to be the height of meanness. Would to God we were both in America with Charles. Do you think it would be possible for us to go from

I. P

Dublin to Philadelphia in an American ship? This is my only
hope, yet I am afraid to indulge it. I beseech you to write to
Charles immediately. I am sure our sister would be delighted
with this plan, and our new brother will of course display all his
energy of character to render it practicable. Was it greatness of
mind or heart which dictated the ever-memorable letter, which has
so stupified me that I know not what I write, for I have incessant headaches to such a degree that it is a torture for
me to take up a pen. Alas! at the end of four long years,
could despair itself have dreamed of such studied cruelty? No inquiries after my present wants, &c.; no wish to see us. Mr
Imlay's silence was a bad omen, and that she could remain in
London a fortnight, and then send poor Bess such a cordial! Oh!
that I could find another Upton, for I never more wish to be near
those I love. The last month with the good and amiable Graux
has been dreadfully embittered. He is now very ill, and thoroughly
hurt at my sublime sister. He sends his love to Everina, whom
he is much more anxious to see than the famous Mrs Wollstonecraft. Write to me immediately. Direct to me at Laugharne, for
an answer cannot reach me here before I leave. Send every
particular relative to the coach at Waterford, and what house will
receive me in Dublin? The visit to my father will add greatly to
my expense: be particular about the terms. I know not what I
say, I am so dull and weary of my miserable life. Is not this a
goodly spring, and is not Bess a lucky girl? The amiable Mary
pined in poverty, while Mrs Imlay enjoys all her heart can sigh
for.

"Good night."   [*Unsigned.*]

The truth, however, was wholly other than Mrs Bishop
supposed. When Mary and Imlay again met in England,
his affairs proved seriously embarrassed, and his affection
had sensibly cooled. There was not as yet, indeed, any
word of a permanent separation; but as they had, in fact,
been actually together during but a short time of their

connection, so now it was evident that Imlay's speculations in trade, which were extended to various countries, would separate them still more ; and nothing was further from his intentions than to settle down on a moderate competence with her who counted herself his wife, and their child.

It proved necessary that some one should go to Sweden and Norway on Imlay's part, on some business, not clearly stated, but connected with his trade; while his own presence was urgently required elsewhere. The voyage, it was thought, would prove of advantage to Mary's health ; and, in the June following their meeting, she made the voyage, and undertook the business.

The document already mentioned remains, in which Imlay spoke of her as his wife, and gave her power to act for him. It is as follows :—

" *May* 19, 1795.

" Know all men, by these presents, that I, Gilbert Imlay, citizen of the United States of America, at present residing in London, do nominate, constitute, and appoint Mary Imlay, my best friend and wife, to take the sole management and direction of all my affairs and business which I had placed in the hands of Mr Elias Bach-man, negotiant, Gottenburg, or in those of Messrs Myburg & Co., Copenhagen, desiring that she will manage and direct such concerns in such manner as she may deem most wise and prudent. For which this letter shall be a sufficient power, enabling her to receive all the money or sums of money that may be recovered from Peter Ellyson or his connections, whenever the issue of the tryal now carrying on, instigated by Mr Elias Bachman, as my agent, for the violation of the trust which I had reposed in his integrity.

" Considering the aggravated distresses, the accumulated losses and damages sustained in consequence of the said Ellisson's dis-obedience of my injunctions, I desire the said Mary Imlay will clearly ascertain the amount of such damages, taking first the

advice of persons qualified to judge of the probability of obtaining
satisfaction, or the means the said Ellisson or his connections who
may be proved to be implicated in his guilt may have, or power
of being able to make restitution, and then commence a new prosecution for the same accordingly. . . .

" Respecting the cargo of goods in the hands of Messrs Myburg
and Co., Mrs Imlay has only to consult the most experienced
persons engaged in the disposition of such articles, and then
placing them at their disposal, act as she may deem right and
proper. . . .

" Thus, confiding in the talent, zeal, and earnestness of my
dearly beloved friend and companion, I submit the management
of these affairs entirely and implicitly to her discretion.

" Remaining most sincerely and affectionately hers truly,

" G. IMLAY.

" *Witness,* J. SAMORIEL."

Her letters to Imlay during this period were afterwards published, when divested of all that was personal and private, under the title, "Letters from Norway,"
and are still thoroughly worth reading, as a picturesque
and graceful description of a summer tour. The more
personal portions may be found among her posthumous
works, and carry on the sad tale of her sorrows.
She returned to England in the late autumn, to meet
letters from Imlay, which made it plain they were to
part, but offering to settle an annuity on her and her child.
This, for herself, she rejected with scorn. " From you," she
writes, " I will not receive any more ; I am not yet sufficiently humbled to depend on your beneficence." They met
once again, when Imlay attempted to gloss over the past, so
that it seemed possible, for the child's sake, that they might
still remain together. But though he had assured her that
he had no other attachment, she discovered in a short time
that he was carrying on an unworthy intrigue under her own

roof. It was then that, driven to despair, and for a time quite out of her mind, she attempted to drown herself by leaping from Putney Bridge; and when that attempt was frustrated, although she was quite insensible when taken out of the water, she still nursed for some time the desire of ending her existence. The letters written during this period are some of the most terrible and most touching ever penned. But calmer counsels, and the loving care of her friends, among whom Mr Johnson was chief, prevailed. She determined once again to support herself by her pen, and resented all attempts of Imlay to induce her to accept support from him. " I want not such vulgar comfort," she says, "nor will I accept it. I never wanted but your heart : that gone, you have nothing more to give. Forgive me, if I say that I shall consider any direct or indirect attempt to supply my necessities as an insult I have not merited, and as rather done out of tenderness for your own reputation than for me." With regard to Fanny's maintenance, she neither accepted nor refused anything. " You must do as you please with regard to the child," was her final decision. Imlay eventually gave a bond for a sum to be settled on his child, the interest to be devoted to her maintenance ; but neither principal nor interest was ever paid.

The following letter to Mr Rowan was written just after the final parting with Imlay.

Mary Wollstonecraft to A. Hamilton Rowan, Esq.

"London, 26*th Jany.*, 1796.

" My dear Sir,—Though I have not heard from you, I should have written to you, convinced of your friendship, could I have told you anything of myself that could have afforded you pleasure. I am unhappy. I have been treated with unkindness, and even cruelty, by the person from whom I had every reason to expect affection. I write to you with an agitated hand. I cannot be more explicit. I value your good opinion, and you know how to feel for me. I looked for something like happiness in the discharge of my relative duties, and the heart on which I leaned has pierced mine to the quick. I have not been used well, and I live but for my child; for I am weary of myself. I still think of settling in France, because I wish to leave my little girl there. I have been very ill, have taken some desperate steps; but I am now writing for independence. I wish I had no other evil to complain of than the necessity of providing for myself and my child. Do not mistake me. Mr Imlay would be glad to supply all my pecuniary wants; but unless he returns to himself, I would perish first. Pardon the incoherence of my style. I have put off writing to you from time to time, because I could not write calmly. Pray write to me. I will not fail, I was going to say, when I have anything good to tell you. But for me there is nothing good in store — my heart is broken!—I am yours, &c. MARY IMLAY."

Still, for the sake of the child, bearing Imlay's name, she began again to enter into London literary society, in which she and Godwin were almost equally conspicuous.

CHAPTER IX.

MARRIED LIFE. 1797.

THE fragmentary notes which Mrs Shelley left, in reference to her mother, are all full of very peculiar interest. They serve to manifest not only the sympathy, partly intellectual, partly physical, felt by the gifted daughter for the still more gifted mother, who died in giving her birth, but also the estimate in which that mother was held by Godwin and by such friends as Mrs Reveley, from whom Mrs Shelley learned all that she knew of her dead mother. Some of these notes are too incomplete for quotation, mere drafts and hints of sentences, which might afterwards be finished; but one, more entire, may here be given, describing the estimate which she had been led to form of Mary Wollstonecraft at the time of her marriage.

" Mary Wollstonecraft was one of those beings who appear once perhaps in a generation, to gild humanity with a ray which no difference of opinion nor chance of circumstances can cloud. Her genius was undeniable. She had been bred in the hard school of adversity, and having experienced the sorrows entailed on the poor and the oppressed, an earnest desire was kindled within her to diminish these sorrows. Her sound understanding, her intrepidity, her sensibility and eager sympathy, stamped all her writings with force and truth, and endowed them with a tender charm that enchants while it enlightens. She was one whom all loved who had ever seen her. Many years are passed since that beating heart

has been laid in the cold still grave, but no one who has ever seen
her speaks of her without enthusiastic veneration. Did she witness
an act of injustice, she boldly came forward to point it out, and
induce its reparation. Was there discord among friends or relatives, she stood by the weaker party, and by her earnest appeals and
kindliness awoke latent affection, and healed all wounds. 'Open
as day to melting charity,' with a heart brimful of generous affection, yearning for sympathy, she had fallen on evil days, and her
life had been one course of hardship, poverty, lonely struggle, and
bitter disappointment.

" Godwin met her at the moment when she was deeply depressed
by the ingratitude of one utterly incapable of appreciating her
excellence ; who had stolen her heart, and availed himself of her
excessive and thoughtless generosity, and lofty independence of
character, to plunge her in difficulties and then desert her. Difficulties, worldly difficulties, indeed, she set at nought, compared
with her despair of good, her confidence betrayed, and when once
she could conquer the misery that clung to her heart, she struggled
cheerfully to meet the poverty that was her inheritance, and to do
her duty by her darling child. It was at this time that Godwin
again met her, at the house of her friend Miss Hayes," having
before done so occasionally before she went to Norway.

Godwin's first impression of her was not a pleasing one.
He wished to hear Tom Paine talk, who was also of the
party, and always a silent man, and he considered that Mrs
Imlay talked too much. He was also an extremely fastidious
critic, and had been offended at some slight verbal inaccuracies, as they seemed to him, in her earlier works. But
after reading the letters from Norway, his views about her
culture were wholly altered. He saw that the blemishes,
if indeed they had really existed, were but superficial, and
he speedily yielded to the charm which all that knew her
recognised. His own exquisitely written description of
their love is published in the Memoirs of his wife, but a

passage may here be extracted from a book which now is scarce, and but little known. He says,

" The partiality we conceived for each other was in that mode which I have always considered as the purest, and most refined style of love. It grew with equal advances in the mind of each. It would have been impossible for the most minute observer to have said who was before and who was after. One sex did not take the priority which long established custom has awarded it, nor the other overstep that delicacy which is so severely imposed. I am not conscious that either party can assume to have been the agent or the patient, the toil spreader or the prey, in the affair. When, in the course of things, the disclosure came, there was nothing, in a manner, for either party to disclose to the other. . . . There was no period of throes and resolute explanation attendant on the tale. It was friendship melting into love."

The description of their married happiness is equally striking. The slight clouds which will appear in the corres-pondence which passed between them, were of an extremely transient character, and arose from Mary Wollstonecraft's extreme sensitiveness and eager quickness of temper, which were perhaps now and then tried by Godwin's confirmed bachelor habits, and also by the fact that he took *au pied de la lettre* all that she said about the independence of women, when in truth she leant a good deal on the aid of others. Into one plan of Godwin's, which may seem strange, his wife willingly fell. His strong view on the possibility that families may easily weary of the society of their dif-ferent members, led him to take rooms in a house about twenty doors from that in the Polygon, Somers Town, which was their joint home. To this study he repaired as soon as he rose in the morning, rarely even breakfasting at the Poly-gon, and here also he often slept. Each was engaged in his and her own literary occupations, and they seldom met, unless they walked together, till dinner time each day.

" We agreed, also," says Godwin, " in condemning the notion, prevalent in many situations in life, that a man and his wife cannot visit in mixed society, but in company with each other ; and we rather sought occasions of deviating from than in complying with this rule."

Before the marriage was declared, but while the intimate relation in which they stood to each other was understood, Southey, then in London, met Godwin and Mary, and wrote to his friend Cottle his views of them.

R. Southey to J. Cottle.

" *March 13th,* 1797.

" . . . Of all the lions or *literati* I have seen here, Mary Imlay's countenance is the best, infinitely the best : the only fault in it is an expression somewhat similar to what the prints of Horne Tooke display—an expression indicating superiority ; not haughtiness, not sarcasm, in Mary Imlay, but still it is unpleasant. Her eyes are light brown, and although the lid of one of them is affected by a little paralysis, they are the most meaning I ever saw. . . . As for Godwin himself, he has large noble eyes, and a *nose* —oh most abominable nose ! Language is not vituperatious enough to describe the effect of its downward elongation."— *Southey's Life,* Vol. i., pp. 305, 306.

The marriage itself took place at Old St Pancras Church on March 29th, 1797, Marshal and the clerk of the church being the witnesses. Godwin takes no notice whatever of it in his diary.

Among those who were entitled to early information was Mr Thomas Wedgwood of Etruria. His correspondence during the early months of this year with Godwin had been familiar and lengthy, chiefly concerned with difficult metaphysical problems in the study of which both were interested. In

one, however, he asks for a loan of £50, and the request
was at once granted, but he did not at once explain the
reason that he required such a sum, though he knew that
his friend would be astonished, since his careful frugality
was well known. The money was in fact required to
enable him to help Mary Wollstonecraft out of some
difficulties, and after the marriage, he again wrote thus ;

W. Godwin to T. Wedgwood, Esq.

" No. 7 EVESHAM BUILDINGS, SOMERS TOWN,
April 19*th*, 1797.

" . . . You have by this time heard from B. Montague of my
marriage. This was the solution of my late application to you,
which I promised speedily to communicate. Some persons
have found an inconsistency between my practice in this instance
and my doctrines. But I cannot see it. The doctrine of my
' Political Justice' is, that an attachment in some degree permanent,
between two persons of opposite sexes is right, but that marriage,
as practised in European countries, is wrong. I still adhere to that
opinion. Nothing but a regard for the happiness of the individual,
which I had no right to injure, could have induced me to submit
to an institution which I wish to see abolished, and which I would
recommend to my fellow-men, never to practise, but with the
greatest caution. Having done what I thought necessary for the
peace and respectability of the individual, I hold myself no otherwise bound than I was before the ceremony took place.

" It is possible however that you will not see the subject in the
same light, and I perhaps went too far, when I presumed to suppose that if you were acquainted with the nature of the case you
would find it to be such as to make the interference I requested
of you appear reasonable. I trust you will not accuse me of
duplicity in having told you that it was not for myself that I
wanted your assistance. You will perceive that that remark was
in reference to the seeming inconsistency between my habits of
economy and independence and the application in question.

"I can see no reason to doubt that as we are both successful authors, we shall be able by our literary exertions, though with no other fortune, to maintain ourselves either separately, or which is more desirable jointly. The loan I requested of you was rendered necessary by some complication in her pecuniary affairs, the consequence of her former connection, the particulars of which you have probably heard. Now that we have entered into a new mode of living, which will probably be permanent, I find a further supply of fifty pounds will be necessary to enable us to start fair. This you shall afford us, if you feel perfectly assured of its propriety, but if there be the smallest doubt in your mind, I shall be much more gratified by your obeying that doubt, than superseding it. I do not at present feel inclined to remain long in any man's debt, not even in yours. As to the not having published our marriage at first, I yielded in that to her feelings. Having settled the principal point in conformity to her interest, I felt inclined to leave all inferior matters to her disposal.

"W. GODWIN."

"We do not entirely cohabit."

Godwin wrote to his mother at once that she might be, as was right, among the first people informed about his marriage. But the fact of Fanny's existence and other details were probably supplied by Miss Godwin. The old lady took time to answer the communication.

Mrs Godwin, Sen., to W. Godwin.

[WOOD DALLING, NORFOLK,]
" 3rd May, 1797.

"DEAR WM.—What you say respecting your dear cousin's deth is very consolitory and a just remark. It was rather the pleasure of knowing she was a live than use we could be of to each other, and upon reflection mater of thankfulness on her account, as the change to her is so far superior to the infirm body she carried about, only this that her letters were always incouraging me to go on trusting in the Lord that had been so gratious to me hitherto, and would not forsake any that reverance his name. Thus did we incourage and comfort one another with passages out of scripture that never failing word. When lover and friend forsake us then the Lord will take us up ; this is the friend that sticketh closer than a brother, and though we should lose all other friends, the unchangable god liveth, for of his years there is no end, blessed for ever be his name.

"Your broken resolution in regard to mattrimony incourages me to hope that you will ere long embrace the Gospel, that sure word of promise to all believers, and not only you, but your other half, whose souls should be both one, as Watts says of his friend Gunston, the sooner the better. My dear Wm., the apoligy I have to make for not answering yours is, Mrs G. was going to send a box to H. soon, and was willing to save ye postage. You might have been so good as told me a few more particulars about your conjugal state, as when you were married, as being a father as well as a husband; hope you will fill up your place with propriety in both relations ; you are certainly transformed in a moral sense, why is it impossable in a spiritual sense, which last will make you shine with the radiance of the sun for ever. Mrs G. and, I may say, all your friends and mine wish you happiness, and shall be glad to see you and your wife in Norfolk, if I be spared. You must not expect great exactness, as I have a young servant, and myself able to do nothing at all. I hope you are good walkers, for I have no horse, and have not entered my Cart, so can go nowhere but to meeting with it. I have for many days had the cramp, I call it, rather than ye Rhumatism. I can't put on my own stockens, and am obliged to stand to eat my vituals, and get up and walk about perhaps 40 times while I write this letter. I intend sending you a few eggs with this in Hannah's box. Could send you a small fether bed, would do for a servant, by wagon, if acceptable. If you give me a direction, you may write by ye return of the box, or Mr Jo. Godwin, whome, John says, intends coming into the country in about a fortnight or three weeks, or by post for me at Mr Munton's, shopkeeper, Foulsham, will cost but 7d., any other way &d. Your poor sister H. is, I fear, a bad oeconomist, her heart too generous for her comings in, and besides that she has lost her good friend Mrs Hague. Many people think her character injured by Marshal, a married man, who, I suppose dines with her on Sundays; is it not so? Do you commend her, tell me freely, or advise her against it yourself? She will hear you sooner than anybody else—faithful are the wounds of a friend. If a righteous man smite me, it shall be a kindness; it's an exelent oil that shall not break my head saith the wise man.

"My dears, whatever you do, do not make invitations and entertainments, that was what hurt Jo. Live comfortable with one another. The Hart of her husband safely trusts in her. I cannot give you no better advice than out of Proverbs, the Prophets, and New Testament. My best affections attend you both.—From y^r Mother,   A. GODWIN.

"I am informed Mr Harwood's mother is dead; that's all I know. Your eggs will spoil soon if you don't pack them up in sawdust, bran, or something of the kind, and turn them often. 'Tis pitty to pay carriage for them if they don't keep."

Mrs Shelley's note on the marriage of her father and mother is as follows :—

"At the beginning of this year [1797] Mr Godwin married Mary Wollstonecraft. The precise date is not known; he does not mention it in his journal, and the ceremony had taken place some time before the marriage was declared. This secrecy partly arose from a slight shrinking on Mr Godwin's part from avowing that he had acted in contradiction to his theories. Such contradictions occur indeed every day, and are applauded. But the fervour and uncompromising tone assumed by the author of 'Political Justice' in promulgating his opinions made his followers demand a rigid adherence to them in action, and to comply with the ordinance of marriage was in the eyes of many among them absolute apostacy. Yet, in fact, all Mr Godwin's inner and more private feelings were contrary to the supposed gist of his doctrines.

The former were all strongly enlisted on the side of female virtue, and he would readily have proved, if questioned, that it was only misapprehension of his doctrines that could lead any one to think that he was opposed to marriage.

" Another cause for the secrecy at first maintained was the stern law of poverty and necessity. My father narrowly circumscribed both his receipts and disbursements. The maintenance of a family had never been contemplated, and could not at once be provided for. My mother, accustomed to a life of struggle and poverty, was so beloved by her friends, that several, and Mr Johnson in particular, had stood between her and any of the annoyances and mortifications of debt. But this must cease when she married. They both however looked on this sort of struggle, in which they had been born, and had always lived, as a very secondary matter, and after a short period of deliberation they, in the month of April, declared the marriage which had before been solemnized. The celebrity of both parties rendered the event of importance in their own circle. It is too usual that when a man marries he commences new habits under such a totally new influence, and that he is lost to all his former friends. Mr Godwin spent a portion of every day in society, and was much beloved; his more intimate friends believed they should suffer from the change. Two ladies shed tears when he announced his marriage—Mrs Inchbald and Mrs Reveley. The former lady seceded from his circle on this occasion, making worldly motives her excuse. Mrs Reveley feared to lose a kind and constant friend, but, becoming intimate with Mary Wollstonecraft, she soon learnt to appreciate her virtues and to love her. She soon found, as she told me in after days, that instead of losing one she had secured two friends, unequalled, perhaps, in the world for genius, single-heartedness, and nobleness of disposition, and a cordial intercourse subsisted between them."

Mrs Inchbald's letter, acknowledging the receipt of the communication, is very characteristic of a woman who, as Godwin remarks, afterwards wished to "shuffle out" of a difficulty. He did not choose to take the hint, and it appears, both from his Diary and a later letter, that he and his wife were present with Mrs Inchbald at the play on the night in question, Wednesday, April 19th, and that then Mrs Inchbald expressed her feelings freely to Mrs Godwin.

Mrs Inchbald to William Godwin.

"*April* 11, 1797.

" I most sincerely wish you and Mrs Godwin joy. But, assured that your joyfulness would obliterate from your memory every trifling engagement, I have entreated another person to supply your place, and perform your office in securing a box on Reynold's night. If I have done wrong, when you next marry, I will act differently."

Godwin merely communicated the fact of the marriage to Holcroft. He knew that his friend would understand to whom he was married. He received from him a very different letter.

Thomas Holcroft to William Godwin and Mary Wollstonecraft Godwin.

"*April* 6, 1797.

" From my very heart and soul I give you joy. I think you the most extraordinary married pair in existence. May your happiness be as pure as I firmly persuade myself it must be. I hope and expect to see you both, and very soon. If you show coldness, or refuse me, you will do injustice to a heart which, since it has really known you, never for a moment felt cold to you.

" I cannot be mistaken concerning the woman you have married. It is Mrs W. Your secrecy a little pains me. It tells me you do not yet know me. T. HOLCROFT."

It will be seen that the above letters are not arranged precisely in the order of their dates, but they appeared to fall in better with Mrs Shelley's note on the marriage than earlier.

The mode of Godwin's married life having been described, a selection from the notes which passed between the pair, both immediately before the marriage and afterwards, to and from the house in the Polygon and his lodgings in Evesham Place, needs no further explanation. Some of them have been taken out of their place in order of date, that the series may be presented consecutively.

Mary Wollstonecraft to William Godwin.

" *Jan.* 5, 1797. *Thursday morning.*

" I was very glad that you were not with me last night, for I could not rouse myself. To say the truth, I was unwell and out of spirits ; I am better to-day.

" I shall take a walk before dinner, and expect to see you this evening, *chez moi*, about eight, if you have no objection."

The Same to the Same.

" *Jan.* 12, 1797. *Thursday morning.*

" I am better this morning, but it snows so incessantly, that I do not know how I shall be able to keep my appointment this evening. What say you ? But you have no petticoats to dangle in the snow. Poor women—how they are beset with plagues— within and without."

The Same to the Same.

" *Jan.* 13*th*, 1797. *Friday morning.*

" I believe I ought to beg your pardon for talking at you last night, though it was in sheer simplicity of heart, and I have been asking myself why it so happened. Faith and troth, it was be- cause there was nobody else worth attacking, or who could con-

I.   Q

verse. C. had wearied me before you entered. But be assured, when I find a man that has anything in him, I shall let my every day dish alone.

"I send you *the Emma*" [Emma, or the Unfortunate Attachment. A novel. London 1773] for Mrs Inchbald, supposing you have not altered your mind.

"Bring Holcroft's remarks with you, and Ben Johnson" [*sic*].

The Same to the Same.

"*Jan.* 27, 1797.

"I am not well this morning. It is very tormenting to be thus, neither sick nor well, especially as you scarcely imagine me indisposed.

"Women are certainly great fools; but nature made them so. I have not time or paper, else I could draw an inference, not very illustrative of your chance-medley system. But I spare the moth-like opinion; there is room enough in the world, &c."

The Same to the Same.

"*Feb.* 3, 1797. *Friday Morning.*

"Mrs Inchbald was gone into the City to dinner, so I had to measure back my steps.

"To day I find myself better, and, as the weather is fine, mean to call on Dr Fordyce. I shall leave home about two o'clock. I tell you so, lest you should call after that hour. I do not think of visiting you in my way, because I seem inclined to be industrious. I believe I feel affectionate to you in proportion as I am in spirits; still I must not dally with you, when I can do anything else. There is a civil speech for you to chew."

The Same to the Same.

"*Feb.* 17, 1797.

"Did I not see you, friend Godwin, at the theatre last night? I thought I met a smile, but you went out without looking round.

"We expect you at half-past four." [She did see "friend Godwin," for the Diary shows that he was there.]

The Same to the Same.

"*Feb.* 22, 1797.

"Everina's cold is still so bad, that unless pique urges her, she will not go out to-day. For to-morrow, I think I may venture to promise. I will call, if possible, this morning. I know I must come before half after one; but if you hear nothing more from me, you had better come to my house this evening.

"Will you send the second volume of 'Caleb,' and pray *lend* me a bit of Indian rubber. I have lost mine. Should you be obliged to quit home before the hour I have mentioned, say. You will not forget that we are to dine at four. I wish to be exact, because I have promised to let Mary go and assist her brother this afternoon. I have been tormented all this morning by puss, who has had four or five fits. I could not conceive what occasioned them, and took care that she should not be terrified. But she flew up my chimney, and was so wild, that I thought it right to have her drowned. Fanny imagines that she was sick, and ran away."

Everina, who had been residing for some time with her sister, but who was not in her sister's confidence as to her relation with Godwin, now left London, to become governess in the Wedgwood family, at Etruria.

The Same to the Same.

"*Mar.* 11*th*, 1797. *Saturday Morning.*

" I must dine to-day with Mrs Christie, and mean to return as early as I can; they seldom dine before five.

"Should you call and find only books, have a little patience, and I shall be with you.

" Do not give Fanny a cake to-day. I am afraid she staid too long with you yesterday.

"You are to dine with me on Monday, remember; the salt beef awaits your pleasure."

The Same to the Same.

"And so, you goose, you lost your supper—and deserved to lose it, for not desiring Mary to give you some beef.

"'There is a good boy, write me a review of Vaurien. I remember there is an absurd attack on a Methodist preacher, because he denied the Eternity of future punishments.

" I should be glad to have the Italian, were it possible, this week, because I promised to let Johnson have it this week."

William Godwin to Mary Wollstonecraft.

[*Between March* 17 *and* 29, 1797.]

" I will have the honour to dine with you. You ask me whether I think I can get four orders. I do not know, but I do not think the thing impossible. How do you do?"

The Same to the Same.

" *March* 29, [*after the Wedding.*]

" I must write, though it will not be long till five. I shall, however, reserve all I have to say. *Non je ne veux pas être fâché quant au passé. Au revoir.*"

Mary Wollstonecraft Godwin to William Godwin.

"*March* 31, 1797. *Friday.*

"I return you the volumes ; will you get me the rest? I have not, perhaps, given it as careful a reading as some of the sentiments deserve.

" Pray send me by Mary for my luncheon a part of the supper you announced to me last night, as I am to be a partaker of your worldly goods, you know !"

The Same to the Same.

"*Saturday, April* 8, 1797.

"I have just thought that it would be very pretty in you to call on Johnson to-day. It would spare me some awkwardness, and please him; and I want you to visit him often of a Tuesday. This is quite disinterested, as I shall never be of the party. Do, you would oblige me. But when I press anything, it is always with a true wifish submission to your judgment and inclination. Remember to leave the key of No. 25 with us, on account of the wine."

The Same to the Same.

"*April* 11*th*, 1797.

"I am not well to-day; my spirits have been harassed. Mary will tell you about the state of the sink, &c. Do you know you plague me—a little—by not speaking more determinately to the land-lord, of whom I have a mean opinion. He tires me by his pitiful way of doing everything. I like a man who will say yes or no at once."

The Same to the Same.

"*April* 11*th*, 1797.

"I wish you would desire Mr Marshal to call on me. Mr Johnson or somebody has always taken the disagreeable business of settling with tradespeople off my hands. I am perhaps as unfit as yourself to do it, and my time appears to me as valuable as that of other persons accustomed to employ themselves. Things of this kind are easily settled with money I know; but I am tormented by the want of money, and feel, to say the truth, as if I was not treated with respect, owing to your desire not to be disturbed."

William Godwin to Mary Wollstonecraft Godwin.

"*April* 20*th*, [1797.]

"I am pained by the recollection of our conversation last night. The sole principle of conduct of which I am conscious in my behaviour to you, has been in everything to study your happiness. I found a wounded heart, and as that heart cast itself on me, it was my ambition to heal it. Do not let me be wholly disappointed.

"Let me have the relief of seeing you this morning. If I do not call before you go out, call on me."

Mary Wollstonecraft Godwin to William Godwin.

"*April* 20*th*, 1797.

"Fanny is delighted with the thought of dining with you. But I wish you to eat your meat first, and let her come up with the pudding. I shall probably knock at your door in my way to Opie's; but should I not find you, let me request you not to be too late this evening. Do not give Fanny butter with her pudding."

The Same to the Same.

"*Saturday morning, May* 21*st*, 1797.

" . . . Montagu called on me this morning, that is breakfasted with me, and invited me to go with him and the Wedgwoods into the country to-morrow, and return the next day. As I love the country, and think with a poor mad woman I knew, that there is God, or something very consolatory in the air, I should without hesitation have accepted the invitation but for my engagement with your sister. To her even I should have made an apology, could I have seen her, or rather have stated that the circumstance would not occur again. As it is I am afraid of wounding her feelings, because an engagement often becomes important in proportion as it has been anticipated. I began to write to ask your opinion respecting the propriety of sending to her, and feel as I write that I had better conquer my desire of contemplating unsophisticated nature than give her a moment's pain.

"MARY."

It does not appear how this knotty point was settled, but Godwin was not long afterwards a companion of Mr Basil Montagu on a somewhat longer excursion, extending over more than a fortnight. The friends hired a one horse carriage, and made a tour into Staffordshire, taking journeys which speak well for the quality of the animal they drove. An abridgement of Godwin's diary will throw light on the correspondence with his wife during the tour.

" *June* 3, *Sa.*—Tour w. Montagu : sleep at Beaconsfield.

    „   4, *Su.*—Wycombe: breakfast at Tetsworth: dine at Horse-man's, Oxford, w. Porter, Mossop, and 3 Swans : Woodstock : sleep at Chapel House.

    „   5, *M.*—Shipston : Welsburn: breakfast at Morley's, Hampton Lucy, w. C. Parr; dine at Boot's, Atherston nr. Stratford, w. Parr, Morley, Bradley, and Philips : Henley : sleep at Hochley House.

    „   6, *Tu.*—Breakfast at Birmingham: Walsal: dine at Caunoc: Stafford: tea, Stone: sup at Etruria, w. Br. Allen and ladies.

    „   7, *W.*—Hobbes's 'Human Nature' p. 14. Dine at Mrs Wedgwood's, w. Miss Ja. Willet: ride to Chesterton w. Montagu.

    „   8, *Th.*—Hobbes, p. 26. View the Pottery: Theatre, Stobe, 'School for Scandal' and 'Catherine.'

    „   9, *F.*—Hobbes, p. 32, fin. Navigate the Tunnel : ladies dine.

    „ 10, *Sa.*—'Life of Hobbse' pp. 20. Ladies dine : ride to Newcastle and Burslem w. Montagu.

    „ 11, *Su.*—'Leviathan' p. 14: 'Logique par Condillac,' p. 30 : Bailly, 'Sur les Sciences,' p. 50 : Ride to Trentham w. J. & T. Wedgwoods and Montagu.

    „ 12, *M.*—'Leviathan,' p. 24, (chap. 6.): Bailly, p. 76. Dine at Mrs Wedgwood's w. Miss Willet junior.

"*June* 13, *Tu.*—Breakfast at Uttoxeter: dine at Derby; call on
  Mrs Darwin: sleep at Burton-upon-Trent.

,, 14, *W.*—Elford, walk w. Bage: dine at Tamworth: Bage
  calls: sup at Bage's w. Davis.

,, 15, *Th.*—Coleshil: breakfast at George in Tree: dine at
  Hatton w. Wynns: walk to Kennilworth w.
  Montagu.

,, 16, *F.*—Guy's Cliff: Coventry Fair: dine at Dunchurch:
  Daventry: sleep at Northampton.

,, 17, *Sa.*—Wellingborough: breakfast at Thrapston: dine at
  Mr Robt. Montagu's, Brampton: tea, Hol-
  worthy's w. Miss Wants.

,, 18, *Su.*—Breakfast and dine at Mrs Montagu's: see
  Hinchinbrooke House: Huntingdon: sup at
  Jones's, Cambridge, w. Woodhouse.

,, 19, *M.*—Breakfast at Otter's: dine at Gunnings Ichleton:
  sleep at Sawbridgeworth.

,, 20, *Tu.*—Breakfast on Epping Forest: Polygon; Fenwick
  calls: A. Pinkerton at tea.

The letters which follow give the journey in detail.

William Godwin to Mary Wollstonecraft Godwin.

"STRATFORD-UPON-AVON, *June* 5, 1797.

" I write at this moment from Hampton Lucy, in sight of the
house and park of Sir Thomas Lucy, the great benefactor of mankind, who persecuted William Shakespeare for deer-stealing, and
obliged him to take refuge in the metropolis. Montagu has just
had a vomit, to carry off a certain quantity of punch, with the
drinking of which he concluded the Sunday evening.

" Is that the right style for a letter ?

" We are going to dine to-day at the house of Mr Boot, a
country farmer, with Dr Parr and a set of jolly fellows, to com-
memorate the victory, or rather no-victory gained last week by the
High Sheriff of Warwick and the oppositionists over the Lord

Lieutenant and the ministerialist, on the matter of the dismission of Mr Pitt and his coadjutors. We sleep to-night at Dr Parr's, 60 miles from Etruria, at which place therefore we probably shall not arrive till Wednesday. Our horse has turned out admirably, and we were as gay as larks. We were almost drowned this morning in a brook, swelled by the rains. We are here at the house of a Mr Morley, a clergyman, with whom we breakfasted after a ride of 22 miles. He is an excellent classic, and, which is almost as good, a clever and amiable man. Here we met Catherine Parr, the youngest, as blooming as Hebe, and more interesting than all the goddesses in the Pantheon. Montagu is in love with her.

"We slept the first night at Beaconsfield, the residence of Mr Burke, 23 miles. The town was full of soldiers. We rose the next morning, as well as to-day, a little after four. We drove about 20 miles to breakfast, and arrived at Oxford, 53 miles from town, about 12. Here we had a grand dinner prepared for us by letter, by a Mr Horseman, who says that you and I are the two greatest men in the world. He is very nervous, and thinks he never had a day's health in his life. He intends to return the visit, and eat a good dinner in the Paragon, but he will find himself mistaken. We saw the buildings, an object that never impressed me with rapture, but we could not see the collection of paintings at Ch. Ch. Library, because it was Sunday. We saw however an altar-piece by Guido, Christ bearing the Cross, a picture I think of the highest excellence. Our escort, one of whom thinks himself an artist, were so ignorant as to tell us that a window to which we were introduced, painted by Jervas (as they said), from Reynolds, was infinitely superior. We had also a Mr Swan and his two wives, or sisters, to dinner, but they were no better than geese.

"And now, my dear love, what do you think of me? Do you not find solitude infinitely superior to the company of a husband? Will you give me leave to return to you again when I have finished my pilgrimage, and discharged the penance of absence? Take care of yourself, my love, and take care of William. Do not you be drowned, whatever I am. I remember at every moment all the accidents to which your condition subjects you, and wish I knew of some sympathy that could inform me from moment to moment how you do, and what you feel.

"Tell Fanny something about me. Ask where she thinks I am. Say I am a great way, and going further and further, but that I shall turn round to come back again some day. Tell her I have not forgotten her little mug, and that I shall choose a very pretty one. Montagu said this morning about eight o'clock, upon the road, 'Just now little Fanny is going to plungity-plunge.' Was he right? I love him very much. He is in such a hurry to see his *chère adorable*, that I believe, after all, we shall set forward this evening and get to Etruria to-morrow.

"Farewell."

[*End torn off.*]

Mary Wollstonecraft Godwin to William Godwin.

"*Tuesday, June 6th.*

"It was so kind and considerate in you to write sooner than I expected, that I cannot help hoping you would be disappointed at not receiving a greeting from me on your arrival at Etruria. If your heart was in your mouth, as I felt, just now, at the sight of your hand, you may kiss or shake hands with the letter, and imagine with what affection it was written. If not, stand off, profane one!

"I was not quite well the day after you left me; but it is past, and I am well and tranquil, excepting the disturbance produced by Master William's joy, who took it into his head to frisk a little at being informed of your remembrance. I begin to love this little creature, and to anticipate his birth as a fresh twist to a knot which I do not wish to untie. Men are spoilt by frankness, I believe, yet I must tell you that I love you better than I supposed I did, when I promised to love you for ever. And I will add what will gratify your benevolence, if not your heart, that on the whole I may be termed happy. You are a kind, affectionate creature, and I feel it thrilling through my frame, giving and promising pleasure.

" Fanny wanted to know 'what you are gone for,' and endea-vours to pronounce Etruria. Poor papa is her word of kindness. She has been turning your letter on all sides, and has promised to play with Bobby till I have finished my answer.

" I find you can write the kind of letter a friend ought to write, and give an account of your movements. I hailed the sunshine and moonlight, and travelled with you, scenting the fragrant gale. Enable me still to be your company, and I will allow you to peep over my shoulder, and see me under the shade of my green blind, thinking of you, and all I am to hear and feel when you return. You may read my heart, if you will.

" I have no information to give in return for yours. Holcroft is to dine with me on Saturday. So do not forget us when you drink your solitary glass, for nobody drinks wine at Etruria, I take it. Tell me what you think of Everina's behaviour and situation, and treat her with as much kindness as you can—that is, a little more than her manner will probably call forth—and I will repay you.

" I am not fatigued with solitude, yet I have not relished my solitary dinner. A husband is a convenient part of the furniture of a house, unless he be a clumsy fixture. I wish you, from my soul, to be rivetted in my heart ; but I do not desire to have you always at my elbow, although at this moment I should not care if you were. Yours truly and tenderly, MARY.

" Fanny forgets not the mug.

" Miss Pinkerton seems content. I was amused by a letter she wrote home. She has more in her than comes out of her mouth. My dinner is ready, and it is washing-day. I am putting every-thing in order for your return. Adieu !"

William Godwin to Mary Wollstonecraft Godwin.

" ETRURIA, *June* 7, 1797.

" More adventures. There are scenes, Sterne says, that only a sentimental traveller is born to be present at. I scaled my last letter at Hampton Lucy, and set off for Mr Boot's, farmer at Atherston, where I expected to meet Dr Parr to dinner. Our way lay through Stratford-upon-Avon, where, after having paid our respects to the house, now inhabited by a butcher, in which Shakespeare is said to have been born, I put your letter in the post.

" But before we entered Stratford we overtook Dr Parr. After a very cordial salutation, he told us that we saw him in the deepest affliction, and forbad our visit at present to his house, though he pressed us to wait upon him upon our return from Etruria. He, however, went on with us upon his trot to the dinner at Atherston. His affliction was for the elopement of his daughter with a Mr Wynn, a young man of eighteen, a pupil of the Doctor's, son to a member of Parliament, and who will probably inherit a considerable fortune. They set off for Gretna Green on the night of Sunday the 4th. To do the Doctor justice, though in the deepest affliction, he was not inconsolable. He had said to the young man the Friday before : Sir, it is necessary we should come to an issue. You must either quit my house, or relinquish your addresses to Miss Parr; if, after having ceased to live with me, you choose to continue your addresses, I shall have no objection to you ; but I will have no Gretna Green work. I allow you till Monday to give in your answer. I cannot help, however, believing that the Doctor is not very inconsolable for the match. What do you think of it? I certainly regard Miss Parr as a seducer, and have scarcely any doubt that the young man will repent, and that they will be unhappy. It was her, and her mother's maxim that the wisest thing a young woman of sense could do was to marry a fool, and they illustrated their maxim from their domestic scene. Miss Parr has now, it seems, got her fool, and will therefore learn by experiment the justice of her maxim.

" I expected to have been rallied by the Doctor upon my marriage. He was in high spirits, but abstained from the subject. I at length reminded him of his message by the Wedgwoods. I mentioned it with the utmost humour, but desired an explanation, as I was really incapable of understanding it. He appeared con-

fused, said he had been in high good humour the evening he
supped with the Wedgwoods, and had talked away at a great
rate. He could not exactly say how he had expressed himself,
but was sure he did not use the word mean. We had a good deal
of raillery. I told him that he understood everything except my
system of ' Political Justice ; ' and he replied that was exactly the
case with me. Montagu afterwards told me that Dr Parr had
formerly assured him that I was more skilful in moral science
than any man now living. I am not, however, absolutely sure of
the accuracy of Montagu's comprehension.

"We left the Doctor at the farmer's house, and came on
on Monday evening to within ten miles of Birmingham and fifty
miles of Etruria. (I forgot to say in the right place that Miss Parr
vowed, upon hearing of my expedition, that she would give me
the most complete roasting she ever gave to any man in her life,
upon my marriage. She, however, has got her husband, and
I have probably lost my roasting. Though I think it not improbable that we shall find Mr and Mrs Wynn at Dr Parr's on our
return.)

"Every night we have ceased to travel at eleven ; every morning we have risen at four, so that you see we have not been idle.
We breakfasted on Tuesday at Birmingham, where we spent two
hours, surveyed the town, and saw the ruins of two large houses,
which had been demolished in the Birmingham riots. I amused
myself with enquiring the meaning of a handbill respecting a wax-
work exhibition, containing, among others, lively and accurate
likenesses of the Prince and Princess of Wirtemberg, and Poet
Fruth. As I had never heard of Poet Fruth, my curiosity was
excited. We found that he was an ale-house keeper of Birmingham, the author of a considerable number of democratical
squibs. If we return by Birmingham, I promise myself to pay
him a visit.

"From Birmingham, we passed through Walsall, a large and handsome town of this county, 8 miles. We went forward, however, and
came at 12 o'clock to Cannock, a pretty little town. Here we
proposed to give our horse some water, and a mouthful of corn.

Montagu had repeatedly regretted the hardship imposed upon the horse of eating his hay with a large bit of iron in his mouth, and here, therefore, he thought proper to take off his bridle at the inn door. The horse, finding himself at liberty, immediately pranced off, overturned the chaise, dashed it against a post, and broke it in twenty places. It was a formidable sight, and the horse was with great difficulty stopped. We, however, are philosophers, so, after having amused ourselves for some time with laughing at our misadventure, we sent for a smith to splinter our carriage. By two we had eaten our dinner, the chaise was hammered together. We paid the smith his demand of 2s., and bid adieu to Cannock, the scene of this memorable adventure.

"Our next town was Stafford, which I viewed with unfeigned complacence, as having had the honour of being represented in four successive Parliaments by Richard Sheridan. We did not, however, stop here (8 miles), but proceeded to Stone (7 more), and nine short of Etruria. Here we took tea, and here I wrote the first 18 lines of this letter. You cannot imagine the state of intoxication of poor Montagu as he approached the place of our destination. It was little less than madness, but the most kindhearted madness imaginable. He confessed to me that he had set out from London in extreme ill-humour, from preceding fatigue, and from doubts of the capacity of the horse to perform the journey, in which, however, he was agreeably disappointed. He added that it was infinitely the most delightful journey he had ever made.

"We reached Etruria without further accident, a little after eight. Our reception appears to be cordial. Farewell, my love. I think of you with tenderness, and shall see you again with redoubled kindness (if you will let me) for this short absence. Kiss Fanny for me, remember William, but, most of all, take care of yourself. Tell Fanny I am safely arrived in the land of mugs.

"Your sister would not come down to see me last night at supper, but we met at breakfast this morning. I have nothing to say about her."

William Godwin to Mary Wollstonecraft Godwin.

"ETRURIA, *June* 10, 1797.

" You cannot imagine how happy your letter made me. No creature expresses, because no creature feels, the tender affections so perfectly as you do ; and, after all one's philosophy, it must be confessed that the knowledge that there is some one that takes an interest in one's happiness, something like that which each man feels in his own, is extremely gratifying. We love, as it were, to multiply the consciousness of our existence, even at the hazard of what Montagu described so pathetically one night upon the New Road, of opening new avenues for pain and misery to attack us.

" We arrived, as you are already informed, at Etruria on Tuesday afternoon. Wednesday I finished my second letter to you, which was exchanged that evening for your letter, written the preceding day. This is the mode of carrying on correspondence at Etruria : the messenger who brings the letters from Newcastle-under-Lyne, two miles, carries away the letters you have already written. In case of emergency, however, you can answer letters by return of post, and send them an hour after the messenger, time enough for the mail.

" I wrote last Wednesday a letter which of course you were to receive this morning. It is probable that you are now reading it : it is between twelve and one. I hope it finds you in health and spirits. I hope you hail the handwriting on the direction, though not probably with the surprise which, it seems, the arrival of my first letter produced. You are now reading my adventures : the elopement of Mrs Wynn, the little, good-humoured sparring between me and Dr Parr, and the tremendous accident of Cannock. These circumstances are presenting themselves with all the grace of novelty. I am, at the same time, reading your letter, I believe for the fourth time, which loses not one grace by the repetition. Well, fold it up ; give Fanny the kiss I sent her, and tell her, as I desired you, that I am in the land of mugs. You wish, it may be, that my message had been better adapted to her capacity, but

I think it better as it is; I hope you do not disdain the task of being its commentator.

"One of the pleasures I promised myself in my excursion, was to increase my value in your estimation, and I am not disappointed. What we possess without intermission we inevitably hold light; it is a refinement in voluptuousness to submit to voluntary privations. Separation is the image of death, but it is Death stripped of all that is most tremendous, and his dart purged of its deadly venom. I always thought St Paul's rule, that we should die daily, an exquisite Epicurean maxim. The practice of it would give to life a double relish.

"Yesterday we dined at Mrs Wedgwood's the elder, Everina was not of the party. They sat incessantly from three to eleven P.M. This does not suit my propensities; I was obliged to have a ride in the whiskey at five, and a walk at half after eight.

"Montagu's flame is the youngest of the family. She is certainly the best of the two unmarried daughters; but, I am afraid, not good enough for him. She is considerably fat, with a countenance rather animated, and a glimpse of Mrs Robinson. Perhaps you know that I am a little sheepish, particularly with stranger ladies. Our party is numerous, and I have had no conversation with her. I look upon any of my friends going to be married with something of the same feeling as I should do if they were sentenced to hard labour in the Spielberg. The despot may die, and the new despot grace his accession with a general jail delivery; that is almost the only hope for the unfortunate captive.

"To-day we went over Mr Wedgwood's manufactory. Everina accompanied us, and Mr Baugh Allen—no other lady. For Everina, she was in high spirits. She had never seen the manufactory before. The object of my attention was rather the countenances of the workpeople, than the wares they produced. . . .

"Tell Fanny we have chosen a mug for her, and another for Lucas. There is a F on hers, and an L on his, shaped in an island of flowers, of green and orange tawny alternately. With respect to their beauty, you will set it forth with such eloquence as your imagination can supply.

" We are going this evening, the whole family included, to see the 'School for Scandal,' represented by a company of strollers at Newcastle-under-Lyne. . . . Your William (do you know me by that name ?) salutes the trio, M., F., and last and least (in stature at least), little W."

Mary Wollstonecraft Godwin to William Godwin.

"Saturday, half after one o'clock.

" Your letter of Wednesday I did not receive till just now, and I have only half an hour to express the kind emotions which are clustering about my heart, or my letter will have no chance of reaching General Tarleton's to-day, and to-morrow being Sunday, two posts would be lost. My last letter of course you did not get, although I reckoned on its reaching you Wednesday morning.

" I read, T[homas] W[edgwood]'s letter. I thought it would be affectation not to open it, as I knew the hand. It did not quite please me. He appears to me to be half spoilt by living with his inferiors in point of understanding, and to expect that homage to be paid to his abilities which the world will readily pay to his fortune. I am afraid that all men are materially injured by inheriting wealth, and, without knowing it, become important in their own eyes, in consequence of an advantage they contemn.

" I am not much surprised at Miss Parr's conduct. You may remember that I did not give her credit for as much sensibility (at least the sensibility which is the mother of sentiment and delicacy of mind) as you did, and her conduct confirms my opinion. Could a woman of delicacy seduce and marry a fool? She will be unhappy, unless a situation in life, and a good table to prattle at, are sufficient to fill up the void of affection. This ignoble mode of rising in the world is the consequence of the present system of female education.

" I have little to tell you of myself. I am very well. Mrs Reveley drank tea with me one morning, and I spent a day with her, which would have been a very pleasant one, had I not been a

I.   R

little too much fatigued by a previous visit to Mr Barry. Fanny
often talks of you, and made Mrs Reveley laugh by telling her,
when she could not find the monkey to show it to Henry, 'that it
was gone into the country.' I supposed that Everina would
assume some airs at seeing you. She has very mistaken notions
of dignity of character.

"Pray tell me the precise time—I mean when it is fixed—I do
believe I shall be glad to see you!—of your return, and I will keep
a good look-out for you. William is all alive, and my appearance
no longer doubtful. You, I dare say, will perceive the difference.
What a fine thing it is to be a man!

"You were very good to write such a long letter. Adieu! take
care of yourself. Now I have ventured on you, I should not like
to lose you.   MARY."

William Godwin to Mary Wollstonecraft Godwin.

"ETRURIA (finished), *June* 12, 1797.

"Having dispatched one letter, I now begin another. You have
encouraged me to believe that some pleasure results to you, merely
from thus obtaining the power of accompanying my motions, and
that what would be uninteresting to another may, by this circumstance, be rendered agreeable to you. I am the less capable of
altering my method, if it ought to be altered, as you have not dealt
fairly by me this post. I delivered a letter of mine to the messenger, but I received none from him in return. I am beginning a
fourth letter, but of yours I have as yet only one.

"The theatre, which was at Stoke-upon-Trent, two miles from
Etruria, was inexpressibly miserable. The scene was new to me,
and I should have been sorry to have missed it; but it was extremely tedious. Our own company, consisting of nine persons,
contributed one-half of the audience, exclusive of the galleries. The
illusion, the fascination of the drama, was, as you may well suppose, altogether out of the question. It was the counterpart of a
puppet-show at a country fair, except that, from the circumstance
of these persons having to deliver the sentiments of Sheridan and

Shakespeare (the School for Scandal and Catherine and Petruchio) their own coarseness and ribaldry were rendered fifty times more glaring and intolerable. Lady Teazle was by many degrees the ugliest woman I ever saw. One man took the two parts of Crabtree and Moses. Another, without giving himself the trouble to change his dress, played Careless and Sir Benjamin Backbite. The father of Catherine had three servants; and when he came to the country-house of Petruchio, he had precisely the same three servants to attend him. The gentleman who personated Charles in the play was the Woman's tailor in the farce, and volunteered a boxing-match with Sir Oliver Surface in the character of Grumio. Snake, who was also footman-general to every person in the play, had by some means contracted the habit of never appearing when he was wanted, and the universal expedient for filling up the intervals, was for the persons on the stage to commence over again their two or three last speeches till he appeared. But enough of these mummers. Peace be to their memory. They did not leave us in our debt: they paid the world in talent, to the full as well as they were paid in coin.

" Which is best, to pass one's life in the natural vegetation state of the potters we saw in the morning, turning a wheel, or treading a lay : or to pass it like these players, in an occupation to which skill and approbation can alone give a zest, without a hope of rising to either?

" Saturday morning our amusement was to go to a place called the Tunnel, a sort of underground navigation, about a mile and a half, at a distance of three miles from Etruria. We went in a small boat, which was drawn along by a horse. As we approached the Tunnel, we saw a smoke proceeding from the mouth, which gave it no inadequate resemblance of what the ancients feigned to be the entrance to the infernal regions. We proceeded to about the middle of the subterranean, the light that marked the place of our entrance gradually diminishing, till, when we had made two-thirds of our way, it wholly disappeared. The enclosure of the Tunnel was by an arch of brick, which distilled upon us, as we passed, drops of water impregnated with iron. We discerned our way by means of candles that we brought along with us, and pushed ourselves along with boat staves, applied to the walls on either side as we passed. Our voyage terminated, as to its extent, in a coal-pit, of which there are several in the subterranean. We had the two elder children with us, who exhibited no signs of terror. I remarked, in coming out, that the light from the entrance was much longer visible in going than returning; and, indeed, in the latter instance, was scarcely visible till it in a manner burst upon us at once.

" The only ladies who accompanied us in this voyage was Mrs Josiah Wedgwood and Mrs Montagu elect. Here, and at the play, where I contrived to sit beside her, I contrived to see more of this latter than I had yet done. I am sorry to observe that she does not improve upon me.

" Another evening and no letter. This is scarcely kind. I re-minded you in time that it would be impossible to write to me after Saturday, though it is not improbable you may not see me before the Saturday following. What am I to think? How many possible accidents will the anxiety of affection present to one's thoughts! Not serious ones, I hope: in that case I trust I should have heard. But headaches; but sickness of the heart, a general loathing of life and of me. Do not give place to this worst of diseases! The least I can think is, that you recollect me with less tenderness and impatience than I reflect on you. There is a general sadness in the sky; the clouds are shutting around me, and seem depressed with moisture: everything turns the soul to melancholy. Guess what my feelings are, when the most soothing and consolatory thought that occurs, is a temporary remission and oblivion in your affections.

" I had scarcely finished the above when I received your letter, accompanying T. W.'s, which was delayed by an accident till after the regular arrival of the post. I am not sorry to have put down my feelings as they were.

" We propose leaving Etruria at four o'clock to-morrow morning (Tuesday). Our journey cannot take less than three days, viz., Tuesday, Wednesday, and Thursday. We propose, however, a visit to Dr Darwin, and a visit to Dr Parr. With these data from which to reason, you may judge as easily as I, respecting the time of our arrival in London. It will probably be either Friday or Saturday. Do not, however, count on anything as certain respecting it, and so torment yourself with expectation.

"Tell Fanny the green monkey has not come to Etruria. Bid her explain to Lucas the mug he is to receive. I hope it will not be broken on the journey."

William Godwin to Mary Wollstonecraft Godwin.

"June 15, 1797.

"We are now at The George in the Tree, 10 miles north from Warwick. We set out from Etruria, as we purposed, at 5 A.M., Tuesday, June 13. We bent our course for Derby, being furnished with a letter of introduction to Dr Darwin, and purposing to obtain from him a further letter of introduction to Mr Bage, of Tamworth, author of 'Man as He is,' and 'Hermsprong.' Did we not well? Are not such men as much worth visiting as palaces, towns, and cathedrals? Our first stage was Uttoxeter, commonly called Utchester, 19 miles. Here we breakfasted. Our next stage was Derby, where we arrived at two o'clock. At this place, though sentimental travellers, we were for once unfortunate. Dr Darwin was gone to Shrewsbury, and not expected back till Wednesday night. At this moment I feel mortified at the recollection. We concluded that this was longer than we could with propriety wait for him. I believe we were wrong. So extraordinary a man, so truly a phenomenon as we should probably have found him, I think we ought not to have scrupled the sacrifice of 36 hours. He is 67 years of age, though as young as Ganymede; and I am so little of a traveller, that I fear I shall not again have the opportunity I have parted with. We paid our respects, however, to his wife, who is still a fine woman, and cannot be more than 50. She is perfectly unembarrassed, and tolerably well bred. She seemed, however, to me to put an improper construction on our visit, said she supposed we were come to

see the lions, and that Dr Darwin was the great lion of Derby-
shire. We asked of her a letter to Mr Bage; but she said she
could not do that with propriety, as she did not know whether
she had ever seen him, though he was the Doctor's very particular
friend.

"Thus baffled in our object, we plucked up our courage, and
determined to introduce ourselves to the author of 'Hermsprong.'
We were able to cite our introduction to Dr Darwin by the
Wedgwoods, and our intention of having procured a letter from
the Doctor. Accordingly we proceeded from Derby to Burton-
upon-Trent, 16 miles. This is a very handsome town, with a wide
and long street, a beautiful river, and a bridge which Montagu
said was the longest he ever saw in the world. Here we slept,
and drank Burton ale at the spring, after a journey of 48 miles.
The next morning, between six and seven, we set out for Tamworth, 15 miles. At Elford, 11 miles, we saw Mr Bage's mills,
and a house in which he lived for 40 years. His mills are for
paper and flour. Here we enquired respecting him, and found
that he had removed to Tamworth five years ago, upon the death
of his younger son, by which event he found his life rendered
solitary and melancholy. The people at the mill told us that he
came three times a-week, walking from Tamworth, to the mill,
four miles; that they expected him at eleven (it was now nine);
and that, if we proceeded, we should meet him upon the road.
They told us, as a guide, that he was a short man, with white
hair, snuff-coloured clothes, and a walking-stick. He is 67 years
old, exactly the same age as Dr Darwin. Accordingly, about a
mile and a half from Tamworth, we met the man of whom we
were in quest, with a book in his hand. We introduced ourselves,
and, after a little conversation, I got out of the chaise, and walked
back with him to the mill. This six or seven miles was very
fortunate, and contributed greatly to our acquaintance. I found
him uncommonly cheerful and placid, simple in his manners, and
youthful in all his carriage. His house at the mill was floored,
every room below-stairs, with brick, and like that of a common
farmer in all respects. There was, however, the river at the

bottom of the garden, skirted with a quickset hedge, and a broad green walk. He told me his history.

"His father was a miller, as well as himself, and he was born at Derby. At twenty-two he removed to Elford. He had been acquainted forty years with Dr Darwin. The other acquaintances of his youth were Whitehurst, author of 'The Theory of the Earth,' and some other eminent man, whose name I forget. He taught himself French and Latin, in both of which languages he is a considerable proficient. In his youth he was fond of poetry; but, having some motive for the study of mathematics, he devoted his three hours an afternoon (the portion of time he allotted for reading) to this subject for twelve years, and this employment destroyed the eagerness of his attachment to poetry. In the middle of life, he engaged in a joint-undertaking with Dr Darwin and another person respecting some iron-works. This failed, and he returned once more to his village and to his mill. The result filled him with melancholy thoughts; and, to dissipate them, he formed the idea of a novel, which he endeavoured to fill with gay and cheerful ideas. At first he had no purpose of publishing what he wrote. Since that time he has been accustomed to produce a novel every two years, and 'Hermsprong' is his sixth. He believes he should not have written novels, but for want of books to assist him in any other literary undertaking. Living at Tamworth, he still retains his house at the mill, as the means of independence. It is his own, and he considers it as his security against the caprice or despotism of a landlord, who might expel him from Tamworth. He has thought much, and, like most of those persons I have met with who have conquered many prejudices and read little metaphysics, is a materialist. His favourite book on this point is the 'Système de la Nature.' We spent a most delightful day in his company. When we met him, I had taken no breakfast; and though we had set off from Burton that morning at six, and I spent the whole morning in riding and walking, I felt no inconvenience on waiting for food till our dinner time at two, I was so much interested with Mr Bage's conversation.

"I am obliged to finish this letter somewhat abruptly, at the house of Dr Parr, where we arrived Thursday (yesterday) about noon, and found Mr and Mrs Wynn, but not the Doctor, he having thought proper to withdraw himself on their arrival. It is most probable we shall be in town to-morrow evening, but may possibly not arrive till Sunday.

"I should have added to the account of Mr Bage, that he never was in London for more than a week at a time, and very seldom more than 50 miles from his home. A very memorable instance, in my opinion, of great intellectual refinement, attained in the bosom of rusticity.

"Farewell. Salute William in my name. Perhaps you know how. Take care of yourself!—Tell Fanny that her mug and Lucas's are hitherto quite safe. I hope I shall find that the green monkey has resumed his old station by the time of my return."

William Godwin to Mary Wollstonecraft Godwin.

"*June* 17, 1797.

"You cannot imagine anything like Mr Wynn and his wife. He is a raw country booby of eighteen, his hair about his ears, and a beard that has never deigned to submit to the stroke of the razor. His voice is loud, broad and unmodulated, the mind of the possessor has never yet felt a sentiment that should give it flexibleness or variety. He has at present a brother with him, a lad, as I guess, of fifteen, who has come to Dr Parr's house at Hatton, with a high generosity of sentiment, and a tone of mind, declaring that, if his brother be disinherited, he, who is the next brother, will not reap the benefit. His name is Julius, and John Wynn, the husband, is also a lad of very good dispositions. They both stammer : Julius extremely, John less : but with the stuttering of Julius there is an ingenuousness and warmth that have considerable charms. John, on the contrary, has all the drawling, loth of voice and thinking, that usually characterizes a clown. His air is *gauche*, his gait negligent and slouching, his whole figure boorish. Both the lads are as ignorant, and as destitute of adventure and ambition, as any children that aristocracy has to boast.

Poor Sarah, the bride, is the victim of her mother, as the bridegroom is her victim in turn. The mother taught her that the height of female wisdom was to marry a rich man and a fool, and she has religiously complied. Her mother is an admirable woman, and the daughter mistook, and fancied she was worthy of love. Never was a girl more attached to her mother than Sarah Wynn (Parr). You do not know, but I do, that Sarah has an uncommon understanding, and an exquisite sensibility, which glows in her complexion, and flashes from her eyes. Yet she is silly enough to imagine that she shall be happy in love and a cottage, with John Wynn. She is excessively angry with the fathers on both sides, who, as she says, after having promised the contrary, attempted clandestinely to separate them. They have each, beyond question, laid up a magazine of unhappiness : yet I am persuaded Dr Parr is silly enough to imagine the match a desirable one.

"We slept, as I told you, at Tamworth on Wednesday evening. Thursday morning we proceeded through Coleshill (where I found a permanent pillory established, in lieu of the stocks), and where we passed through a very deep and rather formidable ford, the bridge being under repair, and breakfasted at the George in the Tree, 18 miles. From thence the road by Warwick would have been 14 miles, and by a cross-country road only six. By this, therefore, we proceeded, and a very deep and rough road we found it. We arrived at Hatton about one, so, after dinner, thinking it too much to sit all day in the company I have described, I proposed to Montagu a walk to Kenilworth Castle, the seat originally of Simon De Montfort, Earl of Leicester, who in the reign of Henry III., to whom he was an implacable enemy, was the author of the institution of the House of Commons ; and, more recently, the seat of Robert Dudley, Earl of Leicester-- the favourite, and, as he hoped and designed, the husband of Elizabeth, to whom he gave a most magnificent and memorable entertainment at this place. The ruins are, beyond comparison, the finest in England. I found Montagu by no means a desirable companion in this expedition. He could not be persuaded to indulge the

divine enthusiasm I felt coming on my soul, while I felt revived,
and, as it were, embodied, the image of ancient times : but on the
contrary, expressed nothing but indignation against the aristocracy
displayed, and joy that it was destroyed. From Dr Parr's to Kenilworth, across the fields, is only four miles. By the road, round by
Warwick, it is nine. We of course took the field way, but derived
but little benefit from it, as we were on foot from half after four to
half after ten, exclusive of a rest of ten minutes. One hour out of
the six we spent at Kenilworth, and two hours and a half in going
and returning respectively, so utterly incapable were we of finding
the path prescribed us.

"To-day, Friday, as fortune determined, was Coventry Fair,
with a procession of all the trades, with a female representative of
Lady Godiva at their head, dressed in a close dress to represent
nakedness. As fortune had thus disposed of us, we deemed it our
duty not to miss the opportunity. We accordingly set out after
breakfast, for Montagu proved lazy, and we did not get off till half
after eleven. From Dr Parr's to Warwick is four miles, from Warwick to Coventry ten miles. One mile on the Coventry side of
Warwick is Guy's Cliff, Mr Greathed's. My description of his
garden was an irresistible motive with Montagu to desire to visit
it, though I by no means desired it. We accordingly went, and
walked round the garden. Mr Greathed was in his grounds, and
I left a card, signifying I had done myself the pleasure of paying
my respects to him, and taken the liberty of leading my friend over
his garden. This delay of half-an-hour precisely answered the
purpose of making us too late for Lady Godiva. We saw the
crowd, which was not yet dispersed, and the booths of the fair, but
the lady, the singularity of the scene, was retired.

"It is now Sunday evening : we are at Cambridge. Montagu
says we shall certainly be in town to-morrow (Monday) night. The
distance is fifty-three miles : we shall therefore probably be late,
and he requests that, if we be not at home before ten, you will
retain somebody to take the whiskey from Somers Town to Lincoln's Inn. If Mary be at a loss on the subject, perhaps the people
of Montagu's lodging can assist her.

" Farewell : be happy : be in health and spirits. Keep a look-out, but not an anxious one. Delays are not necessarily tragical. I believe there will be none."

Mary Wollstonecraft Godwin to William Godwin.

" *June* 19. *Monday, almost* 12 *o'clock.*

" One of the pleasures you tell me that you promised yourself from your journey was the effect your absence might produce on me. Certainly at first my affection was increased, or rather was more alive. But now it is just the contrary. Your later letters might have been addressed to anybody, and will serve to remind you where you have been, though they resemble nothing less than mementos of affection.

" I wrote to you to Dr Parr's ; you take no notice of my letter. Previous to your departure, I requested you not to torment me by leaving the day of your return undecided. But whatever tenderness you took away with you seems to have evaporated on the journey, and new objects, and the homage of vulgar minds restored you to your icy philosophy.

You tell me that your journey could not take less than three days, therefore, as you were to visit Dr D[arwin] and Dr P[arr], Saturday was the probable day. You saw neither, yet you have been a week on the road. I did not wonder, but approved of your visit to Mr Bage. But a *show* which you waited to see, and did not see, appears to have been equally attractive. I am at a loss to guess how you could have been from Saturday to Sunday night travelling from Coventry to Cambridge. In short, your being so late to-night, and the chance of your not coming, shows so little consideration, that unless you suppose me to be a stick or a stone, you must have forgot to think, as well as to feel, since you have been on the wing. I am afraid to add what I feel. Good-night."

Two more notes which follow show that the cordial affection which subsisted between the married pair was not seriously affected by this little outburst.

The Same to the Same.

"*June* 25, 1797.

" I know that you do not like me to go to Holcroft's. I think you right in the principle, but a little wrong in the present application.

" When I lived alone, I always dined on a Sunday with company, in the evening, if not at dinner, at St P[aul's], with Johnson], generally also of a Tuesday, and some other day at Fuseli's.

" I like to see new faces as a study, and since my return from Norway, or rather since I have accepted of invitations, I have dined every third Sunday at Twiss's, nay oftener, for they sent for me when they had any extraordinary company. I was glad to go, because my lodging was noisy of a Sunday, and Mr S.'s house and spirits were so altered, that my visits depressed him, instead of exhilarating me.

" I am then, you perceive, thrown out of my track, and have not traced another. But so far from wishing to obtrude on yours, I had written to Mrs Jackson, and mentioned Sunday, and am now sorry that I did not fix on to-day as one of the days for sitting for my picture.

" To Mr Johnson I would go without ceremony, but it is not convenient for me at present to make haphazard visits.

" Should Carlisle chance to call on you this morning, send him to me ; but by himself, for he often has a companion with him, which would defeat my purpose."

The Same to the Same.

" *Monday morning, July* 3*d*, 1797.

" Mrs Reveley can have no doubt about to-day, so we are to stay at home. I have a design upon you this evening to keep you quite to myself—I hope nobody will call!—and make you read the play.

" I was thinking of a favourite song of my poor friend Fanny's : ' In a vacant rainy day, you shall be wholly mine,' &c.

" Unless the weather prevents you from taking your accustomed walk, call on me this morning, for I have something to say to you."

Holcroft's intimacy with Godwin by no means grew less because his friend was married. The following letter from him when visiting some friends in Norfolk gives a pleasant picture of Mrs Godwin, senior, and of the eagerness which the good old lady really felt to see her distinguished son:—

Thomas Holcroft to William Godwin.

" WOOD NORTON, *July* 26, 1797.

" It was my intention to write, for I feel a kind of vacuity of heart when I am deprived of the intercourse of my accustomed friends. But as I cannot write to them all, and as we have many friends in common, I think there are few whom you may not safely assure on my part that they have their turn in my thoughts. I deferred this pleasant duty however till I had seen your mother, whom I thought it right and respectful to visit. My coming occasioned some little alarm. The Major, Mrs Harwood, and Fanny accompanied me. We were seen from the windows as we came up to the gate. I had my spectacles on, and your sister-in-law ran to inform your mother that yourself and Mrs Godwin were arrived. The old lady stood in the portico; the young ones advanced. There was an anxious curiosity in their countenances, and your sister, addressing herself to me, said, ' I think I know you, sir.' I scarcely knew what to reply. Imagination had winged her and myself to London, where I supposed that some years ago I might have seen her at your lodgings, taking it for granted that she was a relation. But as I did not answer, Major Harwood relieved our embarrassment by announcing my name. The change of countenance that took place was visible, for though your sister could not perhaps have fully persuaded herself that my face was actually yours, yet she seemed rather to trust to her hopes than to her recollection; and these being disappointed, an immediate blank took possession of her features, and the rising joy was damped. Your mother, however, very kindly invited us in, and gave us all the good things she had that could administer to our immediate pleasures. The expectations which Major H. had raised by his description of your mother was not entirely answered. She was neither so alert, so commanding, nor so animated as he and Anne had described; but as they both are apt to deal in the superlative, I make some deductions from their previous description and after remarks, according to which she is very rapidly on the decline. Having quitted her farming business, I have no doubt myself but that her faculties will be impaired much faster than they would have been had she continued to exert them; yet I strongly doubt of the very rapid decline which the Major supposes. Her memory is good, her conceptions, speaking comparatively, are clear, and her strength considerable.

"I have seen more of the County of Norfolk than of its inhabitants; of which county I remark that to the best of my recollection it contains more flint, more turkies, more turnips, more wheat, more cultivation, more commons, more cross-roads, and, from that token, probably more inhabitants, than any county I ever visited. It has another distinguishing and paradoxical feature, if what I hear be true. It is said to be more illiterate than other parts of England, and yet I doubt if any county of like extent have produced an equal number of famous men. This, however, is merely a conjecture, made not from examination, but from memory.

"As it is necessary for me to bathe, I shall immediately depart for Yarmouth, and pass through Norwich, which I have not yet seen. If you or Mrs Godwin, or both, can but prevail on yourself or selves to endure the fatigue of writing to me, I hope I need not use many words to convince you of the pleasure it will give me. And be it understood that this letter is addressed to you both, whatever the direction on the back may affirm to the contrary. Professions are almost impertinent, and yet I am almost tempted to profess to you how sincerely and seriously I am interested in your happiness. But as I am sure my words would ill describe my thoughts, I shall forbear. Pray inform me, sweet lady, in what state is your novel? And on what, courteous sir, are you employed? Though I am idle myself, I cannot endure that any one else should be so. Direct to me at the post-office, Yarmouth. Pray do me the favour to call occasionally and look into the house and library.

"T. HOLCROFT."

CHAPTER X.

MARY GODWIN'S DEATH. 1797.

MARY Godwin had been in remarkably good health during the whole period of her pregnancy. It will have been seen in the correspondence that she consulted Dr Carlisle during this time, but not for any serious indisposition. She had no alarm or even uneasiness on the subject of her approaching trial, since she had suffered but little at the birth of Fanny, and had conceived the idea that women in general made far too much of the difficulties and inconveniences of child-bearing. She had a strong opinion that in all normal and natural cases women were the proper persons to attend their own sex, and therefore engaged Mrs Blenkinsop, matron and midwife to the Westminster Lying-In Hospital to be with her. When Mrs Blenkinsop arrived, soon after Mary Godwin was taken in labour on Wednesday, August 30, all seemed well. She had wished that Godwin should not be in the house, and the notes that follow, written to him during her labour, have probably but few parallels.

Mary Wollstonecraft Godwin to W. Godwin.

"*Aug.* 30, 1797.

" I have no doubt of seeing the animal to-day; but must wait for Mrs Blenkinsop to guess at the hour. I have sent for her. Pray send me the newspaper. I wish I had a novel or some book of sheer amusement to excite curiosity and while away the time. Have you anything of the kind?

The Same to the Same.

"*Aug.* 30, 1797.

" Mrs Blenkinsop tells me that everything is in a fair way, and that there is no fear of the event being put off till another day. Still *at present* she thinks I shall not immediately be freed from my load. I am very well. Call before dinner time, unless you receive another message from me."

The Same to the Same.

" *Three o'clock, Aug.* 30, 1797.

" Mrs Blenkinsop tells me I am in the most natural state, and can promise me a safe delivery, but that I must have a little patience."

The child, not the William so anxiously expected, but Mary, afterwards Mrs Shelley, was born at twenty minutes past eleven, and for some hours all seemed well. But some circumstances then alarmed the midwife, and Dr Poignard, physician and accoucheur to the same hospital, was called in. He did what was deemed necessary, and the danger, which was extreme till about eight the next morning, then appeared at an end. Godwin called in Dr Fordyce, a very old friend of his wife, who confirmed Dr Poignard's opinion that the patient was doing well; indeed, he quoted Mrs Godwin's case the same day "in corroboration of a favourite idea of his, of the propriety of employing females in the capacity of midwives. Mary had had a woman, and was doing extremely well." On Sunday, however, a very alarming change took place, and after a week

I.	S

of terror, alternating with some gleams of hope, she sunk
and died on the following Sunday morning, September 10,
at twenty minutes before eight.

All that medical skill could do was done in the case.
Dr Fordyce and Dr Clarke were constant in their attendance, and Mr, afterwards Sir Anthony, Carlisle never left
the house from Wednesday, Sept. 6th, till the time of the
patient's death. Mr Basil Montagu was constantly with
Godwin, and was full of kindness and sympathy. Through
the whole time Godwin tells us "nothing could exceed the
equanimity, the patience, and affectionateness of the poor
sufferer."

Godwin's diary during these days is very curious. All
that he felt most deeply is recorded in his usual business-
like way ; the hand-writing never falters, the same precise
abbreviations and stops are used, till the last, when occur
the only lines and dashes which break the exceeding neatness of the book. It is as follows :—

"*Aug.* 30, *W.*—'Mary' p. 116. Fell and Dyson call : dine at
      Reveley's : Fenwicks and M. sup : Blenkinsop.
      Birth of Mary, 20 minutes after 11 at night.
      From 7 to 10, Evesham Buildings." [This
      refers to a change of lodgings.]

  „ 31, *Th.*—Fetch Dr Poignard : Fordyce calls : in the even-
      ing Miss G. and L. J. M. Reveley and Tuthil :
      J. G. calls.

Sep. 1, *F.*—Call on Robinson, Nicholson, Carlisle, and M.
      Hays : Johnson calls : favourable appearances.

  „   2, *Sa.*—Carlisle, Montagu, Tuthil, and M. Reveley call :
      worse in the evening. Nurse.

  „   3, *Su.*—Montagu breakfasts : call with him on Wolcot,
      Opie, Laurence and Dr Thompson. Shivering
      fits : Fordyce twice. Poignard, Blenkinsop
      and nurse.

" *Sep.* 4, *M.*—Blenkinsop : puppies [Dr Fordyce now forbade the patient to nurse her child, and puppies were employed to draw off the milk]. Johnson and Nicholson call : Masters calls. E. Fenwick and M. sleep. M. Hays calls. Pichegru, arrested.

,, 5, *Tu.*—Fordyce twice : Clarke in the afternoon. M. Hays calls.

,, 6, *W.*—Carlisle calls : wine diet : Carlisle from Brixton : Miss Jones sleeps.

,, 7, *Th.*—Barry, Reveley and Lowry call : dying in the evening.

,, 8, *F.*—Opie and Tuthil call. Idea of death : solemn communication. Barry : Miss G. sleeps.

,, 9, *Sa.*—Talk to her of Fanny and Mary : Barry.

,, 10, *Su.*—20 minutes before 8 _____

"

It is not easy to characterize the frame of mind in which Godwin sat down a few hours after these agitated pen-marks were drawn, to write himself to those friends to whom as he thought he owed the duty of himself communicating the loss he had sustained. It was probably an attempt to be stoical, but a real indulgence in the luxury of woe. Among the first of these friends was Holcroft.

William Godwin to T. Holcroft.

" *Sunday, Sep.* 10, 1797.

" MY DEAR FRIEND.—The passage in your last kind letter that related to the subject of self-reproach was rather out of season. It has dwelt upon my mind ever since. My wife is now dead. She died this morning at eight o'clock. She grew worse before your letter arrived. Nobody has a greater call to reproach himself, except for want of kindness and attention in which I hope I have not been very deficient, than I have. But reproach would answer no good purpose, and I will not harbour it.

"I firmly believe that there does not exist her equal in the world. I know from experience we were formed to make each other happy. I have not the least expectation that I can now ever know happiness again.

"When you come to town, look at me, and talk to me, but do not—if you can help it—exhort me, or console me.

"W. GODWIN."

He also wrote to Mrs Inchbald, and the whole of the letters which ensued are given consecutively, before passing to other correspondence. Mrs Shelley who had the letters before her, was certainly lenient in her judgment of Mrs Inchbald in her note quoted above. Smart writing and an argumentative temper were sadly out of place over the death-bed of Mary Godwin.

William Godwin to Mrs Inchbald.

"*Sep.* 10, 1797.

"My wife died at eight this morning. I always thought you used her ill, but I forgive you. You told me you did not know her. You have a thousand good and great qualities. She had a very deep-rooted admiration for you.

" Yours, with real honour and esteem,

"W. GODWIN."

Mrs Inchbald to William Godwin.

[*Sept.* 10, 1797]

"You have shocked me beyond expression, yet, I bless God, without exciting the smallest portion of remorse. Yet I feel most delicately on every subject in which the good or ill of my neighbours is involved.

" I did not know her. I never wished to know her : as I avoid every female acquaintance, who has no husband, I avoided her. Against my desire you made us acquainted. With what justice I shunned her, your present note evinces, for she judged me harshly. *She* first thought I used her ill, for you would not. I liked her—I spoke well of her. Let Charlotte Smith be my witness, who received her character from me, such as I gave of her to everybody.

" Be comforted. You *will* be comforted. Still I feel for you at present. Write to me again. Say what you please at such a time as this ; I will excuse and pity you."

The Same to the Same.

" *Sept.* 11, 1797.

" 'The ceremony of condolence is an impertinence, but if you consider mine superior to ceremony, you will accept it.

" I have too much humility to offer consolation to a mind like yours. I will only describe sensations which nearly a similar misfortune excited in me.

" I felt myself for a time bereft of every comfort the world could bestow, but these opinions passed away, and gave place to others, almost the reverse.

" I was separated from the only friend I had in the world, and by circumstances so much more dreadful than those which have occurred to you, as the want of warning increases all our calamities, but yet I have lived to think with indifference of all I then suffered.

" You have been a most kind husband, I am told. Rejoice,— the time *might* have come when you would have wept over her remains with compunction for cruelty to her.

" While you have no self-reproaches to wound you, be pacified. Every ill falls short of that.

" I lament her as a person whom you loved. I am shocked at the unexpected death of one in such apparent vigour of mind and body ; but I feel no concern for any regret she endured at parting

from this world, for I believe she had tact and understanding to
despise it heartily. Mr Twiss received the news with sorrow, and
Mrs Twiss shed many tears. They were not prepared, any more
than myself, for the news, for they had not heard of her illness. I
showed them your note to me, and if you had seen the manner in
which they treated your suspicion of my influence with them
(and that was certainly your only meaning), you would beg my
pardon.

"I shall be glad to hear of your health, and that your poor
little family are well, for believe me concerned for your welfare."
                                                    "E. I."

William Godwin to Mrs Inchbald.

"Sept. 13, 1797.

"I must endeavour to be understood as to the unworthy behaviour with which I charge you towards my wife. I think your
shuffling behaviour about the taking places to the comedy of the
'Will,' dishonourable to you. I think your conversation with her
that night at the play base, cruel, and insulting. There were persons in the box who heard it, and they thought as I do. I think
you know more of my wife than you are willing to acknowledge to
yourself, and that you have an understanding capable of doing
some small degree of justice to her merits. I think you should
have had magnanimity and self-respect enough to have shewed
this. I think that while the Twisses and others were sacrificing
to what they were silly enough to think a proper etiquette, a person so out of all comparison their superior, as you are, should
have placed her pride in acting upon better principles, and in
courting and distinguishing insulted greatness and worth ; I think
that you chose a mean and pitiful conduct, when you might have
chosen a conduct that would have done you immortal honour.
You had not even their excuse. They could not (they pretended)
receive her into their previous circles. You kept no circle to de-
base and enslave you.

"I have now been full and explicit on this subject, and have
done with it, I hope, for ever.

" I thank you for your attempt at consolation in your letter of yesterday. It was considerate, and well-intended, although its consolations are utterly alien to my heart.

"W. GODWIN.

" I wish not to be misunderstood as to the circles above alluded to. I mean not to apply my idea to the sacrifices, for one or two of whom I feel more honour than I can easily express, but to the idols."

Mrs Inchbald to William Godwin.

"*Sept.* 14, 1797.

" I could refute every charge you allege against me in your letter; but I revere a man, either in deep love or in deep grief: and as it is impossible to convince, I would at least say nothing to irritate him.

" Yet surely thus much I may venture to add. As the short and very slight acquaintance I had with Mrs Godwin, and into which I was reluctantly impelled by you, has been productive of petty suspicions and revilings (from which my character has been till now preserved), surely I cannot sufficiently applaud my own penetration in apprehending, and my own firmness in resisting, a longer and more familiar acquaintance."

The Same to the Same.

"*Thursday, Oct.* 26, 1797.

" With the most sincere sympathy in all you have suffered— with the most perfect forgiveness of all you have said to me, there must nevertheless be an end to our acquaintance *for ever*. I respect *your prejudices*, but I also respect *my own*.

"E. INCHBALD."

Mrs Cotton, an old and intimate friend of Mary Godwin, wrote a touching letter of condolence, from Sonning, near Reading. Godwin thus replied,—

William Godwin to Mrs Cotton.

"*Sept.* 14, 1797.

"DEAR MADAM,—I cannot write. I have half destroyed my-self by writing. It does me more mischief than anything else. I must preserve myself, if for no other reason, for the two children. I had desired a friend to write to you. I suppose he has for-gotten it. He is not in the way for me to inquire. She expressed a wish to have had you for a nurse. I wrote a letter to you for that purpose last Wednesday. But the medical attendants told me it was useless to send it. She died on Sunday morning at eight o'clock. She lasted longer than any one expected. She had Dr Fordyce, Dr Clarke, and Mr Carlisle, the last of whom, who is one of the best and greatest of men, sat with her the four last nights and days of her life. Mrs Fenwick, author of 'Secrecy,' a novel, was her principal nurse, and Mr Carlisle said, the best nurse he ever saw. Four of my male friends stayed night and day in the house, to be sent at a moment's warning anywhere that should be necessary. I spent the principal part of my time in her chamber. I will desire Mrs Fenwick to write to you. If you have any inquiries to make, address them to her at my house.

"Believe me to be, with a deep sense of the affection my wife entertained for you,

"Your sincere friend,

"W. GODWIN.

"I find that the address I gave to my friend, Mr Basil Mon-tagu, to write to you, was Mrs Cotton, near Henley-upon-Thames. He has despatched a letter with that address."

The Same to the Same.

"*Oct.* 24*th*, 1797.

. . . "I partook of a happiness, so much the more exquisite, as I had a short time before had no conception of it, and scarcely admitted the possibility of it. I saw one bright ray of light that streaked my day of life only to leave the remainder more gloomy, and, in the truest sense of the word, hopeless.

"I am still here, in the same situation in which you saw me, surrounded by the children, and all the well-known objects, which, though they all talk to me of melancholy, are still dear to me. I love to cherish melancholy. I love to tread the edge of intellectual danger, and just to keep within the line which every moral and intellectual consideration forbids me to overstep, and in this indulgence and this vigilance I place my present luxury.

"The poor children! I am myself totally unfitted to educate them. The scepticism which perhaps sometimes leads me right in matters of speculation, is torment to me when I would attempt to direct the infant mind. I am the most unfit person for this office; she was the best qualified in the world. What a change. The loss of the children is less remediless than mine. You can understand the difference. —I am, madam, with much respect, yours,

"W. GODWIN."

Mrs Fenwick and Miss Hayes, the other friend who was with Mary Godwin in her last hours, each wrote, as did Mr Basil Montagu, many of the necessary letters. Some words of these ladies may serve to complete the picture of a very beautiful character, and a very peaceful death. It was a death, moreover—as here may fitly be remarked in connection with a sentence of her husband's quoted above— brightened by the same faith which has brightened the deathbeds of so many more who have sinned and suffered, faith in the love and mercy of God, whom she had never doubted, though the words in which she would have couched her creed may have changed, since she wrote her early letters to George Blood. Her mind, as Godwin tells us, was undisturbed by the graver doubts on the very Being of God which assailed his own.

Miss Hayes to [*Mr Hugh Skeys.*]

" Sir,—Myself and Mrs Fenwick were the only two female friends that were with Mrs Godwin during her last illness. Mrs Fenwick attended her from the beginning of her confinement with scarcely any intermission. I was with her for the four last days of her life, and though I have had but little experience in scenes of this sort, yet I can confidently affirm that my imagination could never have pictured to me a mind so tranquil, under affliction so great. She was all kindness and attention, and cheerfully complied with everything that was recommended to her by her friends. In many instances she employed her mind with more sagacity on the subject of her illness than any of the persons about her. Her whole soul seemed to dwell with anxious fondness on her friends ; and her affections, which were at all times more alive than perhaps those of any other human being, seemed to gather new disinterestedness upon this trying occasion. The attachment and regret of those who surrounded her appeared to increase every hour, and if her principles are to be judged of by what I saw of her death, I should say that no principles could be more conducive to calmness and consolation." [*The rest is wanting.*]

Mrs Fenwick to Everina Wollstonecraft.

" *Sept.* 12, 1797.

" I am a stranger to you, Miss Wollstonecraft, and at present greatly enfeebled both in mind and body : but when Mr Godwin desired that I would inform you of the death of his most beloved and most excellent wife, I was willing to undertake the task, because it is some consolation to render him the slightest service, and because my thoughts perpetually dwell upon her virtues and her loss. Mr Godwin himself cannot upon this occasion write to you.

" Mrs Godwin died on Sunday, Sept. 10, about eight in the morning. I was with her at the time of her delivery, and with very little intermission until the moment of her death. Every skilful effort that medical knowledge of the highest class could make, was exerted to save her. It is not possible to describe the unremitting and devoted attentions of her husband. Nor is it easy to give you an adequate idea of the affectionate zeal of many of her friends, who were on the watch night and day to seize on an opportunity of contributing towards her recovery, and to lessen her sufferings.

"No woman was ever more happy in marriage than Mrs Godwin. Who ever endured more anguish than Mr Godwin endures? Her description of him, in the very last moments of her recollection was, 'He is the kindest, best man in the world.'

"I know of no consolations for myself, but in remembering how happy she had lately been, and how much she was admired, and almost idolized, by some of the most eminent and best of human beings.

"The children are both well, the infant in particular. It is the finest baby I ever saw.—Wishing you peace and prosperity, I remain your humble servant, ELIZA FENWICK.

"Mr Godwin requests you will make Mrs Bishop acquainted with the particulars of this afflicting event. He tells me that Mrs Godwin entertained a sincere and earnest affection for Mrs Bishop."

Mr Marshal who had been, as might be expected, one of the friends so constant in his attentions, had, with Mr Basil Montagu, the charge of the arrangements for the funeral. Among those asked to be present was Mr Tuthil, a very intimate friend of Godwin, who shared in his views on religious as on other subjects. The correspondence which ensued is honourable to both friends.

Mr Tuthil to Mr Marshal.

"3 CHAPEL COURT, OFF NEW BURLINGTON STREET,
[*Sep.* 13*th*, 1797.]

"I feel very much gratified at finding myself numbered with those who had engaged Mrs Godwin's 'particular esteem,' and should rejoice to pay any honest tribute to her memory. If a funeral consisted simply in the expression of affectionate feelings, I should ardently desire to follow her; but I much doubt the morality of assisting at religious ceremonies; and I cannot place myself where I should be inclined to think I did not look like an honest man.

"It would be painful, very painful to me, if Mr Godwin were for a single instant to suppose my decision incompatible with the warmest affection.—Yours very sincerely,   G. TUTHIL."

William Godwin to Mr Tuthil.

"*Sep.* 13*th*, 1797.

"I think the last respect due to the best of human beings ought not to be deserted by their friends. There is not perhaps an individual in my list, whose opinions are not as adverse to religious ceremonies as your own, and who might not with equal propriety shrink from, and desert the remains of the first of women. I honour your character; I respect your scruples. But I should have thought more highly of you, if, at such a moment it had been impossible for so cold a reflection to have crossed your mind. Think of the subject again. Consult Holcroft. Act finally upon the genuine decision of your own judgment.—Yours in sincere friendship,   W. GODWIN."

Mr Tuthil to William Godwin.

"3 CHAPEL COURT, OFF NEW BURLINGTON STREET,
[*Sep.* 14*th*, 1797.]

"I have reconsidered the subject, and can only arrive at the same conclusion. If there be men who appear to me to violate those principles which they profess to hold sacred, I cannot imitate them. There has been a time when you would have thought as I do : but show me that there is, even at this melancholy moment, a deficiency of true feeling in this reflection, and I will instantly discard it. Indeed, indeed you do not understand me. There is a coldness in my manner which has deceived you.—Yours very sincerely,   G. TUTHIL."

Godwin was too prostrate both in mind and body himself to attend the funeral or meet the friends who did so. He spent the day at Marshal's lodgings and thence wrote to Mr Carlisle.

William Godwin to Mr Anthony Carlisle.

"*Sep.* 15*th*, 1797.

"My dear Carlisle,—I am here, sitting alone in Mr Marshal's lodgings during my wife's funeral. My mind is extremely sunk and languid. But I husband my thoughts, and shall do very well. I have been but once since you saw me, in a train of thought that gave me alarm. One of my wife's books now lies near me, but I avoid opening it. I took up a book on the education of children, but that impressed me too forcibly with my forlorn and disabled state with respect to the two poor animals left under my protection, and I threw it aside.

"Nothing could be more soothing to my mind than to dwell in a long letter upon her virtues and accomplishments, and our mutual happiness, past and in prospect. But the attractions of this subject are delusive, and I dare not trust myself with it.

"I may dwell however with perfect safety upon your merits and kindness, and the indelible impression they have left on my mind. Your generous and unintermitted attendance upon the dear deceased constituted the greatest consolation it was possible for me to receive in that dreadful period when I most needed consolation. I may say to you on paper, what I observed to you in our last interview, that I never, in the whole course of my life, met with the union of so clear and capacious an understanding, with so much goodness of heart and sweetness of manners.

"It is pleasing to be loved by those we feel ourselves impelled to love. It is inexpressibly gratifying, when we find those qualities that most call forth our affections, to be regarded by that person with some degree of a correspondent feeling. If you have any of that kind of consolation in store for me, be at the pains to bestow it. But, above all, be severely sincere. I ought to be acquainted with my own defects, and to trace their nature in the effects they produce.—Yours, with fervent admiration and regard."

By a strange coincidence, Mr Hamilton Rowan was writing on the same 15th of September to congratulate on her marriage her who was then committed to the grave.

Archd. H. Rowan, Esq., to Mary Wollstonecraft Godwin.

"BRANDYWINE, *near* WILMINGTON, DELAWARE,
"*Septr.* 15, 1797.

"DEAR MADAM,—I rejoice most sincerely that you have such a companion, protector, and friend as I believe him to be, whose name the papers inform me you now bear. I have been much to blame. In the more than two years that I have been in America I have written only thrice to you. You were not happy. I had no right to trouble you with my dark reveries. I was displeased with my past and my present conduct and undecided as to my future ; how could I speak comfort to so wounded a mind as yours? Now I may be allowed to croak. You know it was my fashion in Paris. Through my wife's *prudent* conduct she has been permitted to remain in possession of my property, and I have thus become a pensioner of the Irish Government. That I have spent only what was necessary for my subsistence does not satisfy me. Every letter which I receive from Mrs H. R., though couched in the most affectionate terms, yet shows me that what I called acting from principle was in her idea wild ambition or foolish vanity. A mode has been pointed out to me by which I might possibly rejoin my family, but it is a renunciation of principle. I cannot accede to the proposition. I should be for ever unhappy, and, I think, should disgrace my children even as long as it was remembered that I was their ancestor. As my growling, however, signified little, I set about procuring an independence, and with this view have commenced calico printer, &c., on the banks of the Brandywine. I have connected myself with a good *sans culottes* dyer from Manchester, who had two great faults which forced him to quit that place—he could read and he

could speak. I rent the place where we are. Aldred, my partner,
has the stone mansion, and I have in a most romantic corner
built, upon a surface of 18 ft. square, a house in the second stage
of civilization, viz., a log house, where I and Charles, who has a
daughter, live and cook, &c., just as you saw in the Rue
Mousseaux.

"*Nov.* 17.—This has been lying by me, and the last papers
announce a melancholy event—and have you so shortly enjoyed
the calm repose I hoped you were in possession of. I hope the
report is false; if true, let this convey my condolence to Mr G.

"ARCHD. HAMILTON ROWAN."

The funeral took place in Old St Pancras Churchyard,
attended by all the friends, save Mr Tuthil, who had been on
terms of great intimacy with Godwin and his wife. The body
does not now rest there. That churchyard was rudely disturbed when the Metropolitan and Midland Railways were
constructed, before which time Godwin lay by his wife's
side. Loving hands transported their remains to Bourne-
mouth, where they now lie together with those of their
daughter, Mrs Shelley.

This Memoir is a record rather of what was than a
speculation on what might have been. Yet it is impossible
not to think for a moment on the two lives, one shortened
so untimeously, one so blighted. That each had supplemented and improved at once the life and genius of the
other cannot be doubted, in spite of the little clouds which
had arisen on the fair sky of their domestic happiness.
That Mary Godwin's calm faith might have in some degree
softened her husband's ruggedness, that his critical faculty
might have aided to mature her style, and prune her luxuriant fancy, is probable. She too had been more schooled
in the actual work of life than he, and her experience might

have saved her husband from the unfortunate pecuniary
difficulties which were so great a burthen on his later years.
But this was not to be. She died in her prime, intellectual
and physical, leaving to the daughter to whom she gave
birth a mingled inheritance of genius and sadness, of filial
duty, met by coldness at home, of deep wedded joys and
deep widowed sorrows. She passed to her rest, not to be
disturbed by the chorus of vituperation which has assailed
her memory.

> " Thee nor carketh care nor slander,
> Nothing but the small cold worm
> Fretteth thine enshrouded form—
> Let them rave.
> Light and shadow ever wander
> O'er the green that folds thy grave—
> Let them rave."

Yet it may be hoped that in some degree what has here
been written may give some a clearer view of the virtues,
and a more tender pity for the failings and the sorrows of
Mary Wollstonecraft Godwin.

The children were with Mrs Reveley during the few sad
days of extreme danger, and after the death. The infant
was also for a few days alarmingly ill, but recovered after
her return to her father's house on Sunday 17th. Little
Fanny had been brought home the evening before, and Mrs
Fenwick remained a few days to nurse the child. Godwin
removed all his books and papers from Evesham buildings,
and in future took for his study the room which had been
his wife's.

Among those who had been most zealous in offers of
help was Mr Nicholson, who, with his wife, wished to have

charge of the children for a time, had they not been already removed. The letter from him which follows shows not only the interest which " Lavater's Speculations on Physiognomy " then were exciting, but one of Godwin's favourite theories, which he brings out in several books, and notably in " The Enquirer," that education cannot begin too early, and that in the very dawn of infancy the future character begins to develop. The Diary records that Mr Nicholson visited Godwin on Monday, Sept. 18, and on his return home the letter was written.

William Nicholson to William Godwin.

" NEWMAN STREET, *Sept.* 18, 1797.

" DEAR SIR,—When I had the pleasure of seeing your little daughter this morning, and you asked my opinion concerning her physiognomy, I experienced some difficulty, partly from an ill-grounded sense of ridicule in seeming to assume the character of fortune-teller, partly from a consciousness of imperfect knowledge, but chiefly from the little probability that the opportunity would afford time for a calm consideration of the individual, and of my own associated notions, which require meditation and development before I can satisfy myself. My view was, in fact, slight and momentary. I had no time to consider, compare, and combine. Yet I am disposed to think the following imperfect observation may lead you to more than a suspicion that our organization at the birth may greatly influence those motives which govern the series of our future acts of intelligence, and that we may even possess moral habits, acquired during the fœtal state.

" 1. The outline of the head viewed from above, its profile, the outline of the forehead, seen from behind and in its horizontal positions, are such as I have invariably and exclusively seen in subjects who possessed considerable memory and intelligence.

" 2. The base of the forehead, the eyes and eyebrows, are

I.   T

familiar to me in subjects of quick sensibility, irritable, scarcely irascible, and surely not given to rage. That part of the outline of the forehead, which is very distinct in patient investigators, is less so in her. I think her powers, of themselves, would lead to speedy combination, rather than continued research.

" 3. The lines between the eyes have much expression, but I had not time to develope them. They simply confirmed to me the inductions in the late paragraph.

" 4. The form of the nose, the nostrils, its insertion between the eyes, and its changes by muscular action, together with the side of the face in which the characteristic marks of affection are most prominent, were scarcely examined. Here also is much room for meditation and remark.

" 6. The mouth was too much employed to be well observed. It has the outlines of intelligence. She was displeased, and it denoted much more of resigned vexation than either scorn or rage.

" On this imperfect sight it would be silly to risk a character ; for which reason I will only add that I conjecture that her manner may be petulant in resistance, but cannot be sullen. I have chosen to send you these memoranda, rather than seem to shrink from the support of truth by declining to practise what I have asserted could be done without difficulty in the case of my own children.

" That she may be everything your parental affection can desire is the sincere wish of—Yours, with much regard,

" WM. NICHOLSON."

The Diary shows, as might be expected, an almost complete stagnation in Godwin's literary life. Friends were constant in their visits—Holcroft, the Fenwicks, Mrs Reveley, Mrs Barbauld, and many more ; but the only reading recorded is his wife's published works, the letters addressed to her, and the MSS. which she left unfinished, and he found almost at once a comfort in beginning to

compile the memoirs of her which were published in the
following year. Mr Skeys, who wrote very cordially to
the husband of his first wife's friend, aided him with all
the information in his power; but Mrs Bishop and Everina
Wollstonecraft, who had never liked the marriage, gave
as little help as they could, and hence the meagreness and
even inaccuracies, in some parts of that narrative. These
ladies found, or said that they found, difficulties in getting
situations because of their relationship to Mary Godwin;
Mr Skeys, with whom they quarrelled, said it was because
of their own infirmities of temper. At any rate, they closed
as far as possible, and of their own accord, all communication between Godwin and the family of his wife, and for
many years showed no interest in either of the children she
had left.

CHAPTER XI.

A SINGULAR COURTSHIP—FRIENDS. 1798.

EARLY in the year of which the domestic record has been given, Godwin published the " Enquirer." It is a collection of essays, based, as he says in his preface, on conversations. It embraces a great variety of subjects, very much of the character which we have already found he and his friends met to discuss, such as "Of Awakening the Mind," "Of Co-habitation," "Of Riches and Poverty," and the like. The volume elaborated in this manner many of the points which had been treated cursorily in "Political Justice." It did not in any degree detract from his fame, and is admirably written, but since it merely reasserted principles already known as his, it excited no special attention, though it went through several editions. A very furious onslaught on the clergy, however, was one of the causes of a coolness which grew between him and Dr Parr. The Doctor had apparently not seen the book when Godwin paid his visit to Hatton with Basil Montagu.

The beginning of the year 1798 saw Godwin restored to the usual tenor of his life, yet with a sense, constantly expressed in his letters, of a great void in his existence which nothing could fill, with pecuniary cares pressing upon him, and an almost bewildered feeling in regard to the nurture and education of the children his wife had left him. Little Fanny had, from an early period, won his warm affection;

she bore his name, and was always treated by him as a daughter. The Diary of this year shews him again much in society; indeed, rarely at home in the evening. He had no companion there, and it has been seen already that his health did not allow of literary work beyond the time so closely devoted to it in the morning. Yet the amount of work recorded is surprising. Not only was his pen constantly employed, the early part of this year, on the "Memoirs" of his wife, and afterwards on one of the numerous books, of which he had always one or more in hand; but his reading was varied as ever, and the range was still more extended. He read in this year much Latin literature, chiefly the Poets; many French works, mainly the older and standard authors; the old English dramatists; and kept himself *au courant* with all the books of merit which issued from the English press. And there is a curious proof that this reading was, on the whole, thorough and methodical, his extreme honesty with himself leading him always to note in his private Diary whenever he merely dipped into a book, and read it here and there. Those who have turned over his MS. note-books, have been greatly puzzled by an entry occurring at irregular intervals, consisting apparently of the mysterious word, "gala," any explanation of which long seemed quite hopeless. A longer search, however, has shewn that whereas in the earlier note-books he occasionally wrote of an author that he studied him *ça et là*, this phrase gradually became *ça là*, and eventually "gala," the conundrum so difficult to solve. The fact that this is occasional, and always in reference to books into which a man would only care to dip, especially when, as was mostly the case, they had been read before, shews clearly enough the thoroughness of the usual study.

Any regular, more extended notes have for some time ceased, but there are occasional memoranda of value. One such relates to literary work intended during this year.

"1798. The following are the literary productions which I am at present desirous to execute :—

"1. A book to be entitled 'First Principles of Morals.' The principal purpose of this work is to correct certain errors in the earlier part of my 'Political Justice.' The part to which I allude is essentially defective, in the circumstance of not yielding a proper attention to the empire of feeling. The voluntary actions of men are under the direction of their feelings : nothing can have a tendency to produce this species of action, except so far as it is connected with ideas of future pleasure or pain to ourselves or others. Reason, accurately speaking, has not the smallest degree of power to put any one limb or articulation of our bodies into motion. Its province, in a practical view, is wholly confined to adjusting the comparison between different objects of desire, and investigating the most successful mode of attaining those objects. It proceeds upon the assumption of their desirableness or the contrary, and neither accelerates nor retards the vehemence of their pursuit, but merely regulates its direction, and points the road by which we shall proceed to our goal.

"Again, every man will, by a necessity of nature, be influenced by motives peculiar to him as an individual. As every man will know more of his kindred and intimates than strangers, so he will inevitably think of them oftener, feel for them more acutely, and be more anxious about their welfare. This propensity is as general as the propensity we feel to prefer the consideration of our own welfare to that of any other human being. Kept within due bounds, it is scarcely an object of moral censure. The benefits we can confer upon the world are few, at the same time that they are in their nature, either petty in their moment, or questionable in their results. The benefits we can confer upon those with whom we are closely connected are of great magnitude, or continual occurrence. It is impossible that we should be continually thinking of the whole world, or not confer a smile or a kindness but as we are prompted to it by an abstract principle of philanthropy. The series of actions of a virtuous man will be the spontaneous result of a disposition naturally kind and well-attempered. The spring of motion within him will certainly not be a sentiment of general utility. But it seems equally certain that utility, though not the source, will be the regulator, of his actions; and that however ardent be his parental, domestic, or friendly exertions, he will from time to time examine into their coincidence with the greatest sum of happiness in his power to produce. It seems difficult to conceive how the man who does not make this the beacon of his conduct can be styled a virtuous man. Every mode of conduct that detracts from the general stock of happiness is vicious. No action can be otherwise virtuous than exactly in the degree in which it contributes to that stock.

"I am also desirous of retracting the opinions I have given favourable to Helvetius' doctrine of the equality of intellectual beings as they are born into the world, and of subscribing to the received opinion, that, though education is a most powerful instrument, yet there exist differences of the highest importance between human beings from the period of their birth.

"I am the more anxious to bring forward these alterations and modifications, because it would give me occasion to shew that none of the conclusions for the sake of which the book on 'Political Justice' was written are affected by them. I am fully of opinion that the sentiments of that book are intimately connected with the best interests of mankind, and am filled with grief when I reflect on the possibility that any extravagances or oversights of mine should bring into disrepute the great truths I have endeavoured to propagate. But thus my mind is constituted. I have, perhaps, never been without the possession of important views and forcible reasonings; but they have ever been mixed with absurd and precipitate judgments, of which subsequent consideration has made me profoundly ashamed.

"2. A book to be entitled 'Two Dissertations on the Reasons and Tendency of Religious Opinion.' The object of this book is to sweep away the whole fiction of an intelligent former of the world, and a future state; to call men off from those incoherent and contradictory dreams that so often occupy their thoughts, and vainly agitate their hopes and fears, and to lead them to apply their whole energy to practicable objects and genuine realities. The first Dissertation would be applied (1) to shew that the origin of worlds is a subject out of the competence of the human under-standing; (2) to invalidate the doctrine of final causes; and (3) to demonstrate the absurdity and impossibility of every system of Theism that has ever been proposed. The second Dissertation would treat of the injurious and enfeebling effects of religious belief in general, and of prayer in particular. The consideration would be wholly confined to the most liberal systems of Theism, without entering into superfluous declamation upon the pretences of impostors and fanatics.

"3. A novel, in which I should try the effect of my particular style of writing upon common incidents and the embarrassments of lovers.

"4. Five or six tragedies."

Godwin's most constant associates at this time were those named already as his friends and those of his wife; Basil Montagu, T. Wedgwood, the Fenwicks, the Reveleys, Mrs Cotton, Charlotte Smith : he received at his own house very frequently the members of his family who were in London. These, as his mother's letters imply, were doing but little to their own advantage, and were a great drain on Godwin's limited resources. Beyond this inner circle, he mixed with almost all people then well known in the world of liberal politics and of letters, and much also in theatrical society : he seems to have attended the theatre almost whenever he had no other evening engagement. Wordsworth and Southey appear among the more note-worthy literary acquaintances of this year, the dinners with

Horne Tooke and with King were frequent, different as was the society which assembled at the two tables.

It will be convenient to take first among the correspondence of this year that which relates to Godwin's domestic life, and this requires a few introductory remarks. The care of the children, and the superintendence of the household at Somers Town, was undertaken by Miss Louisa Jones, a friend of Harriet Godwin. The position was not an easy one to fill; there were difficulties with the servants in consequence of little Mary's requiring a wet-nurse; not all people could understand or be prepared for Godwin's constant uncertainty about dining or not dining at home; the combination of friend and upper servant has inconveniences of its own, and is open to misconceptions. Besides, there is some evidence from the poor lady's letters that she would willingly have been a tender stepmother to the children, while nothing could be further from Godwin's thoughts than any relation whatever beyond that of housekeeper and governess to his children. The arrangement, therefore, was but temporary, and after Miss Jones ceased to reside in the house, she, Miss Godwin, Mrs Reveley, and other lady friends, seem to have given a kind, but at the same time necessarily casual superintendence to the nurse in charge of the children, who was devoted to them, and especially to little Mary.

This was among the circumstances which induced Godwin to think it possible, even at a very early date after his wife's death, that he might marry again. Experience had modified his views on this as on some other matters. He did not find that the ideal best was always practicable, and the comfort he had found tended to change his ideal. Mrs Shelley writes that his sentiments on the subject were entirely changed, that—

" the happiness he had enjoyed, instilled the opinion that he
might, at least in a degree, regain the blessing he had lost, if he
married a woman of sense, and of an amiable disposition. Instead
of, as heretofore, guarding himself from the feelings of love, he
appears rather to have laid himself open to them. The two orphan
girls left in his charge of course weighed much in the balance ; he
felt his deficiency as the sole parent of two children of the other
sex.   In March 1798, he left town, as he was in the habit of doing
for a short time in every year.   He visited Bath, and spent ten
days in that city, where he met the authoresses of the Canterbury
Tales, Sophia and Harriet Lee." [These ladies were the daughters of John Lee, an actor at Covent Garden ; and after their
father's death they kept a school at Bath. They afterwards retired to Clifton and died there, Sophia in 1824, Harriet in 1851,
aged 94.   They each wrote, separately, several novels, and, con-
jointly, "The Canterbury Tales."]   "The latter soon attracted
his admiration and partiality ; to the end of his life he always
spoke of her with esteem and regard, though it was not till his
papers were placed in my hands that I learned the nearer tie that
he sought to establish between them.   The feeling of love was
awakened on their first acquaintance, and his immediate desire
was to study her mind."

He made, on returning from visits to her house, in the
course of those few days, elaborate analyses of her conversation, in which they had discussed books together, Rousseau's works, Richardson, and others, and soon made up his
mind to win her, if possible, for his wife. They had only
met, as appears from the Diary, four times, but on Godwin's return to London he wrote as follows to Miss
Lee :—

William Godwin to Miss Harriet Lee.

[*April* 1798.]

" When I last had the pleasure of seeing you, you said you supposed you should hear of me. What was your meaning in this, I

do not think proper to set myself to guess, lest I should find that
you meant nothing, or what in my estimate might amount to
nothing. In saying, therefore, that you *supposed* you should hear
of me, I am determined to understand that you *expected* to hear
from me. It is indeed a very displeasing thought to reflect, when
one's ideas of a person have just been raised by their writings, and
afterwards confirmed by a direct communication of sentiments and
feelings, that possibly years may elapse before that communication
is renewed, and that possibly it may even never be renewed.
There are so few persons in the· world that have excited that
degree of interest in my mind which you have excited, that I am
loth to have the catalogue of such persons diminished, and that
distance should place a barrier between them and me, scarcely
less complete than that of death. Indulge me with the knowledge
that I have some place in your recollection. Suffer me to suppose,
in any future production that you may give to the world, that while
you are writing it, you will sometimes remember me in the number
of your intended readers. Allow me to believe that I have the
probability of seeing you in no long time here in the metropolis.
You said, if I recollect right, that this was rather the less likely as
the friend with whom you used to reside in London had lately
removed to some other place. Why should not I venture to suggest the practicability of your substituting my house, instead of
the accommodation you have lost? I do not perceive that there
could be any impropriety in it. A sister of the Miss Joneses, with
whom I resided at Bath, lives at my house upon the footing of an
acquaintance, and is so obliging as to superintend my family, and
take care of the children. I am sure she would be happy to do
everything to accommodate you. I should imagine, therefore,
that you might accept the invitation without sinning against the
etiquette that you love. It is true that my establishment is a
humble one, but you could not, perhaps, be under the roof of a
person who does more justice to your merits." [Here follows
some criticism on Miss Lee's writings, of no sort of interest
now.]

" Be so good as to express to your sister my sense of the flattering politeness and attention she was so obliging as to bestow upon me. Farewell.—Yours, with much regard and esteem,

"W. GODWIN."

This letter remained unanswered, and the lover became tormented by a thousand doubts. Three drafts of letters remain, which show his great perplexity. Had he offended? He was sometimes impelled to pour out his feelings with fervour and frankness, sometimes to be as guarded as possible. The first draft is little more than a concise announcement of his intention to revisit Bath, the second is an open confession of all his feelings, and of this there are three copies, but neither the first nor the second of these letters seems to have been sent. The third which reached Miss Lee is a curious mixture of confidence and reticence, and half measures did not please Miss Lee.

William Godwin to Miss Harriet Lee.

[LONDON], *"Saturday June 2, 1798.*

"DEAR MADAM.—I have been extremely mortified at receiving no answer from you, to the letter I wrote soon after my late excursion to Bath. I am not sure indeed whether, in perfect strictness I was entitled to an answer. But silence is so ambiguous a thing, and admits of so many interpretations, that with the admiration I had conceived for you, I could not sit down tranquilly under its discipline. It might mean simply that I had not been long enough your knight, to entitle me to such a distinction. But it might mean disapprobation, displeasure, or offence, when my heart prompted me to demand cordiality and friendship. My mortification has since been increased, by finding that you have been in town lately, and had left town before I knew of your presence: though having a kind of suspicion that the 'Two Emilys' would bring either Miss Lee or yourself to London, I had made some enquiries on the subject.

" I am obliged to be at Bristol next week. I remember as my greatest good fortune and pleasure in my last excursion the repeated and long conversations I enjoyed at Belvidere House. May I hope that now, having a right to call myself an acquaintance, I have not without intention or consciousness on my part forfeited the kindness I then experienced as a stranger. Whether next week shall be a week of pride or humiliation to my feelings will depend on the solution it will afford to this question.

" Present my best remembrances to your sisters, and believe me, with the highest regard and esteem, yours,

"W. GODWIN."

On reading this letter Miss Lee underlined and bracketted in pencil such words and sentences as she especially noticed, or to which she took exception, then wrote a sort of minute on the margin. This was returned to the writer, after the final cessation of their correspondence.

[*Note on the above by Miss Harriet Lee*].

"The tone of this letter appears to me to betray vanity disappointed by the scantiness of the homage it has received, rather than mortified by any apprehension of discouragement. If any offence was given by the former letter this is calculated to renew and increase it; for it is equally presuming without being more explicit, except in two sentences so alien to the temper, or distant from the express reach of the rest, that they should be made under all circumstances to leave the letter. An alternative proposed by the second clause presents itself to me thus: this journey to Bristol has no reference to me; as far as that is concerned he visits me simply as an acquaintance; but his title to be received as such has been lost by his forwardness to employ the privileges, and claim the rights of a more endeared relation. The purpose of his journey is addrest to me, and it may be dictated either by humility or assurance. I doubt that the former interpretation would be given to a letter in which the same air and accent reign as in this."

She wrote, however, a civil but formal note, expressing her readiness to see him, and on his arrival at Bath on June 5th, Godwin formally paid his addresses to Harriet Lee, and there is a note in his diary of a "conference" on the subject. That the lady admitted "regard and esteem," appears from a correspondence which afterwards ensued, and with this the lover was prepared to be content. Miss Lee herself was not disinclined to marriage, but feared what would be thought of it by her sister and the world. Almost persuaded to treat this objection as lightly as in reality it deserved to be treated, there remained what was to her a very grave question; were Godwin's own opinions such as would promise a happy marriage with a woman who held strongly her faith in God, and the divine guidance of the world?

It is not possible to fix exact dates to Godwin's letters to Miss Lee, because only the undated drafts remain, but they were subsequent to the conference. Arguments to induce the lady to reconsider her determination are urged with a pertinacity and elaboration which would be wearisome to all but the principal performers in this little domestic drama, perhaps to all but the writer. Extracts, however, will prove interesting, not only as a specimen of love-letters which are probably unique, but also as a statement of Godwin's own opinions, thoroughly honest, of course, but placed in what he considered the most favourable light.

William Godwin to Miss Harriet Lee.

[*June* 1798.]

". . . We got thus far, I think, in our last conversation, that the decision you shall be pleased to make will be of the greatest importance, since, though it may be easy for either of us to marry, supposing the present question to be decided in the negative, yet it is not probable that either of us will, elsewhere, meet with a fit and suitable partner, capable of being the real companion of our minds, and improver of our powers. We must remain in that separate and widowed state of the heart, which is no part of the system of nature, or must, as St Paul says, be unequally yoked.

". . . Pass over in your mind everything which, if we were united, would employ us from day to day, and from week to week. Things in which we perfectly sympathised, in which we acted in concert, in which our feelings would vibrate to each other. In the exercise of the benevolent and social affections, in the improvement of our understandings, in taste, in the admiration of natural beauty, or the beauties of human productions; in the expressions—the refined, the delicious, but evanescent expressions—of mutual attachment, those expressions in which the true consciousness of life consists, that attachment which converts this terrestrial scene into a paradise, we should, I hope, fully coincide, nor should one discord intrude into the comprehensive harmony.

". . . What will the world say? In the first place, I am not sure that you do not labour under some mistake in this case. I must be permitted to say on this occasion, that among those who personally know me, the respect and love I have obtained is, I believe, fully equal to any reputation I may be supposed to have gained for talents. I believe no person who has so far run counter to the prejudices and sentiments of the world has ever been less a subject of obloquy. I know that many whose opinions in politics and government are directly the reverse of mine, yet honour me with their esteem. I cannot, therefore, be of opinion that your forming a connection with me would be regarded as by any means discreditable to you.

". . . I have said to you once before, Do not go out of life, without ever having known what life is. Celibacy contracts and palsies the mind, and shuts us out from the most valuable topics of experience. He who wastes his existence in this state may have been a spectator of the scene of things, but has never been an actor, and is just such a spectator as a man would be who did

not understand a word of the language in which the concerns of
men are transacted. The sentiments of mutual and equal affection, and of parental love, and these only, are competent to unlock
the heart and expand its sentiments—they are the Promethean
fire, with which, if we have never been touched, we have scarcely
attained the semblance of what we are capable to be. When I
look at you, when I converse with you, it is more, much more the
image of what you might be, and are fitted to be, that charms me,
than the contemplation of what you are. I regard you as possessing the materials to make that most illustrious and happiest of all
characters, when its duties are faithfully discharged—a wife—a
mother. But if you are eminently and peculiarly qualified for
these offices, it is the more to be regretted, and shall I not add?
the more to be censured in you, if you peremptorily and ulti-
mately decline them."

The Same to the Same.

[*June* 1798].

"I sit down as a disinterested friend to give you an opinion,
the result of what has lately passed between us. It is little likely
that anything of consequence to me should arise either way from
what I am going to state. I give up the point I have hitherto
sought to enforce. You have erected an insurmountable wall of
separation between us. Henceforth we shall be no more to each
other than persons that had heard of each others' names, that
remember there was a period when for a short time they had the
habit of seeing each other, and who may now and then have occasion
to say, 'Dear me! no, I believe he is not dead, is he?' It might
have been otherwise. It ought to have been otherwise. But you
have made your election. I have neglected nothing that became
me. I have brought the whole subject laboriously before you;
but you have remained pertinacious and immoveable. Certainly
my opinion of you is not altered; my partiality is not diminished;
if it were yet possible that you should view the question between
us with fairness and liberality, it would afford me a gratification
much, much beyond the power of words to express. It would

change me into a new creature, and open to me afresh the most pleasing prospects of life. I know that your heart—the bias and leaning of your heart—is on my side. But you have found the secret of suppressing the feelings of your heart, and subjecting them to the mystery and dogmas of your creed. Suppose, then, that you are reading the reflections of an impartial friend, who has the courage to communicate to you the truth; suppose that the person whose visits you have lately had occasion to receive is dead. Such a supposition may easily be made, and will cause little difference in anything to which you look forward. The friend who addresses you, as he has the courage to treat you ingenuously, so I hope will not forget what is due to your sex and your merits, or utter a word that it would misbecome you to hear.

" You tell me, that if it were not for your religion, and your ideas of a future state, you believe you should adopt a system of conduct selfish and licentious. I do not credit you when you say this; if I did, it would be impossible for me to have the smallest respect for you. I am not so unfair as to suppose that your opinion has the effect of rooting out all liberal and ingenuous sentiments from your mind, but I think it a serious misfortune that you conceive it has. Every parent and preceptor perfectly knows that a conduct adopted from the hope of reward or the fear of punishment is not virtue. If I make myself useful to my fellow-men merely because I expect to be rewarded for it, it is clear that I have no love of utility or virtue, and that if the reward were placed on the other side, I should immediately become as mischievous a creature as lives. Virtue is not a form of external conduct,—it is a sentiment of the heart. I am a base and low-minded creature, whatever be my external conduct, if I do not seek to confer happiness from a genuine principle of sympathy, and because I have a direct and heartfelt pleasure in the pleasure, the improvement, and advantage of others. If Omnipotence itself were to annex eternal torments to the practice of benignity and humanity, I know not how poor a slave I might be terrified into; but I know that I should curse the tyrant, while I obeyed the command. In reality, the virtue of every good man is built upon the stable basis

I. U

of what he sees and daily experiences, and not upon the precarious foundation of the retribution which he rather endeavours to credit than certainly believe.

"The second error I have to notice is that your creed, as you understand it, inculcates the worst part of bigotry. You look, as in fact you tell me, with suspicion and incredulity upon the virtue of almost all that was most illustrious in ancient times, and upon half the most unprejudiced and exemplary men of our own day. This is the very quintessence of bigotry, to overturn the boundaries of virtue and vice, to try men, not by what we see of their conduct and know of their feelings, but by their adherence to, or rejection of, a speculative opinion. You have a certain Shibboleth, a God and a future state, which if any man deny, you assert he can have no firm and stable integrity. And, which is most curious, you say to him, ' If you have only the sentiment of virtue, if you only do good from a love of rectitude and benevolence, and do not feel yourself principally led to it by a foreign, an arbitrary, and a mercenary motive, I can have no opinion of you.' I am happy to know that these errors of yours have no necessary connection with either Deism or Christianity.

"I am happy to say that I have known many Deists and many Christians, who confess that morality is an independent rule, by a comparison with which they pronounce on the goodness of providence itself, and of which the rewards of a future state are not the source, but merely an additional sanction. Thinking thus, they are not backward or timid in applauding the virtues of the patriots and sages of ancient times, or of those benefactors of mankind in their own day, who have discarded the opinions which they cherish. I know it has been fashionable among divines to pretend that no man rejects religion but because he wishes to be profligate with impunity, but liberal-minded believers despise the shameless assertion.

"But I have done. I entertain no hopes of a good effect from what I now write, and merely give vent to the sentiments your determination was calculated to excite. I have made no progress with you. When you have dropped an objection it has been only afterwards to revive it; when I have begun to entertain fairer prospects, you have convinced me I was deluding myself. My personal qualities, good or bad, are of no account in your eyes, you are concerned only with the articles of my creed. I am compelled to regard the affair as concluded, and the rational prospect of happiness to you and myself as superseded by something you conceive better than happiness. I have now discharged my sentiments, and here ends my censure of your mistake. If ever you be prevailed on to listen to the addresses of any other man, may his success be decided on more equitable principles than mine have been."

Miss Lee's next letter was intended to close the correspondence.

Miss Harriet Lee to William Godwin.

[BATH], "*July* 31, 1798.

"You distress me, sir, extremely, by again agitating a question which ought to be considered as decided. I had full opportunity, when in Town, to hear, and attentively to weigh your opinions concerning the point on which we most differ: for perhaps I do not fully agree with you in supposing our minds at unison on many others; but that is immaterial—the matter before us is decisive. All the powers of my understanding, and the better feelings of my heart concurred in the resolution I declared before we parted; every subsequent reflection has but confirmed it. With me our difference of opinion is not a mere theoretical question. I never did, never can feel it as such, and it is only astonishing that you should do so. It announces to me a certain difference in—I had almost said a *want* in—the heart, of a thousand times more consequence than all the various shades of intellect or opinion. My resolution then remains exactly and firmly what it was: it gives me great pain to have disturbed the quiet of your mind, but I cannot remedy the evil without losing the rectitude of my own.

"I have taken from my sister the unpleasant task of telling you what you are unwilling to credit. She does justice to your understanding, she wishes you every good that you can reasonably demand, but recollect how improbable it is that I should cherish opinions she has not entertained long before; and even if I did, self-dependent as I am both in mind and years, how little likely is it that I should look to another for a rule either of duty or happiness.

" You tell me that you are individually beloved by those who know you, and I can easily believe it, but I will tell you that even among the number of your friends, or at least well-wishers, there are to my knowledge those who much lament, and even blame the lengths to which your systems of thinking have carried you, and who recede insensibly from your opinions, while they preserve a respect for your intentions.

" If, in our conversations, I have ever appeared in any moment undecided, it was only at those when it occurred to me that truth and genuine feeling were so strongly on my side, that while you were collecting arguments to enlighten my mind, I felt persuaded of the possibility of a change in your own. And why should I not? A doctrine so necessary to the heart, so consonant to the reason, as that of a just and all-powerful Diety will I hope one day find its way to both.

" My own good wishes and those of my sister attend you. Nothing further can or ought to be said by either of us. Farewell —but let it be a friendly Farewell. H. L."

Godwin, however, was not so to be put down, and wrote a flood of letters in one week, of which the following extracts may serve :—

William Godwin to Miss Harriet Lee.

[*Early in August,* 1798.]

" . . . What you have done is in the genuine style of the eleventh and twelfth centuries. You have put out of sight the man, and asked only what he believed. In the midst of the vast world of conjecture, before the beginning of all things, that appropriate field of wild assertion, in which proud man, ignorant of the essence and character of what immediately passes under his eyes, delights to expatiate, you have chosen a creed. You have done well; it amuses the fancy, it is the parent of a thousand interesting pictures, it soothes the heart with pleasing ideas. This is the deism of those persons whom I have known, who, having shaken off the empire of infant prejudices, yet differ from me in the point in which you differ. They frankly acknowledge that it is a matter of taste, and not a matter of reason. What can you know of the origin of the universe? Wert thou present when the foundations of the earth were laid? Didst thou see whereupon they are fastened, or who laid the corner stone thereof? Knowest thou it because thou wert then born, or because the number of thy days is great? Still more unsupported in reason is the notion of a future state. We see a man die; we can lock up his body in a vault; we can visit it from day to day, and observe its gradual waste; and we say that an invisible part of him is flown off, and inhabits somewhere with a consciousness that that, and that only, is the man. The evidence that we had of his existence was speech, and motion, and pulsation, and breath. All this is changed into a motionless and putrid mass, and we still say the man exists. We pretend to infer the character of infinite benevolence from what we see in a world where despotism, and slavery, and misery, and war continually prevail, and then, reasonably growing discontented with the scene, we piece out most miserably another world with hallelujahs and everlasting rest, according to our fancy, and we call this evidence. We first infer the goodness of God from what we see, and then infer that this world is not worthy of the goodness of that being whose existence we deduced from it. I have no disrespect for these opinions; far from it. I regard them as the food of a sublime imagination and an amiable temper. But I expect the unprejudiced man that cherishes them to know them for what they are—the creatures of taste, and not of reason. I expect him to be moderate and forbearing in assertion. I know that such a man will never regard this invisible world, with which he has no acquaintance, and which is the mere creature of his conjecture, as a balance for the realities around him ; will never, instead of inquiring what is a man's understanding, what is his genius, what are his morals, what is his temper, what the improvement, the pleasure, the mode of happiness he proposes to him ; will never, I say, instead of this, inquire, what is his creed, and judge him by that . . . ."

The Same to the Same.

[*Early in August*, 1798.]

" . . . Bigots have pretended that the will of God is the foundation of morality, that what He commands is therefore right, and what He forbids is therefore wrong. But rational theism teaches that morality is antecedent to the divine will, and is a rule to which God himself delights to conform. Rational theism teaches that God is good ; and to prove that He is so, compares His providence and works with the immediate standard of rectitude to which God and good men equally adhere. The will of God therefore is by no means the foundation of morality, but merely its sanction, an additional reason why we should conform to it. . . ."

Miss Lee wrote a letter on August 7th, which seems to have been taken as final, in which she hopes that friendly remembrance may still subsist, unchecked by " minute misunderstandings," and so concluded this singular correspondence. After a time, however, friendly though somewhat formal intercourse was renewed, and there is a letter extant, written in the following year by Miss Lee in reference to a literary criticism by Godwin on some new publication by her. But there is no allusion to the more intimate terms on which he had once desired to stand.

It was just as well that Godwin's plan of keeping house with Thomas Wedgwood was never carried out. Their correspondence shows the not unexampled state of things in which two men who were intellectually complementary to each other, who had for each other a sincere friendship, were yet antipathetic when they met, and suited each other only at a distance. Wedgwood had discovered this earlier than Godwin, and though still writing very cordial letters, though helping his friend with most liberal loans, or rather presents of money, in his need, he yet, in his now failing health, preferred that they should not meet, and that their discussions should be conducted only on paper. Godwin, on the contrary, characteristically desired that they should meet and discuss rationally the questions whether they were or were not more cordially and kindly disposed to each other when apart. Only portions of one letter and of its answer are generally interesting.

Thomas Wedgwood to William Godwin.

"PENZANCE, *Jan.* 6, 1798.

"It is hardly necessary for me to inform you that the contents of your letter were highly agreeable to me. You are almost the only person whose judgment is valuable to me on speculative points, and on that account I feel continually the necessity of your sanction. On the subject of friendship, no person ought to think with so much charity of others or to speak with greater diffidence than myself. I was not satisfied with the propriety of my last letter, though, as it has happily led to an explanation agreeable to both of us, I cannot now repent of it. Perhaps I am incapable of friendship—my habits and disposition are certainly so unfavourable as to require a concurrence of fortunate circumstances for its birth and support. 'Sickness,' says Johnson, 'makes scoundrels of us all,' it impairs and destroys sympathy. But feebleness of constitution and spirits is not the only obstacle; I have to contend with a timidity of disposition which has long harassed me inconceivably, and which in a thousand ways is obstructive to the growth of an entire and affectionate intimacy. . . .

William Godwin to Thomas Wedgwood.

[LONDON], " *Jan.* 10, 1798.

" . . . I am pleased with the style of writing you have lately employed. I have more taste, though I have sometimes suspected and often been told that it is a vicious taste, for letters and conversations of feeling than of discussion.

" Allow me to recommend to you a very cautious admission of the moral apophthegms of Doctor Johnson. He had an unprecedented tendency to dwell on the dark and unamiable part of our nature. I love him less than most other men of equal talents and intentions, because I cannot reasonably doubt that when he drew so odious a picture of man he found some of the traits in his own bosom. I have seen more persons than one or two, whom sickness has neither converted into scoundrels, nor stripped of a sympathetic disposition.

" Your paying the postage of your letters to me is contrary to established etiquette. It is scarcely worth while to enter into an argument about it, but I think I could prove to you that it is wrong.

" W. GODWIN."

Though Godwin was now a middle-aged man, though his habits were methodical, and his manner somewhat cold and formal, the fact that his opinions were progressive, and his soul full of what would now be called the enthusiasm of humanity, continued to attract to him young men of hopeful and vigorous minds, whom he never failed to receive with kindness, and set forward to the best of his ability. Their fresh youth, and the earnestness of their minds, served to keep his own mind buoyant, even in the midst of sorrow and disappointment, and as his relations with Webb and Cooper served in some degree to show what he was, in

his inner life, so now does a correspondence with a young
Scotchman named Arnot, who, coming to London to seek
his fortune, attached himself to Godwin. He left no mark
on his generation, but he wrote excellent letters, and incidentally the correspondence throws light on Godwin as
showing the kind of lad who still attracted him. A note
by the second Mrs Godwin to Mrs Shelley describes
Arnot as

"a tall young man, pale faced, with large blue eyes with much
meaning in them, in shabby clothes. Whenever your father spoke
of him he extolled his intellectual powers, saw infinite folly and
danger in the intemperance of his impulses and pursuits, and
expressed his fear that he must be mad. At one period his sister
and her husband, Mr and Mrs Fyler from Edinburgh, put him in
confinement, and had a great dislike to your father, on account of
'Political Justice,' ascribing their brother's conduct to the principles it contains. Arnot and L. Jones [the lady who lived with
Godwin as housekeeper] were in love with each other. Arnot was
desperately attached afterwards to some German lady of rank. I
think this is in the letters."

The immediate reason why Arnot left Scotland does not
appear, but he walked the whole way from Edinburgh to
London, and wrote the account of his journey to a friend
whom he left behind him. These letters afterwards came
into Godwin's hands, and are preserved among his papers.
An extract from one of them is characteristic of the young
man, and is valuable as a picture of a scene not unfamiliar
at this time.

John Arnot to Peter Reid.

" CAMBO [NORTHUMBERLAND], *April* 24, 1798.

. . . "At some distance from the village of Elsdon, through
which I passed to-day, I observed a large post erected on the top

of the hill.   I conceived it might be an intimation about the roads
leading to such a place.   Being thirsty, I went into a house near
it to buy some milk.   I sat down to drink it, and inquired what
the post meant.   ''Tis a Gibbet, Sir.'   'A Gibbet! why was it
erected amongst the hills?'   'For murder; an old woman was
killed there, and two men and a woman were hanged for it, upon
that gibbet.'

   "What a train of horrid ideas did that introduce into my mind.
I looked at the man who told it me; he is a sour-looking fellow.
His wife, a little shrew, in a red jacket, was present.   I thought
her a devil.   I took care to keep my stick near me, it was my
only means of defence.   I felt a strong aversion to them both, and
was glad to get away.

   "I went up to the gibbet.   The bones are still hanging, kept
together with iron.   This, no doubt, is intended as a conspicuous
monument of retributive justice.   Is it thought this will have a good
effect?   I cannot help being of an opposite opinion.   Surely the
people who live near it cannot be happy.   They cannot even feel
easy and contented till their minds become hardened.   The ideas
of hanging and of murder must first become familiar to them.   I
don't like them.   Let me get away from this place.

   "I walked as fast as I could, but could not walk long.   I was
fatigued, and my right foot began to give me pain.   I sat down,
therefore, upon a stone at the roadside, pulled out my little octave
flute, and began to play a tune, but it only added to my melancholy.   I looked around.   This is a wild, barren country; no
trees to be seen, no bushes or enclosures, no fine cultivated fields.
All is a dreary waste; this gibbet its only ornament; the sheep
its inhabitants.   They were feeding within a few yards of me.
I looked on them with an emotion which I never felt before.   Ah!
innocent people, as Thomson calls you, how much happier are
you than man—man who butchers you and his fellow-creatures
indiscriminately.

   "Such is the nature of the present state of society.   It punishes,
with the utmost severity, crimes to which it holds out irresistible
temptations."

Arnot, after he had spent a short time in London, formed
the design of visiting the less known portions of Europe on
foot, at once to learn the German language, and to take
notes for a book of travels, to be published on his return.
Godwin warmly approved of this plan, and aided Arnot to
carry it into execution. France was of course closed to an
English subject, and he therefore went to Germany in a
Baltic ship by way of Russia. The letters that he wrote to
Godwin are all extremely good, but only portions of them
can here be given.

John Arnot to William Godwin.

" PETERSBURG, 10 *August* 1798, *New Style.*

" DEAR SIR,—I shall leave this place to-morrow. I am so happy
that I have got my passport! And I assure you that it was no
easy matter. It has detained me here for three weeks, living at
no little expense, in the British tavern. . . .

" I arrived at Cronstadt after a tedious and very disagreeable
passage of 30 days, and in 5 days more got my passport to Petersburg. It was rather odd that I should have pitched upon the
worst ship in every respect, perhaps, of the whole fleet; my patience was tried more ways than one. I don't think Job himself
had more patience when he was my age.

" I declare I am afraid to write any more. I am writing to
Godwin just as if I was writing to my good friend Peter Reid,
scribble, scribble, scribble, I have fifty thousand things to say, and
don't know which to say first. I dare say my pen has run mad.
If I were beside you, you would think my tongue were mad. . . .

" I intend to walk to Riga, and from Riga to Vienna. Indeed,
I am determined to be at Vienna this winter, that is, if nothing
happens to me by the way, which you know is possible. 'Walk
to Riga!! The poor lad has lost his wits. Do you know what
you are doing? Such weather, such roads, such a country, and
such a people. You may as well think of walking to the moon.'
But I'll walk it for all that. 'Tis nothing at all.

" I don't think I am half so courageous as when I left Scotland.
I believe I could have taken a bear by the ear as coolly as you
could take your dinner. But now that I have the prospect of
being happy when I return—am I not happy already, at least at
this moment?—I begin to think I am worth the taking care of,
and therefore I am determined to take care of myself, and never
to meddle with a bear unless the bear meddles with me, and to be
wondrous civil to the boors and the booresses. . . .

" I have been obliged to lighten my parcel very much. I gave
away ' Tristram Shandy' about five weeks ago, and my two flutes.
I have laid aside all my pistol bullets, except about 20, and am
thinking to throw away the only shirt and pair of stockings I have
to spare. . . .—I am, with great esteem, yours, &c.

" JOHN ARNOT.

" I keep no journal on my way to Vienna. I dare not."

The Same to the Same.

" DRESDEN, *Wednesday, 7th Nov.* 1798.

" DEAR SIR.—Here I am. Fol lol de rol, nay I will give you
the very notes. No I will not; for you don't care for music, at
least for the music that I care for. . . .

" I cannot get a grammar. There is none here. I shall apply
very hard, for I wish to be master of the language in 4 months,
and then I may go to the Play, and where else I please. I must
also study French, which in Dresden is the only language that is
spoken in *fashionable* company. I shall have enough ado. I
wish also I had English books, but I cannot have everything while
I have no money.

" I don't recollect whether I mentioned to you that I had brought
with me from Edinburgh, sets of the best old Scotch songs. By
publishing them here, and perhaps also at Leipsig, or Prague, or
Vienna, or at all of these places, I hope not only to procure a
subsistence for the winter, but to be able to pay such debts as I

have contracted. Germany as you know is a very musical country, and the Scotch songs are very fine. . . . Adieu, yours sincerely,

"JOHN ARNOT."

" *P.S.*—I heard something of a great victory obtained over the French. If you have any of the old newspapers containing an account of that, or of any other remarkable public occurrence, I shall be obliged to you for them. But first it would be proper to enquire whether it is allowed to send papers abroad, for I would rather want them than run the risk of losing your letters. . . . "

William Godwin to John Arnot.

[LONDON, *Nov.* 23*rd* 1798.]

"DEAR ARNOT,—I derived exquisite pleasure from the receipt of your letter. I have thought of you a thousand times with inexpressible anxiety. I have been accused, as you know, of countenancing a young man, in whom I felt a powerful interest, in entering unprovided, and unsupported, upon an attempt the most perilous and insane, from which it was next to impossible he should not reap intolerable calamities, and hardly probable that he should come off alive. Without an accuser I should have sufficiently felt the high responsibility that devolved on me. Yet what could I do? The first sensation your project excited in me was envy. I wished I could have been a lad like you to undertake what you proposed. I saw in you many qualifications, fitting you for the design, courage, though not an uniform courage, and an easy and assured manner, calculated to smooth a thousand difficulties, and prepossess strangers in your favour. Feeling approbation, could I belie my sentiment?

" Under these impressions it seemed to me very long before I heard from you. I saw you for the last time on the 13th of June, and your first letter did not reach me till the 10th of November. You promised me to write from Petersburgh. My active imagination passed in review all the dangers of your route, immense deserts, rude forests, fierce Cossacks, hunger, assassination and death. These evils would have impressed me more strongly, had

not the various reports of the vigilance of Russian police created
in me a persuasion that you would not be permitted to enter that
empire.   I confess I had my fears that you would return, looking
like a fool, by the same vessel in which you sailed.   I considered
however that if all activity and enterprise did not desert you, you
would in case of the worst, find means to push for the other
side of the Baltic, and find rest for your foot on the dry land of
Sweden.

"And now, will you forgive me, if I acknowledge, in spite of the
heart-felt pleasure with which I received your letters, my satisfaction was not unmixed with disappointment.   The first consisted
of five poor lines, with a morsel of postscript.   The kindest
construction I could put upon this was that you were so sunk in
spirit that if you had written more, you felt your melancholy and
dejection would break out, and therefore out of pure generosity
you stopped while you could.   But if this were the kindest
construction, it was not the most consolatory.   Your second letter
has in some degree removed this uneasy apprehension.   It reached
me last night, November 22nd, in fifteen days from its date.   But
in neither do you tell me where you have been, what you have
seen, not even whether you took the route of Livonia, Poland,
and Silesia, or of Sweden, Denmark, Holstein, &c.; whether you
took shore at Petersburgh and continued your route by land, or
whether though first at Vienna, and now at Dresden, you have
seen no other country than Germany.   Another fault I find is,
that I trace in your letters no feature of the mind I loved, no
sterling observations of man, no agreeable naiveté of adventure.
I hope while your body has been in restless motion, your mind
has not slept.   But I suppose you reserve all your good things to
surprise the world with.

"I think your famous Dr John Brown affirms that the natural
genuine state of man is death.   I know not what physical truth
there may be in this, but morally I greatly fear that the man who
would truly be alive must obstinately spur his mind into a much
better state than that into which, if neglected, it will sink.   I hope
you keep a copious journal.   I hate travels into the four quarters

of the world written after all is over, within sight of St Paul's
Church. Perhaps it would be better for your book, and better for
yourself that you should visit some countries that are not travelled
every day, such as Hungary, Spain, &c. You ought too, to take
some precautions respecting your manuscripts, that in case of
an accident your name and your usefulness may not be wholly
lost. But above all take care of yourself. I had rather be
refreshed by the sight of John Arnot in person than John Arnot's
book. . . . Study language elaborately, you cannot know man
without understanding his speech.

"You ask for news. . . . The grand topic is Egypt. Buonaparte
sailed for that country in May. Our Admiral Nelson pursued him,
arrived before him, and returned to Europe. Buonaparte landed
his forces July 1st. Nelson having refitted, sailed again to Alex-
andria, where he found the French Fleet still at anchor. Nelson
with 14 ships attacked the French with 13 on August 1st, took 9
and burned 2, so that only 2 escaped. Buonaparte, on the other
hand, seems impregnably established in possession of Egypt. The
Turk has in consequence declared war against France.

"Coleridge and Wordsworth, two names that I believe you will
find in the list I wrote out for you, landed some time ago at
Hamburgh. They are at no great distance from that place, but I
cannot learn where. You may perhaps meet with them in your
rambles. They are both extraordinary men, and both reputed
men of genius. Coleridge I think fully justifies the reputation . . .

"I wish you all manner of prosperity, improvement, and happiness."

John Arnot to William Godwin.

"DRESDEN, *Saturday, 8th Dec.* 1798.

"DEAR GODWIN,—Your letter has given me no small degree of
pleasure, but I confess it has also given me anxiety. It seems the
letter of a man who once thought well of me, but who now finds
with regret that he has reason in a great measure to retract his
good opinion. It is worse. It seems to me to be written in a
tone of melancholy despondency. I don't know what to think of

it. What a disappointment that you have not said a word of my friends. Not a word of Louisa [Jones]—not a word of Fanny— not a word of sister Mary, who was so fond of me—nor of Miss Godwin, nor Marshall, nor Dyson, nor Dibbin, nor anybody. Ah, Godwin, you would not have forgot that, had you received my letter from Petersburg, or had you known how nearly I feel my happiness allied to theirs. Are they well? or have they forgot me? or can you think I have forgot them?

"Curse the news—what care I for Egypt? But that was my own thoughtlessness and impertinence. . . .

"I took the route of Livonia, Poland, and Silesia. I passed through Riga, Warsaw, Cracow, Teschen, Olmütz, Brünn, to Vienne. So far from having kept a copious journal; between Petersburg and Warsaw I marked only the days of the month, and the place where I slept each night, when that place had a name and I knew it. Before I reached Warsaw I lost my inkholder—a loss which in the capital of Poland could not be supplied, so that I did not afterwards write another word, but trusted solely to my memory. I regret this. . . .

"I am quite of your opinion that it would be better to visit countries which are not traversed every day. Hungary, however, I scarcely expect to see, or any part of the Emperor's dominions, so difficult is it to procure admittance, and so closely are you watched when admitted. . . . Fortune, indeed, has not smiled upon my early youth, and my infant years have been years of misery; but among the few happy periods of my life I shall ever rank the time I spent in walking through Poland. And yet I met with nothing there to make me happy; the generality of young men in my situation would have considered their condition as most desperate and deplorable. My happiness was founded in hope, and in thinking of the Polygon. . . ."

There can be no doubt that Godwin had, during his married life, withdrawn himself in some degree from those acquaintances who did not lie within his immediate circle of friends, and had also taken less interest in the more abstract questions connected with life and politics than he had done before. His life on the whole was so happy, rounded, and complete, his literary work had been so sharply defined during that period, that he had less time and inclination for pursuits and companions once, and to be again, full of interest for him. But he now began once more to see and correspond with literary and distinguished men beyond his intimates, though many letters written by him are unfortunately lost. Such is the case with that to which the following letter is an answer, but the document itself is of sufficient importance to call for insertion.

The writer, the Rev. T. R. Malthus, published anonymously his " Treatise on Population " in 1798, but no secret was made of the authorship, and he gave his name to the fourth edition, published five years later. Mr Malthus, who was born in 1766 at Albury, was Fellow of Jesus College, Cambridge, and afterwards, from 1804 till his death in 1831, Professor of History and Political Economy at Haileybury College, then the place of education for Writers in the East India Company's Service. The main doctrine of the Treatise is that assistance should be refused to poverty for the purpose of preventing over-population—which he declares to be the main cause of the evils apparent in human life—though his name is more often associated with some of the details of his argument.

The Rev. R. Malthus to William Godwin.

" ALBURY, *August 20th* [1798].

" DEAR SIR,—I went out of town almost immediately after I left you on Wednesday morning, and therefore did not receive your obliging letter till I arrived at Albury, whither Mr Johnson was so good as to send it.

I.   X

" In the view in which you now place the subject, do you not in some degree change the question from the perfectibility and happiness to the numbers of the human race ; and it may be a matter of doubt whether, without looking to a future state, an increase of numbers without a perpetual increase of happiness be really desirable.

" Could we suppose any country, by the most extraordinary exertions, to arrive at the *ne plus ultra* of subsistence and population, in one or two centuries we have reason to think that the pressure of population in its utmost weight, would be felt in frequent famines and pestilences, and particularly in the small recompense of labour ; for I think you yourself must allow that under the present form of society the real recompense of labour depends upon the increase of the funds for its maintenance ; and when these funds are completely stationary, and have continued so some time, this recompense will naturally be the least possible. You think that the present structure of society might be radically changed. I wish I could think so too ; and as you say I have completely failed in convincing you on this subject, will you have the goodness to remove a few of those difficulties which I cannot remove myself, and allow me to be convinced by *you ?*

" I set out with granting the extreme desirableness of the end proposed—that is, the abolition of all unnecessary labour, and the equal division of the necessary labour among all the members of the society. I ought also to premise, that in speaking of the present structure of society, I do not in the least refer to any particular form of government, but merely to the existence of a class of proprietors and a class of labourers, to the system of barter and exchange, and to the general moving principle of self-love.

" I can conceive that a period may arrive when the baubles that at present engage the attention of the higher classes of society may be held in contempt ; but I cannot look forward to a period when such a portion of command over the produce of land and labour as cannot be within the reach of all will cease to be an object of desire. Moderate cloathing, moderate houses, the power of receiving friends, the power of purchasing books, and particularly the power of supporting a family, will always remain objects of rational desire among the majority of mankind. If this be allowed, how is it possible to prevent a competition for these advantages? If the labour of luxuries were at an end, by what practicable means could you divide the necessary labour equally? Without the interference of Government, which I know you would reprobate as well as myself, how could you prevent a man from exchanging as many hours of labour as he liked for a greater portion of these advantages? Were the island of Great Britain divided among a great number of small proprietors, which would probably be the most advantageous system in respect to produce, it would be the natural wish of each of these proprietors to get the labour of his farm done for as small a part of the produce as he could, that he might be able to gratify his inclination in marrying without transgressing the rules of prudence, and provide for a large family, should he have one. The consequence of this desire in the proprietor to realise a sufficiency to maintain and provide for a family, together with the desire in the labourer to obtain the advantages of property, would be that the labourer would work 6, 8, or 10 hours in the day for less than would support 3, 4, or 5 persons, working two hours a-day. Consequently the equal division of the necessary labour would not take place. The labourers that were employed would not possess much leisure, and the labourers that were not employed would perish from want, to make room for the increase of the families of proprietors, who, as soon as they were increased beyond the power of their property to support, must become labourers to others, who, either from prudence or accident, had no families. And thus it appears that, notwithstanding the abolition of all luxuries, and a more equal division of property, the race of labourers would still be regulated by the demand for labour, and the state of the funds for its maintenance.

"The prudence which you speak of as a check to population implies a foresight of difficulties; and this foresight of difficulties almost necessarily implies a desire to remove them. Can you give me an adequate reason why the natural and general desire to remove these difficulties would not cause such a competition as

would destroy all chance of an equal division of the necessary
labour of society, and produce such a state of things as I have
described? If you can satisfy me on this head, I will heartily
join with you in invectives against the increase of labour, and in
the general sentiments of your essay on avarice and profusion.
Excuse my descending to particulars, as I am of opinion that the
great object of our researches, *truth*, cannot be attained without it.

" Your objection against the present form of society, on account
of its preventing the greatest practicable population, would, in
some degree, hold against your system of prudence, the object of
which, as I conceive, would be to keep the population always considerably within the means of subsistence. Should such a system
ever prevail so generally as to remove the constant want of an
increasing quantity of food, it is highly probable that cultivation
would proceed still more slowly than it does at present. I only
approve of the present form of society, because I cannot myself,
according to the laws of just theory, see any other form that can,
consistently with individual freedom, equally promote cultivation
and population. Great improvements may take place in the *state*
of society; but I do not see how the present form or system can
be radically and essentially changed, without a danger of relapsing
again into barbarism. With the present acknowledged imperfections of human institutions, I by no means think that the greatest
part of the distress felt in society arises from them. The very
admission of the necessity of prudence to prevent the misery from
an overcharged population, removes the blame from public institutions to the conduct of individuals. And certain it is, that almost
under the worst form of government, where there was any tolerable
freedom of competition, the race of labourers, by not marrying,
and consequently decreasing their numbers, might immediately
better their condition, and under the very best form of government, by marrying and greatly increasing their numbers, they
would immediately make their condition worse. As all human
institutions will probably be imperfect, and consequently always
open to censure, it is not surely fair to charge them with evils
of which, as far as I can judge, they are totally guiltless. And in

all projected changes of human institutions, it appears to me of the highest importance previously to ascertain as nearly as possible how much evil is to be attributed to these institutions, and how much is absolutely independent of them.

"I have made this letter much longer than I at first intended ; and I certainly ought to apologise for taking up so much of your valuable time : but if your avocations will not permit you to answer it, I shall hope for some future opportunity of hearing your opinions upon the subject, when I have the pleasure of seeing you.—I am, dear sir, yours sincerely, A. MALTHUS."

A letter from Mrs Godwin, senior, will close the record of the year.

Mrs Godwin, senior, to William Godwin.

[WOOD DALLING, 1798.]

"MY DEAR W^M—I'm a poor letter writer at best, but now worse than ever. After thanking y^o for y^r genteel present of the Memoirs of y^r wife. Excuse me saying Providence certainly knows best, the fountain of wisdom cannot err. He that gave life can take it away, and none can hinder, and tho we see not his reasons now, we shall see them hereafter. I hope y^a are taught by reflection your mistake concerning marriage, there might have been two children that had no lawful wright to anything y^t was their fathers, with a thousand other bad consequences, children and wives crying about ye streets without a protector. You wish, I dare say, to keep y^r own oppinion, therefore I shall say no more but wish you and dear babes happy. Dose little Mary thrive? or she weaned? You will follow your wives direction, give them a good deal of air, and have a good oppertunity, as y^o live out of ye Smoke of the city. You will be kind enough to let y^r Sister know Mr and Mrs G. and self wish to know if she rec^d a box with eggs whole, they were all new, and sundry trifels I sent her, with a new piece of print for my grand-daughter Mary for a gown, with 2/6 to pay for the making, a pr. little

Stockens and Hat for yr. Ch. 16 March last. Am greatly concerned to hear yr. Bro. has lost his place at Wright's ; am affraid
it's from the old cause ; Seneca's morals he bostes off is not
sufficient, there is something else wanting of greater moment and
importance. I dont write to him because he gives me such hard
names, as that I don't act up to the carrector my blessed Saviour
has set me, &c., though I wish him well, and think I discharge
my duty towards him. He wrote me word he wish'd he had done
with Sirvitude or with life, I'm afraid he is prepared for neither.
I have been burning a great number of old letters, but when I
came to yours, it was with great reluctance that I destroyed them,
there is such a kind and benevolent spirit in them towards your
dear S. and J. in their necessities. What a burthen has John been
to yo. ! Poor creature, what will become of him I tremble to
think. He trusts providence, but its in a wrong way, not in ye
way of well doing. I have sent him a new shirt for Mr Sothren to
send by private hand, directed to Hanh. I coud send him my
riding-coat, its so very heavy, and I so very week I cant wear it,
and perhaps Natty a waistcoat, but imagain the use he will make
of them will be to lay them in pawn, but so he must if he will,
who can help it ? Money is of no use, nor is it much otherwise
with some others which I shall not name.

"By seling a little Timber, and frugality in my expences, hope
to be able a little after Mic[haelmas] to help you and the rest to
£10 a-piece, taking yr. notes for it, perhaps will just keep their
heads above water. I wd. reserve somthing to keep yr. S. from
starving, but yt. will be difficult. If I leave her a place for her life,
and she be deep in debt, and have interest to pay, she will be
nothing ye better. I wish you to write very soon by post with
your opinion of the matter, and also how Joe conducts himself
towards his wife and family. I sent Mary a pritty mourning ring
with an emethist and 2 sparks in it ; do you ask to see it, also a
box for it ; hope she will not loose it. Would not wish yo. to
declare the contents of my letter : my best wishes attend you and
yours. Yr. Bro. Hull and wife and Natt join me in the same,
Mrs G. is in ye increesing way ; their eldest has got the measels

is very full, but hope no danger. I see in ye news a Miss Foster married of Wisbeach.—From y^r. affec^ate. Mother, A. G.

"I wish you woud let me know if there is any better way of directing letters or parcels, are they no more than letters to London when directed to Somers Town.

"What I send Han wou'd be glad y^o. to be her director what use to make of it. She has told me some former letters she was affraid she sh'd be put to trouble, and often exprest y^o. have been a father to her, but it stands y^o. in hand to take care of yourself; an aspiring temper will be beat down, while the humble shall be exalted."

CHAPTER XII.

ST LEON—MRS REVELEY. 1799.

TIIE year 1799 began with a breach with Mackintosh, which afterwards grew wider. Mackintosh delivered early in that year, in the hall of Lincoln's Inn, a course of lectures on the Law of Nature and Nations. To some expressions in the first of these Godwin objected, as unfairly directed against himself. His letter is not preserved, but its purport can be in great measure divined from the following reply :—

Mr, afterwards Sir, James Mackintosh to William Godwin.

"SERLE STREET, LINCOLN'S INN, 30*th Jany.* 1799.

" DEAR SIR,—I read your very candid and good-tempered letter with real pleasure. I owe you an honest answer. I think I am disposed to make it a perfectly good-natured one. The strongest expression you quote, 'Savage Desolators,' you will find on reperusal to be a half-pleasantry directed against metaphysicians in general, amongst whom I have sometimes the vanity to number myself. 'Those who disguise commonplace in the shape of paradox' is most certainly not an allusion to you. The thing is so common as an art of literary empiricism that I rather think no particular writer was present to my mind when I wrote the passage. Your opinions do not stand in need of any contrivances to make them *appear* more singular than they *are.* As to Turgot, Rousseau, and Condorcet, I have the highest reverence for the first of these writers. The second I have long considered as the most eloquent

and delightful madman that ever existed. The third I always
thought a cold and obscure writer; I never could think very
highly of his talents, partly perhaps because I am no great judge
of his mathematical eminence, which is, I believe, the principal
part of his reputation. His conduct did not appear to me to have
been that of a good man. But in none of the phrases which you
have selected have I even so much as insinuated that he or any
other mistaken speculator was influenced by bad motives. A
man may be 'mischievous' with the best 'motives' in the world.
In all discussions of 'Speculative Principles' it is always a most
unfair act of controversy to load the author whom we oppose with
the 'immoral consequences' which we suppose likely to flow from
his opinion, not to mention that it is a sorry and impertinent
sophism to urge such consequences as an argument against the
truth of a speculative proposition. But the case is very different
in moral and practical disputes. There the consequences are
everything, and must be constantly appealed to, especially by
those who, like you and myself, hold utility to be the standard of
morals. To apply this to the present subject. With respect to
you personally, I could never mean to say anything unkind or
disrespectful. I had always highly esteemed both your acuteness
and benevolence. You published opinions which you believed to
be true and most salutary, but which I had from the first thought
mistakes of a most dangerous tendency. You did your duty in
making public your opinions. I do mine by attempting to refute
them ; and one of my chief means of confutation is the display of
those bad consequences which I think likely to flow from them.
I, however, allow that I should have confined those epithets, which
I apply to denote pernicious consequences, merely to doctrines.
Though these epithets, when they are applied by men to me, are
never intended to convey any aspersion upon the moral or intellectual character of individuals, but merely to describe them as
the promulgators of opinions which I think false and pernicious,
yet I admit that I should not in any way have applied the epithets
to *men*. I feel gratitude to you for having recalled my attention
to this great distinction which I shall observe in my proposed

lectures, and in the work which may one day be the fruit of them, with a caution which is prescribed equally by a regard to my own character, and to the interests of science. I assure you that I never felt any desire that our intercourse should be lessened ; having never experienced anything but pleasure from it. Distance, accident, occupation, and laziness have contributed to make it less ; inclination has had no share. I, on the contrary, hope that we shall continue to exhibit the example, which is but too rare, of men who are literary antagonists but personal friends.—I am, with great regard, yours,   JAMES MACKINTOSH."

Godwin's Diary for the year exhibits him engaged in the same, or even greater intellectual labour than before. The conscientious accuracy which impels him to state the fact when a book was read only superficially, "*ça et là*," serves to bring into greater prominence the number of books of all kinds, and in many languages, which were read thoroughly. He wrote in this year his novel of "St Leon," on which he bestowed extreme pains, a tragedy, and many Essays and Articles. "Caleb Williams" had proved so great a success that he had been much urged to write a second novel, but he hesitated ; he "despaired of finding again a topic so rich of interest and passion." At length, however, he thought that if he could "mix human passions and feelings with incredible situations," he might conciliate even the severest judges. The situations of "St Leon : a Tale of the Six-teenth Century," are indeed sufficiently incredible, since the hero, St Leon, has the secrets of the Philosopher's Stone and the Elixir Vitæ ; and Godwin took as his motto to the work a quotation from Congreve, "Ferdinand Mendez Pinto was but a type of thee, thou liar of the first magni-tude." The aim of the tale is to show that boundless wrath, freedom from disease, weakness and death, are as nothing in the scale against domestic affection, and "the charities of private life." For more than four years he had desired to modify what had been said under that head in " Political Justice," while he reasserted his conviction of the general truth of his system.

Though it had a considerable reputation, and went through many editions, it never had the popularity of " Caleb Williams ; " its even greater improbability removed it still more from the region of human sympathies. But the description of Marguerite, drawn from the character of Mary Wollstonecraft, and of St Leon's married life with her, idealized from that which Godwin had himself enjoyed, are among the most beautiful passages in English fiction, while the portrait of Charles, St Leon's son, stands alone. No such picture has elsewhere been drawn of a perfectly noble, self-sacrificing boy.

It does not appear that the tragedy was ever published, nor is any trace of it now to be discovered.

When his books were laid aside for the day, he entered into society, and very few days indeed are now mentioned as spent at home. There is little mention of the children, who, indeed, were a great and increasing embarrassment to him, but such allusions as there are in the Diary and Letters, show great tenderness and affection. He took Fanny out with him to the houses of his intimate friends, and there are two or three entries of "Astley's with Fanny." While his chosen friends and most constant companions remained the same as in former years, he was attracting to himself many literary men—Wordsworth, Coleridge, and Lamb,—though the intimacy with these scarcely ripened till the following year. Frequent visits also to Sheridan and other political men show a great revival of the old political interests,

though the questions were not so burning nor were men's
minds so keenly exercised about them, as had been the
case a few years before.

But neither literary work, politics, nor society, welcome
as Godwin was to all his friends, could make up for the
want of the home-life which he had so greatly enjoyed,
even when from his dislike of constant "co-habitation," he
had striven to minimize the time he gave to it. The correspondence with Miss Lee has shown that he was anxious
to contract another marriage, and in this year it seemed
possible, at least it seemed so to him, that the way was
open to such a marriage, in which his feelings no less than
his reason might be once more deeply engaged. Mrs
Shelley's note will explain the circumstances.

"An event happened during this year which gave a new turn
to Mr Godwin's feelings : this was the death of Mr Reveley,
which occurred suddenly from the breaking of a blood-vessel on
the brain, on the 6th of July 1799.

"His widow has often described to me her horror at this event.
He did not die at the moment of breaking the vessel ; he became
gradually stupefied, and his senses, one by one—first his taste,
then his sight—failed him. He was unaware of his danger in the
first instance, and as the thought that he was really dying flashed
across his wife's mind, her terror became ungovernable. Mrs
Fenwick, the ever kind, cordial, womanly friend, had called in the
morning, and finding Mr Reveley indisposed, remained to assist
in waiting on him. At this moment of horror she looked out of
the window, and saw Marshal passing up the street on horseback.
She called to him, and he was in an instant with the frightened
women, ready to devote his whole time to their assistance. A
physician was called in, but it was a case past all medical aid from
the moment the vessel broke. He died in a few hours.

"From the chamber of death his widow rushed to a remote
and desolate room at the top of the house, in a state bordering on

frenzy,—for a week she remained in the same place, in the same
state. She and her husband had at times disagreed, and believed
themselves unsuited to each other. But he was the husband of
her early youth, the father of her adored son, the friend and companion of nearly fifteen years. She was endowed with the keenest
sensibility, and her heart received a shock from which she could
with difficulty recover.

"Mr Godwin heard of Mr Reveley's death at the house where
he dined on the same day." [This is a mistake of Mrs Shelley's,
as it appears from the Diary that on Saturday, July 6, Godwin
did not dine out, and he went to the theatre in the evening.
But on the *next* day, Sunday, he dined with his sister, Harriet
Godwin, to meet Mr and Mrs Fenwick, and there probably
heard of what had occurred on the previous evening.] "He
became thoughtful and entirely silent—he already revolved the
future in his mind. Maria Reveley had been a favourite pupil, a
dear friend, a woman whose beauty and manners he ardently admired. After his wife's death, his visits and attentions had excited
Mr Reveley's jealousy, and they became to a great degree discon-
tinued. His uprightness and candour of character made him disdain the suspicion, but he withdrew, unwilling to be the cause of
domestic feud. It was, however, his plan to yield but little to
form and etiquette, and before Mr Reveley had been dead a
month, he did not scruple to ask to see his widowed friend, and
to make her understand the feelings and prospects with which her
visits would be paid. She at first refused to see him, and several
letters passed between them."

Mrs Reveley's letters have not been preserved, but copies
of those which Godwin sent to her still remain.

William Godwin to Mrs Reveley.

[*July* 1799].

"How my whole soul disdains and tramples upon these cow-
ardly ceremonies! Is woman always to be a slave? Is she so
wretched an animal that every breath can destroy her, and every

temptation, or more properly every possibility of an offence, is to be supposed to subdue her?

"This ceremony is to be observed *for some time*. What miserable, heartless words! What is *some time?* this phrase, upon which all feeling, all hope of anything reasonable is left to writhe, and to guess, as it can, when its sufferings shall have an end. You know in what light such ceremonies have been viewed by all the liberal and wise, both of my sex and yours.

"If you mean any more than ceremony, say so. You are free ; with this stroke of my pen I sign your freedom. But think, what must be my sensations, and my tranquillity, while you leave me in doubt whether this freedom is or is not to be used against me.

"I am the furthest in this world from wishing to give you a moment's pain. You, with your entrenchment of ceremony, have forced me, very, very contrary to my own inclination, to say thus much. I ask not a word of answer from you. I have no wish that you should know what it is you are doing, and what are the feelings which you are imposing, and are resolved, for some time, to impose upon me.

"The conduct which propriety and a generous confidence in the rectitude of our sentiments dictated to us both was too plain to be mistaken ; to see each other freely and honestly as friends ; to lay down no beggarly rules about married and unmarried men ; and to say nothing, *for some time*, but what was the strict and accurate result of friendship. If you had that confidence in me which every sentiment of my heart proclaims to me I deserve, you would have felt no want of these ceremonies.

"I use no form of superscription, because I know of none that can at all represent the interest I take in your welfare.

"W. GODWIN.

"I give this to Mrs Fenwick to transmit to you, because whatever I think of your rules, I will not without your consent break through them in any point in which I can avoid it.

"Do you think you can be more anxious about the propriety and rectitude of your conduct than I am?

"You cannot be displeased with the above. I do not pretend

to prescribe to you any article of your conduct. That I should take care to let you know what my feelings are can never be imputed to me as a crime."

The Same to the Same.

[*August* 1799.]

" I think you have the courage to excuse the plainness with which I am going to speak. The game for which we play, the stake that may eventually be lost is my happiness and perhaps your own.

" You have it in your power to give me new life, a new interest in existence, to raise me from the grave in which my heart lies buried. You are invited to form the sole happiness of one of the most known men of the age, of one whose principles, whose temper, whose thoughts, you have been long acquainted with, and will, I believe, confess their universal constancy. This connection, I should think, would restore you to self-respect, would give security to your future peace, and insure for you no mean degree of respectability. What you propose to choose in opposition to this I hardly know how to describe to you. You have said you cannot live without a passion; yet you prefer a mere abstraction, the unknown ticket you may draw in the lottery of men, to the attachment of a man of some virtues, a man whom you once, whom you long believed you loved. Your temper is so gentle and yielding, in those moments in which your heart is moved, that you indeed want a protector and an amulet. I cannot bear to think of what, but for the sake of warning you, I would not suffer to remain a moment in my thoughts, the new difficulties, embarrassments, and repentance in which this amiable softness of your character will, too probably, involve you. I offer you a harbour, once your favourite thought ; you prefer to launch away into the tempestuous treacherous ocean. I should not forgive myself in case of any new misfortune to you, if I had not ventured to say thus much.

" How singularly perverse and painful is my fate. When all obstacles interposed between us, when I had a wife, when you had a husband, you said you loved me, for years loved me ! Could you for years be deceived? Now that calamity on the one hand, and no unpropitious fortune on the other, have removed these obstacles, it seems your thoughts are changed, you have entered into new thoughts and reasonings." . . . [The end of the letter is lost.]

The Same to the Same.

[*Sept.* 1799.]

"I am surprised, and will you forgive me if I add, pleased, at Mrs Fenwick's intelligence, that your objection to what you once desired is wholly grounded upon your opinion of my understanding. I cannot persuade myself to regard this as an invincible objection. If Mrs Fenwick has misunderstood you, if your objection have any other basis beside this, I think you owe it to me to correct my mistake.

"And so you would really demand in a partner an understanding too little comprehensive to see into many things, and a heart, for these are wholly or nearly inseparable, of too little sensibility to feel many things? Surely to state such a requisition is sufficiently to display the misapprehension on which it is founded. I should have thought experience would have shown you how little is to be hoped from characters of this kind. Make one generous experiment upon a man of a different sort. Can you fail to be aware that the man of real powers will infallibly, at least when he loves, be affectionate, attentive, familiar, and totally incapable of all questions of competition or ideas of superiority; while the man of meaner or middling understanding may almost always be expected to be jealous of rivalship, obstinate, self-willed, and puffed up with the imaginary superiority he ascribes to himself? Can you fail to be aware of the inferences which you ought to draw from the respective characters of the two sexes? We are different in our structure; we are perhaps still more different in our education. Woman stands in need of the courage of man to defend her, of his constancy to inspire her with firmness, and, at present at least, of his science and information to furnish to her resources of amusement, and materials for studying. Women richly repay us for all that we can bring into the common stock, by the softness of their natures, the delicacy of their sentiments, and that peculiar and instantaneous sensibility by which they are qualified to guide our tastes and to correct our scepticism. For my part I am incapable of conceiving how domestic happiness could be so well generated without this disparity of character. I would not, if I could, marry a man in female form, though that form were the form of a Venus.

"You say you are incapable of reasoning with me. Believe me, there is no good to myself I would not cheerfully sacrifice, rather than consciously be guilty of an atom of sophistry. Ask yourself whether any word I have put down on this subject be not unquestionable truth, and I might almost say put down dispassionately. This, as I have just said, is the privilege of our sex, from superiority of education, to collect the materials of decision : your sex, though feeling both exquisitely and admirably, are often in danger of deciding from a partial view of the subject.

"But what I have just said was not the purpose for which I sat down to write, though I could not prevail on myself to omit it. I am willing to leave this question to time. There is no character I have so much repugnance to act as that of a tormentor. The point I have principally to press is one which, so far as I at present see, tends to decide whether you have a heart or have no heart ; I mean the point of the continuance of our acquaintance.

"We have now lived on terms of the most cordial and unreserved friendship for six years. For more than four of those six years I suffered no thoughts respecting you, but those of single and unmixed friendship, to find harbour in my heart. You showed, in a thousand instances, that you valued my friendship, as I hope it deserved to be valued. On my part, at a moment when what would have happened without my interference I regarded as your ruin, I spared no exertion of my faculties or my industry, I defied misrepresentation and obloquy in every shape they might assume, so I might rescue you. Esteeming me probably more than you ever esteemed any other man, you, with a resolution that does you the highest honour, preserved my acquaintance, often in spite of Mr Reveley, once in spite of myself. Again and again, when he

I. Y

was unwilling to receive my visits, by your perseverance you conquered his inflexibility : at another time, when I was no longer
willing to pay them to him, you conquered me. If, the moment
all these complicated obstacles are removed, you of your own
accord cease from all further intercourse with me, what, I beseech
you, would you have me think of you? You always professed the
highest regard for Mrs Godwin ; naturally it would be expected
you should feel some interest in her children and mine : are these
motives all at once become nothing to you ?

"You cannot form so despicable an opinion of me as to suppose
that I can view you with no eyes but those of a lover. You saw
the contrary for years ; and believe me, I know what I say ; I can
conquer myself again and again, as often as the conquest shall be
necessary. There is nothing upon earth that I desire so ardently,
so fervently, so much with every sentiment and every pulse of my
heart, as to call you mine. But dispose of that point as you
please, I am too vigorous and robust of soul ever to be made the
suicide of my body or the suicide of my mind. No objection to
our intercourse can therefore arise from that point.

"If you are all at once become so thoroughly the slave of a
miserable etiquette that you must not even risk the seeing me alone,
you may dine here with my sister ; she comes to me every other
Sunday through the year : next Sunday is her day : or order me to
invite Mrs Fenwick : when the heart is willing, such trifles are
easily adjusted.

"It is, however, more than probable that in all I have said
respecting our intercourse, I have been fighting a shadow. In one
of your first intimations to me since your widowhood, you said
you could not see me, or any unmarried man, *for some time :* that
did not sound as if our intercourse was to be closed for ever. I
think, however, you pay too little attention to my feelings. Two
months of etiquette have now nearly elapsed, and no elucidation
of this *some time* has yet reached my ears. You ought perhaps to
have known that respecting persons in whom I feel myself interested, uncertainty fills my soul with tumults, and tortures my fancy
with a thousand painful and monstrous images."

Whatever answer Mrs Reveley returned to this was probably accepted as conclusive, and Godwin no longer prosecuted a suit which was unwelcome, or strove to anticipate the date at which it would be possible that those between whom so strange a correspondence had passed should meet on the old terms of intimacy. They did not in fact meet till December 3d, as it appears from the Diary, and then Mrs Reveley was in the company of Mr Gisborne, whom she afterwards married. And thus ended a curious wooing.

A considerable number of letters from Arnot to Godwin were written during this year. He was in Dresden after his tour from Vienna, often in great poverty, during which he had seriously thought of hiring himself out as a footman to obtain the very necessaries of life. But his desire of writing his travels, and making, as he believed, a very important book, was never laid aside, in spite of much discouragement from those who encountered him, Tuthil, Godwin's friend, now residing at Dresden, among the number. From Hamburg his journals were despatched to England, with the intention that they should be simultaneously published in English, French, and German. There is, however, no trace of such a work discoverable, his family strongly opposed the publication, and it is probable that their objections prevailed. The letters written to Godwin are less full than those presented already of his personal experiences of travel, because these were recorded in the now missing journal, but some shrewd observations are worthy of extraction as showing what subjects he knew would interest Godwin, while they are moreover striking in themselves, because, though coming from a young man at

such a time, they breathe such an essentially modern
spirit.

John Arnot to Godwin.

" HAMBURG, *Sunday, 4th August* 1799.

" . . . Having first delineated the character of the [Russian]
people, I meant then to have pointed out to the English, and to
every civilised nation, how much they had to dread if ever such a
people, or rather if such machines should be put in motion against
them as enemies, and to have called their attention to the pro-
digious extent of the Russian Empire, and the gradual encroach-
ment of its Sovereign, first in Asia from south to north, and now
in Europe from north to south. After a due consideration of
these facts, I flattered myself that I might be able perhaps to persuade the English to dissolve their present alliance with Russia.
In this I now think I was too sanguine, but it is not improbable
that my representations might in time have produced a good
effect. . . .

" Another project soon occurred, which would not have been
difficult to execute. I had not pored long over my books before
I was struck with the difference in the combination of the words
in the German and in the English languages ; the one the language
of imagination, yet minutely accurate and metaphysical in its distinctions ; the other the language of reflection, simple and philosophical, for such do these languages appear to me to be. When
I shall have considered them better, it may be that I shall find
myself mistaken. As I proceeded with my reading, this difference
of arrangement became to me still more remarkable, and at length
suggested the idea of attempting an analysis of the German language, and a comparison of it with the English. With the
minutiæ of the grammar of both I had no concern ; that would
have been more than I could have grasped ; I meant only, from
several well chosen sentences in both languages, to select of each
that sentence which should seem to me most complete for my
purpose, to analyse them both, tracing the order of ideas, and
placing them in various points of view, and then to compare them

together. The study of philosophical grammar is generally supposed to be a very dry study. I had long been of opinion that no study was dry if it were pursued in a proper manner; I thought I had now an opportunity of making the experiment, and for two months I continued collecting remarks and preparing materials, all of which were to me agreeable and entertaining, and, as I hoped, would have proved so to others."

In the winter Arnot was again at Vienna, where Godwin sent him money, and though the amount is not stated, it was clearly no inconsiderable sum. It came when he was in great poverty, in want of food, and with scanty clothing, one pupil, a Polish Count, to whom he taught English, his only means of livelihood, but with still undaunted purpose of writing a great book of travel, which should supersede all existing books on the subjects treated, and come as a very revelation to his countrymen. What might be done by a determined walker appears in the following extract :—

The Same to the Same.

"VIENNA, *26th Novr.* 1799.

". . . I left Hamburgh with a few shillings in my pocket, but instead of taking the straight road to Vienna, or even to Frankfort-on-the-Main, where I had addressed my portmanteau, I turned aside to Bremen. I then went to Ferden, Hanover, Hildesheim, Göttingen, Cassel. From Cassel I turned to the left to Mülhauser, and from thence to Gotha, Erfurt, Weimar, Jena. At Weimar I saw Wieland and Heider; I called also upon Göethe, but was not admitted. At Jena, where I saw Tuthil, I staid a few days, and then travelled over Coburg, Schweinfurt and Würtzburg to Frankfurt; from Frankfurt I returned to Würtzburg, and went to Bamberg, Nurnberg, and Ratisbon. Ratisbon is said to be about 270 or 280 English miles from Vienna, which, however, I might have reached in four days by sailing down the Danube, at the expense of perhaps six shillings, but instead of doing that I turned to the north, and, travelling through the Upper Palatine, and crossing those mountains of Bohemia covered with wood that go by the name of the Bohemian Forest, I arrived towards the end of October at Prague. Here I wished to have staid for a short time, but being in great want, I was obliged to depart in three or four days for Vienna.

"The weather during the summer was as extraordinary as during the winter. The long continuance of the rain was equally astonishing, vexatious, and ruinous. Having no change of clothes, and being amongst a most unfeeling and inhospitable people, and frequently without a penny, you may conceive that I endured many hardships, and that my health was not thereby improved. Yet whatever effect this may have had upon me at the time, it has upon the whole acted differently upon me from what might naturally have been expected,—instead of disheartening me it has increased my ardour, and rendered me doubly sanguine in my hopes of favourable weather for my travels through Hungary. Having endured so much, I wish to have now some compensation. . . .

"Perhaps I shall pay a visit to the Black Sea. But I don't know if this would be advisable, and I confess I am not fond of venturing into the Turkish dominions.—I am, with much esteem, &c.,   JOHN ARNOT."

On the receipt of Arnot's MSS. towards the end of this year, Godwin lent them to Arnot's brother, from whom remains an angry letter in regard to them, protesting against their publication. According to this gentleman, "the ingenuity and knowledge which he may have evinced is prostituted in the support of sentiments which are visionary, and subversive of all social order, and yet (thank God) totally irreducible to practice." He requires Godwin "in the most particular manner not to publish these MSS.," or if it be not in his power to withhold them from the press, he desires that the publication may be an anonymous one.

Of Godwin's friends on the Continent, Arnot had met

not only Tuthil, but Holcroft also, who was residing for a considerable part of this year at Hamburgh. His reasons and plans appear in the correspondence, where also appears a renewal of the squabbles which had from time to time interrupted the usual cordiality between the friends, but with this difference that the "little rift" which now was made was never again completely closed, as it had been on former occasions.

Thomas Holcroft to William Godwin.

> "HAMBURG, *July* 19*th*, 1799.
> " *At Wm. Cole's, No.* 100 *Cathermen Strasse.*

" We have been in this place eight days, and, had I time, the description of what I have already seen would be certainly more than sufficient to fill eight pages. But it is not my present intention to say anything on this subject, except to remark that though there may be few essential differences in the morals, or great outlines of behaviour in two nations, yet the numberless little particulars produce so striking an effect upon the eye and imagination, and we are so apt to wonder and laugh at what we are not accustomed to, that for some few days young and unpracticed persons might imagine themselves suddenly transported to another, and, certainly not in their opinion, to a better world.

"I received your second volume, and made enquiries immediately after my arrival, but have not yet met with any person who could give me sufficient information relative to the translating and publishing it in the German language. I think it right to tell you that Louisa and Fanny have read the two volumes, and are both of opinion that Leon is a second Falkland, but much his inferior. I was present when Louisa several times laid down the book to exclaim against his feeble and absurd conduct, to which I made no reply whatever. But it was a consolation to me to find they were both delighted with Marguerite. They think, however, there is by no means the same degree of interest created as that which they felt in reading 'Caleb Williams.' I inform you of this because you have always wished to enquire into the feelings of your readers, and because I consider such experiments as beneficial.

" I was somewhat moved, and rather surprized at the note included in the parcel. You reproach me for not having consulted you on my travelling plan, which you say you have always dis-approved and loathed. I have been frequently amazed at your forgetfulness, but never more than in the present instance. It is full two years, I believe indeed much more, since I first conceived the project. I spoke of it frequently, and I dare affirm oftener to you than to any other person. I cannot recollect whether you then made any objections, but had they been very serious and pointed they would surely have been attended to, and not forgotten. My reasons, however, I think you have already heard, and when again brought to your recollection will scarcely be thought feeble. I had a house and establishment, which, my family being dis-persed, were a heavy and unnecessary expense; my debts were great, and several of them of so long standing that I remembered them with a poignant anxiety, neither were my creditors, however they might forbear to dun me, entirely satisfied. These debts could only be discharged by the sale of my effects, and the breaking up of what was become in my opinion an immoral establishment, to support which I subjected myself to unnecessary labours, turmoils, and obligations. Persecuted at the Theatre as I continually have been from the appearance of ' Love's Frailties ', whenever a piece was known to be mine, what could I do better than disappear from the scene, and no longer excite malice or anger, call it which you will, that I could not appease? This was my train of thoughts, this train of thinking you have often witnessed, and in it, in my apprehension, you have acquiesced. That I was the first to recommend, both in language and practice, an unreserved communication, I well remember, and though certainly it has not existed between us of late in the same high and unspeakably gratifying degree it once did, its decline as far as I am a judge did not begin with me. This decline had I think two marked and decisive periods. The first was that which immediately preceded your marriage, and the second the lamentable event by which it was terminated. The anguish of heart I felt, first from the event itself, and afterwards from circumstances which I cannot endure to repeat, was such as never can be forgotten. You will not, I am sure, wound me by saying I do want or ever have wanted, since I have known your worth, confidence in you. Question me on any possible subject, any act or thought of my life, and I will answer you with the openness due to the honesty of your intentions, and the sincerity exacted by truth. No one, however, better understands than you do how impossible it is to be totally unreserved on one side, where there is a conviction of reserve being practised on the other. Of this you have given a fine picture between your St. Leon and Marguerite. That I shall never cease to have an unequivocal and active friendship for you I am certain, and what I have said has been accidentally drawn from me. . . .   T. HOLCROFT."

William Godwin to Thomas Holcroft.

"POLYGON, SOMERS TOWN, NEAR LONDON,
September 13th, 1799.

" DEAR HOLCROFT.—I know I have been guilty of what the world calls a crime, in suffering your letter to be so long by me unanswered. But for this you were prepared : you knew there were few offices I loathed more than that of sitting down to write, without having my mind previously filled with some subject on which to discourse. I come to the employment with the utmost repugnance ; and I hate myself, and for the moment half hate my correspondent, all the time I am engaged in it. I believe this is a defect ; but there are some propensities in the mind, whether taking their date from before or after the period of birth, that to say the least, almost surpass all human force to conquer. Supply me with a subject, and I will discourse upon it most eloquently ; believe that scarcely a day passes without your being in my mind, but do not expect me to amend.

" What could I have said ? ' I bear you in the highest regard ; I think of you continually ; I felt the loss of you an irreparable one.'

This and no more, however honest and cordial, discovering itself in the folds of a letter, would have looked dry and repulsive. It would have been still worse, if I had made you pay postage for it a second time. I did not like to enter on the point which makes the principal topic of your letter. If I had I could have shewn, demonstratively to my apprehension, that the breach of confidence and reserve came first on your part. This I might perhaps never have known, but for Mrs Inchbald. I afterwards discovered it in other instances. This was the true St Leon and Marguerite point between us ; you date it too low.

" I should have been much mortified if my friend Arnot had taken your advice and returned to England. It would have snapped the series, and broken the goodly harmony of his undertaking. I always thought, and his manuscript confirms me in the opinion, that he was happily formed for a traveller, and I have never been able to repent that I encouraged his purpose. There is nothing relative to the publication of his remarks that may not be managed full as well in his absence ; wherever he was, he must have subsisted in the meantime, and subsistence, as I take it, is as cheap on the continent as here.

" I am glad that you treated him kindly ; I can perceive that it had a good effect on him. In some things indeed you failed ; in your marginal annotations you were too rude and harsh, especially to a stranger. In one place you say 'This is the knave's morality.' This he took considerably in dudgeon ; you had not been long enough acquainted with him to be able to form a regard for the author, distinct from his work. Mrs Cole, he says, treated him with the most supercilious neglect ; in that case I am more sorry for her than for him. Observe, neither of these things were mentioned in his letter to me, but are merely noted in his private journal put down every night, which he has sent me. I know that according to the maxims of the world, I am guilty of a breach of decorum in mentioning them to you. But I think one of the crying sins of society is that we do not sufficiently explain our feelings to one another, and I am willing to make this solitary experiment whether it will not do more good than harm.

"No alteration, so far as I have observed, has taken place in the politics or tone of this island, since you left it. If there had, I should be almost afraid to state it. Parliament is to meet on the 24th instant, a period uncommonly early.

"Nicholson, Col. Barry, and Opie (your friend, no friend of mine) are well. I have seen the two latter once, the former several times, since your absence. I am unable to say whether his school will succeed; it goes on, like its master, at a slow and German-sort of a pace, but he appears sanguine. . . .

"You say nothing in this new communication by means of Arnot respecting my novel. I could send you another volume : there will be four.

"You are so anxious with your machine to get a legible copy of your letter, that you make a very devil of the original, and one has scarcely courage to attempt to decipher it. You water it too copiously.

"The above letter is to Mr Holcroft ; but as he may not be at Hamburgh, and I would not willingly lose a moment in transmitting the enclosed £20 to Mr Arnot, I have addressed it so that Mr Cole may open it, who, I am happy to hear by Mr A., is well. Advise me of the receipt.   W. GODWIN."

The letter is addressed, "Mr Cole, 100 Catherinen Strasse, Hamburgh."

Thomas Holcroft to William Godwin.

"HAMBURG, CATHERINEN STRASSE, 100, *Nov.* 22*nd*, 1799.

". . . Do not imagine you have been long out of my thoughts. Your novel, your tragedy, your well-being and happiness in every sense, are the frequent and serious subjects of recollection. Having made four at least fruitless attempts in Hamburg to make the first productive of some small gain to you, I hoped to have been more successful at Berlin, where I am told the book-sellers are more liberal and enterprising. Two men of consider-able literary merit here have read it, and, after considerable praise of the style, have pronounced it cold and uninteresting : at least

they plead, when I endeavour to controvert them, as far as they
are judges of the taste of readers in Germany. I have not read it
since I left England, but the impression it then made cannot have
been so entirely false as for their decision to be entirely true,
though I never felt satisfied with your choice of a subject. In
your last I learned with pleasure you have extended it to four
volumes, for I suppose you would not have done this, had you not
found incidents and passion grow upon you, and where these are,
success must be.

" For your Tragedy I am still more, I may say, irritably anxious.
I saw it only in its half-finished state. Give me the history of its
theatrical progress. When is it to be performed? What are your
feelings? Do you remain thoroughly concealed? Are you yet
thoroughly under the scourge of Managerial tyranny? I am very
desirous to hear this, and anything else you can tell me on the
subject.

". . . Let me know if Opie has received my pictures, what
you think of them, and what he and others say. In my opinion,
the ' Guide' is a masterpiece, though it will not appear so, perhaps, till it has been deeply considered. . . . Care has been taken
of young Arnot.	T. HOLCROFT."

The expressions about the pictures refer to a scheme of
Holcroft's of buying art treasures at a cheap rate abroad,
and sending them home for sale. It is scarcely necessary
to say that he was about as successful as amateur buyers
usually are when in competition with professional dealers.

The Same to the Same.

"HAMBURG, *December* 13*th*, 1799.

". . . My second motive for writing relates to yourself. I became acquainted here with a man of letters who wished to trans-
late your novel, but who could not find a bookseller that approved
the undertaking. This gentleman, whose name is Bulow, is now
at Berlin, and I have received a letter from him to-day, to inform
me that a publisher of that city, named Unger, will give ten

guineas if I will send him the sheets I have, and the remainder as soon as possible. The novel being now published, I made no difficulty of answering by to-day's post that I would accept the terms; and I hope I have acted as you would have advised. Bulow himself is a man of indifferent character; I therefore wrote that the copy should be delivered on payment of the money, of which, the moment it is received, you shall have notice, and either a draft on London, or payment by some other means. Do not, therefore, neglect to send me the remaining sheets, with a copy inclosed for myself.

" Being at this distance, my heart revolts at concluding without signing myself—Ever and ever affectionately yours,

"T. HOLCROFT."

The following extract, which ends for the year the correspondence between the friends, is interesting for the mention of an almost forgotten book and its translator, but which once produced a profound sensation. It is curious, too, as showing the extreme difficulty of holding any communication between England and France :—

William Godwin to Thomas Holcroft.

" *December* 31, 1799.

" . . . Mr Marshal desires me to add that he has conceived the intention of writing to Volney, who is now at Paris, and printing, as we understand, his travels in America, to request him, upon the strength of having been the translator of his ' Ruins of Empires '—a translation which has been very successful and much praised here—to send him, if he felt no impropriety in it, the sheets of his present work before publication. But our laws relative to corresponding with an enemy are so complicated and severe, that Mr Marshal, upon trial, has found it impracticable to send his letter. He thinks it not impracticable that, through Pougens, you might effect his object for him. He observes that the reputation of Volney as a traveller has been so puffed by

Gibbon and others, and is consequently so unprecedentedly high, that, if he could obtain the work in time, he would think of publishing the translation on his own account."

Godwin was still extremely anxious to make up his quarrel with Mrs Inchbald. He sent her a copy of his novel, "St Leon," with a letter requesting a renewal of the old friendly intercourse. After giving her reasons for delay in reading it, the seeing a new play through the press, and other engagements, and after a promise to give her sincere opinion on his work, she continues—

Mrs Inchbald to William Godwin.

"LEICESTER SQUARE, *Wednesday morning, 4th Dec.* 1799.

" . . . In respect to the other subject, you judged perfectly right that I could not have expressed any resentment against you, for I have long ago felt none. I also assure you that it will always give me great pleasure to meet you in company with others, but to receive satisfaction in your society as a familiar visitor at my own house I never can.

" Impressions made on me are lasting. Your conversation and manners were once agreeable to me, and will ever be so. But while I retain the memory of all your good qualities, I trust you will allow me not to forget your bad ones ; but warily to guard against those painful and humiliating effects, which the event of my singular circumstances might once again produce.—Your admirer and friend,　　　　　　　　　　　　　　E. INCHBALD."

Three weeks later she sent an elaborate and very clever critique on "St Leon," written with some bitterness, but it dwells too much on details to be interesting to the general reader, who has not the work in his mind.

That Godwin, in spite of his own difficulties, had sent £20 to Arnot has been already recorded in his own letter.

There are other indications of large and self-denying charity, extending to most distant and unexpected quarters. One such is a letter from Mrs Agnes Hall, of Jedburgh, acknowledging the receipt of £10 for some poor lady whose name is not mentioned, in which Mrs Hall says that, " though grief like my friend's can admit of no remedy, yet your judicious bounty was a means, by enabling her to procure the necessary comforts to her dying children, of preventing that grief from becoming absolute despair."

The name of James Ballantyne, the Edinburgh printer, needs no note. The Dr Bell whom he introduces to Godwin was probably Dr James Bell of Edinburgh, who died in Jamaica in 1801, and is still remembered by his writings on professional subjects.

James Ballantyne to William Godwin.

"KELSO, *Nov.* 14, 1799.

" SIR,—About three years ago there dined in your company at Mr Holcroft's, introduced by the late Mr Armstrong, a young man from Scotland, on whose mind your wisdom and benevolent condescension have left impressions of affection and gratitude, which no time will efface. The writer of this letter is the person so delightfully distinguished ; but as he is sensible that an interview which constituted so prominent a period of his life may long ere this have melted into the common mass of uninteresting events which consume your time without attracting your attention, he begs leave to mention a circumstance which may recall him to your memory. He promised to send up to London a distinguished portrait, which promise remains to this day unfulfilled. He was not to blame that on enquiry he found every impression of that portrait was sold off; but he severely condemns the mingled indolence and timidity which prevented him from stating that circumstance to account for apparent neglect.

"The customs which fetter man in his intercourse with his fellows do not justify this tardy intrusion on your leisure ; but these customs Mr Godwin will disregard when they interfere with his power of communicating instruction and extending happiness. The gentleman who will deliver this letter is Doctor Bell, an amiable and accomplished physician, whose mind since his earliest perusal of your writings, has been filled with the most exalted respect for your talents, and affection for your heart.

"The Jamaica fleet which sails in a few days, conveys him from his country, perhaps for ever. His situation will be one of high influence and authority, and I know he will exert his power to lighten the woes and diminish the horrors of slavery. Once only will he be able to avail himself of this introduction, but to see and converse, for however short a time, with Mr Godwin, will prove a source of pleasure, both in enjoyment and reflection, which he cannot leave his native soil without endeavouring to attain. It is no common motive which would incline me to trespass thus on your leisure.

"I beg to be considered, my dear sir, with the utmost respect and affection, your obliged friend,

"James Ballantyne."

"*One line* from you to say you forgive what the world would term my presumption would give me supreme pleasure. I confess I would rather be assured of this by yourself, than by the report of my friend."

A few lines from the good old lady at West Dalling contain the only domestic facts worth recording.

Mrs Godwin sen. to William Godwin.

[Wood Dalling], "*Sep.* 21*st*, '99.

"Dear Wm.—I hope yo rec^d. a letter from me dated 5 July by ye hand of y^r sister. I wish you happy. If you be not I shall have ye sattisfaction in my own mind that I have tryed to make y^o so.

" Terms are agreed upon to sell Dalling Estate to y^{r.} brother Hull, that he may not be thrown out of business when I die with his young family which he must mortgage. What will be y^{r.} shares I don't know yet the notes each have given will be considered as past and disstroyed. Is all I can say at present. I have wrote a few lines to John y^o may show yours to him if y^o please. Have not wrote to Jo. or Han^{h.} because ye affair is not finish'd.

" Y^{r.} affec. Mother,

" A. GODWIN."

" I'm sorry to put y^o to this expense, however its not necessary y^o shoud write till yo hear from me again."

" MY DEAR W^{m.}—Since the above I've recieved y^{r.} very kind letter of ye 16 Sep. The little dear boy Johny's arm was not out, and was quite well in a day or two. Your bro. Nath came home ye 7 of July, very poorly indeed, went to Norwich next day for advice of Dr. Alderson, whose prescription with the blessing of God was of service. He returned in 3 weeks to his place again, repeated the physick several times, is better, but fear he will never get clear of his laxating dissorder, but like John wishes to be in buissness for himself but fear he will not be a good ecconomist, especially without a good wife, and they are as hard to be met with as farms. However its the last I can do for him in my life time. Your share and John's will fall short of a Hundred, Natt's and Hull's a little more, Han^{h.'s} least of all, because she have had most. I purpose clearing of that I gave to Wright, on Jo's account I should have said, and White the former is dead a year or two agoe insolvent, the latter broke lately. I'm not sure I shall not send this in a parcel to Han^{h.} If I do I shall write a few lines to her. I do put much trust in your advice and management for John and your sister, who has always told me you was a father to her.'

I.   Z.

CHAPTER XIII.

GODWIN'S acquaintance with Coleridge rapidly increased, and had now developed into a most cordial and confidential friendship. It will be remembered that Coleridge was the fourth and last of those persons whom Godwin names as having made on him a profound intellectual impression. The change of thought and view which he attributed to Coleridge coincided, however, with that which was brought about also by other causes. He had recommenced the habit, now for some time laid aside, of placing on paper the results of his constant self-introspection. He examined the state of his belief, and the causes of his mental change, and then are recorded, truly enough as it would seem, other influences contemporaneous with that of Coleridge. The extract which immediately follows was written indeed some years later, though it chronicles the reading which mainly occupied him about this time.

"A great epocha, or division in my life, which may as well deserve to be recorded as almost any other event, is that at which I began to read the old English authors. This was in 1799-1800, when I had completed my forty-third year.

"During the term of my college life, from 1773 to 1778, I endeavoured to take a survey of the world of knowledge, and to select the branches to which in preference I should devote my attention, I was deeply impressed with the maxim that *art is long,* and *life is short.* My judgment dictated to me that it would be best to read few things but to read them well. In fact life is to a young man entering on the era of manhood, a term of ten or twenty years; to look further than that with any certainty, and as to a period in which given things are to be done, seems deviating into the visionary and romantic.

" I resolved to read the classics; but I purposed to confine myself to a few of the greater classics, Virgil, Horace, Cicero, Livy, Sallust, and Tacitus, among the Romans, and Homer, Sophocles, Xenophon, Herodotus and Thucydides among the Greeks. I considered this list as admitting of enlargement, but such was the general outline.

" It is surprising how much men are guided in their whole plan of life by a few external circumstances—the creatures of accident. I was brought up to a profession, that of a preacher among the dissenters. This I was very likely to exercise, at least at first, in a rural situation. My pecuniary means were much confined; my income was likely to be small; I should have few books. On this account I was well pleased with this plan of classical reading, in which, as my education in this branch of knowledge had been a very imperfect one, one author might last me for six months.

" The same principle that guided me in the field of classical reading, was of still more obvious and necessary application in the literature of my own country. Contemplating the immense library that might be filled with our vernacular authors, I resolved that my reading should be select; and one of the first rules I was induced to adopt was, that I would, for the most part, confine my reading to our modern authors. History was a study to which I felt a particular vocation; and I should say now what I thought then, that the modern writers of history in English are eminently superior to their predecessors. Their narrative is more free and unincumbered; they have more taste; their views are more extensive; they philosophise better on the principles of evidence and the progress and vicissitudes of human society. One of the first trials of comparison I was prompted to make, was between Hume and the

English translation of Rapin; and, to be sure, there can scarcely
be a comparison in which all the advantage is more clearly on one
side. I believe I should hardly have found the superiority of the
moderns to the ancients so decisive in any other department as in
this of history. The result of my feelings and habits in this kind
is strikingly exhibited in the Essay on English Style, at the close of
the ' Enquirer,' written when I was forty.

"A rule of study which I adopted at College, and adhered to
with exceptions and interruptions for many years, was to divide
my day into several parts, adapting a particular species of study to
each part. Thus there was not a day passed in which I did not
read a portion, first of the Greek, and then of the Roman classics,
another part of the day was appropriated to metaphysics, theology,
and books of reasoning, a third to history, and so forward. This
habit was very beneficial in giving system to my mind and clearness to my reasonings.

" It was not till 1799 that I broke in upon my rule of confining
my English reading principally to the moderns. The only considerable exception to this rule was Shakespeare. That was an
exception hardly to be avoided by a native of this island. At the
period I have mentioned, and often before, my thoughts were
turned to the Drama, and I had designed, if my talents had been
found sufficient for the undertaking, to look to it as one of my
sources of subsistence. About this time I got possession of a copy
of Beaumont and Fletcher; and looking into them at first with
reference to the object I had in view, I found in them a source of
sentiment and delight of which I had not before had the smallest
conception. This opened upon me a new field of improvement
and pleasure, and engaged me in a course of reading which, from
that hour [to 1813], I have never deserted.

" I soon felt that I had gained an uncommon advantage from
this discovery made at this time. While I was at College, I had
thought that *art is long* and *life is short.* In the course of years
that had elapsed since, I had sometimes felt inclined to alter my
mind : in other words, I had felt that the scheme of reading I had
prescribed to myself was rather too narrow. I remember, when I

was a very little boy, saying to myself, ' What shall I do, when I have read through all the books that there are in the world?' and my sensation in this limited application of the question was now somewhat similar. I had gradually a little enlarged my plan in the matter of classical reading.

" But on the present occasion a new world was opened to me. It was as if a mighty river had changed its course to water the garden of my mind. I was like a person who, for many years, had subsisted on a slender annuity, and had now an immense magazine of wealth bequeathed to him. I looked over the inventory of my fortune, and felt that these treasures would never be exhausted. This illustration does not come up to the idea I felt, that everything enumerated in this inventory was new, and that I was, therefore, suddenly put in possession of a museum of untried delights. What a blessing for a man at forty-three years of age, a period at which we are threatened with the blunting of some of the senses from the monotonous repetition of their gratifications, to enter into the lease of a new life, where everything would be fresh, and everything would be young !"

Such were his recollections of this time some thirteen years later, but they have about them a ring of truth, which shows they were as genuine as unforgotten. Here is also another note, undated, but probably somewhat earlier than the last, which records the change in his religious creed.

" In my thirty-first year I became acquainted with Mr Thomas Holcroft, and it was probably in consequence of our mutual conversations that I became two years after an unbeliever, and in my thirty-sixth year an atheist.

" In my forty-fourth year I ceased to regard the name of Atheist with the same complacency I had done for several preceding years, at the same time retaining the utmost repugnance of understanding for the idea of an intelligent Creator and Governor of the universe, which strikes my mind as the most irrational and ridiculous anthropomorphism. My theism, if such I may be permitted to call it, consists in a reverent and soothing contemplation of all that is beautiful, grand, or mysterious in the system of the universe, and in a certain conscious intercourse and correspondence with the principles of these attributes, without attempting the idle task of developing and defining it—into this train of thinking I was first led by the conversations of S. T. Coleridge."

A fragment of an analysis of his own character, not merely looking back upon, but actually written about this time, will serve to give other indications of what Godwin now was, subject, however, to the unavoidable drawback, that no man, however desirous of truth, is a fair judge of himself.

"Why does a man feel any degree of eagerness to expose his character to the world? For the most part it is a disclosure made to enemies, who will study it for purposes of degradation, and to find, if the writer acquired any degree of applause, that it was impossible he should have owed it to his merit. Such a disclosure is, however, of high value; it adds to the science of the human mind, and, by the operation of comparison, enables each reader to make an estimate of himself.

"A timorous advocate, both of men and opinions, on individual occasions—afraid to advance opinions lest I should be unable to support them—always beginning with a kind of skirmishing war. This owing to frequent miscarriage, and experience of my own inaccuracy.

"Too sceptical, too rational, to be uniformly zealous. Nervous of frame, mutable of opinion, yet in some things courageous and inflexible.

"So fond of disinterestedness and generosity that everything in which these are not has always been insipid to me—inextinguishably loving admiration and fame, yet scarcely in any case envious. Habitually disposed to do justice to the merits of others; never depreciating an excellence I felt, and eager for the discovery of excellence, yet in some cases too languid an assertor of it—ever addicted to reflection and reasoning, frequently to ardour.

" I am extremely modest. What is modesty? First, I am tormented about the opinions others may entertain of me ; fearful of intruding myself, and of co-operating to my own humiliation. For this reason I have been, in a certain sense, unfortunate through life, making few acquaintances, losing them *in limine*, and by my fear producing the thing I fear. I am bold and adventurous in opinions, not in life ; it is impossible that a man with my diffidence and embarrassment should be. This, and perhaps only this, renders me often cold, uninviting, and unconciliating in society. Past doubt, if I were less solicitous for the kindness of others, I should have oftener obtained it.

"I am anxious to avoid giving pain, yet, when I have undesignedly given it, I am sometimes drawn on, from the painful sensation that the having done what we did not intend occasions, to give more.

" My nervous character—to give it a name, if not accurate, well understood—often deprives me of self-possession, when I would repel injury or correct what I disapprove. Experience of this renders me, in the first case, a frightened fool, and in the last, a passionate ass ; in both my heart palpitates and my fibres tremble ; the spring of mental action is suspended ; I cannot deliberate or take new ground ; and all my sensations are pain and aversion— aversion to the party, impatience with myself. This refers merely to active scenes, not to colloquial disquisition ; in the latter my temper is one of the soundest and most commendable I ever knew.

" Perhaps one of the sources of my love of admiration and fame has been my timidity and embarrassment. I am unfit to be alone in a crowd, in a circle of strangers, in an inn, almost in a shop. I hate universally to speak to the man that is not previously desirous to hear me. I carry feelers before me, and am often hindered from giving an opinion, by the man who spoke before giving one wholly adverse to mine.

" I am subject to sensations of fainting, particularly at the sight of wounds, bodily infliction, and pain : perhaps this may have some connection with my intellectual character.

" I am feeble of tact, and occasionally liable to the grossest
mistakes respecting theory, taste, and character ; the latter experience corrects the former consideration ; but this defect has made
me too liable to have my judgment modified by the judgment of
others ; not instantaneously perhaps, but by successive impulses.
I am extremely irresolute in matters apparently trivial, which occasionally leads to inactivity, or subjects me to the being guided by
others.

" I have a singular want of foresight on some occasions as to the
effect what I shall say will have on the person to whom it is
addressed.   I therefore often appear rude, though no man can be
freer from rudeness of intention, and often get a character for
harshness that my heart disowns.

" I can scarcely ever begin a conversation where I have no preconceived subject to talk of ; in these cases I have recourse to
topics the most trite and barren, and my memory often refuses to
furnish even these.   I have met a man in the street who was liable
to the same infirmity ; we have stood looking at each other for the
space of a minute, each listening for what the other would say, and
have parted without either uttering a word.

" There are many persons that have gone out of life without
enjoying it—that is not my case.   I have enjoyed most of the
pleasures it affords.   I know that at death there is an end of all,
but I have not lived in vain for myself ; I hope not for others.

" There is an evenness of temper in me that greatly contributes
to my cheerfulness and happiness ; whatever sources of pleasure I
encounter, I bring a great part of the entertainment along with
me ; I spread upon them the hue of my own mind, and am satisfied.   Yet I am subject to long fits of dissatisfaction and discouragement ; this also seems to be constitutional.   At all times agreeable company has an omnipotent effect upon me, and raises me
from the worst tone of mind to the best.

" No domestic connection is fit for me but that of a person who
should habitually study my gratification and happiness ; in that
case I should certainly not yield the palm of affectionate attentions
to my companion.   In the only intimate connection of that kind

I ever had, the partner of my life was too quick in conceiving resentments; but they were dignified and restrained; they left no hateful and humiliating remembrances behind them, and we were as happy as is permitted to human beings. It must be remembered, however, that I honoured her intellectual powers, and the nobleness and generosity of her propensities; mere tenderness would not have been adequate to produce the happiness we experienced.

"If it is curious to observe those propensities of the mind which appear so early that philosophers dispute whether they date their origin from before or after the period of birth, it is no less curious to remark how much is indisputably to be attributed to the empire of circumstances. I had an early passion for literary distinction, but an extreme uncertainty as to the species of literature by which it was to be attained. Poetry may be said to have been my first, my boyish passion. Afterwards, abandoning poetry, I hesitated between history and moral philosophy, dreading that I had not enough of elaborate exactness for the former, or of original conception for the latter. My first attempt, in 1782, a very wretched attempt, was history. To this I was immediately, and at the time reluctantly, spurred by the want of money. In 1790 I wrote a tragedy on the story of St Dunstan, which has since been laid aside. In 1791 I planned and begun my 'Political Justice.' In 1793 I commenced my 'Caleb Williams,' with no further design than that of a slight composition, to produce a small supply of money, but never to be acknowledged: it improved and acquired weight in the manufacture. To the choice of each of these kinds of composition I was more or less determined by mercantile considerations. If I had been perfectly at my ease in this respect, I cannot tell when I should have gravely attempted original composition, and in what species of literature.

"My mind, though fraught with sensibility, and occasionally ardent and enthusiastic, is perhaps in its genuine habits too tranquil and unimpassioned for successful composition, and stands greatly in need of stimulus and excitement. I am deeply indebted in this point to Holcroft."

These observations are but fragmentary, and the remainder is lost. In some points Godwin's knowledge of
self is remarkable ; in others it may be doubted whether
his extreme minuteness of detail did not lead him astray
in regard to the whole truth of his picture.

The Diary for this year throws some light on a portion
of the above. His tendency to faintness seems to have
increased about this time to a somewhat alarming extent,
and there are frequent notices of "deliquium" as having
taken place when he was in society as well as when alone.
In the early part of the year Coleridge was in London, and
the intercourse between the two friends was constant, while
during the rest of the time it was maintained by very
frequent letters. With Lamb also Godwin became now
intimate ; and there are many notes of suppers at Lamb's
and at the Polygon, where are also to be found the names
of all that circle of friends known to the readers of "Lamb's
Life and Letters." There was indeed scarcely a name
of any literary, artistic, or theatrical eminence, that does
not appear in these brief notes as among Godwin's circle.

In May 1800 Mrs Reveley married Mr Gisborne. The
engagement was kept a profound secret from all but the
family of the gentleman, and from Mr and Mrs Fenwick,
old friends both of Mrs Reveley and of the Godwins. It was
not only a severe blow to Godwin, who had never abandoned the hope that he might overcome the lady's objections to a marriage with him, but he was greatly wounded
at having been kept in the dark. What he felt, however, can
only be gathered, not from any words of his own, but from
Mr Fenwick's manly and sensible letters to him, excusing
himself from any unfriendliness in having kept a secret

which Mrs Reveley had a right to require him to keep.
Friendly relations were afterwards renewed, but Godwin
was not sorry to make a longer tour than usual during this
year—to accept Curran's invitation to Ireland, in the hope
of driving from his thoughts a sentiment which was probably
much deeper than any he had ever felt, except his love for
Mary Wollstonecraft.

In July he went to Ireland, after repeated invitations, of
which the following is a sample :—

J. P. Curran to William Godwin.

"DUBLIN, *June 8th,* 1800.

" . . . I have yet two months to remain here. I am too much
of a slave to have as much of your company as I would wish, but
I will treat you with perfect candour, and promise you that I will
act as your host as I would as your guest. I have an house in
town and a cottage in the country within three miles of it; a spare
bed in each, books in each, and a bottle of wine in each, and in
each you will find the most absolute power of doing what you
please as to idling, working, walking, eating, sleeping, &c. There
are many here that know you in print, and are much pleased with
the hope I have given them of knowing you in person. One of
them, Lady Mountcashel, who is now settled in Dublin for the
summer, speaks of you with peculiar regard, mixed with a tender
and regretful retrospect to past times and to past events with
which you have yourself been connected.

"Let me add, this is the pleasantest time of the year. The
journey is but little : a sit down in a mail-coach and a ferry brings
a philosopher, six shirts, his genius and his hat upon it, from
London to Dublin, *et vice versa,* in fifty-four hours. I think, too,
you would feel a curiosity to see a nation in its last moments.
You would think that slavery is no such fearful thing as you have
supposed in theory. I assure you our trees and our fields are as
green as ever. Thus have I stated the *pro* and *con* with as much
fairness as can be expected from a person so much interested in

your decision. If, therefore, it does not interfere with some material object or engagement, in the name of God, even trust yourself to the hospitality of these Irish barbarians, with whom your nation is about to communicate her freedom and her wealth. One word or two more on this subject, which, as an old traveller, I may speak with some authority. There are only two things that make a journey a grievance, preparation and luggage. During the former, a man travels it over a thousand times, instead of once ; and travelling in idea is a thousand times more tiresome than travelling in fact. Say to me, then, by a line, that I may put your sheets to the fire. If you land here in the night, you will find your bed ready at No. 12 Ely Place at any hour. . . .

"Will you give my very kind respects to Mrs Inchbald, if you should see her?—Yours truly, JOHN P. CURRAN."

He also visited Skeys and Lady Mountcashel, by both of whom he was cordially welcomed ; and at the house of the first he again met the sisters of his wife, Everina Wollstonecraft and Mrs Bishop, on amicable if not wholly cordial terms. He did not, however, go beyond the immediate neighbourhood of Dublin, and was absent from London less than six weeks, the last week or ten days having been spent in a homeward tour in North Wales.

His own record of the tour is contained in letters to Marshal, which follow without break, as they all relate to the same subject.

William Godwin to J. Marshal.

[DUBLIN, *July* 11, 1800.]

" I received your letter this morning, four days from its date. I forget now what I said in my last letter about the poor little girls, but in this letter I will begin with them. Their talking about me, as you say they do, makes me wish to be with them, and will probably have some effect in inducing me to shorten my visit. It is the first time I have been seriously separated from them since

they lost their mother, and I feel as if it was very naughty in me
to have come away so far, and to have put so much land, and a
river sixty miles broad, between us, though, as you know, I had
very strong reasons for coming. I hope you have got Fanny a
proper spelling-book. Have you examined her at all, and discovered what improvement she has made in her reading? You do
not tell me whether they have paid and received any visits. If it
does not take much room in your next letter, I should be very
glad to hear of that. Tell Mary I will not give her away, and she
shall be nobody's little girl but papa's. Papa is gone away, but
papa will very soon come back again, and see the Polygon across
two fields from the trunks of the trees at Camden Town. Will
Mary and Fanny come to meet me? I will write them word, if I
can, in my next letter or the letter after that, when and how it
shall be. Next Sunday, it will be a fortnight since I left them, and
I should like if possible to see them on the Sunday after Sunday
20th July. . . . .

William Godwin to J. Marshal.

[DUBLIN, *Aug.* 2, 1800.]

" Mrs Elwes tells me in her letter that I shall be at home on
the 3d of August. Probably she had the intelligence from you.
From what premises the conclusion was drawn I know not, but I
am apprehensive it will prove in some measure erroneous. My
original purpose was to have quitted Dublin the 27th of July, last
Saturday, and exactly four weeks from the day I quitted London.
I am now writing on Saturday, the 2d of August, one week later,
and am seated quietly in Mr Curran's bookroom, in his rural
retreat he visits from Dublin. It was originally proposed between
him and me that the week now concluding should be spent in an
excursion to Wexford, whither he expected to be called for the
assizes. That expectation has been frustrated, and he has now
prevailed on me to attend him to the assizes at Carlow, and has
promised that I shall be on board the packet for England on
Thursday evening, the 7th inst. That Thursday, however, will
probably be Friday. I then propose, as I believe I have told you

already, to walk three days amidst the natural and almost unrivalled beauties of N. Wales, and have a letter of introduction from Mr Grattan to Lady Harriet Butler and Miss Di Ponsonby, two old maids in the vale of Llangollen, with whom I propose to spend a couple of hours. I shall, however, certainly endeavour to give you precise notice of the time of my arrival at the trunks of the trees, which I can at any time by despatching a line from any part of N. Wales, twenty-four hours before I quit it in person. . . .

"I wish also that you would write to Arnot immediately, *poste-restante*, at Fünfkirchen, if there is any chance of your letter reaching its destination in time to cheer the beloved wanderer. Tell him of my absence from London, tell him of my increasing affection and anxiety for his welfare, tell him of my increasing admiration and respect for his narrative. Beg him to give me under his hand an explicit permission to publish his journal in case of any unhappy accident to himself, and an approbation beforehand of my conduct, whatever it shall happen to be. Keep a copy of your letter.

"I have kept pretty good company here. Last Wednesday I dined with three countesses—Countess-dowager Moira (it was at her house), Earl and Countess Granard, and Countess Mountcashel, and on Sunday I am to dine at Lady Mountcashel's. I mean to call on Lady Moira the moment I have quitted this letter. But I have not yet seen either Grattan or Ponsonby. They are however, I believe, to dine with us at Mr Curran's barn (as he calls it) to-morrow. He wishes me to go with him to the assizes at Wexford, but that I believe I must decline. They are in the beginning of August. Hitherto there have been daily sittings of the courts of law, and I see nothing of him from breakfast till five o'clock. This will last ten days longer, and I wish much to spend one week with this charming creature when he is at full leisure. On that computation I shall not cross the channel till about the 28th inst.

"I am fully sensible to your care of my children and my establishment. Every minute particular that you will be so good as to write to me respecting them will be highly gratifying. . . . .

" I depute to Fanny and Mr Collins, the gardener, the care of the garden. Tell her I wish to find it spruce, cropped, weeded, and mowed at my return; and if she can save me a few strawberries and a few beans without spoiling, I will give her six kisses for them. But then Mary must have six kisses too, because Fanny has six.

" It would be highly gratifying if on my return I could find the elaborate repairs and papering of my house finished, the garden-door erected, and the household linen ready for use. Do not forget the directions of this or my preceding letter, though they should not be repeated in any of my subsequent ones. . . .

The Same to the Same.

" DUBLIN, *Aug.* 2, 1800.

" I begin another letter immediately on despatching its predecessor, as much, I believe, by way of recording my own feelings and adventures, as with a view to any amusement you may derive from the narration. Two persons, as you know, exclusive of Mr Curran, I was particularly desirous of seeing in Ireland, Mr Grattan and the Countess of Mountcashel. This desire I have had a reasonable opportunity of gratifying; and, in addition to this, have been a spectator of a considerable portion of most interesting scenery, which was not in my contemplation when I left England. I saw Mr Grattan, for the first time in Ireland, at Mr Curran's country house, on Saturday the 12th of July, ten days after my arrival at Dublin. He then dined with us, but it was a numerous company, that afforded me very little opportunity of diving into his characteristic qualities. The next day, however, we went over to Grattan's own house, where we arrived in the evening, and slept that and the succeeding night. Mr Curran was obliged on Monday morning to go to Dublin to attend the courts, in consequence of which I had Grattan almost, though not entirely, to myself till dinner-time, when Curran and another person, his companion, returned from Dublin, about 18 English miles. The Sunday of this week I had dined at Lady Mountcashel's, about the same distance from Dublin, and 4 miles from Grattan, in company with

Mr Curran. These two days, July 13, 14, were the first time in which I saw any of the beautiful scenery with which Ireland, and especially the county of Wicklow, abounds. I was particularly struck with a scene they call the Scalp, which has, I think, a finer effect than Penmanmawr in N. Wales, as in this latter instance you pass between two vast acclivities of rocks, with immense fragments broken off, and tumbled round you to the right and the left.

"With this quantity of gratification I might have rested satisfied. No more than this obtruded itself on my acceptance. But I invited myself to a second and a third dinner with Lady Mountcashel, July 21 and 28, and a second at Grattan's, July 29. On the 28th, Lady Mountcashel conducted me in her cabriole to the Devil's Glen, 20 or 30 miles from Dublin, and infinitely the most stupendous scene I ever saw. You travel for at least a mile and a half surrounded by rocks and mountains, varied and magnificent in their form beyond all imagination, and with a current all the way at the bottom, encumbered with stones of astonishing dimensions, and terminating at the further end in a grand waterfall, which changes its direction two or three times in the descent. You are not here, as in a similar scene nearer Dublin, fettered and hemmed in by the too great nearness of the opposing rocks, but, while cut off, on the one hand, from the whole world, your soul has room to expand in its desert, and savour its divinity. My visit at Grattan's, July 29, was peculiarly fortunate. I spent two mornings with him alone.

"And now let me recollect with what degree of kindness and cordiality I have been received in this country. No one has been ignorant who I was; to no one in that sense have I needed an introduction; and by none, so far as I know, have I been received with an unfavourable prepossession. Yet, believe me, I feel no atom intoxicated by the kindness of this people. I am not aware that I have been received with distinguishing or inordinate favour, except by a few. The good opinion of Joseph Cooper Walker, an Irish antiquarian, seems to have been marked with sufficient explicitness. Hugh Hamilton, whom I conceive to be the most eminent painter in Dublin, has shown himself enthusiastically partial to me. Mr Curran's kindness has been satisfactory, cordial, animated and unceasing. Grattan conversed with me with perfect familiarity, and answered me on all subjects without reserve, but not one word of personal kindness and esteem towards me ever escaped his lips. Let me observe by the way, that the characters of the two most eminent personages of this country, though sincere and affectionate friends to each other, are strongly contrasted. They are both somewhat limited in their information, and are deficient in a profound and philosophical faculty of thinking. They have both much genius. Grattan, I believe, is generally admitted to be the first orator in the British dominions ; and variety and richness of picturesque delineation perpetually mask the slightest sallies of Curran's conversation. But Grattan is mild, gentle, polished, and urbane on every occasion on which I have seen him ; Curran is wild, ferocious, jocular, humorous, mimetic and kittenish ; a true Irishman, only in the vast portion of soul that informs him, which of course a very ordinary Irishman must be content to want. He is declamatory, and his declamation is apt to grow monotonous, so that I have once or twice on such an occasion, felt inclined to question the basis of my admiration for him, till a moment after a vein of genuine imagination and sentiment burst upon me, and threw contempt and disgrace on my scepticism. I have had the good fortune to hear from him a speech of two hours, in the cause of Latten *versus* the publisher of a pamphlet by Dr Duigenan, which was tried a little before in England, Erskine being advocate for the plaintiff. Erskine got £500 damages and Curran 6d. ; so disgracefully high does the spirit of party, even in courts of law, run on this side the water.

"Lady Mountcashel is a singular character : a democrat and a republican in all their sternness, yet with no ordinary portion either of understanding or good nature. If any of our comic writers were to fall in her company, the infallible consequence would be her being gibbetted in a play. She is uncommonly tall and brawny, with bad teeth, white eyes, and a handsome countenance. She

I.   2 A

commonly dresses, as I have seen Mrs Fenwick dressed out of poverty, with a grey gown, and no linen visible ; but with gigantic arms, which she commonly folds, naked and exposed almost up to the shoulders.

" Monday, July 14, was rendered memorable here by the execution of Jemmy O'Brien, a notorious informer, for murder. He had been accustomed, I am told, to sell warrants of imprisonment on suspicion of treasonable practices for 2s. 6d. a-piece. Persons came out of the country 30 and 40 miles barefoot to enjoy the spectacle of his exit. One exclaimed, he was the death of my husband, and another, my two brothers were brought to the gallows by his instrumentality. An individual stationed himself on the highest pinnacle in the neighbourhood, that the whole population, however remote, might join in one shout of deafening and unbounded rapture the moment the scaffold sunk from under him. For the rapture, however, you will observe that they were partially indebted to the apprehension which both he and they entertained to the last moment, that the government would interfere with a pardon. When his execution was completed, his body was for a few moments in the hands of the populace, and they tore away fingers and toes with the utmost greediness, to preserve as precious relics of their antipathy and revenge.

" I am exceedingly offended with Mrs Elwes for her fiction, equally wilful and malicious, of a quarrel between me and Mrs Robinson. There is not a shadow of foundation for it. I was somewhat displeased with her (Mrs R.) the last time I saw her for her copious vein of vulgar abuse against a quondam, most despicable friend of hers, and endeavoured in vain to stop it, but I scarcely imagined she was even sensible of the degree of pain and displeasure she inspired.

" And now what shall I say for my poor little girls? I hope they have not forgot me. I think of them every day, and should be glad, if the wind was more favourable, to blow them a kiss a-piece from Dublin to the Polygon. I have seen Mr Grattan's little girls and Lady Mountcashel's little girls, and they are very nice children, but I have seen none that I love half so well or

think half so good as my own. I thank you a thousand times for
your care of them. I hope next summer, if I should ever again
be obliged to leave them for a week or two, that I shall write long
letters to Fanny in a fine print hand, and that Fanny will be able
to read them to herself from one end to the other. That will be
the summer 1801."

The Same to the Same.

" I see by my memoranda that it is now near a fortnight since
I wrote to you last. On that day I wrote to you two letters,
both of which, I take it for granted, you have long before this
received. What I said in them I cannot now with exactness
recollect. I had, however, by that time made my contract with
Mr Curran to go to the assizes at Carlow, for which place we set
out, Sunday, Aug. 3, the day after I closed these letters. On our
road, we called on Mr Geo. Ponsonby. . . . We, however, only
spent an hour or an hour and a half at his house, and I saw no
more of him. At Carlow I was introduced to my Lord Judge,
Michael Kelly, Esq., eighty years of age, and by his invitation had
the honour to sit on the bench with him. Here we hanged a post-
master, worth by his own evidence £1000 a year, for opening letters
and robbing the mail (he was appointed for execution this morning), and procured an estate for a friend of Mr Curran, by setting
aside a last will in favour of the testator's relations, or a last
will but one, in behalf of their friend, who was no relation at all.
Poor old Kelly made a grand speech in summing up, the most *ex
parte* pleading I ever heard, the famousness and effort of which,
as I was assured, was all prepared for the ears of the author of ' St
Leon.' (*N.B.*—'St Leon' is a much greater favourite everywhere in
Ireland than ' Caleb Williams.') These trials last two days. Tuesday and Wednesday, Aug. 5, 6, at Carlow I also made acquaintance with Mr Whaly, commonly called Buck (in the Irish idiom
Book) Whaly, who made himself famous, a few years ago, by
undertaking for a wager, to go to Jerusalem and return in the
space of 2 years. This man, as a traveller, is really a curiosity :

he affirmed that Georgia was the capital of Circassia, and that Moesia (a province) was the original name of the ancient Byzantium (a city). We returned by a famous old monastic ruin called the Seven Churches, and slept on Wednesday night at Hackets' Town, lately distinguished for its flourishing streets, but of which every house but two, including the church and the barracks, was reduced to a heap of ruins by the late rebellion. We arrived at the Seven Churches about 5 o'clock Thursday afternoon, when we found neither inn, nor even alehouse, but a camp, the officers of which, generously spying our distress, and hearing the name of Counsellor Curran, supplied us, starving as we were, with dinner, tea, supper, and bed. Friday, Aug. 8, we called for the last time on Grattan, and arrived in Dublin to dinner. Saturday, I proposed starting for England, but the wind was contrary, and I was prevailed on to stay till Monday (Sunday there is no packet), by which I gained two days in Ireland, and lost but one day in England : for if I had sailed on Saturday, I could only have left Holyhead by the Tuesday morning's mail-coach, so tedious was their passage : and, sailing on Monday I was in time, though the passage was 24 hours, for the Wednesday morning's mail. Wednesday, therefore, Aug. 13, at 4 A.M., I once more landed on my beloved native isle. At 6 A.M. I got into the mail-coach, and dined with the passengers at Conway at 1 P.M. There I left them, being determined, as I told you before, to penetrate on foot through some of the most delightful scenery of N. Wales. I slept last night at Llanrwst (the w is pronounced like oo), and breakfasted this morning, by the most purely accidental recommendation, at the house of a most stupid dog, Mr Edwards, a brewer, whose town house is in Portman Square, and who has built himself a mansion in the vale of Llanrwst, because in this valley he passed the most pleasing years of his childhood. Llanrwst is 12 miles from Conway, this place 10 miles more, where I am just sitting down to dinner, and Corwen, where I propose to sleep, is 13 miles further. Llangollen, to which I purpose to proceed to-morrow, is 14 miles beyond Corwen. . . . Whether I shall leave Llangollen Friday or Saturday will depend pretty much on

these ladies [Lady Eliza Butler and Miss Ponsonby], but I think
I will contrive to be in town so as to be able to give you an
accurate previous notice of the time, for the sake of the dear little
girls and the trunks of the trees: perhaps you may have a letter
by Monday's post, to tell you exactly of the final particulars of my
arrival the day after.

"Tell Fanny and Mary I have brought each of them a present
from Aunt Bishop and Aunt Everina. I love Aunt Bishop as
much as I hate (you must not read that word) Aunt Everina: and
therefore Fanny, as the eldest, must, I believe, have the privilege
of choosing Mrs Bishop's present, if she prefers it. Will not Fanny
be glad to see papa next Tuesday? It will then be more than
seven weeks since papa was at Polygon: I hope it will be a long,
long while before papa goes away again for so much as seven
weeks. What do you think, F.? But he had to come over the
sea, and the sea would not let him come when he liked. Look at
it in the map. . . .

"A further object of curiosity with which I have been gratified
was, that Mr Grattan introduced me to a poor man who had been
twice half-hanged by the King's troops in the rebellion. I had,
therefore, the account of the transaction from the fellow's own
mouth. The first time, seven cars were brought, and set on end,
that seven villagers might be suspended from the tops of their
shafts, to extort a confession of arms from them. The second
time, the poor fellow's wife, who was on her death-bed, crawled to
the threshold to entreat for mercy for him in vain. She survived
the scene, of which she thus became the spectator, exactly ten
days. God save the king!"

[*Enclosed in letter.*]—"I have just closed the week with a
very interesting conversation with Curran, upon the charge I had
heard alleged against him of insincerity and prostitution of friendship. I am convinced it has no shadow of foundation to lean
upon. I like him a thousand times better than ever.

"We are now going to set out for Carlow, and shall spend an
hour or two this morning with Geo. Ponsonby, who is by most
persons pronounced the third orator in Ireland, and by the devo-

tees of chaste and level declamation, is affirmed to be the first.
I have never yet seen him, except for a few minutes, in England.

"Ah, poor Fanny! here is another letter from papa, and what
do you think he says about the little girls in it? Let me see.
Would pretty little Mary have apprehension enough to be angry
if I did not put in her name? Look at the map. This is Sunday
that I am now writing. Before next Sunday I shall have crossed
that place there, that you see marked as sea, between Ireland and
England, and shall hope, indeed, to be half way home. That is
not a very long while now, is it? My visit to Ireland is almost
done. Perhaps I shall be on the sea in a ship, the very moment
Marshall is reading this letter to you. There is about going in a
ship in Mrs Barbauld's book. But I shall write another letter,
that will come two or three days after this, and then I shall be in
England. And in a day or two after that, I shall hope to see Fanny
and Mary and Marshall, sitting on the trunks of the trees. . . ."

The tender domestic tone of these letters is in strong
contrast to the acrimony which now began to mark Godwin's intercourse with Dr Parr. According to Godwin's
own testimony at a later date, the Doctor had always been
"an advocate of old establishments," and even "of old
abuses." But "his heart had always seemed better than
his logic," he had a ready sympathy for those with whom
his reason did not wholly agree, as was shown in his letter
to Godwin at the time of the political trials, he could take
Godwin with all his heresies as a chosen friend.

But his opinions, in common with those of many others,
had insensibly become more reactionary. The French
Revolution had proved a test which few could bear. Mackintosh became, according to Godwin, "an apostate," and
though Godwin could not apply the term to Dr Parr, he had
soon to find that the division was no longer only of creed
but of sympathy, and that the friendship was fading away.

He sent a copy of "St Leon" to Hatton, but heard nothing of its reception, and after waiting more than a reasonable time, wrote to his friend.

William Godwin to Rev. Dr Parr.

"POLYGON, SOMERS TOWN, *Jan.* 3, 1800.

" DEAR SIR,—I received a visit more than twelve months ago from Mr Morley of Hampton Lucy, the express purpose of which was to vindicate himself from any supposed concern in a foolish story that was propagated of my having been, through the influence of a certain melancholy event, converted to Christianity. This was the first time I had ever heard his name joined with that story. His vindication with me was therefore easy. From all that I know of Mr Morley, I should feel great difficulty in persuading myself that a conduct pitiful and unmanly could justly be imputed to him, and I had no hesitation in completely acquitting him.

" I felt some inclination on that occasion to have written to you for the purpose of removing any unpleasant impression that might remain on your mind in connexion with that story. This inclination, after an interval, was renewed in my mind with still greater force, in consequence of my being told, though I cannot now recollect by whom, that you had been heard to do me the honour to express your regret at some unfortunate misunderstanding that had arisen between us. But procrastination is of very fatal influence. I deferred my explanation ; I reserved it for the occasion that now presents itself, which I calculated would have occurred much sooner than it has done. I said, I will request Dr Parr's acceptance of a copy of my second attempt in the way of a novel, and will then write to him on the subject at large.

" The story was first brought to me by a very amusing and good-natured young man, Mr Basil Montagu. He represented you as the assiduous propagator of the tale. If his representation had been true, I should have regretted the circumstance, but I should have looked upon it as a ground of misunder-

stan ling with a man I so profoundly value and esteem as Dr
Parr. I saw you soon after in town (June 1798), and with my
customary frankness related to you what I had heard. You instantly assured me that you had heard the tale, only to contradict
it. No answer could be more satisfactory. From that moment
the circumstance ceased to give me the slightest uneasiness, and,
but for the incidents related in the preceding page, would, I am
satisfied, long since have vanished from my mind. I hope this
explanation will be received by you as complete. There are few
things I regret so much as that petty considerations of miles and
hours should now for a year and a half have withheld from me the
improving conversation, and the cordial assurances and encourage-
ments I might otherwise have held with and received from Dr
Parr.

" I ordered my bookseller to send you a copy of my new novel.
I hope you received it in due course. It would give me great
pleasure if you did not hold it lost time to communicate to me,
with your usual manliness, your sentiments respecting it : if you
would give yourself the trouble, in case of your discovering in it
any fundamental mistake, to set up a beacon to direct me better
in my future efforts, and in case you thought it did not disgrace
me, to cheer me with one breath of your applause, that I might
proceed with greater confidence and strength to future exertions.

"You made a long visit at Norwich last summer. If I had heard
of it in time, I should, perhaps, have been tempted to review the
scene of my boyish years. You saw, I am told, a good deal of
Mackintosh ; you therefore, no doubt, settled accounts with him
as to your opinion of his political lectures. I am, myself, exceedingly disgusted with some of their leading features. Sheltering
himself under, what I think, a frivolous apology of naming nobody,
he loads indiscriminately the writers of the new philosophy with
every epithet of contempt,—absurdity, frenzy, idiotism, deceit,
ambition, and every murderous propensity dance through the
mazes of his glittering periods : nor has this mighty dispenser of
honour and disgrace ever deigned to concede to any one of them
the least particle of understanding, talent, or taste. He has to

the utmost of his power contributed to raise a cry against them,
as hollow, treacherous, noxious, and detestable, and to procure
them either to be torn in pieces by the mob, or hanged up by the
government. There is a warmth in this style of speculation, that
does not well accord, either with the conclusions of my understanding, or the sentiments of my heart. I have noticed it
accordingly, *en passant*, in the third volume, p. 247, of my novel.
—I remain, with sentiments of much regard, dear sir, yours,

" W. GODWIN."

To this letter Dr Parr returned no answer by way of
letter, but he replied to it with a vengeance on the following Easter Tuesday, April 15, 1800. He was selected to
preach the annual "Spital Sermon" before the Lord
Mayor, and delivered a great manifesto on "the new
philosophy" with direct and unmistakeable reference to
Godwin and "Political Justice."

The remaining letters may speak for themselves, with the
remark only that Godwin's "notes" to Dr Parr's letter of
April 29 form the first draft of a pamphlet published by
him in the following year, called "Thoughts occasioned by
the Perusal of Dr Parr's Spital Sermon." He complained
in this with considerable vigour of the treatment he had
received from Parr and Mackintosh, and of the "flood of
ribaldry, invective, and intolerance which had been poured
against him and his writings." So ended a friendship which
once had been close and cordial.

William Godwin to Rev. Dr Parr.

" POLYGON, SOMERS TOWN, April 24, 1800.

" DEAR SIR,—I was very desirous to see you. I have called
twice for that purpose. Saturday, unfortunately, you were on the
point of going out : to-day you slept in the country.

" If I had seen you, I designed to ask whether you had received

a letter from me, written in December [January] last. I meant to
have listened, to know whether intention or simple forgetfulness
had caused it to remain unanswered. It did not appear to me an
ordinary letter, but one the author of which was entitled to a
reply.

" This subject dismissed, I should then have mentioned your
sermon of Easter Tuesday. I spoke in that letter of Mackintosh's
letters, in which that gentleman, without the manliness of mentioning me, takes occasion three times a-week to represent me to an
audience of a hundred persons, as a wretch unworthy to live.
Your sermon, I learn from all hands, was on the same subject,
handled, I take it for granted, from what I know of your character,
in a very different spirit. I am sorry for this. Since Mackintosh's
Lectures, it has become a sort of fashion with a large party to
join in the cry against me. It is the part, I conceive, of original
genius, to give the tone to others, rather than to join a pack, after
it has already become loud and numerous.

" These subjects were better adapted for a conversation than a
letter, and I much wish they had been so treated. Every difference of judgment is not the topic for a grave complaint.

" If, however, both my letter and my visit would have passed
unnoticed, I am entitled to conclude that you have altered your
mind respecting me. In that case I should be glad you would
answer to your own satisfaction, what crimes I am chargeable with
now in 1800, of which I had not been guilty in 1794, when with
so much kindness and zeal you sought my acquaintance.—I am,
dear sir, yours, with the warmest regard,   W. GODWIN."

Rev. Dr Parr to William Godwin.

" 38 CAREY STREET, *April* 29, 1800.

" SIR,—I have read your letter attentively, and I believe that you
know enough of my serious and importunate avocations in London
to consider them as a sufficient excuse for the delay of my answer.

" ' You designed,' it seems, ' to ask me whether I had received
a letter from you written in December last.' ' You meant,' also,

' to have listened to know whether intention or simple forgetfulness had caused it to remain unanswered.' You further represent it ' as appearing to yourself not an ordinary letter, but one, the author of which was entitled to a reply.' If you had seen me and spoken what you thus wrote, I should not have given you the trouble of *listening* to hear my answer. Without professing to adopt your system about the undistinguishing disclosure of truth, I shall follow my own, which appears to me equally sound and salutary.

" A parcel came to my house in December last, when I was absent. Upon my return I opened it, and found four volumes, together with a letter, which from the direction I knew to be from you. I read only the preface to your novel, and afterwards, having heard from Mrs Parr some account of its contents, I felt no anxiety at the time to look into them. I happened to be then very busy upon subjects which were far more interesting to me ; and perhaps, if I had been more at leisure, yet I might not have found myself disposed to read your book till I knew the opinion entertained of it by the very sagacious person whom I had desired to peruse it. Certainly, sir, I was not for one moment insensible of your civility in sending it to me. But I had determined to return it to you ; and the reluctance I felt to do what might seem to you ungracious, made me put off from day to day the execution of what I intended. I now thank you, sir, for sending me the book. I also apologise to you for not having made my acknowledgments sooner, and after my arrival at Hatton I will take the earliest opportunity of conveying back to you the volumes which for obvious reasons I cannot keep without impropriety.

" Your letter I laid aside, and as I did not expect to find the contents of it agreeable to me, I laid it aside unopened. With some uncertainty whether I should or should not venture to read it, I afterwards looked for it in my library and could not find it. But my search was not very diligent, and I suppose that some day or other it will fall into my hands. I cannot, however, pledge myself, either upon finding to read, or upon reading, to answer it.

" I have told you, sir, with all possible plainness, every circumstance I remember about your letter and in the books : and in consequence of what you wrote to me the other day, I think myself justified in confessing that I am now not disposed towards you entirely as I once was.

" Your letter of April 24th goes on thus : ' This subject dismissed, I should then have mentioned your sermon of Easter Tuesday. I spoke in the letter above referred to of Mackintosh's Lectures, in which that gentleman, without the manliness of mentioning me, takes occasion three times a week to represent me to an audience of an hundred persons as a wretch unworthy to live.' Indeed, sir, I must congratulate myself upon not opening a letter containing a passage so offensive to me as this misrepresentation of Mr Mackintosh, be it accidental or voluntary. From various quarters I had heard of the ability and success with which Mr Mackintosh had combated opinions which you are supposed to hold, and of which I am accustomed to disapprove. But I never was told by other men that he had been guilty of any unbecoming personalities towards you ; and by Mr Mackintosh himself I have been informed that he never insulted your character, never pronounced your name, never even opposed your tenets, as holden by yourself exclusively. You will therefore permit me to express my fixed belief, that what you wrote in your former letter, and have repeated in your last, is utterly unwarranted by the conduct of Mr Mackintosh in his lectures. Of his genius, his judgment, his erudition, and his taste, I have always thought and spoken with high admiration. From the doubts which I may now and then have entertained of his firmness, I am happily relieved. By experience I am convinced of his sincerity in friendship, and for the important services which he is now rendering to a cause which is most dear to my heart, I gladly give him the tribute of my thanks and my praise.

" I return to your letter, in which you say, ' Your sermon, I learn from all hands, was on the same subject, handled, I take it for granted, from what I know of your character, in a very different spirit. I am sorry for this.'

" Be assured, sir, that you have done me no more than justice, when you acquit me of describing you 'as a wretch unworthy to live.' I hope, sir, you are not sorry *for this.*

" For the principles which I defend from the pulpit, I am conscious of an awful responsibility, not only to society, but to Almighty God, and it is at my own peril that, in speaking of my fellow-creatures, I forget the obligations which lie upon me to preserve the candour of a gentleman, and the charity of a Christian. Let me hope, that for this also you are not sorry.

" In your letter you thus proceed : ' Since Mackintosh's lectures, it has become a sort of fashion with a large party to join in the cry against me. It is the part, I conceive, of original genius to give the tone to others, rather than to join a pack, after it has already become loud and numerous.'

" So far as the foregoing passage contains a statement of facts relating to other men, it may or may not be just. So far as it contains your general opinion upon the duty of men who are endowed with original genius, I am inclined rather to admit than to contradict it. But if it be meant in any degree whatsoever to contain a particular accusation against me, I must lament the want of precision, and the want of fairness in the writer. Sir, I lay no claim ' to that original genius which is to give the tone to others.' But I have too delicate a sense of decorum to join a pack because it is loud and numerous, or to act with a party because it is large, or to repeat any cry against you because it is fashionable. I trust, sir, that, upon reconsidering what you have thus written, you will be very sorry for it, and, let your motives be what they may, when you wrote the passage above mentioned, and let your feelings be what they may, when you have reconsidered it, I have no hesitation in pronouncing it quite unauthorised, either by what you know of my general character, or from what you can have heard from any man of sense about my sermon at Christ Church.

" ' These subjects,' you proceed to say, ' were better adapted for a conversation than a letter ; and I much wish they had been so treated. Every difference of judgment is not the proper topic for a grave complaint.'

" Confessing myself at a loss to find any close connection be-

tween the beginning and the conclusion of the foregoing paragraph, I am under the necessity of replying to them separately.
If the subjects upon which you meant to speak to me were those
upon which you actually have written to me, I think that they may
be discussed more temperately and more correctly by letter than
by conversation ; and, of course, I very much rejoice that they
have not been treated in the manner you say you very much wish
to treat them.　True it is, that every difference of judgment is not
the proper topic for a grave complaint.　But if I had joined a
pack against you, there would have been reason for very loud
complaint on your part ; and if you in conversation had accused
me, as you seem to accuse me in writing, of having acted thus
unbecomingly, I should have complained of you, not for weakness
in judgment, but for rashness in reproach, not for differing from me
on a point of opinion, but for calumniating me as a point of fact.

　　" I now quote your concluding paragraph :—' If, however, both
my letters and my visits would have passed unnoticed, I am entitled to conclude that you have altered your mind respecting me.
In that case I should be glad you would answer to your own satisfaction what crime I am chargeable with now in 1800, of which I
had not been guilty in 1794, when with so much kindness and
zeal you sought my acquaintance.'

　　" The letter you wrote to me on the 24th of April does not pass
unnoticed.　Your visits entitled you to civility, and yet I am under
the painful necessity of acknowledging that I do not wish you in
future to give yourself the trouble of writing to me any more
letters, or favouring me with any more visits.　Upon the alteration
of my mind towards you, I can speak entirely to my own satisfaction, though not without some doubts upon the degree in which
you will be glad to find I am satisfied.

　　" I never sought your acquaintance, sir, with any zeal.　I received you with kindness when you were introduced to me by Mr
Mackintosh.　I have treated you with the respect that is due to
your talents and attainments.　But before the year 1800, I had
ceased to think of you so favourably as I thought of you in 1794.
I had not in 1794 read in your Enquirer the passage where you

speak so irreverently and unfavourably about the Founder of that religion of which you know that I am a teacher, and of which you can have no reason for doubting but that I am a sincere believer. And in truth, sir, though I found in that book many judicious observations upon life, and many pleasing instances of your improvement in style, still your mis-statement of Christ's meaning, and your insinuations against his benevolence, have occurred to me again and again, and from the resemblance they bear to the impious effusions of Mr Voltaire, which I have lately read, they have displeased, and ever will displease me more and more.

"I had not in 1794 been shocked, in common with all wise and good men, by a work which you entitle 'Memoirs of the Author of the Rights of Women.'

"I had not then discovered the dreadful effects of your opinions upon the conduct, the peace, and the welfare of two or three young men, whose talents I esteemed, and whose virtues I loved.

"I had not then seen your eagerness and perseverance in employing every kind of vehicle to convey to every class of readers those principles which, so long as they appeared only in the form of a metaphysical treatise, might have done less extensive mischief.

"Above all, sir, I had not considered the dangerous tendency of your tenets with the seriousness which the situation of the moral and political world has lately produced in my mind upon subjects most interesting to the happiness of society, and to the preservation of that influence which virtue and religion ought to have upon the sentiments and the happiness of mankind.—I am, Sir, very sincerely your well-wisher and obedient servant,   S. PARR."

Notes on Dr Parr's Letter.

"'As I did not expect to find the contents of it agreeable to me," &c. This is a very curious remark. What disagreeable contents did the Doctor divine he should find in my letter? There was not the shadow of a misunderstanding between us. The most obvious interpretation is, that the Doctor expected to find in my letter expressions of consideration, kindness, and friendship, and that these expressions, under the circumstance of the secret alienation of mind he had harboured against me, would have been disagreeable to him.

" ' Misrepresentation of Mr Mackintosh.' This remark is sufficiently answered in my " Thoughts occasioned by Dr Parr's Sermon."

" ' Never pronounced your name,' ditto. Here Dr Parr converts, with what propriety I will not decide, my allegation against Mr Mackintosh in a defence of his conduct.

" ' I hope, sir, you are not sorry for *this*.' Be it recollected that my letter was written instantly upon my return home, with the suspicion upon my mind of Dr Parr's desertion of his former friendship for me. The instances I had repeatedly observed of warm and affectionate temper in Dr Parr had produced in me a considerable attachment to him. I beg pardon for this, as well as for having been so far disturbed at the moment by the first apprehension of his unkindness as to have fallen into the inaccuracy of making the pronoun the Doctor amuses himself with, refer in strict construction to the latter member of my sentence, while in spirit and intention it refers to the former.

" ' I never sought your acquaintance, sir, with any zeal.' In August 1793 the unfortunate and illustrious Mr Gerrald, whom I then saw for the first time, communicated to me the favourable opinion he entertained of the E[nquirer] and P[olitical] J[ustice], and his anxiety to be acquainted with the author. Soon after Mr Mackintosh made me a similar communication. In February 1794 the Doctor was in town, and at Mr Mackintosh's desire I attended him to the Doctor's lodgings. He received me with the cordiality and warmth which have so often delighted me. To Mr Mackintosh he said, ' Jemmy, I was very angry with you yesterday, but now you have brought Godwin to me, I cannot help forgiving you.' Dr Parr invited me to spend some time with him in Warwickshire. I went thither in October. The Doctor introduced me to all his neighbours. We dined out almost every day, and his manner of announcing me was in the highest terms of eulogium and regard. After a stay of six days, I was unexpectedly called to town by some circumstances connected with the state trials at the Old Bailey. The Doctor dismissed me with reluctance, complained of the shortness of my visit, and insisted that, when the affair was over, or if not then, in the following summer, I should return and make up to him the injury he now sustained. In November following, the Doctor, at my particular instigation, visited Mr Gerrald in the prison of the New Compter. I repeated my visit to the Doctor in 1795, and staid sixteen days: still the same round of distinguishing kindness and panegyrical introductions. In April 1796 Dr Parr invited himself, his family, and a party of ten or twelve persons to dine with me in a little hovel which I then tenanted near London. In June 1797 I was in Warwickshire on a journey northwards. I then saw Dr Parr, who regretted to me his absence from home, but insisted I should make some stay at his house on my return. In June 1798 I had another cordial interview with him in London.

" ' The passage in which you speak so irreverently and unjustly of the Founder, &c.' In the period of the Doctor's greatest cordiality and friendship, he was accustomed to call and believe me an atheist. This remark brings to my mind a passage in Hume's History of England, where he says : ' At God's altar in Canterbury, there were offered in one year £3, 2s. 6d. ; at the Virgin's, £63, 5s. 6d. ; at St. Thomas's, £832, 12s. 3d. But next year the disproportion was still greater ; there was not a penny offered at God's altar ; the Virgin's gained £4, 1s. 8d., but St. Thomas had got for his share £956, 6s. 3d.'

" ' I had not then discovered,' &c. Whether any, and what meaning is to be ascribed to this mysterious and terrible sentence, Dr Parr only, I suppose, is able to explain.

" ' Above all,' &c. Thus, by Dr Parr's own confession, the E[nquirer] and P[olitical] J[ustice] which originally induced him to seek my acquaintance, is the great and principal reason why he now desires that ' in future I will not give myself the trouble of writing any more letters, and favouring him with any more visits.'

" The above remarks I have put down under the idea that Dr. Parr's letter may one day be printed. I feel the utmost delicacy in exercising any jurisdiction over the communications of private

I. 2 B

correspondence ; but I do not regard the letter a man writes me, for the purpose of dismissing me from all future intercourse with him, as private correspondence.

" (If Dr Parr's letter should ever be printed, mine of April 1800 should stand as a general introduction, and of January in the same year.)"

From Dr Parr to William Godwin.

"HATTON, *Oct.* 28, 1800.

" For reasons which were some time ago communicated to Mr Godwin, Dr Parr takes the liberty of returning him a book which has been read by Mrs Parr, Mrs Wynne, and Catherine ; and he begs leave to unite with them in thanks to the courtesy of the writer. In the sincerity of his soul, Dr Parr wishes Mr Godwin health, prosperity, and such a state of mind, united with a possible and proper use of his great talents, as may obtain for him a lasting reputation among wise and good men, and secure his happiness both here and hereafter."

Unfinished draft of letter from William Godwin to Dr Parr.

"SIR,—I very sincerely thank you for your letter. I feel the most pungent grief in witnessing your disgrace ; but, since it must be so, I am well satisfied to possess this evidence of your disgrace, subscribed in your own hand and with your own name.

" If I could ever be prevailed upon to present to the public the luxuriant but short-lived vegetation of your professions of regard, as they now lie by me in my closet, contrasted with the expressions of this letter, and the frivolous reasons by which they are attempted to be supported, your character would be placed in a light in which it was never yet the lot of a human being to be exhibited.

" I rejoice that there are not many men like you. If there were, there would indeed be little inducement to the attempting public benefit by the acquisition of talents, when the very production which first obtained for its author the attention of one who was a stranger to him, is afterwards unblushingly assigned as the ground, and, 'above all,' the ground of alienation and a tone of reproach that I think it would rather unmanly to apply to the most atrocious criminal that ever held up his hand at the bar of Old Bailey.

"My 'unwarranted misrepresentation' of Mackintosh's lectures, stated in my own terms, I am ready to support, if necessary, with a body of evidence as complete as ever obtained the attention of a court of justice in a public trial."

WISBEACH.